S Y N F U L

S NFUL

CHARLOTTE
FEATHERSTONE

Spice

Recycling programs
for this product may
not exist in your area.

Spice

SINFUL

ISBN-13: 978-0-373-60543-9

For questions and comments about the quality of this book
please contact us at Customer_eCare@Harlequin.ca.

Spice and the Colophon are trademarks used under license and
registered in Australia, New Zealand, Philippines, United States Patent
and Trademark Office and in other countries.

www.Spice-Books.com

Printed in U.S.A.

To my awesome editor, Lara Hyde, because you were the first to see the beauty in him, and I thank you for that! By loving him as he is, you made it so easy for me to write his story. Thank you for letting me write him how he is; darkly beautiful. I'm so glad we got to work together on this book!

To Barbara from the Happily Ever After blog, and Ashley (aka VampFanGirl) from the Lovin' Me Some Romance blog. Thank you for all your support and enthusiasm for my writing, and all things Wallingford. I am so happy to have found you. You bring so much fun to what is sometimes a solitary career. And to all the blog hussies who carefully gathered all those "Sinful breadcrumbs" I spread on my blog. I hope his story satisfies and gets the inner hussy purring.

And last, but never least, to all the readers who e-mailed me, requesting Wallingford's book, I hope his story doesn't disappoint.

And the day came when the risk to remain tight in a bud was more painful than the risk it took to blossom.

—Anais Nin

1

With a jaded outlook and a black heart, Matthew, Earl of Wallingford, knew exactly what human nature consisted of. Temptation and physical pleasure. At least he had it in him to acknowledge the flaw. Unlike so many of his peers, he did not pretend to be otherwise. He was an unconscionable wastrel without thought or feeling. A rake with insatiable appetites. A disreputable heartbreaker, women said with disgust as he strolled by. Yet it was these same women who entertained him in their husbands' homes, with anything but disgust.

Ah, the facade of Victorian morality. What a jest.

It was a wonderful time for someone like him to be alive. Someone who didn't believe the innate nature of humans was anything more than self-serving. He had seen very little goodness in his life. But then he had been the furthest from kind or good himself.

Every day he was confronted with man's startling avarice. And nowhere on earth was the confirmation of mankind's selfish, pleasure-seeking ways more evident than in London, among the aristocracy's elite.

Behind fluttering silk fans, and beyond the fashionable ballrooms where champagne and polite conversation flowed, lay a cesspool of immorality and vice. It was this dichotomy that Matthew found so amusing. He enjoyed watching the members of the nobility feverishly working to implement the queen's moral views on religion, family and sex. These were the men who married, fathered children and touted the merits of the married state thither and yon. They were the leaders whom the queen respected, whom she believed in. The ones who championed social reform, who rallied vigorously and vocally at parliament to keep the whores off the street and sex buried beneath a cloak of piety. It was these same men, he thought with amused cynicism, that he greeted in the evening as he toured the brothels, the gambling halls and the supper clubs. Hell, he even, on occasion, shared a cheroot and a glass of port with them while watching the naked dancers parade about, jiggling their breasts and bottoms from the stage where they danced seductively to a bawdy tune.

Pious and moral, indeed. Even now the mayor's secretary had a woman's face in his lap and another's breasts in his hand. And the mayor? He had taken his leave a few minutes earlier with his long-standing mistress hanging on his arm. Matthew wondered if the mayor had given his young wife and two-day-old son a second thought this evening. Not likely.

The world-weary space where his heart and soul had once lain laughed at the ever-opposing sides. Morality and London were not symbiotic. Human nature and temptation, now *they* were synonymous. He, more than anyone, understood that.

Glancing around the smoky supper club he suddenly realized that it never ceased to amaze him, the variety of proclivities offered in the metropolis. Vice of every kind was available in Victorian London. One didn't even need a fortune to secure one's pleasure. Some vices came cheap. Others, not so much. Some men would part with their souls for a chance to taste the sweet nectar of forbidden delights. It was that fact, coupled with his knowledge of what his peers lusted for, that had him here tonight.

He knew a thing or two about lust and selling one's soul. A painful, haunting lesson that, but one that had served him well. One that would pay him back tonight.

Considered a connoisseur of the more pleasurable vices, Matthew was a leader in things such as depravity and scandal, and tonight he was using his reputation to further his goals.

While the gentleman of the ton played at morality by day whilst indulging in sin at night, Matthew could not be bothered to pretend to be the former. He never was one for hypocrisy. Why act the gentleman when he was nothing but a bastard? He had never understood the need to act like two separate people. It seemed a lot of work, and for what? He respected these men no more than he would a thief or a convict. Perhaps, he thought with a small smile, he respected them even less. There was a certain honor among thieves, and these men, in their evening dress and smooth smiles, had no honor.

So, not desiring to be a hypocrite, he lived his life in sin, day and night. And he would have it no other way.

He probably should have felt a measure of mortification that he could so easily admit to such a flaw, but he was incapable of shame. He had no conscience or soul. No heart, either. That had broken and died years ago. The leftover pieces had petrified in his chest, leaving stone shrapnel in a black, empty place that felt nothing. Just a yawning void of…*nothing*. And he liked it that way.

He didn't get close to any of the women he took his pleasure from. And he never took them to his home, either, and preferred to rut on anything but a bed. Proclivities, he reminded himself. London could provide for even the most bizarre perversions. Finding women who would give him what he wanted wasn't a trial. The only real difficulty was avoiding those irritating emotional entanglements that women liked to enmesh with the act. Fucking was fucking as far as he was concerned. The act was nothing but cock, cunt and the grunts of pleasure. There was nothing more to it than a physical connection in which a male and female's genitals met. Of course, the poets would fiercely argue otherwise, and his best friend, Lord Raeburn would strenuously work to dissuade him of his slanted view. But Matthew knew better. He'd never been with a woman who didn't spread her thighs for nothing. There was always a reason: coin, advancement, even something as mundane as making a husband or other lover jealous. There was always motivation behind it.

It hadn't taken a lot for Matthew to discover that women manipulated men with sex. It was a female's most lethal and effective weapon. And being a man who rather enjoyed getting off, he had no recourse but to submit to them, despite their manipulations.

"Evening, guv." The sultry voice was followed by the brush of an ample breast along his arm. He stiffened, striving to put the old anxiety and distaste back in that gaping void where his soul had once resided. He didn't care to be put upon by a female who took the lead. In this chase, he preferred the part of predator. But this one, with her doe eyes and pouting mouth would not easily be run to ground. Her air of innocence was an illusion. She was as calculating as they came, and any submission on her part would be feigned.

"I could suck the Thames dry, you know."

Focusing on the stage, where the dancers were strutting about in drawers and bare breasts, Matthew ignored her throaty voice and the subtle sounds that were designed to mimic sucking lips. "I'm not in the mood for mouth play."

"What are you in the mood for then, guv?" she whispered while she raked her hand through his hair.

A bundle of money, he thought savagely, hating how he had to sit there and endure her attentions. Her perfume was suffocating him. So were her tits, which she kept shoving in his face.

"That 'andsome gent over there tells me you've painted a naughty picture, and it's going to be auctioned off tonight."

Matthew glanced at the gent in question. *Broughton*. His friend never could keep his mouth shut. Broughton caught his scowl. The bastard actually grinned.

"Why don't you give me a try, guv?" she purred, running her hand along his thigh. "I could be naughty."

He ignored her, even as her fingertips traveled down the leg of his trousers. "Cor, yer hard," she cooed. "Big strong thighs, I bet yer built like a bull, aren't ye?"

Wrong words. Any erection that was mounting despite his mental distaste deflated like a hot-air balloon. "Excuse me," he growled, nearly toppling her to the ground when he jumped up from the chair.

"Come back, guv," she called. "We can have a merry party."

With a sense of relief, he saw that the woman had now fixed her attentions on Broughton. She was crawling all over him as Broughton leaned back in his chair allowing her attentions.

Matthew had never been one for that sort of play, preferring something more direct, like his cock in a quim without preamble. What was the point of foreplay when it didn't interest him? When he wanted to fuck, he wanted his pleasure. The rest could all go to hell.

Reaching for a glass of champagne from a passing tray, Matthew made his way to the back room where the portrait he had painted was going to be auctioned off. He had heard enough crude remarks this night, and seen enough antics to know that this was the perfect venue for his art auction. The clientele of the supper club was a good mix of old and new money. They would pay a fortune for his portrait, and in return he would use their money to fund his art gallery.

Downing the champagne, he felt the slow burn along his throat, wishing it was something stronger, even though he was already well on his way to being drunk. More and more, he found himself *on the way,* he thought morosely. But when one lived the sort of life he did, dissolute and isolated, one needed the company of *something* that understood.

Taking another glass, he watched the men swarming into the room with the club girls and their mistresses. There were no wives here this night, a fact that Wallingford did not belabor. He was here for the money to fund his art gallery. Plain and simple.

"Everything is going well," Raeburn said as he slapped Matthew against the shoulder. "What a bloody crush."

Matthew grunted and took a drink of his champagne as he looked about the room. It was a bloody crush. There wasn't a corner free of slobbering lustful men waiting for a chance to see the portrait he had dangled and teased before them. Hopefully the piece would be inspiring enough to force the men to bid heavily. He needed the blunt if he was going to get his gallery opened. And the gallery had been the only thing of importance in his life for a very long time.

Finally he tore his gaze away from the crowd and settled it on his best friend. "I wasn't aware your prison cell had an escape route," he muttered.

Raeburn laughed, motioning away a serving girl as he did

so. "Prison?" he said, his eyes glinting. "If you call having a beautiful woman at my beck and call prison, then so be it. I'll die a convict."

Matthew arched his brow in annoyance. Raeburn was madly in love, a fact he could not decide was a blessing or a curse. "I do call monogamy prison," he grumbled as he looked away from the glimmer in Raeburn's eyes. "It would be a death sentence to me to spend my life tied to one woman."

"You haven't found the right one yet."

He snorted. "Out of numerous samplings, I think I would have found *her,* if indeed, *she* even existed. Admit it, Raeburn, you're an oddity."

His friend shrugged. "There are many men who find themselves in love."

Not like this, Matthew thought churlishly. He had never seen a love like Raeburn shared with Anais. Even he, a depraved muff chaser, had marveled at the beauty of it. And if he were being honest with himself, which he rarely, if ever was, there were times, like now, when the wicked little fingers of jealousy crept up to choke him.

"So, I've heard nothing but excitement since I entered the club. Everyone is wondering what scandalous thing you've done."

Matthew shook himself free of all thoughts of love and fidelity. "Why do you not stay and see for yourself?"

"I won't be bidding, of course. I doubt it is something my future wife would welcome in our home. However, I had to come for just a peek. And what an eyeful it was. Lucky bastard." Raeburn leered. "Imagine being tucked in your little studio with those naked women spread before you. How you must have been in your glory."

Matthew listened while he kept his eye on the staff. The champagne was being passed about as freely as water from a

fountain. Soon the men would be drunker and itching to begin the bidding.

"Not that I would have done such a thing, of course,"
Raeburn continued, "I'm quite happy with Anais. There isn't
another woman who could tempt me."

"I am well aware of your irritating attachment to your
intended. I find it rather annoying, if you must know."

"No, you don't." Raeburn grinned as he rocked on his
heels. "You're just jealous."

"The hell I am," he growled.

"Miserable again tonight," Raeburn taunted. "Don't worry
about a thing, old boy. I have a feeling the bidding will go on
for quite some time. Everyone is panting to get a glimpse of
the infamous portrait."

"I never worry," he muttered. But his insides were tight and
he felt as though he couldn't catch his breath. It wasn't like
him to be nervous.

"I had Anais invite Lady Burroughs to our wedding," Raeburn said, chatting away. "Thought it might make the
weekend more enjoyable for you. I know how you feel about
weddings and such. No need to thank me," Raeburn added
when Matthew frowned. "Well then, I think I shall be on my
way. Anais, you know, is home alone." Raeburn waggled his
eyebrows at him. Matthew rolled his eyes.

"You have the rest of your life to bed the girl. Why you do
not find the idea of monogamy stifling, I will never understand."

"With the right woman, Wallingford," Raeburn drawled,
"you will never get enough of her. In the right woman's bed,
you will never grow bored."

Could he be monogamous, even if he desired to be? He
didn't think so. He was a different man than Raeburn. Cold.
Distant. He was not the sort to make a woman happy. With

him, a woman would only find loneliness and emptiness, hardly conducive to conjugal contentment.

"I'm off, then," Raeburn said as he set his glass upon a passing footman's tray. "Do not forget you're the best man. There isn't anyone else I'd want by my side as I marry the woman of my dreams."

"I will be there."

"I thought weddings give you rashes."

Matthew shrugged and reached for another glass of champagne. "I will simply instruct my valet to put a salve in my portmanteau."

Raeburn grinned. "Good luck tonight."

Matthew saluted his friend with his glass and meandered about the room. Beside a table was the infamous portrait that was still draped in canvas. One corner was beginning to slip, and Matthew saw the elaborate gilt frame peeking out from beneath the sheet. The candles from above flickered, making the gold sparkle in the light, like diamonds in a necklace.

"Gentlemen," the loud voice of the auctioneer boomed. The cacophony of voices and laughter immediately died to an eerie quiet.

"Damn me, Wallingford, you've dangled this pretty little piece before us long enough. Give us a glimpse, man," Lord Ponsomby said irritably as he tossed more brandy down his fat throat.

"Yes, you've had your fun, now give us a peek," cried someone near the back of the room.

"Gentlemen," the auctioneer yelled, hitting his gavel against the wooden podium. "All in due time, gents. Now, we will start the bidding for this exceptional piece at five hundred pounds."

"Let's see it first," shouted Frederick Banks, an investment banker. Matthew found himself smiling. Old money never cared what they bought, but new money, they wanted to hold on to it, watching it grow, making certain they got good return for their investment. Old Banks was new money, trying to take a pence and press it into two.

Matthew was reasonably certain that Banks would find his portrait an infinitely prudent investment, if indeed, the old roué's reputation was to be believed.

"Gentlemen, ladies…I give you the *Dance of the Seven Veils.*"

With a whoosh, the sheet was pulled away from the portrait by the club's butler. A collective murmur of appreciation rippled out from the center of the crowd to the fringes of the room. There was a hushed awe, a sort of reverence in their silence that made Matthew turn his head and gaze at the portrait.

It was as stunning as it was erotic. Beautiful, tasteful, yet titillatingly explicit.

He heard a series of appreciative murmurs. *Simply stunning. Sensually beautiful,* as well as *Erotically elegant.* All words that made him immensely proud.

When he had the idea for the auction, he had known the piece would need to cause a stir. Something that would make the wealthy part with their money, preferably *lots* of their money.

It had started out as a piece of lewd portraiture, but had morphed and changed into something tasteful, but decadent. Any man who adored the female form would shed his own blood to own this painting.

Standing back, Matthew tried to dissect his work. To pick it apart and focus on the imperfections, yet he could not find anything to criticize. It was perfect, even down to the way the women's bare breasts were being displayed and how some of their ankles and wrists were bound with their veils.

Each woman, white, black, Asian, Arabic, East Indian, was depicted in elegant repose with brilliant colored silk veils that set off the hue of her glowing skin. All were naked and spread for the admiration of the male voyeurs before them. Some were sprawled out on a crimson velvet chaise. Others were kneeling. Two women were bound together by a blood-red veil tied around their bosoms, their mouths locked in a passionate kiss. Two other women explored each other's bodies, while one looked on, touching herself, her face awash in pleasure.

In all, the seven women were stunningly beautiful, well endowed, and most of all, supremely comfortable posing for him. It was not conceit, but the truth, as well as the mark of a good artist. The easy confidence shone in their faces, in the way their eyes seemed to sparkle and the way their lips curved in secret, provocative smiles and pouts.

"A thousand pounds," someone cried.

"Two thousand," Banks, the frugal investor, rebutted.

The numbers continued to be shouted out, climbing at a most pleasing rate. With this amount of blunt, he could purchase the building he wanted, an old little shop in Bloomsbury with a lovely bow window. It needed work, and while he was a shameless rogue, he was not above working up a sweat. He wanted this gallery. It had been the only thing he'd wanted in the past sixteen years.

"Six thousand pounds," the auctioneer cried. "Going once…going twice. Sold to Mr. Banks."

With a satisfied smile, Matthew watched Frederick Banks jostle through the crowd, toward him.

"Damn me, what a pretty picture," Banks said excitedly as he pumped Matthew's hand with his damp one. "I'll deposit a draft in your account in the morning."

With a nod, Matthew glanced once more at his painting.

"I will have one of my footmen deliver it to you. Perhaps the bank would be the best place?"

Banks's eyes widened. "Yes, yes." He laughed. "My wife would have a fit of the vapors, although it might teach her a trick or two, wouldn't it?"

From what he had heard, Mrs. Banks was well versed in a number of delightful little tricks.

"Thank you, Mr. Banks," Matthew muttered, wanting to depart from the burgeoning crowd that seemed to swell before him. "I think I shall take my leave."

He never was one for being smothered by bodies. And he had no interest in carrying on idle conversation.

"You look like you could use a drink. A celebratory drink."

He knew that voice. His rod hardened in his trousers as he took the glass filled with the mysterious green liquid and stared down into a lovely face that looked up at him with hunger. "Ah, the green fairy. How did you know?"

"A woman never tells her secrets," the woman said with a coy smile as she passed it to him. "Absinthe, it does do wonders for the mind, doesn't it?"

"Mmm," he murmured, drinking it down. Nothing made him forget who and what he was like absinthe.

"What a wickedly debauched painting," she said. Her eyes flickered over the portrait with appreciation. "I would wager that those women actually liked posing for you."

"Perhaps," he murmured, looking her over. He had seen her a few times before, but had never approached her. Tonight she was wearing a red dress, with a low square-cut bodice. He liked what he saw falling out of the cheap gown.

"I would like posing for you," she whispered. "Are you up for it tonight?"

Christ, he was already hard and straining. The effects of the absinthe and the euphoria of getting six thousand for his painting only made the ache more unbearable. "The question is, my dear, are you up for it?"

Her lashes fluttered, concealing eyes nearly as cynical as his. "That, my lord, depends on what you want."

"You. Tied up."

Taking the now-empty glass from him, she set it down on the arm of a chair. "That will cost extra, of course."

He smiled, one he knew could only be described as world weary. "It always does."

"I have a room upstairs. With a delightfully large bed."

"What of a wall?" he inquired as he trailed behind her, assessing her hips, which swayed erotically beneath the tawdry red satin. "It's my usual preference."

The woman gazed back at him as she headed for the stairs. "For another ten pounds."

He nodded in agreement. What was ten pounds when faced with fucking in bed? It was an investment in pleasure and what little of his sanity still remained.

"You're an odd duck," she said to him, her painted eyes softening in the glow of the wall sconce. "Broken, I think."

"Broken?" He laughed. "Madam, I am completely and unequivocally damaged beyond repair. Don't bother to try to fix me. I'm utterly ruined and fit only for the rubbish bin. Now, where the blazes are you taking me?" he asked as the absinthe began to find its way to his brain, making his thoughts fuzzy. Maybe a bed would be all right tonight. He was drunk enough, he supposed.

"Just a little farther up," she whispered.

"That's the exit," he barked, trying to clear his vision. "I thought you said you had a room upstairs?"

"Well, I lied," she snapped in a voice that turned from siren to spinster. "I'm broken, too. Now hand over your money and your jewels and be quick about it."

He laughed at the absurdity of her trying to rob him, then snarled as someone came from the dark shadows and shoved him out of the club and into the alley. "Now, guv," came the cockney accent, followed by a thick arm around his throat and the stench of foul breath and rotten teeth. "Give us the goods and we'll let you live."

"Oh, what a treat," he drawled. "Another morning. A new, mundane day. You do know how to depress a man, don't you?"

He felt the man turn to glance at the woman, no doubt silently questioning Matthew's mental state.

"I don't know," his would-be assignation spat. "He's as mad as a hatter but rich as Croesus."

"Right and wrong, love. Mad, indeed. Rich? 'Fraid not."

The man holding him paused and loosened his hold a fraction, allowing Matthew to get in his surprise left hook.

"Ow! 'E broke me nose," the man cried, stumbling back. Matthew was on him, using the skills he'd honed over the years studying pugilism. He was as big as an ox with the stamina of a stallion—the frail cockney indigent would be no match for his fists.

"Afraid you chose the wrong target, mate. I'm no weak guvnor. I've boxed for the past ten years."

There was an angry cry from the depths of the alley, followed by three more ruffians who emerged through the darkness. Fists flying, legs kicking, Matthew fought them off even through his drunken haze.

Wait till he got his hands on that bitch, he thought savagely as he landed a jab into the throat of one of the thieves.

He was about ready to dispatch the last by planting his fist in his face when a glimmer of white whisked past his right eye. In a blinding whirl, he felt something crash against his temple. The last thing he felt was the slime-covered cobbles of the alley as his cheek cracked against them.

"Pick him clean," the woman ordered. "I saw the winning bidder come up to him. I'm certain he passed him some money. Once you've found it, make it so he won't be identifying me."

2

The stench of the wards was always a little overpowering at the beginning of the shift. But tonight it was particularly putrid. The scent of excrement, vomitus, death and disease was literally breath stealing.

Two full pails of water and a pair of mops were placed at her feet—the water too clean to have been put to any use.

"Have you washed the beds and walls yet?" Jane asked the two petulant nurses standing before her.

"Whot fer? They only piss on them again."

Jane glared at the one, a brunette with a comely face and sinfully curved body. She'd come from the workhouse after being arrested for prostitution. It was clear that the idea of nursing the ill and dying was less appealing than that of selling her body for coin. But for Jane Rankin, a woman of suspect birth, an opportunity to have any sort of respectable job was her idea of heaven.

"When you arrived here, I explained your duties thoroughly. At the beginning of the night you're to clean the beds and walls before you begin your rounds."

"And what's it yer doing, Miss Hoity-Toity, when we're breaking our backs cleaning?"

Jane straightened her spine. Illegitimate or not, she still had a measure of her aristocratic father's arrogance. "I am head sister of the ward. Your superior," Jane stated, prickled by the woman's insolence. "I take this profession very seriously. If you have no respect for it, then you may leave."

The new nurse seemed to settle her ire, although anger still flashed occasionally in her eyes. "I like the pay. I 'ate the work. Besides, it's nothin' but worn-out whores and old washerwomen doing this work. It's not like yer an archangel saving lives. More dies in 'ere than lives." She snorted with amusement. "And alls the men want a tup with their sponge bath. Don't see 'ow this is any more respectable than whoring."

"Stop that talk," Jane commanded. "If we're to make a go of this, then we must adhere to a strict code of morality and respect. If we want others to see nurses as something other than worn-out women, then we must first believe in the profession ourselves."

The pair of them snorted. "And whot would the likes of ye know about bein' on the outs, earnin' yer coin by spreadin' yer thighs?"

Jane softened a bit. "I know enough. My mother was a working girl."

"Yeah? Well it's not the same as when it's you gettin' pawed for a pence."

"I am well aware of that. And here is your chance to make your life better. You'll see, in a few years nurses will be respected. As much as a governess, or a…a tutor. Now, go on and see to your duties."

"Whatever ye say, *Sister*," Abigail jeered. "But nothin' will come of it. You'll see. It's just another form of slavery for women."

Jane watched the two new employees of London College Hospital saunter back to the wards, which tonight, were overflowing. They might take the profession of nursing lightly. They might scoff and laugh at it, but Jane could not. How could a girl, born in the gutter and raised by a mother who prostituted herself be anything but grateful for a chance at employment such as this? No, nursing, while in its infancy, had a long way to go, but already, in the short year she had worked here, it had provided so much for her.

She was no longer an illegitimate bastard castoff. She had purpose. Knowledge. And the power to know that when her other employer, Lady Blackwood, left this earth, she would not be left destitute and alone unable to support herself.

It was knowledge like that, that gave a woman power. She would not be dependent upon a man for her survival. She could rent a small room and furnish it in a home with other women who were making their way in the world. Independent women, she thought with satisfaction. There was a new generation of women such as her. Women who believed they could make it on their own. Women who counted on no one for their survival or happiness but themselves.

The world was changing, albeit slowly. Too slow, as far as Jane was concerned. But she took comfort in knowing that there were others out there like her, trying to live a respectable life without the encumbrance of a man.

It was Lady Blackwood's doing, Jane thought with a wistful smile. It was her employer's teaching of this radical new thinking. Many people laughed at Lady Blackwood. She had been blackballed by more than one hostess in the past few years, but Jane knew if someone like Lady Blackwood could make her way in a world dominated by men and their laws, then Jane could, too. Lady B. had grown up in a world where she had everything to lose. Jane had grown up with nothing, and everything to gain.

No, nursing was far better than lowering herself by selling her body in the streets. Or worse, being a mistress. There was something so abhorrent to Jane about the thought of a man owning a woman for his pleasure. For Jane, it would be more than the exchange of her favors, it would be the selling of her dignity, her identity—her soul. She may have precious little in the way of material things, but the things that mattered most to her, her ideals and beliefs, made her wealthier than most women she was acquainted with.

As was her nightly routine, Jane strolled down the dark hall, lantern in hand, quietly making her way from bed to bed, ensuring all the patients were tucked in. Most were lying two to a bed. The blankets, threadbare and some moth-eaten, were too thin to ward off the dampness of the April night. Inside the ward, the air was ripe with disease and the melancholy of death. Bad air, she thought as she gently covered up a child who lay with its mother. She wanted to open a window, but knew the cold would make the patients suffer more. Still, the sickly stench wasn't much better than a damp draft.

There were sixty patients tonight, all suffering from a menagerie of ailments, and that was not including the five who already died since she arrived for her shift. Such were nights at London College Hospital. At first, she had been horrified by what she witnessed night after night. The beatings, the diseases, the air of hopelessness. But Jane had grown in strength these past twelve months, learning more about herself and human nature than she ever thought possible. The human soul was an amazing thing; the willpower to survive, humbling. The capacity to love, frightening.

She, herself, had never loved—not a passionate love. Of course she felt love for Lady Blackwood who had saved her from the streets and given her a life. But that was a different kind of love—a familial one. Sometimes, Jane would watch the other nurses with the male patients, flirting and flaunting themselves. She was no fool; she knew what went on in certain wards. She had been no stranger to the baseness of men. She had seen prostitutes with their clients. She knew of the acts. Knew that sex could be pleasurable. But what she had never been able to understand was how a passionate connection could be forged between two people. A connection that went beyond the few minutes that sex provided.

Perhaps there was something wrong in her makeup. Some flaw that prevented her from warmth of feeling. It was not that she hadn't longed for that sentiment, or yearned to discover what sex was all about, it was just that she had never felt moved enough by a man to embark upon the journey that might very well enlighten her about the aspects of pleasure and passion.

She was old by the standards of the day. Twenty-seven, to be precise. She had been kissed only once, and it had left a lackluster feeling inside her. Of course, being a lady's companion by day and a nurse by night did not exactly bring about ardent suitors. It didn't help that most found her shy and plain, two facts that Jane had never bothered to worry over. She could not help the way she was born. She would be lying, of course, if she said she hadn't questioned why she had not been born with her mother's beauty. Her mother, despite being born in the stews, had managed to capture the notice of an earl's son, who decided right then and there that she must be his mistress. That aristocrat had been Jane's father. Homely though he was, he had been a prize for someone like Lucy Rankin. But their life had taken a horrible spiral downward when Jane was six and her father had married another. Lucy had still been his mistress, but his visits were less and less frequent, and Jane had been forced to watch her mother's beauty, as well her spirit, decline. When her father had kicked them both onto the street without anything to live on, or a roof over their heads, Jane, at the tender age of seven, had made her first promise to herself. And that was, never be a mistress, and never allow a man to dictate your life or your happiness.

At twenty-seven, she was proud to say she had upheld that promise, and without any regrets. Still, she would be a liar if she refused to admit to at least herself, that there had been the occasional time, lying in her bed, that she found herself wondering what it would be like to share a bed and her body with a man.

"How is the consumptive child who arrived tonight?"

The whispered voice drifted over her shoulder, pulling her out of the unwanted, yet haunting, reminders of her past and the eager yearnings that had recently begun to plague her. Turning, Jane held the lantern aloft, illuminating the intelligent face of Dr. Inglebright, the younger. Dr. Inglebright, the senior, was a crusty old bear, with a wrinkled face and a deep mistrust of the new phenomenon of nurses. Inglebright, the younger, was a man with a kind smile, and gray eyes full of genuine concern—and respect.

"She sleeps at last, sir. Although her breathing is not so easy."

"Give her a quarter dram of laudanum then."

"Yes, Doctor," she murmured, unable to look into his eyes. For the past month, Dr. Inglebright had been looking at her most queerly, and it made her insides turn inside out. Why, she didn't know. She only knew that her response to the presence of Richard Inglebright had dramatically changed over the course of the year that he had taken her under his wing, teaching her about medicine, and showing her how to care for the ill. Perhaps it was only gratitude. After all, without Richard, she would never have had an opportunity to become a nurse. Mayhap it was friendship. They did talk very easily and freely between themselves.

"How is Lady Blackwood?" he asked, concern evident in his eyes. "I wanted to stop by this morning, but I found myself engaged in sewing up a young lad after removing his appendix."

Richard Inglebright was far more dedicated to the pursuit of healing than his father. If she had any say at all, she would, without batting an eyelash, request the younger Inglebright, despite the fact that his father was very often called to care for the elite of the city. It was episodes such as these, Richard staying on after his shift to care for others, that endeared him to Jane.

"You must be utterly exhausted," she said with concern. "You performed four surgeries last night."

Inglebright's eyes flashed. "Your concern warms me," he murmured in a deep voice that flustered her and made her look away. "No one cares about my needs like you do, Jane."

The statement felt far too familiar, and Jane, unsure of herself around men, did the only thing she could—she retreated behind her veil of coolness.

"As you inquired, Lady Blackwood is very well," she said, stumbling to get their conversation on a safe course. "That tincture you sent for her has helped immensely with her arthritis."

He smiled, making Jane wonder if he was laughing at her. "Good, good," he mumbled, his gaze traveling over her face and the white apron she used to cover her gown with. "You do credit to her, Jane. I know of few lady's companions who would deign to become a nurse."

"You give me too much credit, sir. You know very well I came to the hospital to work off my, as well as Lady Blackwood's, mounting debt to your father."

His smile softened as he pressed in closer to her. "But you didn't have to stay once it was repaid."

A little frisson of excitement snaked along her spine at his closeness. It was most improper how close they were standing. "I found I liked helping the ill. And what is closer to the truth, I saw it as a means for future employment. We both know that Lady Blackwood will not be with me forever. And where would I go? There is not another Lady Blackwood out there who would overlook my pedigree and bring me into her home to act as companion."

"There are many that would overlook your upbringing, Jane." His smile was like a full kiss on the lips. Jane felt it in every cell of her being.

"Doc, we've got somethin' fer ye."

Irritation flickered in his eyes, and Jane held the lantern higher. The annoyance swiftly passed as he saw two burly night men carrying in the body of what looked to be an unconscious man. A rather large man, Jane thought.

"'E's bleedin', he is. Head's mashed to bits."

"My theatre," Richard commanded, taking charge. "Jane, wash your hands and assist me."

"Yes," she said, obeying him with a slight curtsy. She ran to the end of the ward where a porcelain sink and a pitcher of clean, soapy water awaited her.

Pouring the now-tepid water over her hands, she rubbed her palms together, using friction to clean between her fingers and beneath her nails. Richard was fastidious about washing, a fact his father laughed about. But Jane had noticed over the months here that Richard's patients had less wound infections than those of his father.

Drying her hands on a clean towel, Jane walked briskly to the wooden doors that swung open. The hem of her black gown was swishing around her legs, the starched white apron itching against her neck, which had started to perspire. It was not fear that made her sweat, but excitement.

"We have a significant head wound, Jane," Richard announced as she entered the room where Richard performed his operations. "And perhaps some broken bones."

Richard's hands, covered in blood, searched through the tumble of black hair on the man's head.

"'E's a rich cove, 'e is," the burliest of the night men said. "Look at 'is clothes and that waistcoat."

"Never mind that now," Richard growled. "Help me to get him undressed so I can see if there is more damage. Jane, bring over the tray with the ether. I have a feeling when this giant awakes, he will not be in pleasant humor."

The two men began pulling off the bloodstained jacket and waistcoat. Jane turned her back, preparing the silver tray with the ether and an assortment of tools she thought Inglebright might need. For certain, this man would require needle and thread to close the gaping wound in his head.

"Damn me, the man's been through a rounder!"

Whirling around, Jane caught sight of a very muscular chest and arms. On the man's ribs were black smudges, which she knew were bruises.

"Spleen and liver feel intact, and there isn't any swelling or firmness," Richard muttered as he palpated the man's belly, which was etched in muscle. "His limbs seem to be intact, as well. I don't know how he managed it, but he seems to have avoided breaking any bones. Bring a cloth and water, Jane. Let's find out where all this blood is coming from."

Jane set the silver tray down on a wooden table, and began dabbing at the wound. The scalp wound, while large, was not overly deep. More of a superficial gash, really. The blood was already starting to dry, and the wound no longer wept.

Cleaning the cloth in the water, Jane wrung it out, watching the clear water turn red. She turned to his face, bending over him to work. He snarled, his white teeth bared like a rabid animal's as he grabbed her wrist.

"Givens and Smith, if you please," Richard said, motioning to where the man held her.

"None of that now, guv," Givens said. "The chit is only tryin' to help."

The man came off the table, swinging and hitting, as the night men struggled to hold him down.

"Get off," he cried. Like a madman, he swung at anything that moved. "Get the fuck off me, you whoreson!"

"'E don't talk like a gent," Mr. Smith grunted as he twisted the man's arm, forcing his torso back onto the table. "Talks like 'e was born in the rookery."

The man burst into a litany of profanity about being tied down. He struggled, his strength incredible considering his wounds.

"Give him two drops of ether, Jane."

With a dropper, she administered two drops of the liquid onto a folded cloth and pressed it tightly against the man's face.

He struggled, roaring, but it was not a cry of rage, Jane thought as she watched him, it was one of terror. He tossed his head from side to side trying to dislodge the towel, but Jane held firm.

"No," he said, muffled beneath the cloth, his voice weakening, as was his strength. "Don't do this. No binds…"

Jesus Christ, not again. He was being held down, his body unclothed, hands, cool and damp, stroked his flesh. He retched, trying to fight through the fog that clouded his brain. Fumbling at his waist told him his trousers were being removed, and he gathered the last of his evaporating strength to fight off his assailant.

The old fear seized him and he began to shake and breathe too fast.

"Shh," came a female voice. "You're safe."

He stilled, going limp, then realized it was a trick. This was no angel in disguise.

Violently he tossed his head, trying to fling off the cloth that was smothering him.

"It's all right," came the softly spoken voice, directly in his ear. "Take a slow deep breath, and hold it. That's right. Now let it go."

His body seemed to go languid. He felt hands in his hair. They were gentle and soothing. Not like the other hands that had always plagued his dreams. Hands that clawed and pinched. Hands that had awakened him many times in his sleep. Hands that had ruined him.

"You're bleeding, and we want only to help you," the voice whispered again. "You're safe here. I promise."

The world was blackening. He felt disembodied, weightless. Yet his hearing remained nearly perfect.

"There," she soothed, her breath caressing his cheek. "There is nothing to fear." The cloth fell away from his mouth as his body stilled. "Sleep now," she encouraged.

"You truly are an angel, Jane," came the voice of a male.

Before the blackness settled in, his fingers reached for her wrist, which he sensed was near his hip. He grabbed her, holding on to her like an anchor clutches the sand at the bottom of the sea.

"Be here," he scratched out through his cracked lips and dry throat.

She squeaked at the shock of knowing he was not asleep, but then she recovered swiftly. The tension in her hand lessened, and Matthew entwined his fingers with hers, holding on to the only thing that felt safe.

"I'm here," she said, her voice like that of an angel.

"No," he growled. "Later. Be here…*later*."

"He's out at last. Jane, hand me the scalpel."

Jane did as she was told. Thankfully, it was nearly automatic now, for she could not take her gaze off the stranger. He was beautiful, she realized, allowing her gaze to wander along the length of his unclothed body. He was very tall and broad. His were muscles honed and sculpted, reminding Jane of a diagram she had once studied while she learned anatomy. She tried to still her pulse as she ran through the anatomical terms. *Pectoralis.* His were large and firm, his nipples small and brown. On the left one, above his heart was a tattoo. A crest of some sort.

Rectus abdominis. Stomach muscles. All six of his were prominently displayed. So too was a tantalizing trail of soft black hair that disappeared beneath the white sheet.

"Jane."

The sharp voice drew her attention and she blushed. Sliding her spectacles back on her nose where they belonged, Jane met Richard's annoyed gaze. "Needle and thread," he repeated.

"Yes, Doctor."

She'd been caught staring. She was no better than the two new employees she had scolded a short time ago. But really, how could a woman possessed of a pulse not notice the man lying before her. He was stunningly masculine, and his face, while exceedingly handsome, held a beauty that was dark and sensual.

She noticed his lips were cracked and smeared with blood. She went to wipe them. "Not now, Jane," Richard commanded. "I need your hand."

In the light, he held a shining object between a pair of tweezers. "From a gin bottle most likely," Richard murmured as he held the tweezers up to the light. "It was lodged in the corner of his eye. You'll need to sew the outer lid back together. That is what is bleeding. You've a steady, delicate hand, Jane. You'll leave less scarring if you do it."

"Yes, Dr. Inglebright."

Richard nodded and reached for the towel. His hands were drenched in blood to his wrists. "He's an aristocrat," he muttered as he tossed the towel into the wicker basket they used for laundering. "I don't want him coming back displeased with me because I've bungled his looks."

Jane hid her smile. She knew Richard's opinion of the titled populace. It was not gracious.

Bending over her patient, she tried to forget that Richard was watching her, and that her patient's face lay pressed against her ample bosom as she bent low over his eyes.

Concentrating on steadying her hand, Jane tried to ignore the way the man's warm breath caressed her exposed skin above the edge of her bodice. Never before had she been so discomposed to be sitting this close to a man. He was asleep from the ether, yet her body was as aware of him as if he were awake, caressing her with his gaze, his hands, his beautiful mouth.

"He'll need his head bandaged. We don't want that gash to get putrid, or his eyes. You can see to that, can you, Jane?"

"Yes."

"Givens and Smith will find a bed for him. I think it best if he stay the night here in my room. He doesn't need to be out with the others. Whoever he is, he has money. I think he would be rather dismayed to find himself amongst the consumptives and typhoids."

Squeezing her shoulder, Richard passed behind her, studying her skill with the needle. "It's unfortunate the college doesn't allow women in, Jane. You'd be a superb surgeon. Lucky bastard, I doubt he'll even have a scar."

That was praise, indeed. No other compliment could have meant more to Jane. It carried far more substance than one based on the superficialities of beauty and feminine wiles. She was not a beauty. She knew and accepted it. But she was smart, and eager to learn all she could. She was a woman of worth, and would continue to be so, despite her looks.

"How do you do it?" Richard asked, peering over her shoulder. "Your stitches are so slight."

She laughed despite the closeness of Richard at her back, and the stranger's face at her front. "Sometimes it pays to be a woman," she whispered, smiling secretly to herself.

"We'll, you've a fine hand, and a quick mind, Jane. I'm glad I found you first."

3

Warm water sluiced from the cloth over the large expanse of the man's shoulders and chest. The water turned to rust, taking the remnants of dried blood away from his skin.

His skin tone was darker than most, tanned almost, she mused as she dipped the cloth once more into the basin and squeezed it over his pectorals. The water shimmered over the blue ink of the tattoo, and she bent closer trying to see what the image was of.

She still couldn't make it out. Tracing it with her finger, she saw him flinch and she pulled away, afraid to waken him—afraid to touch him.

Like a child caught stealing a sweet, Jane felt utterly guilty to be taking delight in washing this stranger.

Even with his head and eyes bandaged, he was beautiful. His nose, straight and refined, told of his aristocratic breeding. His lips, however, full and soft yet masculine, were made for pleasure.

Jane didn't dare touch them. She had wanted to, but had not allowed herself the wicked pleasure of such a thing. He was her patient. It was wrong. Had she not long ago given her two new charges the devil for their misconduct? Moral responsibility, Jane reminded herself. *Respectability.*

Yet Jane could not stop thinking of how hard he felt beneath her fingertips and how her body seemed to soften as her hands gently touched him. She had never once been physically affected by a patient. She had never felt the slow deep burn inside her, the vague tightening of her loins and her womb. Not even Richard had this effect on her. She knew the words that made her feel this way, but was at loss to explain why they suddenly consumed her.

Desire. Attraction—*compulsion.* Desire and attraction were what she felt at this precise moment. Compulsion was what she was trying so diligently to fight.

Her gaze fixed on his chest, watching how slowly his chest rose and fell. She allowed her hands to traverse the width of his torso under the pretence of counting his respirations. She heard the breath enter his lungs, felt his heart beating slow and steady against her palm. Saw his lips part as the air escaped through them.

Even when she was certain he was breathing easy, she could not push away. Her hands simply would not let go of him.

It was wrong to be this close to him, to sit on the edge of his small cot, to be leaning over him as she watched him sleep. He was clean now, yet still she bathed him, refusing to take her hands off his body.

He stirred against her, the bandages hiding his brow and facial expressions. Every once in a while, he would tremble, and his mouth would move as if he was trying to speak. His head would then begin thrashing, his body tensing despite the deep sleep produced by the ether.

What demon gripped him? She knew it was something evil that held him now. He should be peaceful from the ether, not grimacing and tensing, as if he was trying to fight.

Perhaps he was dreaming of his attack.

He cried out, his head arching back as his torso and buttocks lifted from the cot. The white sheet slid down, exposing the line of fine black hair that continually captured her attention.

"Shh," she soothed, pushing him gently back with her hands on his shoulders. "You're safe here."

He settled easily, falling back into the slow, even breathing of before. His body was still. His muscles quiet.

As Jane sat back and watched him, she allowed herself to take her fill of his naked chest. She had never seen a man like this before. One who was so large and muscled. One whose shaving soap and cologne still clung to his skin.

His chest was smooth and hairless, all except for the line of onyx down that swirled around his navel and worked its way lower. Without thinking, Jane ran her forefinger along the pathway of hair, marveling at the softness and the steely muscles beneath his skin. It was a contradiction, how something could feel so soft and innocent, yet just beneath so hard and unyielding.

She was utterly captivated by him, by the secrecy of his identity, not to mention the mysteries to be found on his body. Like a child with a new doll, she could not stop looking at him, or prevent herself from running her hand along his chest.

What would it feel like to have his length atop her? To be encased by his strong arms? To lay her head on his chest and listen to the steady cadence of his heart beating as she traced the outline of his tattoo?

What would it be like, she wondered, to have a man this handsome and virile buried deep within her?

As if he could discern her wayward thoughts, the sheet moved as his penis began to swell, the outline of which was pressed urgently against the thin, graying cotton.

Jane was not an innocent. She did not smother a cry of hor-

ror and launch herself from the bed. Instead, she allowed
herself to pull the sheet down, slowly exposing the man to
her curious eyes.

He was as large and beautiful there as he was everywhere
else.

His erection continued to fill, and Jane watched, mesmerized as the pink rod filled with blood. He was long and thick.
The foreskin pulling back, revealing a heavily veined staff and
engorged head.

She was consumed by the thought of feeling him,
touching the hardness that still grew. The devil whispered in
her ear, and she obeyed, reaching out to skim her fingertip
along the veined shaft.

He moaned, and hastily Jane pulled the sheet up, ashamed
by her actions. She had no idea what had gotten into her. She
had seen many male patients naked before, and never once had
she been tempted to touch them, to learn whether or not the
skin was as smooth and velvety as it looked.

Perhaps she had her mother's harlot blood after all, for that
could be the only reason for these new thoughts that suddenly
began to cloud her thinking and judgment.

"Are ye done yet?" Givens, the night man asked as he entered
the room. "We've brought a bed and we'll get him onto it for
you."

"Yes," Jane said in a voice that belied her thoughts. "I'm
finished. But do be careful, he took a nasty blow to his head.
I'm afraid I'm going to have to check on him frequently
tonight to ensure he wakes up."

She had seen many patients die in their sleep from blows
less severe. Tonight she would have to return to him hourly
and wake him, ensuring that he did not slip into unconscious-
ness and ultimately death.

One of the men reached for his ankles, and the other, his

wrists. The third shoved the bed closer so that the mattress of one was pressed against the wooden operating table. Beneath his weight, they grunted as they lifted him, affording Jane a glimpse of how tall he was. Well over six feet and solid as marble.

"Ye better take good care of 'im, miss," the one grunted with exertion. "'E's part of the fancy and there's no tellin' what will 'appen if 'e cocks up 'is toes here."

"I am aware of that."

Jane watched as they plopped him down onto the small bed. The mattress was thin, but it was clean. So, too, was his pillow. It was the best of what London College Hospital had to offer, yet Jane knew it was not even close to what the man was used to.

"Will there be anythin' else?"

"No, thank you. I'll call if I need help."

Jane pulled the screen around his bed, trying to afford the man some privacy. News traveled fast throughout the wards, and there was no doubt that the news of an aristocrat having arrived after being beaten unconscious would be fodder for those well enough to spread the word. Many of the patients, Jane knew, would risk their own health to leave their beds, if for nothing more than a glimpse of the man. Jane was determined to keep him safe and quiet, and not a spectacle on display for the others' amusement.

"Who are you?" she asked as she drew up a blanket, covering him to his shoulders. "And where do you belong?"

"Who are you?"

The words burned his brain, which throbbed in an unrelenting tattoo against his skull. He swallowed, tasting bile, and knew with sickening certainty the voice would come again, no matter how hard he tried to shove it aside and suffocate it until he could hear it no more.

"Who are you?"

"Your slave." The words erupted in his mind. Words said in his voice. Words that opened the floodgates of revulsion. Fear and panic swelled as he felt hands sweep over his chest.

He lay still and quiet, hoping that the words and memories would fade, along with the touch, but they rushed back, smothering him.

His heart was racing, his skin sweating, yet he felt chilled as the hated memories came back.

"You know, this is all you're good for—fucking."

No. He tried to say it, to scream it in his mind, but no sound emitted from his lips.

"You like this. If you didn't, you wouldn't be hard. Wouldn't be leaking your seed, anticipating what we're going to do to one another."

He shook his head denying it. Hating that the truth could not be hidden. But it couldn't. His cock was hard and throbbing, screaming for the release he had begun to crave with frightening regularity.

"Open your eyes and watch me."

No, he couldn't. It was dirty. Sinful. *Unnatural.*

But it felt so damn good, the devious little voice in his head whispered. And it did. No matter how shameful it was, he had never felt anything so good. And if he kept his eyes closed, he didn't have to see what was happening. Didn't have to watch the person between his thighs, sucking his cock deep into a hot mouth that knew how to get him off every time.

He was so close, he could feel it in the way his cods tightened up in the palm that handled them. He felt it in the way his seed raced up his shaft. And then it stopped. That hot sucking mouth and probing tongue abruptly abandoned him.

He cried out and reached for his prick, holding it out, offering himself, pleading and panting as he stroked his swollen cock with his hand. Even with his eyes closed he could feel those lascivious eyes watching him masturbate. *Harder.* He could hear the word whispered in a harsh rasp of growing arousal. Yes. He liked it hard, and his lover liked watching him toss off with ferocious jerks, spewing his seed over his palm.

"Beg me to take you in my mouth."

No. He wouldn't. But the word *please* was pulled from his lips before he could stop it. He was humiliated that he had shown such weakness and need—such perversity to want this—with this person. Yet despite that, he wanted the mouth on him, finishing him off, drinking him down and dry.

He felt the swipe of a tongue as he continued to stroke himself, the tongue teasing him with its elusive touch. *"You aren't going to tell. Are you?"*

It was a demand, not a question. No. He wouldn't tell. *Couldn't.* He hated himself for what he was doing. Hated the person who was once again pulling his cock so deep, sucking him until he had nothing left to give.

"No one would believe you if you did, you know. They would believe me, not you."

Yes. He knew that. No one would believe it, no one would understand.

"Open your eyes," the voice demanded.

He was loath to do it, to confront the wickedness and shame that played out between his spread thighs. But he was at the mercy of that mouth, and the hands that strayed to his buttocks, pulling them apart in time to the ravaging mouth on his cock. A finger slipped inside at the same time his cock was pulled deep, and the first spurt of come shot from his cock.

His eyelids flew up, and their gazes met. He was shocked by what he saw looking up at him. Despite all the times they had been together, the image still stunned him. Indignity flooded him, mixing with the pleasure he felt at seeing his cock being so greedily sucked as he continued to fist his hand up and down his swollen shaft, milking himself.

Dirty and unnatural. A slave to desire. A prisoner in a prison of his own making.

"You want to come, don't you?"

He wanted to, yet he despised admitting it.

"You hate me for what I do to you, but you can't resist, can you? You can't bring yourself to put a stop to our illicit meetings because you like what I do to you. You like these lessons I'm teaching you."

He was panting, anger and desire curling within him. *I hate you, I hate you, I hate you,* he chanted in his mind while a hot tongue glided over the swollen head of his member.

He hated this, lying here at his prick's mercy, but he could not move away, knowing how degraded he would feel after. He could not think about that now. All he could think of was coming and spewing it all over, making his sinful, secret lover feel a measure of degradation at his hand.

He came, pulsing in long powerful spurts. The low moan at once inflamed, yet angered him. His lover should have been dishonored by what he had done, but instead the act had aroused.

"My turn."

He found his body handled, moved to how his lover desired him. His lips were against a straining sex that pressed against his open mouth. He licked and sucked as he had been taught, listening to the growing sounds of pleasure. His cock was hard again, and his lover worked it, tugging and pulling hard.

He felt eyes on him, watching him. Felt that greedy gaze devouring his body. A hand smacked his buttock, stinging him before a finger traced his opening, and plunged in.

"You are such a dirty, sinful boy," his lover moaned.

He bit down, angry and mortified. He felt his lover fall apart and he came once more, empting into a hand that refused to release his cock.

Dirty. *Sinful.* He could never erase the taint. The smothering feel of his body being consumed with his unnatural lust, with his sick perversions.

He had a secret. A secret he must hide. A secret he wished he could hide from himself.

"Water," the angel's voice whispered, chasing away the old memories. He felt his head being lifted and cradled in a supple arm as something pressed softly against his lips, which felt swollen and cracked, and he winced. Immediately his head began to throb in a relentless pulsation.

Disoriented, unable to see, he shook off the hold and clamped his mouth shut. Where was he? He struggled to get out the words, but they came out in a growl that was incomprehensible.

"You're safe. It's only water."

The voice was soft, lyrical, with a hint of sensuality to it. It was a woman's voice, throaty and beckoning, yet it held a measure of authority that forced him to sip at the tepid water.

She tried to get him to drink more, but he refused, and finally she released him back against the pillow. The scent of her rushed over him as she bent down, fluffing the pillow and pulling up the sheet high on his chest. *Soap.* He inhaled again, discovering the essence, tasting it. She smelled clean—pure. Not overpowering as so many women did, with their flowery oils and perfumes.

He liked the way this woman smelled. Simple, yet enticing.

When she was about to pull away, he clasped her wrist, holding her still against him. He heard her gasp, felt her pulse quicken beneath his thumb.

For a moment he welcomed the feel of her, the heat of her body so close to his, the scent of her. What a novelty, for he hated the feeling of being smothered by another.

"Sir, you will reinjure yourself."

The voice, still soft and beckoning, was laced with a huskiness that belied her words.

"Where am I?" he asked while he licked his dry lips.

"London College Hospital," she replied as she tried to extract herself from his hold.

"Who are you?" He gripped her tighter, pulling her down lower until he could smell the starch in her clothes and the delicate scent of feminine sweat beneath the scent of her bathing soap.

"Jane."

The word exploded in his brain. Such a simple word. Such a plain name. Yet for all its simplicity and its single syllable, Matthew could not help but repeat it in his thoughts and marvel at how exotic and sensual her name could sound on his tongue.

"Jane…" He murmured the name, liking the resonance when murmured in his deep voice. He liked the sensuality of it said in a dark whisper of longing. *Jaaaane….* He drew out the syllable, allowing it to echo within the confines of his aching brain.

"Your name?"

He fought through the fog, trying to replay the events of the night, and instead he got lost in her voice once again, tripping along in his blindness and mental fog, waiting to hear her speak to him.

"What is your name, sir? Can you not remember it?"

Licking his lips once more, he savored the way her voice washed over his body like honey dripping from a spoon—slowly, in golden, hypnotizing rivulets, unraveling in soothing waves.

Christ, what the devil had they given him to make him think such queer thoughts?

"Sir?" she asked, concern taking away a measure of the sensuality he had heard.

"Matthew," he finally admitted. He heard her breath stop for the tiniest second. *She knew.* He was not simply a man, but an aristocrat. No aristocrat gave his Christian name—not when their identity revolved around a title. He didn't know why he didn't give her his title. The fog, he thought, that was the reason he was not thinking clearly. Perhaps, though, he wanted to be someone else—anyone else—here with this woman whose name alone aroused him.

"Matthew, will you release me? My back is hurting."

It was the shock that freed her. He had not heard his Christian name in years. He'd been ten the last time anyone had uttered it. He had always only been Wallingford, or my lord. Never Matthew. The intimacy of it rocked him, aroused him until he felt his cock stir, filling with need. He had released her as though she were fire and he was singed.

"You've taken a very bad blow to the head. Do you remember anything at all about your attack?"

"I recall your voice," he murmured. Intimacy swelled up once more between them, and he searched for her hand that lay in the wrinkles of the sheet. "You spoke to me."

"Yes, when the doctor was helping you."

"Come closer." Desire made his voice thick. "You are much too far away."

He felt the mattress dip slightly, heard the crinkle of fabric and petticoats as she arranged her skirts. He felt the weight of all that fabric as it pressed against his thigh.

"There now, is that better?"

"No." He reached for her, pulling her by her wrist until he felt the edge of her bodice graze his chest. The warmth of her skin met his, and she gasped, steadying herself with her hand against his shoulder.

She was too close, his brain warned, but his body over-ruled logical thought, and he wanted her closer, until her breasts were crushed against him, and his mouth was buried in her throat.

"Sir, release me."

"Jane…" He released his hold and brought his hand up, connecting with what felt like a soft, plump cheek. She had ample time to retreat from him, but even with his blindness, he could see that she moved closer. "Jane," he murmured again, not understanding this strange fascination with her name, or the sound of it coming from his mouth. She held still, although he heard her breathing change from slow and steady to shallow, unsteady rasps as he caressed her cheek, the tip of her nose, her full mouth that inflamed him.

He discovered her with his fingertips, painting her in his mind's eye. Her cheeks were full, her face narrow and her nose little, the tip slightly pointed. Her skin was smooth, like warm butter, her lips full and pouting. He moved his hand upward, to trace the contours of her eyelids, but she inched back, evading his touch, which exposed her throat and the swell of her breasts. His hand fell away from her face and glided down her throat to the apex of her heart, which beat furiously be-neath the stiff fabric of her gown. Her breasts were high, full, soft, and the sound she made, part cry, part surrender, had him stirring beneath the sheets.

"You…you've had an injury," she stammered as he traced the contours of her breast over her gown. "You're confused."

Yes. He was confused. He wanted to touch her. To learn her, and her lush form. He wanted her to touch him despite the fact he hated to have his flesh stroked. He wanted to stay like this, with his hand roaming over her.

"Matthew," she gasped, pulling away, "this is most unseemly."

"Stay, Jane." A beat of silence whispered between them.

"All right. But you must promise that you will sleep."

"And what if I dream of you?" he asked as he searched for her hand, and found her fingers trembling.

"You won't," she said in a quiet voice he knew he wasn't supposed to hear. "Men don't dream about women like me."

He tried to reply—*wanted*—to say something, but the blow to his head, combined with the alcohol he had consumed, swiftly robbed him of speech. He was asleep, struggling to return to Jane and her angel's voice.

How long he slept, he could not say. He only awakened for brief moments when Jane would rouse him, and ask him his name. Carefully she would check the bandage that wrapped around his head and eyes. Gently she would cover him up, and whisper to him that it was all right to return to sleep.

And always he would reach for her, grasping at her wrist, tugging her down beside him until he could feel the outline of her thigh against his.

"Stay with me, Jane," he mumbled hours later as he clasped her small hand to his chest.

"I cannot," she replied quietly. "The dawn has arrived."

"I despise the morning," he murmured, tracing the satiny nails of her fingers with his fingertips. "I am a creature of darkness, whose element is night and shadows. I belong in the dark with the other sinful creatures."

She caressed his cheek, and he did not flinch and shrink away in revulsion. Instead, he savored that gentle touch, eating it up like a starving man given a few scraps of bread. Why had he admitted such a thing? Christ, he was making himself vulnerable. Instantly he regretted saying those words, that secret truth. He never wanted to be weak, never wanted to show anyone that there was a chink in his armor. Yet there was something about this woman, this female he could not even see, that invited his trust, that lured the demon within him.

He clutched her tight as she pulled away, trying to keep her with him. "I will return tonight, Matthew."

"Then I will sleep until you do, and then, Jane, I will stay awake the night with you."

4

Mrs. Blackwood's old town coach awaited her outside the black iron gates of the hospital, just as it did every morning.

"Good morning, miss, I trust you had a decent night."

"Thank you, George," Jane replied as her driver helped her up into the coach. "It was relatively uneventful."

Well, if you can consider fondling a patient and being fondled in return uneventful.

"How was Lady Blackwood's night?" she asked, trying to think of anything other than Matthew's hand on her body.

"Mrs. Carling didna' say anything, so I imagine it went very well."

With a nod, he closed the door and hefted himself up onto the carriage box. With a whistle, the horses began their slow canter from the east end to the small house in Bloomsbury where she lived with Lady Blackwood.

On the nights when Jane worked at the hospital, Mrs. Carling, the housekeeper and cook, took over the duties of companion. Theirs was a small household—Mrs. Carling,

Jeanette, the maid, herself and George, who acted as coach driver and stable hand. Yes, it was a small household, and a ragtag one at that, but they were all satisfied with their lot in life. Lady Blackwood paid them on time, and treated them with respect. None of them bothered to concern themselves that they hadn't had a raise in a few years. What was money, if one was treated like a slave? Lady Blackwood treated them as though they were family, especially Jane. A fact she would be forever grateful for.

Long ago, Lady Blackwood had lived in one of the largest town houses in Mayfair. She had been young and beautiful and full of gaiety. She had been the wife of the Earl of Blackwood, and appeared to have held the world in her palm. That had been the outside image. Inside, however, her world had been one of terror and pain. After years of suffering physically from her husband's beatings, Lady Beatrice Blackwood had scandalized society by leaving her husband and seeking a divorce.

What courage it must have taken her to decide on such a course. She had been a pampered lady from the womb. Everything had been handed to her, and yet, she had left everything she had known to become a woman who was ostracized by her peers and her friends, a woman who'd had to learn to live by her wits and the very small monthly sum the courts demanded her husband pay her, as well as the small inheritance left to her by her father.

Divorce was still a stigma. Jane wondered how Lady Blackwood had endured it, being a social pariah all those years ago.

The carriage rounded the corner, and Jane glanced out through the warped glass to the sidewalk where women and children were setting up carts of fruits and vegetables. A fishwife, busy tossing the early-morning catch onto the table, shooed away a stalking cat, which curled its body around her gown's tattered hem.

The black soot and the acrid scent of coal permeated the air, mixing with the heavy veil of fog that had rolled in from the Thames. This was the East End, and the place where Jane had been raised.

Every morning on her way home from the hospital, she watched the activity, the hollow faces, the worn expressions of the women. And every time, she thanked God that Lady Blackwood had found her that one night and taken her in from the pouring rain. Jane shuddered to think about what her life would have been like had she not been found and whisked away from this place. Would she have survived long enough on her own to have a similar hollow, empty expression on her face as the women before her had?

Her life had been drastically altered that night. She had been given shelter and food. A bed, free of bugs, and a blanket that could not be seen through. Lady Blackwood had tutored her, teaching her to read and write, to sew and do needlepoint. She had taught her how to conduct herself in society, but most important, she had showed her what it was to live by your convictions.

Years ago, Lady Blackwood had taken an illegitimate, homeless waif without a future, and given her a life. Jane knew she could never repay such a debt.

She had been, and still was, beholden to Lady Blackwood for the life she'd been given. Lady Blackwood was a most excellent employer, providing Jane with food, clothes and lodgings, as well as permission to work as a nurse. She had two afternoons off per week, to do whatever it was she wished. She had a mother of sorts in Lady B., and no amount of money could ever replace that.

She was content with her life. Happy, she thought. Yet now, after leaving work, a little kernel of discontent began to gnaw at her. She could not stop thinking of her patient—

Matthew—and what he had done to her, what he had made her feel.

During the years spent with Lady Blackwood, Jane thought she had learned all she needed to know about being an independent, free-thinking woman. Tonight, she had discovered that she had never learned how to indulge her female needs. She'd had needs before, and she was not ashamed to admit that she had eased them with self-discovery and her own touch. But nothing compared to that heated searing deep within her as Matthew's skin connected with hers.

The rumble of the carriage ceased, and the conveyance swayed to the left, then halted, abruptly bringing Jane's thoughts to the present. She should have been tired after being awake all night, but she felt an odd hum in her body, as if the stale, coal-sooted air had given her a second wind. Not even the thick fog that still rolled throughout the city was enough to make her eyelids droop.

"'Ere ye are, miss. Home at last."

"Thank you," she said as she took George's hand and alighted from the carriage. Although her feet and back ached like the devil, Jane felt a buoyant energy coalesce within her. She wondered if it had to do with the thought of returning to the hospital and her patient that night.

Through the thickening drizzle, she saw the warm glow of the oil lamp that sat on the rosewood table before the bow window of the small town house. The soft, lumpy outline of Mrs. Carling could be seen lighting the other gas lamp that rested on the hearth. The house was awake, and that would mean that a pile of warm scones and butter, and a pot of hot tea would be awaiting her.

Picking up the hem of her gown, Jane ran up the steps that lead to the home she shared with Lady Blackwood and let herself inside. The scent of cinnamon and sultana raisins greeted her, and she closed her eyes inhaling the aroma as her stomach protested loudly.

"C'mon in, gel," Lady Blackwood announced from the breakfast room. "I can hear your insides rumbling from here."

Tossing her cloak and bonnet onto the hall chair, Jane swept into the breakfast room and took the chair opposite Lady Blackwood, who was dressed in her morning gown and cap.

Her employer was a large woman, with kind, sparkling eyes and a heart the size of her body. Her hair, once a dark walnut and given to curl, was gray and thinning.

When was it, Jane wondered, that Lady B. had grown so old and frail? How had she missed it?

"Well, tell me all about it. What mischief did you get up to last night?"

Jane felt her face flush as the image of Matthew's naked chest flared to life. "The usuals—consumptives, carousers and a few inebriates."

Lady B. arched her brows, even as her intelligent gaze strayed and lingered over Jane's glowing cheeks. "I do not like you working there, Jane. It's a dangerous part of the city."

Which made Jane ask herself what Matthew, with his obvious aristocratic blood, had been doing in the East End last night.

"How was your night?" Jane asked as she reached for a scone. "It was damp last night."

"That tonic young Inglebright sent over works like a charm. I slept like a babe."

"Lovely. He said it would. Dr. Inglebright is most knowledgeable."

Lady Blackwood's shrewd gaze traveled over her. "My dear, has the young doctor claimed your heart?"

Jane chuckled and smeared a large pat of butter over the steaming scone. "Of course not."

"Then why do you stay there, Jane? If not to see Inglebright every night?"

"Because I must."

"I am truly grateful to you for all you have done. Old Dr. Inglebright is well satisfied with our account and agrees that the debt is settled. There is no need to keep on at the hospital."

Jane took a sip of tea then a bite of her scone, fortifying herself for the argument to come. It always arrived every morning.

"Jane, that part of the city is just not safe—at any part of the day, let alone the dregs of night."

"Have you no other concerns than my safety?"

"I do not like to see you working so hard, Jane. I know I haven't much, but I do have some put aside to pension you and the others off when I depart this earth."

The scone turned to ash in Jane's mouth. She did not want to think of living in a world without Lady Blackwood. "You know I do not—"

"Yes, I know." Lady B. sighed. "You do not wish to take from me, but, Jane, it is my fondest wish to see you settled. And see you settled I will."

"I like working. It gives me purpose. *An identity.*"

Jane shrank away from the blue gaze that bored into her. "You do not need to exhaust yourself to be of notice."

But what of purpose? Jane wondered.

"There are times when I wonder if I haven't instilled too much independence in you, Jane. It can be a burden to only rely on oneself."

"I am grateful for everything you've given me. Independence is a gift, my lady."

"Sometimes it can be a curse," she replied, staring at her with eyes, that despite their rheuminess, showed deep understanding. "And it can be lonely, too."

"Nonsense," Jane scoffed while brushing off a few crumbs from her fingers. "A lady's independence is invaluable."

Lady B. pursed her lips, but said nothing. "Very well. You have won this morning, Jane, but we will have this conversation tomorrow morning, and the morning after, and the one after that until I have prevailed upon you to quit that place. Now, then, on to other business. I have had a letter from my niece," she said, reaching for a folded missive that was placed near her left hand. "She fares well, but her sister, Ann, has taken ill. Measles, I'm afraid."

An image of the breathtaking Ann flared to life in her mind. She would no doubt still break men's hearts despite the red dots that marred her usually flawless skin.

"Anais has written, wondering if there is anything they might give her for relief of the pain. Naturally, she is hesitant to use laudanum."

Jane could well understand the reason for that. Anais's fiancé was recovering from an opium addiction. Anais would naturally fear the worst. "I do have some holistic recipes she might try, herbs and powders. I'll write to her this afternoon when I wake up."

Lady Blackwood's expression darkened. "You work yourself to the bone, Jane, I can't bear to see it."

Jane patted her employer's wrinkled hand. "I like my job, *both* jobs," she clarified. "And I'm not working myself to death."

"Well, you shall have a break soon, for you will be accompanying me to Bewdley for my niece's wedding. And there, I will assure you that I will make every attempt to play matchmaker. You mark my words, Jane, I was quite a strategist in my youth."

Jane laughed and left the breakfast room, all the while thinking of her patient, and how impossible it would be to be matched with someone like him. Ah, well, she mused as she climbed the stairs to her room, that was what dreams were for.

The wards were loud that night as Jane entered the hospital. Shouting and the sound of metal hitting the stone floor echoed off the lime-washed walls. A woman's shrill voice cut through the ringing, followed by the deep rumble of a man's, full of indignation and anger.

Pulling her bonnet strings, Jane tugged off her hat and placed it atop the hook in the storage room. Her cloak came next, then she reached for the starched apron. She was tying the strings around her waist when the day nurse came in, her face flushed and her gown and apron soaked through.

"Maggie, what have you done to yourself?" Jane asked, watching the agitated woman reach for her wrap.

"I quit," Maggie snapped. "That devil of a man has been the death of me today."

"What man?"

"His lordship," she replied, out of breath from her anxiety. "He's been nothing but a pill today, he has. Always grumbling about somethin' and fighting me at every turn. Couldn't do a thing right for him. He's been asking for you since breakfast, maybe you can set him on the right track."

"All right," Jane murmured. Her body was suddenly filled with little prickles at the thought of seeing him again. *He had asked for her.* A ridiculous little thrill warmed her blood.

She had not slept well during the day, her slumber interrupted by the most improper dreams and thoughts. She had told herself on the carriage ride over that she would not seek him out. She would not think of him as a healthy, vibrant man, but as an ill patient. And nurses did not have erotic thoughts about their patients.

She had succeeded in putting him out of her mind, that

was, until Maggie had mentioned him. How little it had taken to flame the flicker of desire she tried so hard to snuff.

"He's burning with fever, and he won't let anyone near him to check beneath the bandages," Maggie grumbled as she searched through her purse for a crown for the hansom cab. "Dr. Inglebright fears the wound is festering, but his lordship won't let him get within a hairbreadth of him. He calls for you, Jane, and the doctor awaits you."

Jane touched the sleeve of Maggie's damp gown. "You aren't serious about quitting, are you, Maggie? It would be such a loss."

The woman, who was in her late forties, flushed again, but this time it was not with agitation, but pleasure. "Perhaps a good night's sleep will change me mind."

"And a different patient tomorrow morning?"

Maggie nodded and squeezed her hand. "Good luck, miss. You'll be in for a time of it. His lordship is quite the handful, and he's got a tongue that will slice you to ribbons."

Jane had come across many difficult patients in her time at the hospital—she was certain the mysterious lord would not get the better of her.

Leaving Maggie, she walked down the long corridor that led to Dr. Inglebright's private room. She heard Richard's voice through the wood.

"Damn you, if you don't cooperate, you'll get the ether."

"Sod off," came the deep reply. "I'll break your goddamn hand if you come near me."

"May I be of some help?"

The door swung closed behind her, and the two men froze in place. Richard was looking at her, a pair of scissors in one hand and a roll of fresh bandages in the other. Her patient was lying on the bed, thrashing his limbs as the two night men tried to hold him down. His chin lifted and he quieted. She saw his nostrils flare, as if he was smelling something, and then his head turned in her direction.

"Jane," the two men said simultaneously. The sound of the patient's voice, deep and seductive, made her tremble, and she was grateful for Dr. Inglebright's stern voice, for it made it easier for her to hide her response to Matthew's hushed whispering of her name.

"He burns with fever and rages like a lunatic. I need to check beneath the bandages, but he lashes out."

"How long has he had the fever?"

Jane came closer to the bed and watched as Matthew's head turned, as if he was following her path. He could not see, yet somehow he knew where to find her.

"All day, and I'm afraid the wound is full of putrefaction."

Jane could not smell anything that might lead her to believe the wound was festering, but there was a shadowing of old blood and yellow fluid beneath the layer of binding, which could be pus. The fact he burned with fever was sign enough.

Richard caught her gaze, his eyes pleading silently for her assistance. His gaze said it all, the patient was an aristocrat, and Richard could ill afford the man's death on his hands.

"Will you not let the doctor look?" she asked as she came to stand beside Matthew's bed.

"No," came the hoarse voice, "but I will allow you to look, Jane."

Richard arched his brow, staring at her in stunned silence before he handed her the scissors. "I will need to cut off the binding. Be still for a minute," she said.

Bending over him, she gently cut the white bandage and slowly began to unwind it. When she got to the back, she cupped his head in her palm and lifted, allowing the wrapping to come free. His mouth was close to her bosom and she felt the incredible heat rising from his body, as well as the dry warmth from his breath as it caressed her décolletage.

"Jane," Matthew murmured, and she heard him inhale the scented valley of her breasts. "Help me," he whispered.

"I am. I will," she replied as she lowered his head onto the pillow. Dr. Inglebright was watching her with scrutiny, and her fingers nervously fluttered against the white cloth.

"There," she murmured, pulling the long strip of binding away from his eyes. Inglebright stepped closer and reached out to examine Matthew's head, when his hand shot out and captured Richard's throat. "I want Jane," he growled. "Only Jane."

"Very well," Richard gasped as he pried off the fingers that held him. "Jane will look."

The hand fell away, and Jane pressed in, allowing her fingertips to gingerly part the clumped strands of hair that covered the cut. Blood had dried to his hair and scalp, making it difficult to visualize the wound. From what she could see, there was naught but redness. When she shook her head, telling the doctor that the fever did not stem from the head wound, he ordered her to peel back the dressing over Matthew's left eye.

"I want to remove the bandage over your eye, but I'll need to wet it to loosen it. Will you let me?"

He nodded and Jane rinsed the cloth that sat in the basin on the table beside his bed. Carefully, she wet the bandage, saturating it and dissolving the bits of dried blood that stuck to it. As she pulled, she felt him stiffen, and she whispered soothing, encouraging words to him. He responded to her voice, and settled deep into the bed, allowing her to pull the bandage free and probe his swollen eyelids. Both lids were grossly distended and bruised, and Matthew was unable to open his eyes. Standing back, Jane looked at him, studying the face that was still so beautiful despite the bruising and swelling.

"His eyes look fine," Richard grumbled behind her. "I've no idea why he has developed the fever."

"Perhaps it is the body's response to all he's been through."

"Maybe," Richard mumbled. "He's safe enough from his wounds, but if this fever continues to rage unchecked, it could be disastrous."

"I will get the fever down," she replied.

"If he allows it."

"He will."

Richard reached for her hand when she retrieved the cloth from the basin. With a squeeze, he forced her to look up at him. "I don't like the thought of leaving you alone with him. He's violent."

Jane glanced at Matthew, and something in her seemed to liquefy and soften. "He will not hurt me."

Richard stared at her curiously, as if he would see inside her, discovering for himself the tempest of emotion that stormed within her. She was at a loss to explain it, or to understand how it had happened—this connection she sensed she shared with Matthew.

"I will return, Jane, to check on you." Richard's gaze traveled along her body, before it once more rested on her face. "You will have a care, won't you, Jane? I'd truly hate it were anything to happen to you."

"You needn't worry."

"Ah, but I do, Jane. And never more since he has arrived. I *will* return to make sure you are safe."

As Jane watched Richard leave with the two night men in tow, she realized that it was not a statement from Richard, but rather a warning. He was coming back to check on her, to make sure that she was behaving as she should. Were her thoughts so transparent? Could Richard have any idea?

She turned to Matthew and pulled a chair close to his bed.

He was sweating, and the sheet that covered him was damp. His hair was mussed, and black stubble covered his upper lip and angular jaw. He was everything that was beautiful and masculine, and Jane could not look away from him, or the tiny rivulet of sweat that trickled between his pectorals.

"Jane," he murmured, then cried her name again, his voice rising when she did not immediately answer him.

"I am here." She covered his hand with hers and was astonished by the heat of it. "You burn."

He swallowed, then turned his head toward her voice. "I can't see you."

"Your eyes are swollen shut. The one is still stitched closed, but the thread will come out in the next day or two. In a few days, you'll be on your way, right as rain."

He scowled, changing his face from that of a beautiful angel, to demon. "I waited for you, all day. Where did you go?"

"Home. And I've only been gone the morning and afternoon. 'Tis early evening yet."

"It felt like a lifetime, waiting for you to return to me."

Her traitorous heart skipped a beat. She had never had anyone speak to her in such a fashion, let alone a man who looked like this.

"Will you stay, Jane?" he asked as he curled his fingers between hers. "Will you sit at my beside and nurse me through the long, dark hours of the night?"

"Yes, of course. It is my job, after all."

"Is that the only reason you are here?"

She glanced away, despite the fact he could not see that her eyes were busy taking in every inch of his body. No, she thought in silent answer. It was not her job that brought her to his bedside, but some other invisible force that pulled her to him.

He licked his cracked lips. "I dreamed of you today."

The cloth she was lifting from the basin sloshed back into the water, spilling over the rim and onto the table. She struggled for composure and reached for the rag once more, ringing it out, focusing on the task ahead of her. *I dreamed of you today....* She let the words echo in her mind, savoring the feeling they gave her. The words were like a soft caress along her body, intimate, alluring, slightly unnerving.

Jane's hand trembled as she brought the cloth to his face and carefully wiped his cheeks and lips with it. He caught a drop of water with his tongue as it landed on his mouth, and Jane watched, mesmerized, thinking it the most erotic thing she had ever seen.

"I heard your voice speaking to me," he continued as she moved the cloth down his neck. "It brought me comfort."

She swallowed and allowed him to talk as she cooled the cloth once more in the water. "Did you dream of me, Jane?"

"No," she lied as she watched her hand smooth the cool material down his chest, toward his navel.

"Then why did you scent your breasts?"

She paused, glanced up at his face and saw the devilish grin on his lips. How could he have known?

"Last night you smelled of soap, tonight you smell of perfume."

"Is it not a woman's prerogative to use perfume?"

"Yes, but why waste something so expensive if not for a certain purpose? Especially here, in a hospital full of the ill and dying?"

"Perhaps it has nothing to do with you, or any other man."

He laughed, and Jane felt herself flush. He knew. Knew she had thought of him, desired him.

"Lower, Jane," he rasped as she washed his abdomen. "I'm burning all over."

She absolutely refused to dip her hand beneath the edge of the sheet, but he reached for her wrist and stilled her. With the merest pressure, he pulled her down so that her ear was to his lips.

"I want to touch you, Jane. To learn you with my hands and mouth. I want to paint you in my mind."

Her breathing became much too heavy as her corset pressed and squeezed her chest even tighter. "My lord, you rage with fever."

"Yes," he replied, the sound husky and deeply male. The maleness was what made her body answer with feminine response.

"You do not know what you are saying, sir," she whispered, her voice trembling.

His hand left her wrist to touch her throat. With a gentle glide, his hot fingers swept up and down the column of her neck. "Swallow, Jane," he whispered. When she did, he kept his fingertips pressed against her, feeling the action of her throat moving sensuously up and down. He made a sound, a strange, guttural noise, and she tried to break free, but his arm came around her waist, holding her.

"I can see you, taking me in your mouth, swallowing me down. My cock has ached for it all day."

Shocked, aroused by his honesty, Jane pulled away, off-centered by the fleeting visual of her, bending over his body and taking him between her lips.

"Stay," he commanded. The fingers that were pressed against her throat were now skating down to gently caress the quivering flesh of her breasts. The arm that was wrapped around her rose up, his hand perilously close to the underside of her breast.

"My lord," she gasped.

"Let me touch you, Jane. You're such a novelty. I can't understand it, this need I have to feel you, to share myself with you. I never share, Jane—*never.*"

He cupped her, his hot palm holding her breast, squeezing and molding until she squirmed in his hold. Despite his wounds and the fever that ravaged his body, he was strong, too strong for Jane to fight off, if she had wanted to defend against him. A small voice whispered that she should, that she must, but a larger voice, a dominant one, told her to accept his touch, encouraged her to enjoy it, explore it, *return it.*

While she warred with herself, Matthew had somehow loosened the top three buttons on the front of her gown. Cool air kissed her bosom as his burning hand reached into her corset and pulled her breast free of the whalebone and linen.

She gasped as he moaned when her breast fell into his palm. She was startled by the sight of her pale breast being held in his tanned hand. The pink nipple, hardening, was stroked by the tip of his thumb.

Jane could hardly breathe for the pleasure that flooded her. As he fondled her, she grew languid. Her core seeping with wetness seemed to open—open to him.

"How wonderfully proportioned you are. I can see you in my mind, and what a treat it is. I can see myself doing all kinds of very wicked things to these breasts, Jane."

He freed her other breast, and now both were hanging out over her corset, the nipples hard and pointing. He pulled her forward, his hands spanning the expanse of her ribs, her waist, then down to her hips.

"I can see you, naked, lips parted in anticipation. Do you know in anticipation of what, Jane?"

"I can't imagine," she said breathlessly.

He held her waist tightly, his fingers pressing into her skin through the layers of her gown and chemise and corset. Her breasts bobbed as she leaned over him.

"Please," she whimpered. But was it a plea for him to stop, or to ignore her protest? She didn't know. She only knew her body was trembling everywhere.

His hot palm pressed into the soft flesh of her breast as he rubbed the flat of his hand along her nipple, sending it straining against his smooth skin.

"So beautiful," he whispered. "Ripe, succulent, waiting for my mouth and tongue." It unnerved her, all that passion she heard. Yet it made her soul soar to hear his praise.

Unable to stand the torture, she looked down and saw how he used his fingertip to trace the circle of her nipple; her areola puckered in response to the featherlight caress. Sharp stabs shot through her, straight to her belly, as he rolled both nipples between his thumbs and forefingers, lengthening them as he gently tugged and plucked. Suddenly she was wet between her thighs, restless with the need to curl her fingers in his hair and guide his mouth to her breast.

When he brought her close enough so that he could brush his chin and lips over them, she cried out and reached for his shoulders, anchoring herself onto him.

He nuzzled her, burying his face between the valley of her breasts. He brushed his chin and cheeks and damp lips over the mounds, before holding her up by the waist, her pointed nipples hovering over his mouth.

Jane watched his tongue snake out between his lips, flicking one engorged tip now a dark shade of pink. She moaned and shifted so that he could take it deep into his mouth, but he refused, and instead amused himself by flicking and licking her nipples with the tip, and sometimes the flat of his tongue.

"Are you watching, Jane?"

"Yes," she rasped as he circled her nipple then flicked his tongue in a series of feathering flutters.

"Do you like it?"

Her core damped, and she drove her short nails into his shoulders.

"I can feel that you do," he answered for her. Then he took her into his mouth and suckled. Slowly at first, then fiercely, as though he was starved for her.

His mouth broke away from her, and he gasped. "Jane, touch me. Learn me, too."

Jane gazed down at him. Her breasts, wet from his mouth, glistened at her. The sheet that covered his lower half slipped, and Jane reached for the edge.

"How?" she asked. "How should I touch you?"

5

He was delirious, not from fever, but Jane. The scent of her, the incredibly arousing feel of her petal-soft skin against his face made his flesh and blood blaze until he thought he would be consumed by the heat of longing.

He was amazed by her presence, the calm she washed over him. He had never been able to bear the feel of another atop him, yet he craved Jane like this, her breasts against him, the beat of her heart in his ears. He was starved for this, for the touch, the contact of another human being.

If he had been in his right mind, he would have refuted that wayward thought with a snort and a callous remark. But he was not in his right mind. Desire like nothing he had ever experienced before ruled him now. It was the same driving, relentless need that had fueled him with his first lover. But that had been lust, and animal need. The fucking had been hard, angry, soul stealing, yet the danger of it, the threat of being caught and punished, had made it arousing, made it just as good as the actual fucking.

But this moment with Jane was soft and tender, soul stealing, as well, as he felt something that had long lain dormant begin to awaken. There was need here, too. It was not animal lust, but something else. Something he could not name, something he had never felt before.

"You burn with fever, my lord."

"Matthew," he corrected. He did not want to be Wallingford here with her. He did not want to be an earl and heir to a dukedom. He wanted only to be a man, a painter and lover. He wanted Jane, not as a damaged soul who could not enjoy the feel of another, but as someone who was whole, untainted.

She was good and kind. He sensed it in her, and the devil inside him wanted to have a bit of her goodness all to himself. He had never known what it was to be good, or kind. He was cold and callous, purposefully hurtful. Yet here was this angel lying against him, allowing herself to be corrupted by a demon in a gentleman's disguise.

"We must stop this," she breathed in a husky pant that sent his cock lifting beneath the sheet that had grown just as hot as his body. "I must see to ridding you of this fever."

"Yes, you must," he agreed, his mind taking a turn down a wicked, wicked path. It was bad enough that he had envisioned her taking his cock into her lush mouth and swallowing him down, something he could never allow in any real way. Now he thought of her touching him, every inch of his body. When he felt the cool cloth return to his chest, he reached for her wrist and brought it low, guiding her. With his hand leading hers, he brought the cloth, which she clutched steadfastly, to his cock. He heard her gasp; it was followed by the rustle of starched muslin, and he imagined her shifting on the bed, her waist turning so she could look down at him, and the heavy sex that lay between his thighs. Her breasts would still be exposed, and he knew the image of her like this would be forever imbedded in his mind. He would paint her the minute he arrived home.

"Touch me, Jane," he choked out as he forced her hand to release the cloth, and instead hold him. He groaned, threw back his head and gritted his teeth as her palm engulfed his thick shaft. With little pressure, he moved her hand up, then down. The image of his fingers locked atop hers as he worked his cock made his excitement grow. He was rasping in shallow, hard breaths, which mingled with hers.

She was watching, he could feel her eyes searing into the spot where their hands wrapped around his shaft. It aroused him, not angered him, knowing her eyes were upon him. He did not feel defiled as he once had when his lover had watched him masturbate. His lover had taken perverse delight in ordering him to pleasure himself and come all over his hand. His lover had enjoyed barking out orders. Even now he heard them: *harder, faster, now slower, stop…*

But Jane did not say anything. Their breaths were the only sound in the room. It had a strangely calming effect on him. Normally he was tense, his big body taut with urgency, but tonight, he felt himself go limp and fall into the thin feather-ticking mattress. He allowed himself to enjoy the feel of their joined hands on him, and the images that played out in his mind, how she would look like this, taking him in hand and tossing him off.

It seemed forever he lay like that, his pleasure building, Jane's breaths frenzied. The scent of her wafted over him and he used his free hand to tug at her nipple in the same rhythm she used to stroke him.

"Matthew!"

The sound of his name in her angel's voice weakened him, and he came, exploding in a hot jet onto both their hands. He heard her cry of shock, but she did not pull away, slowing her strokes instead, watching as his cock pulsed with his seed.

My God, he had not come into someone else's palm in fifteen years. The shuddering orgasm unnerved him, and he turned his head, not wanting Jane to see his expression of terrified wonder. For he was alarmed by the emotions that suddenly ruled him.

Mercifully she said nothing as she rose from the bed. He heard the water in the basin softly slap against the porcelain sides. It was followed by the wringing of a cloth, then the sound of Jane's fingers buttoning her gown.

Was she ashamed? Horrified he could be such a beast? He was ill, burning with fever, and yet he was *still* ruled by the needs of his body and cock.

"The water has turned too cold. Tepid is best for bringing down a fever."

"Go then," he said in a hoarse voice. He wanted to add a request that she return to him, but he bit his tongue, refusing to ask or beg. Yet as soon as he heard the door swing shut behind her, he heard her name, whispered in his broken voice, "Jane, come back."

Scooping the water from the rain barrel, Jane watched as the clear liquid splashed into the bowl. Her hands were shaking, as was her body. The sounds of the wards inside the hospital were a distant whisper compared to the husky groan of male satisfaction that was ringing in her ears, even now.

Good God, what had she done?

Setting the bowl on the steps, she sat down and brought her head to her knees, trying to regain her innate sense of calm and composure. She refused to close her eyes and instead stared down at the starched white cotton of her apron. It was no use. Even with her eyes open she could see Matthew's fine, strong body lying on the bed beside her, completely naked, the sheet thrust to his thighs, his phallus thick and long, heavily veined, engorged with desire. *Desire for her.*

Jane still could not understand, or make sense of the way she had instinctively known what he wanted. She had never done such a thing before, yet the feel of him, heavy and hot in her hand, had felt so right, as if she had pleasured many a man before. She gazed down at her palm and studied the lines in the moonlight. She could still feel it in her hand, still hear her own thoughts whispering in her mind, *I want to know what this would feel like inside me.*

It shocked her to hear such an admission, and in her own voice. She was not a naive prude. She had seen much growing up in the rookeries of the East End. Yet it still shocked her that she could want such intimacy with a stranger. Never before had she looked at a male patient and wondered what it would feel like to take his body inside hers. She had not even thought of Richard in such a way. Strange, since she felt a measure of affection for the young doctor.

Jane closed her eyes and forced an image of Richard to mind. Gray eyes, pale skin and golden hair. He was handsome in a typical English way. He was tall, too, although not as tall as Matthew, and much, much leaner. In all, he was very pleasing to the eye, and there was no shortage of nurses and patients who flirted with him. To Jane's knowledge, he had never taken up their offers. She knew with one-hundred-percent certainty that Dr. Inglebright would never have touched, in a sexual manner, a patient under his care.

How far she had fallen for the touch of a man. Jane had no idea she yearned for such things. Certainly there were some nights when she felt the urge to touch her breasts and quim. She had found it naughty, in a forbidden way, to touch herself. And it had felt good. Now, those times of self-pleasure paled when put beside this brief, erotic interlude with Matthew. She sensed that what he had done to her, what she had done to him, was merely the starting point of where their shared passion might go.

She yearned to explore it, she realized, giving honesty to her feelings. But to do so could be disastrous. Besides, there could be nothing out of it except a few stolen moments, hardly worthwhile when one thought of what she could lose if it ever got out what they were doing behind that swinging wooden door.

Her job at London College would be lost. Her name and that of Lady Blackwood would be further tarnished. The profession, which she was trying so hard to make credible to the eyes of the world, would be thrust back down. Only old harlots and washerwomen are nurses...that would be accurate, if the truth about what she had just done got out.

No, she could not repay Dr. Inglebright or Lady Blackwood by sullying her name, her profession or the hospital.

Standing up, Jane retrieved her basin of water and determinedly stepped back into the ward, resolute to rid her patient of his fever and survive the long night ahead without further thinking on how much she wanted to lie on top of him and feel him thrusting that beautiful phallus deep inside her.

The tepid water trickled over his skin as Jane changed the cloth that she had folded on his forehead. His fever was higher, despite the hours of sitting at his bedside, bathing him.

"I don't understand it," Richard mumbled behind her. "Where is this fever coming from?"

"I do not know," she whispered, worry clouding her thoughts. "He's so strong and healthy, I don't know why it holds him."

"He smelled of spirits when he arrived. Perhaps he is a

chronic drinker. I've seen the fever in the gin addicts when they don't have it."

Jane glanced at Matthew's face, which was drawn tight. Occasionally he would frown, as if he was being plagued by dreams. Taking her fingers and dipping them in the basin, she brushed them over his cracked lips, while Richard continued to pace behind her, deep in thought.

"Perhaps it is the head trauma that is causing it. The body's natural response to pain and injury."

Jane did not respond. She knew no answer was necessary. This was Richard trying to solve a medical puzzle. Instead, she continued to bathe Matthew, studying the way his body felt taut with tension.

"Don't touch me," he suddenly cried, and thrashed in the bed, his arms flaying wide, nearly hitting her in the head. "Jesus Christ, get off me."

He knocked her off the bed with a blow to her shoulder. With a thunk, she landed on the floor, and the ceramic basin smashed to bits around her.

Richard ran to her and helped her up. "Are you cut?"

"No, I don't think so," she muttered as she looked at her shaking hands then back at Matthew. "He rages with fever. He didn't mean it."

Richard looked at her skeptically. "From now on I will assign another nurse to care for him."

"No!" The rebuttal was out of her mouth before she could stop it. Richard looked startled, then his gaze slipped past her shoulder to where Matthew lay still on the bed.

"No?"

Jane swallowed hard. She could not bear the thought of another woman sitting beside him. He was hers—her patient. The thought that perhaps he was already married or engaged did not enter her thoughts. For Jane, he was hers. It was the last remnant of growing up in the East End that still clung to her. She had grown up with nothing, not even a decent parent. As a result, anything that was hers, she held steadfastly on to with a selfish single-mindedness. Matthew was something she knew she had to keep hold of, if only for this night.

"Very well, then, Jane. But only because you are my most skilled nurse, and he is a man of good breeding."

Jane nodded. "Have you any idea of his identity?"

"My father thinks he knows. He's gone to Mayfair tonight after learning a few things at his club this afternoon."

"I see."

"Well then, I will let you tend to him, but I will be back," Richard murmured as he ran his palms down her shoulders. He squeezed her arms gently before leaving. He didn't say anything to her, but the look in his eyes said it all. He knew. Somehow Richard had discovered her fascination with Matthew.

Someone was touching him, but it was not that filthy lover in his past whose hands were covering his body. It was Jane. Amazing how he had the wherewithal to discern such a thing. Yet he knew it was not the other.

The other one had come, though, for a visit in a dream. He loathed those dreams and the way his body felt after them. But it was Jane's body here with him now.

"Jane?" he asked, croaking through his dry lips and raw throat.

"Here," she whispered, "take a sip, slowly."

The cool water that slipped down his throat felt so good that he could not sip, but only gulp, despite her warnings. When he sat back, he felt weak and exhausted. He recalled what they had done, and the effects on his body still pleasantly lingered.

"You must rest," she ordered, her voice now cool and detached.

"I have slept enough."

"Sleep is the body's best medicine."

"No, Jane. You are the tonic I need."

Silence blanketed the room, and Matthew cursed himself for his loose tongue. He was not a talker, not unless he was cutting someone off at the knees, but tonight, with Jane, he couldn't seem to hold his tongue, or hide the strange emotions that bubbled beneath his skin. In truth, he had no idea if he desired to or not. His brain knew he should lie in silence and leave her to her work. But his body cried out for her presence at his bedside, her voice in the quiet, her hands on his flesh. He refused to wonder if it was the fever provoking these thoughts, or some deeply hidden need he had never known that lurked within him. Neither reason mattered now, the only thing that mattered was getting Jane back close to him, drawing her into him.

"Will you not sit with me?"

"No. There are other patients who require care." She brushed past him. He heard her stiff skirts brush the sheet and he reached out, grasping for anything that he could hold.

"I wish I could see you," he whispered. "Here, help me to, Jane." He held his hand out in the air, waiting for her to take it.

"Matthew," she said in a voice full of pleading, "please don't."

Despite his blindness he found her hand and pulled her down so that she was sitting beside him on the bed.

"If you are in pain, or in need of something—"

"I am in need of you." Their fingers entwined and he ordered her to bring their hands to her face.

"I don't understand what this will prove."

"I want to paint you in my mind."

He found the soft curve of her chin, and traced his trembling fingertips over the downy skin. In his mind he saw unblemished peaches-and-cream skin. His fingertips skated over the bridge of her nose down to her lush mouth. She turned her head when he reached the corner of her lips. Despite his coaxing words, she held herself away from his touch.

"Let me touch your mouth."

"No." She tried to move away, but he held her to him and brought her forward, capturing her mouth with his. It was a soft, lingering kiss, just lips brushing, and his soul stirred.

She pulled away, his lips kissing the air. "We can't do this, Matthew."

"Why? Is there another?"

"It doesn't matter, does it?"

He smiled and reached for her once again. "No, it really doesn't."

"Matthew, stop."

"What color is your hair?"

There was hesitation before she answered, "What does it matter what color it is?"

"Because I want to know what color to visualize when I'm dreaming of you and your hair spilling over me."

"Please," she whispered, "do not say such things."

"Why?" he asked, the fog from his fever lifting, giving increasing clarity to his thoughts. "Did I shame you by forcing your hand to pleasure me?"

"You did not force me."

"But I did shame you?"

The accusation hung heavy and he heard Jane leave the bed and walk to the corner of the room, her heels clicking against the floorboards.

"Why do you run, Jane?"

"I do not run."

"Aye, you do. Every time the rope that is wrapped between us pulls you closer to me, you pull away, untangling us."

"There is no us, Matthew. You're confused. Febrile."

"There could be an us," he replied, hating the desperation he suddenly felt flare in his breast. "Jane," he whispered, "come away with me."

He knew he had caught her attention when he heard her movements stop altogether.

"When I leave here, come with me. Let us explore this… this…whatever has brought us together. Let me paint you, pleasure you. Be my muse," he added, tossing in anything that might persuade her to come to him.

"Your muse?" she questioned.

"Yes. I've done nothing but paint you in my mind with nothing but my fantasies. Let me see you with my own eyes. Let me paint my fantasies."

The door opened, and the sterile odor of Dr. Inglebright flowed around them. "Jane, the carriage is here. I ordered it 'round early. You've had a long night."

Hatred fused his thoughts. Was Jane the doctor's lover? Wife? Bloody hell, he had not thought of her as anyone but his.

"How very kind of you, Dr. Inglebright, but I will stay to finish my shift."

There was no feminine welcome in that tone. No gratitude, either.

"I insist, Jane. There will be no argument."

"Very well," she muttered, and Matthew heard the clicking of her heels on the floor once more. This time they belied her true thoughts. She was not happy to be ordered about by the good doctor.

"Jane," he called. "Sleep well. And you might do me the favor of reflecting on my offer."

The door swung shut, and Matthew sensed the doctor staring him down where he stood at the foot of the bed.

"Lord Wallingford," Inglebright growled, "you'll be leaving us now, returning to your side of the city."

"Why didn't you tell her?" he asked, feeling his heart sink back into the black depths of his chest.

"Tell her what, that you're a licentious rake who feeds off women and discards them when your amusement fades? Amusement, I have been told, that is rather dark, and decidedly not the sort of entertainment that Jane would find amusing."

Matthew growled, "Yes, why didn't you tell her I'm a soulless bastard?"

"Because it would have made you all the more attractive. Now then, my lord, your father has sent a carriage around to fetch you. The night men will make a litter for you—"

"The hell they will. I will walk out of here on my own two feet if it's the last damn thing I do. And the last thing you're going to do, Dr. Inglebright, is give me Jane's direction."

6

"Lord Raeburn to see you, milord."

Matthew looked up from his easel and over to the paneled door where his aging butler peered at him with rheumy eyes. The man's fingers, gnarled with arthritis, gripped the edge of the door as he pressed his frail frame against the wood for support. He really was going to have to see to pensioning off the old retainer, and soon by the looks of it.

"You may send him in, Thomas."

"Very good, milord."

"I had to come and see for myself, days holed up in bed, and without anyone for company. It must be the end of the world."

Paintbrush poised in the air, Matthew arched his brow in annoyance as he watched Raeburn, breeze into his studio. "I am well, as you can see. Nothing untoward after my brush with death."

"I do see. Incredible the way you can reconstitute yourself. Are you certain you're human and not a vampire?"

Matthew grumbled and motioned to the settee by the window. "Trust me, I would need more than blood to sustain me. Just toss the papers onto the floor. I haven't the heart to ask Thomas to clean up in here. He and the rest of the staff are working themselves ragged."

"Slave driver, are you?" Raeburn chuckled as he lowered his tall frame onto the settee. "Working them to the bone?"

"Had my father not decided to cut back my living expenses by nearly twenty-five percent, I would not be forced to run my household on the barest-minimum requirements. Hence, the servants may thank my father. It is his fault they have had to work their fingers to the bone."

Raeburn grinned and gazed into the hearth. A small fire burned in the grate, dispelling the chill in the air from the rain that had not let up since midmorning. Odd, but Matthew had felt chilled since leaving London College Hospital a week ago. He had not been cold then, when he had Jane pressed against him. He could still feel the warmth of her body as he pressed against her breasts, still tasted her on his tongue, smelled her on his hand. He could hardly paint, so consumed was he by thoughts of her. He had relived that night with Jane over and over, and each time he marveled at how beautiful it had been.

Damn Inglebright for refusing to divulge any information in regard to Jane or where she lived. And damn him for not giving up the idea of pursuing her. Already the day's letter had been shipped off to the hospital. Another missive for Jane requesting that she come away with him. *Anywhere.* Just him and her and a place that was private, so he could fuck her senseless and purge her from his body and mind.

"I was worried, you know, when I heard you had been ambushed in the East End. Nasty work, that."

"You, of all people, know that I have an exceedingly hard head. It would take much more than a few rookery ruffians to do me in."

"Still, I was worried."

"No need. I'll still bear witness to your nuptials, if that is your concern."

Raeburn sent him a scathing glare. "I'm here because I care for you, damn you, not because I'm concerned I'll need to find myself a new best man. Devil take it, Wallingford, you know I care."

Of course he did. Raeburn wore his emotions on his sleeve, unlike himself who buried emotions to the pit of his being. Feelings led to weakness and he never again was going to weaken. Despite that, he did love his friend, and acknowledged the sentiment with his usual hauteur and a deep grunt that Raeburn was able to interpret. Theirs was a long-standing friendship that no longer required words. And Matthew thanked the Fates that he still had such a friend in his life. Raeburn understood, and wisely chose a different tack for his visit.

"You know, if this business of money has got you tied in knots, why not set your cap for an heiress?" Raeburn suggested as he continued to study the flickering flames. "It's a simple enough option, and it's all the rage, you know. The nouveau riche are clamoring for titles as illustrious as yours. What railway magnate's daughter would not swoon for the opportunity to become a countess, not to mention a duchess? You could have your pick of them, you know. Your reputation could easily be swept under the carpet. No one would bat an eye once you made it clear you intended to actually do right by the girl. You could easily become the most sought-after bachelor, with your looks and your estates, and your other—" Raeburn waggled his brow "—sizable attributes."

"Sod off," Matthew cursed, swiping his brush along the canvas while he ignored Raeburn's taunting. 'I'd rather become a damn eunuch than find myself married to some simpering, weeping girl."

"Get yourself a feisty American chit, one with a large dowry and a minx of a body. That should change your mind about spending the rest of your life living without your bullocks."

"Surely to God you have not traveled to Berkeley Square to talk to me of marriage."

"Well—" Raeburn shrugged as he tossed a pillow aside and stretched his booted feet out on the settee, lounging in negligent repose "—I did come to see you to make certain you were on the mend. Thomas told me you had the fever."

"I am recovered, as you can see."

"But still stewing over money."

"There is very little in my life to occupy my thoughts. Naturally it falls to money to become my fixation."

"Fucking used to be your fixation."

"What does your future wife think of your crudeness," he snapped. "Does she find it as tiresome as I do?"

Raeburn threw his head back and laughed. "I assure you, crudity has its place in the bedchamber. And while we're talking of the fairer sex, I was introduced to an extraordinarily lovely young lady last night. I thought she might do very well for you. Beautiful face, quite perfect breasts, at least from what I could tell—I don't really look, you know, as I'm very devoted to Anais. However, I could not help but notice—"

"Stop." Matthew held out his hand and glared at his friend. "I am not the least bit interested in meeting some young twit who cannot string two words together. Furthermore, I am not interested in virgins. Innocence is highly overrated and more often than not, feigned. Give me the jaded whore any day over a naive virgin. Give me a woman who can indulge her passion without blushes and remorse. If we're exchanging currency for fucking, I'd rather do the buying instead of being the one sold off. It's much more palatable to know I can toss a few pound notes on the bed and leave forever, than it is to fuck a wife, knowing she's purchased your cock just for your title. I'll not be bound like that—*never.*"

"Christ, you're so bloody cynical," Raeburn grumbled. "Not every woman is the devil disguised behind a good set of tits."

Matthew arched his brow and peered at Raeburn over the top of his easel. "I've yet to meet one that is an angel."

But that was not entirely true. He did not think of Jane as he did all the other women who had come and gone in his life. She was not made of the same stamp as the women he had taken to his bed.

"Right, then, since a rational discussion of marriage seems to be out of the question, let us talk of something else." Raeburn inclined his head to the easel. "What are you painting, now that your masterpiece is completed?"

"Nothing, really." Matthew looked at the portrait he was just starting. Pale lines lay in contrast against the vanilla-colored canvas. It was the shape of a woman, all soft curves. She was reposed on a lounge, naked, her fingers tangling in her blond hair. She was faceless. Frowning, he realized he had painted Jane without even thinking.

Raeburn cocked his brow and studied him. "You're in fine fettle this morning. Up a bit too early, or is it you've gotten to bed too late?"

Matthew ignored him and proceeded to close the lids on his ink pots.

"Damn me, man, you are not yourself. You've become as dull as a vicar's wife. It is not like you to not have gotten into some sort of illicit scrape with a lord's wife or infamous actress. Or perhaps you've managed to seduce a maid who was taking care of you on your sickbed?"

"No...no scrapes."

"What of the famous Lady Burroughs? How goes your pursuit of her?"

Christ, he had not thought of her in a week. Not since Jane had entered his life.

"Word is that the young countess is looking for someone to warm her bed. Her husband seems incapable of pleasing her. I'm quite certain, from what I've heard from your past paramours, that you are more than up to the challenge of pleasing Lady Burroughs."

"You're remarkably well informed in the latest gossip."

Raeburn shrugged and crossed his legs. "I had not stepped foot in Lord Halifax's ballroom last night for more than five minutes before I was inundated with gossip and questions."

"Tell them all to go to hell, that's what I usually say."

Raeburn shrugged off his rebuttal. "Has your father come to you yet, about the portrait and auction?"

"No."

"I wonder what the duke will say when he finds out about it?"

"With any luck, this one might finally kill the old bastard."

There was no love lost between him and his father. In fact, he rather relished the confrontation that would ensue when the news of his auctioning off of a scandalous piece of art reached his father. He smiled, thinking of the blows they would come to.

Served the pompous bastard right for systematically denying him of his rightful income. Bloody hell, the man had no right to do such a thing. He was the heir. He'd been reminded of that fact more times than he could count. Well, damn him, didn't the heir deserve more than what his father was currently having his solicitor pay him?

Bugger the old bastard. He had found another way to pay for his art gallery. If it was not going to come from respectable money, it could damn well come from another source. Yes, let the bastard come to him after learning of his latest scandal. What was another one in a long list of outrageous behavior? Scandal was his way of life. He was completely and utterly immune to shame and the whispers behind his back. He was a ne'er-do-well and a muff chaser. He cared for no one but himself. Everyone knew that.

But does Jane? Did Jane know of his true reputation, or was she blissfully unaware? A little niggling of hope entered his breast that she did not know him.

"Has some hussy bit off your tongue?" Raeburn said on a laugh. "Bloody hell, man, what the devil is wrong with you?"

"Nothing," he said with a scowl.

"Nothing? Good God, you've taking up woolgathering, you haven't bedded a lord's wife in God knows how long and you've been relatively scandal free for days. And don't bother to deny it."

"I've been occupied."

"With what?"

"None of your damn business."

"Ah, a woman, then. Tell me, is it the lovely countess? Have you succeeded in getting her into your bed?"

"Go to hell, Raeburn."

But his friend only smiled. "Oh, come now, Wallingford, pray do not play the gentleman now. You've never been one to keep your exploits to yourself—" Raeburn halted midsentence and watched him thoughtfully, a sly grin suddenly parting his lips. "Don't tell me that the infamously debauched Lord Wallingford has found a woman he would actually like to talk to, as well as fuck. Christ, is the world coming to an end? I never thought to see the day that you—"

"Don't be ridiculous, Raeburn," Matthew growled as he leaped up from his chair and prowled about the room. "My notion of the proper woman has not changed since you decided to get married. My concept of a proper woman is still one who raises her skirts, spreads her legs and lets me have my way with her, then puts up little fuss when I leave her without a backward glance."

A thought of Jane flashed through his mind, and he felt ill. This was something he didn't want with her, the coldness, the distance.

Jane. Lovely, mysterious Jane. Jane, whose body was full and curved beneath her plain woolen gown. Jane, whose voice alone made him shiver in longing.

Bloody hell, he was a man possessed. *A man obsessed*. Never had his need to know a woman been this strong. The only needs he had ever had in regard to women were sexual. He never really talked with women, unless of course it was in double entendres and sexual innuendos. And yet, he craved Jane's company. He yearned to be with her, sitting beside her. He needed to know her—all of her. He wanted her carnally. Emotionally. Spiritually.

It didn't make sense, she was just a woman. Weren't they all the same? Yet somehow he knew she was different from all the others. Somehow he knew she was forbidden. Forbidden to be tainted by someone as debauched and amoral as himself. But damn him, he could not resist this temptation—this woman who made him yearn. Made him dream. Made him hope.

Christ, it was dangerous to hope.

It was dangerous to feel alive.

"Are you ill?" Raeburn asked once more.

"Quite possibly," he muttered.

Alive….hope…he hadn't felt those things since he was a ten-year-old boy. He should have been frightened, terrified by the whole damnable idea. However, he was not. He welcomed the feeling, hoping that this afternoon would bring Jane's reply to him.

She was going to go to him. Jane could hardly countenance such a thing, but here she was, standing at the iron gate of the hospital, waiting in the drizzle beneath a black umbrella, sporting her finest cloak and reticule. She wore a bonnet and veil, shielding her identity from any passerby. From Matthew.

This was only for a few hours, she reminded herself. A few hours of indulgence. Today was her regular afternoon off, and tonight she was not scheduled at the hospital. These few hours were hers to do what she desired, and what she wanted was to see Matthew once again.

Jane was nervous. She could hardly breathe as each carriage passed her by, wondering if it would be the one to stop before her. It had only been a week since she had seen him, yet if felt like a month. Nervous butterflies made her insides quiver— with dread, or anticipation, she could not tell.

Perhaps she was making a mistake, agreeing to meet him. What if he didn't come? What if he saw her standing there in the drizzling rain and thought her someone else? What if, she finally admitted, he found her lacking? That was the crux of her uneasiness, she finally admitted. She was afraid to see him. It was one thing to carry on when he could not see her, quite another when he was able to see her. He had painted her in his mind, he had said. She doubted the image had been of a red-haired spinster who sported spectacles and a top lip that had been scarred from the back of a man's hand. No, he had seen her as a beauty. He had elevated her to the status of a goddess in his mind and she knew it was lie. She was not a goddess. Plain was the most honest description of her.

Her gloved hands fidgeted against the handle of her bag as the drizzle changed to raindrops, which began to fall earnestly above her head. What was she doing here? she questioned. She took a step to leave, when a large black town coach, led by four gray horses stopped at the sidewalk. Raising her head, she took in the gleaming black exterior and the shining gold accents. A lump formed in her throat. He really was rich, she reminded herself, and so far removed from her humble upbringing. They had little to offer each other, except the pleasures of their bodies. Nothing could come of this, and Jane did not know whether to feel satisfied or saddened by the notion.

"His lordship awaits inside," the coachman said from his perch. As if on cue, the door opened, revealing black velvet squabs on the door. The interior was gently lit by tiny oil lamps. Shadows played deep in the interior, and Jane nearly ran, frightened like a silly little pea wit.

The wind gusted, sending the flame of one lamp sputtering, then dying as a large shadow moved across the width of the carriage. It was followed by the appearance of a black boot. With a swift movement, the stairs unraveled with a clang, and his lordship appeared.

Jane could not breathe. She felt her pulse beating frantically through her throat. She could not look up at him, despite knowing the heavy black veils concealed her face. She was out of her league here, unsure of how to proceed. She did not like the feeling, nor did she like feeling at the mercy of a man and her carnal appetites. Her mother had lost herself to a man, and Jane refused to follow that path.

Standing alone on the sidewalk, she felt small and unsure, *afraid*. Part of her wanted to walk away, another part wanted to run to him and throw herself into his arms for safekeeping.

Seconds of indecision went by in which Jane thought a

hundred different things. It was only when he held out his hand to her, waiting patiently for her to come to him as the rainwater ran off the brim of his hat, that Jane had the absurd sense that somehow everything would be all right. He would make it right. She trusted him. Believed in him, even though she knew nothing about him. His name was Matthew, and he was a painter. If he was a lord or baron, he had not disclosed that information in his letters. To her he was simply Matthew. They were two people standing on the sidewalk, in the rain, waiting to discover one another. The only question left to be answered was, who Jane was. Was she an independent woman who yearned to discover pleasure in this man's arms, or was she the shy woman, allowing her fears to rule her, and to rob her of this once-in-a-lifetime chance?

She didn't know. In that second, both women ruled her. Both sought to control her. There was only one thing that Jane knew for certain. If she entered that carriage with him her world would never look the same. It would be different. *She* would be different. She didn't know if she could bear it, not knowing who she was. She was used to her world, yet she hungered for the smallest glimpse of the world that Matthew could show her.

She only had to reach out to grasp it. To take his hand and allow herself to be taken to a place she had never thought she would discover.

7

Matthew's gaze burned into her, memorizing everything about Jane, standing alone on the sidewalk waiting for him. She wore a gray mantelet that was plain and unadorned. Her gloved fingers trembled nervously against the wooden handles of her purse, and he ached to soothe her fears, yet he could not think of moving as he catalogued the way the skirt of her gown fitted over her hips and thighs, the unadorned train trailing out behind her, allowing him to study the contours of her figure. Of its own volition, his gaze slowly caressed her belly and breasts, which were hidden from him beneath the mantelet, till it rested on the black veil that concealed her face.

Damn it, his hands were shaking. He was nervous, strange for a man whose life was filled with nothing but clandestine meetings and couplings. But something told him that this meeting was going to be different. Jane was different.

Ignoring the strange tremors, he extended his hand to her. "Come to me."

With a moment's hesitation, she glanced behind her at the

filthy windows of the hospital, as if seeking permission. He half wondered if Inglebright was in there, watching from behind a curtain. But he forgot all about the doctor when she began to slowly walk to him. The few steps it took seemed to take forever. He hungered for her, for the feel of her in his arms. Swallowing hard, he reined in the mad urge to cross the remaining distance between them and crush her to him. But he couldn't do such a thing. No, he had wanted this, to watch her coming to him, offering herself to him of her own free will.

Their fingertips touched and he felt as though he'd been punched in the middle. As their fingers entwined, he felt something that was at once welcoming yet terrifying. Looking down at their locked hands, he realized it was a sense of…completion. Instinct told him to block the feeling. But then she spoke, her voice causing a warmth to spread throughout his body.

"I almost didn't come this afternoon."

Instinct be damned. His past and who he was need not intrude here, not with Jane. He was only Matthew with her, not the scandalous Earl of Wallingford, not the libertine society knew him to be.

Pulling her close, he removed her glove then raised their joined hands to his mouth, pressing a kiss to the soft flesh above her thumb. Closing his eyes, he inhaled the scent of them together—hers the clean, pure scent of soap and his, the warmth of eastern spice. Together, it was an erotic, heady scent that went straight to his head.

"I…I…" She swallowed and looked away. "I'm not sure—"

"Let me come to you, Jane," he said, unable to stop himself from pressing his lips against her hand once more. Opening his eyes, he looked down into her upturned face and saw the flash of what looked like green eyes watching him carefully from beneath the veil. "No questions, Jane. I will take only what you are willing to give me."

He watched the line of her throat move up and down as she swallowed hard. He trailed his fingers along that smooth skin and felt how fast her heart was beating for him.

"Come to me, Jane," he murmured, pulling her closer. "My carriage is waiting. It's waiting for you. *I'm* waiting for you."

Her breath caught, and the sound wreaked havoc within him. Nodding, she took a tentative step closer and allowed him to guide her around a large puddle, then to his waiting carriage. Bowing her head, she concealed herself from the coachman who sat as still as a statue on the box, his gaze never straying from whatever object he was staring at straight ahead of him. Inside, the shades had been drawn, and once Matthew closed the carriage door behind him, the lamp blew out, making the interior black as pitch.

With a rap of his walking stick, the carriage lurched into motion. It was so dark, so unnaturally quiet, that he swore he could hear Jane's heart beating from deep within her chest. He could smell her—soap and feminine arousal—and his cock stirred, hungry to be inside her.

"You said you almost did not come today. Why?" he asked, feeling a burning in his chest as he awaited her answer.

"There is much risk for me. My job at the hospital. My name." She swallowed hard, he heard it in the quiet, along with her fidgeting fingers.

"That is the reason for the veil."

"Yes."

"Do you regret it now, Jane, coming to me?"

"I do not know," she said in a hushed breath.

"Come," he whispered, reaching for her, knowing exactly where she sat, and wrapped his hands around her waist, bringing her forward so that she was sitting beside him. He reached up, his fingers resting against the veil, and her breathing stilled. "Do not be afraid," he said as he lifted the veil from her face and reached for the satin ties of her bonnet strings. "I will take such good care of you, Jane. You have nothing to fear from me."

Taking her bonnet in his hands, he reached across the carriage and placed it atop the opposite bench. Then he twisted his body so that he was pressed up against hers, and he turned his gaze to hers, unable to see anything—only hear and smell and feel—and lowered his mouth to her forehead, kissing her softly, reverently. His lips brushed her skin and hair and he could not help but glide his fingertips along the sweet curves of her face, tracing her, memorizing her, *imagining* her. Christ, he wanted her more than he had ever wanted anything, and that included his art gallery. What madness had she inspired in him? He had never felt this way before, this need to connect so deeply with another.

He wanted to share things with Jane: his body, his heart, the secrets he kept locked inside his withering soul. She took a ragged breath, and he felt her body tremble against his arms, shattering his control.

His mouth found her pulse above the lace she had tied around her throat. Its frantic, fluttering beat caressed his lips, and he sat there, feeling her heart beating against him.

"Jane," he said softly as he removed the strip of lace and tucked it into his pocket, "come to me. Give yourself to me— only me. Let us share this…this passion that has consumed us. Say yes, Jane," he murmured as he began to gently suck the tender, supple flesh of her throat. "One word, Jane…*yes.*"

Her heart was racing at a dangerous pace. Jane felt the pulsations bounding in her throat, felt the tightening of her bodice against her breasts. Her breathing was coming in short, sharp pants as her body, which was no longer her own, trembled like that of a newborn fawn.

She could not hide her response to him. She had not expected this so soon, nor had she thought to allow him to remove her veil. But it was shadowy, the afternoon grew late, and with the black clouds and the rain, it was dark. With the blinds closed it was like midnight in the carriage.

An absurd sense of relief flooded her. She had removed her spectacles while she waited for him to come to her, and in the dark, she could be the kind of woman he desired. The kind of woman she had fleetingly wished she was.

As his lips and tongue blazed a path down her neck, and his hands began to search her body, Jane was stunned by the thought that it was all really happening. Although she had thought of him nonstop this past week, and dreamed of him, she had thought never to see him again. But it was true. She was here with him. His hands truly were on her flesh. It was really his breathing she heard, his lips she felt kissing her cheek. She felt the heat of his gaze travel lower, away from her face, and fix on the bounding pulse in her throat. She knew she was right about that heated gaze when he reached out to put his fingertip to her neck. Pressing toward her, he inhaled once, softly, almost imperceptibly, then again, deeper. The leather squabs creaked as his body shifted, and Jane felt her own body grow limp and warm as he pressed his face against her. Then his lips were brushing against the quivering pulse that leaped with his touch. A deep sound resonated in his chest.

"I thought to talk with you, Jane, to woo you, but I have no skill at it. I haven't the words to make polite conversation. Need has robbed me of speech. I need you, Jane," he said in a dark, fevered whisper.

She didn't want to talk. She wanted him to touch her, to

make her feel the way he had that night when he had bared her breasts and touched them. Besides, she didn't trust herself to speak.

"Jane, I want to be with you—*in* you."

"Yes," she murmured huskily. She worked up the courage to unclench her hands, which rested in her lap, and rake her fingers through the luxuriant softness of Matthew's hair.

Her lips trembled as both his big hands stroked the sides of her neck, caressing her with soft sweeps. Slowly his palms descended the length of her throat and back up again, his thumbs brushing her wildly beating pulse. Closing her eyes, Jane weakened and tilted her head farther back, her lips parting just enough to allow the barest movement of air between them. He groaned and she felt the smooth tip of his finger trace her bottom lip. "Innocent, perfect lips. Such perfection," he whispered darkly, stroking his thumb along her mouth. "I want to feel them beneath mine. I want to feel them sliding along my body. I want my cock between them."

Her stomach flipped and she clutched his hair, forcing his head down to her mouth. Jane savored the slow descent of his mouth to hers, felt his lips part and settle atop hers. It was wonderful, intimate, almost as if he was treasuring her. His lips pressed once more against hers, then he angled his head and kissed her over and over with his hot open mouth, a mouth that was hungry and devouring and causing havoc not only with her body but with her mind, as well.

She couldn't think, her head was a whirlwind of thoughts and emotions, as if she were drugged, disembodied. She was conscious of the moan that escaped her when he slanted his mouth against hers, encouraging her to open for him.

"Let me in. Let me taste you."

He parted her lips and slid his tongue deep inside. He groaned and his hand left her face and cupped her breast as he pressed his hard body up tightly against hers. Fiercely he kissed her, his mouth slanting over hers, faster and faster. His tongue drove into her, and she could do nothing but reach for him and wrap her arms around his neck and hold on as he swept her away. The intimacy of him invading her mouth was nothing like she expected. It was hot and arousing, and it did little to relieve the ache in her womb, but deepened it until she could feel it eating away at every corner of her body. She felt him in her blood, in the pulse of her heartbeat. She heard him, his sounds of desire in her thoughts, felt him knocking at the door of her soul.

With one kiss he owned her.

Jane held on to him, her fingers digging into the shoulders of his jacket while their tongues tangled wildly together, when suddenly he broke off, and breathing as though he was out of breath, he said, "I need to touch you. I need to feel you naked against my hand."

His hand snaked through the opening of her woolen wrap, and his heat seemed to seep through the thin muslin of her gown, straight to her own skin that greedily absorbed his warmth. She trembled, aware of his large hand resting beneath the curve of her breast. He seemed to know, to understand her response, for he parted the cloak more, and she instinctively knew that he was looking up at her despite the fact he could not see her reaction when his hand slid along her waist to her belly.

She wanted him, with frightening need. She could think of nothing else but shedding her clothes and lying naked here with him. She wanted to ask for it—*beg for it,* but she didn't know how. What words to use. So she lay still, feeling his hand torturing her as it kneaded and lowered, drawing closer and closer to the mound of her sex, wondering what thoughts were going through Matthew's mind.

★ ★ ★

Lovely warm, soft skin, he thought, wishing he could see his hand resting atop her. Despite the layer of her gown and chemise, he could feel the suppleness of her skin, could feel her body heat enveloping him, teasing him with the thought of feeling the hotness from her core seeping onto his hand. He could not wait to be wrapped in her heat, in her welcoming body, or to feel this gently mounded belly beneath his mouth and hands. He thrust the mantelet from her shoulders. She shivered, but he knew she was not cold, she was too damn hot for that. He could almost see it radiating from her body. He could definitely feel it reaching for him and drawing him in, chasing away the dampness, and the demon inside him.

Christ, she was perfect. Her nipples were hard little points, pressed against the bodice of her gown. He felt, with satisfaction, the mounds of her breasts swell, just like the flesh between his legs that had now grown to an impressive size. How he was going to enjoy giving her that flesh and reveling in her scalding heat.

"Such beautiful breasts," he said appreciatively, cupping them. "I've thought of them nearly every minute this past week. You cannot know how you have captured my attention." *And held it,* he silently added. "I'm going to paint you naked and have them cupped in your hands. I'm going to paint them swollen with desire, just as they are right now."

She squirmed beneath his palms. His cock was now so heavy and engorged that it was painful, trapped as it was beneath his trousers. He wanted her hand on his cock—*not hard*—just light and teasing. He wanted to feel his orgasm slowly build. He wanted to come in her hand once more, empty himself into her palm. He wanted the peace of lying with her like this after the last of his climax melted away. "I want to please you. Christ, I do," he moaned as his lips caressed the soft skin of her breasts that crept above her bodice. His hand found its way beneath her skirt and his palm made the slow, sensual glide up her stocking-clad leg. "I want to taste you, Jane, to feel your core weep against me. I want you to call my name, score my back as I pleasure you with my mouth."

She gasped, clutching wildly to his jacket, and his fingers pressed into her firm, lush thigh. He had shocked her with his talk, and he discovered he was aroused by her naiveté. He pushed her farther into the bench, so her back was pressed against the side of the carriage and her legs were draped over his thighs.

He wanted to strip her of that innocence, to tutor her to pleasure. He wanted her to know passion, and he wanted her to learn it from him. Her hand left his shoulder and rested low on her belly. He placed his hand on hers, rubbing it in soft circles.

"Do you ache for it, Jane?"

Her teeth chattered, her whole body trembled, but she wasn't cold, indeed she was warm, so very hot. Together their hands moved, him bringing his palm lower and lower until it rested between the apex of her thighs, which squeezed their joined hands like a vise.

"You feel it here?" he asked. "Release the pressure then, Jane," he encouraged. He lifted his hand, and felt, as well as heard, her small palm move between her thighs. Her breath caught in her throat, and she made an inarticulate sound that aroused him.

"I burn, Jane." His tongue traced the cleft of her breasts, while his thumb circled and hardened her nipple. Jane whimpered with each probe of his tongue, and he rubbed his engorged, throbbing cock against the soft vee of her thighs as her hand played overtop her gown.

This is where he wanted to be, between her thighs, cushioned and welcomed. He wanted inside her, to feel her quim sheathing him, tightening around him as he took her deep, rocking against her.

He shoved against her and she cried out, shocked, alarmed, frightened by the size of him. She tried to push away from him, but he followed her, pressing his chest against her, pinning her against the wall of the carriage. She was panting now and her fingers were tightening in his hair, at times almost painfully clutching, and it drove him wild. No, she was not afraid, he thought with relief, just anxious and eager.

"Matthew," she panted between brushes of his lips and the plunging of his tongue. "I ache, I burn, I hurt."

"I will fill that hurt, Jane," he promised. He reached for the tapes at the back of her gown and opened them, clumsy in his hurry. But he needed her. Needed to feel her, taste her. The bodice came free and he pulled it away from her skin. She had pressed herself against the wall, arching her neck and thrusting her breasts forward. His hand brushed the hot skin of her breasts, and he slid his mouth lower, wetting a wet path down to the full swell. His hand resting beneath her breast, he could feel the delicate ribs beneath her skin, could feel her breast quivering against his thumb in anticipation and escalating desire. He felt reckless now. Any pretense to gentleness was slowly being eaten away by his own mounting excitement.

"Ask me," he murmured against her, his mouth coming so close to her nipple. "Ask me, Jane, to suckle you."

"Take me in your mouth, *please,* Matthew."

He went to his knees, his tongue trailing along the soft tip of her nipple. It furled and budded. He opened his mouth, then slipped the nipple inside and sucked, slowly, drawing it deep and hard between his pulling lips. He imagined that her insides were already tightening and she was feeling her honey slide out of her body. He wanted that honey on his mouth, his tongue. He wanted Jane in the worst possible way. And he was going to have her, naked and spread and completely at his mercy.

Oh, God, Jane chanted over and over in her mind. What was Matthew doing to her, making her feel this way? He was suckling her so deeply, slowly, erotically that her entire body felt weak. When his strong palm reached the apex of her thighs, she whimpered, and instinctively spread her legs, allowing him to shoulder his way between them. She felt herself blush as he ran his hand along her curls. When he skimmed his finger along her wet cleft, she whimpered in anticipation.

"I want you there," she cried, shoving his hand against her. He made a growling sound then was fully atop her, capturing her mouth with his. His kiss turned greedy, frantic. His hands were everywhere. Sliding down her arms, her hips. His fingers cupped her buttocks, then slid up to knead her breasts. He took her nipples between his thumbs and fingers, squeezing, rolling, pulling until she gasped beneath him, all the while kissing her with unfettered passion.

Jane had never felt anything so sinfully wicked in all her life. Her body was awakening, flickering to life, as it responded to his touch, heating her flesh as he made her burn for more. Her breasts ached for his lips, his tongue. The place between her thighs throbbed with a longing that was much stronger than when she pleasured herself.

She mewled as he settled his body more intimately over hers. He felt hard and heavy. The throbbing length of his arousal rubbed against her thigh, burning her. He groaned deeper and plunged his tongue in and out of her mouth as he pressed his erection rhythmically onto her leg.

"Touch me," he breathed harshly as he rocked his hips against her.

She clutched him tightly, stroking him through his trousers as she had that night at the hospital. Needing to feel him in her hand, she tore at the buttons with trembling fingers. She was clumsy and unschooled, and impatiently he tore at them, opening them, freeing himself onto her palm.

"God, yes, touch my cock," he moaned as he pulled at her nipples. His words, so dark and full of need, urged her open. Jane cupped him, feeling the hot length of him scalding her palm. Exploring him, she ran her fingers up and down, her hand firming as it slid up the thick length. His breath quickened, rasping harshly against her neck as her hand worked up and down his shaft.

His excitement fueled her own, and when finally his hand cupped her intimately, her thighs fell open. Immediately his fingers slid inside her—filling her. She moaned at the invasion, the feeling of fullness and the slickness that pooled there.

"My God," he whispered thickly. "I cannot wait to watch your cunt take me."

Oh, yes, she wanted that, too. To see his penetration of her body. It was base and primitive, yet Jane wanted it. To watch her body accept him.

But then he was sliding down the length of her, parting her slick sex with both hands and she could not think any more thoughts. Stubble grazed her thighs as he lowered his head to her flesh, the sensation sending jolts of awareness straight through her.

He licked her then. His hot tongue scorched a path up the length of her, each time using the flat of his tongue to fully cover her sex. He opened his mouth, covering her, kissing her there as he had her mouth. She was wet, sticky, mortified that he would know, that he would feel and taste...

"No," she whimpered, squirming in his iron grasp.

"Don't pull away from me," he murmured, his finger stroking that sensitive part of her. "Just come for me, Jane. Come…"

With deliberate strokes, he sucked and teased, and then, when her body tightened and bowed beneath him, he sucked harder and made the world shatter around her.

"Matthew!" she cried, gasping, clawing at his hair.

"Let me take care of you," he whispered.

"Oh, God, please, Matthew," she begged, struggling for air. "Yes," she cried, then began to shake uncontrollably in his arms.

His lips and tongue tasted the sweet skin of her throat and the swells of her breasts. Her hands were fisted in his hair, clutching and tugging, begging him for more.

"Jane, come home with me," he whispered softly against her ear. "Let us take this passion where it wants to go. No questions. No demands. Only pleasure."

Jane couldn't think. She felt as though she had died and been reborn in Matthew's arms. The pleasure…she had never felt such bliss. Her whole body seemed to glow with it.

"Let me paint you, Jane. Let me inside you."

She swallowed hard, trying to think, to not be impulsive and rash, but "yes" was out of her mouth before she could stop it.

"When, Jane?" he asked while he nuzzled the soft patch of skin beneath her ear. "When will you come to me?"

"In two days, that is my next afternoon off."

"An afternoon is not enough, Jane. I need more than a few hours with you."

She tried to think, and didn't want to. Getting more time off would involve lies and deceit. She didn't want to lie, yet she could not stop thinking of spending hours with Matthew.

"In two days," she whispered, "I will spend the night with you."

8

Jane buried the guilt she felt for lying to both Lady Blackwood and Richard. She was not proud of what she had done, but she could not change her mind now. She was meeting Matthew today, and he was taking her somewhere where they could be together. She didn't care where that somewhere was, what mattered was that she'd be with him.

The past two days had felt like a dream. He had written her darkly sensual letters that promised every kind of forbidden pleasure. Pleasures that would be hers in a matter of moments, when Matthew pulled up to the sidewalk in his elegant carriage, to carry her off, like Hades had done to Persephone.

Meeting him like this went against everything she believed in, but she was too weak to resist the temptation he offered. She had never been tempted, never known how pleasurable it could be to heed the cry of enticement.

She would not feel guilty, she told herself for the thousandth time. It was only going to be one more time. *One night*. She would give herself to him because she was, she thought with startling amusement, falling in love with Matthew.

Could one love a man one knew nearly nothing about? Was it love or simply lust? Some might say it was only lust, but she would argue it. Love, albeit tender and new, was what was in Jane's heart. She knew it was silly, that it could never be, and that come the morning it would be done. But tonight, she could share that love, indulge it, gift it to him, and it would be enough, it would have to be.

Their spheres were different. Their worlds divided by class, money and titles. She could not live in his world, and he could not live in hers. But they could forge a new world tonight. One that transcended the realities of their birth and social standing. It would be a world based on mutual passion, of shared feelings. Of love, Jane thought.

The sun peeked through a cloud, and Jane tilted her face to the warm rays. It was a glorious day. A fine day for an assignation.

The clatter of hooves drew her attention, and she glanced down the street to see a familiar set of gray horses cantering along the cobbles. The street was busy, and Jane moved to the side to avoid being jostled by the crowd.

Excitedly, she watched the carriage pull to a stop, and the door swing open to reveal Matthew. Butterflies circled in her stomach like mad, but Jane quelled them as she watched him, looking like a dark angel, descend the carriage steps.

He stood in front of the carriage, his head turning left and right, scanning the bustling street. With a frown he drew his pocket watch from his waistcoat pocket and flipped the silver lid open before settling it back into his pocket.

With a deep breath, Jane walked through the crowd toward him. He glanced at her, then turned his attention back to the iron gates of the hospital. *He didn't know her.*

Of course he didn't, she reasoned. She had worn a veil the last time they had been together, and the times before that, his head had been bandaged.

"Hello," she murmured as she came up to him.

He ignored her and gave her his back. Jane swallowed back the slight.

"Are you looking for someone?"

He turned and glared at her, and Jane actually shrunk back, shocked by the change in his expression. "Yes, but not the likes of you," he snapped.

Rendered mute, Jane stood there for long seconds, trying to breathe. With a scathing glance he took her in, from the top of her green bonnet to the tips of her scuffed half boots. His assessment, she knew, was not a positive one.

His rebuke stung. And for some ungodly reason, her hand automatically flew to her hair. She saw how he was staring at it, the bright red hue beneath her bonnet. She could not bear to see the way he was looking at her—*right through her*—without seeing her. He did not see a woman. He did not see Jane, the woman he had been so passionate with two days before. He saw... Jane swallowed hard and looked away, hating the weakness of her spirit. She was more than this, a wilting flower. She was stronger than this. But damn it, this hurt.

It hurt because he was the man responsible for making her burn. For making her feel like a woman. It hurt because it had been a trick. An illusion. And it hurt most of all because he did not see her, the woman she was behind the unfashionable spectacles and garish hair.

"Is there something you need?" he asked in a most uncivilized tone.

"No," she whispered, glancing away so he wouldn't see the tears in her eyes.

"Do I know you?" he asked, suspicion growing in his voice. "Have we met?"

She could hear the fear in his voice, and it killed what remained of the hope she held in her heart. She searched for anything to say, anything at all that might save her further humiliation, but her pride would not let go.

"Do you...do you know who I am?" she asked quietly, at last able to look up at him. His eyes...Jane was struck breathless at the sight of them. They were dark blue, the color of india ink. Faint bruising marred his eyelids but it in no way detracted from his handsomeness. The way he looked at her, with those beautiful eyes glaring at her, cut her to the quick.

His gaze narrowed for a brief second as if he did, indeed, begin to recognize her, but he straightened and stepped back. "Should I know you?" He looked her over from the top of her cap to the tips of her worn boots as if she were an insect on a stick that he found rather revolting.

"From the hospital," she said, adopting her native cockney accent, while disguising herself from him. Jane shoved her wounded pride aside and instead tilted her chin up a notch and stared him down through the lenses of her spectacles.

His mouth worked, and Jane saw the horror in his eyes. He was afraid she was his lover. He was horrified by the thought of it, and Jane was just as horrified that she had allowed herself to be such a fool. Men were men. They all wanted beauty. Such shallow, fickle, *heartless* creatures.

"Yer 'ere to meet Jane," she grumbled, and he saw his expression grow hopeful.

"Yes, have you seen her?"

"Yes, I expect she's on her way 'ome by now."

"Home?" he thundered, his expression growing dark. "We planned to meet here."

"Oh, she had no plans to meet with you, milord," she

countered, growing more venomous by the second. "She paid me a crown to wait 'ere to tell ye she wouldn't be coming today, or any other day fer that matter."

He looked crestfallen, and Jane, for an instant, felt badly, but the stinging of her pride and the burning ache of her heart soon shoved any softening feeling aside.

"What do you mean she's not coming?" he growled. "We had an appointment."

"She changed 'er mind."

He swore, and slapped his gloves against his thigh. "I don't believe this."

Jane wondered what was so incredulous to him, the fact that Jane had not fallen into his grasp, or the fact that Jane, as a poor, working woman would have the audacity to turn down a lord. Either way, it made her rage and seethe inside. She had grossly misjudged him. That had been her own fault. A fault she wouldn't allow ever again.

"Would you give her this?" he asked. He reached into his pocket and removed a silver case. He pulled out an ivory card and handed it to her.

The Earl of Wallingford. Jane nearly choked on her tongue. Wallingford was her Matthew? *The* Wallingford? The man was the most vile, most reprehensible skirt chaser in the realm. She knew of his infamous reputation, even with her limited association with the ton. Lord, what a fool she had been. His exploits were legendary. His callous attitude toward women shameful. He was a beast, a misogynist, and Jane felt abused and violated that she had allowed herself to be taken in by his silky tongue.

How had she not recognized him? she wondered. She had met him once, while she had been visiting Anais. Wallingford and Anais had been friends for years. Jane didn't expect him to recall their introduction, for she was nothing but a servant in his eyes, nothing worth remembering. But why had she not realized who he was? How had she not remembered his rugged handsomeness?

Because he was beaten. Because he was in the East End, her mind tried to rationalize. Oh, Lord, what the devil had she done?

"I will give you half a crown," he muttered, "if you tell me where she lives."

Jane glared at him, and turned her back, preparing to leave. He reached for her and held her arm in his grip. "All right, a crown. Tell me where to find Jane."

"She doesn't want to be found by the likes of you."

"All right, five pounds. Now give me her direction."

She knew her eyes were glittering with rage. "Get yer paws off me, or I'll scream for the constable."

His lips turned mulish. "He'd hardly believe I was ravishing you, now, would he? You're hardly the ravishing type."

Jane gasped at his cruelty. "You'll never find her," she hissed. "She's run off, far away from you."

"Nothing evades me when I want it bad enough." He dropped her arm and stared down at her. "Now then, how much is it going to cost me to get what I want out of you?"

Jane's entire being filled with hatred for him. How had she misjudged him? How could this puffed-up, arrogant beast be her sweet Matthew? She looked up at him, stunned, trying to understand how there could be two so very different sides to him.

"Simple, as well as plain, I see," he growled. "Here, there's ten pounds, now tell me where to find Jane. *Now.*"

She took the money, dropped it to the ground and stepped onto the bill, grinding her boot on it. "There's much for purchase on these streets, milord, but you'll find I'm not one of the items."

With a flare of her skirt and head held high, Jane strolled down the street and waved down a hansom cab. As they drove past the spot where she had waited for him, she noticed that Matthew—no, it was Wallingford now—was marching his way into the hospital.

She was right when she thought her world would look different if she got into that carriage with him. Her world had changed. It had gone from gray to black in the span of a kiss.

She was ruined now, broken by the Earl of Wallingford.

The rain was pouring down in a blinding sheet.

Heedless of the bone-raking chill of the wind and driving rain, Matthew gripped the iron bars of the fence and stared at the empty spot where he'd once held Jane's hand.

Stark reality slapped him in the face. He had driven her away from him. What had he done? Had he been too bold in his embrace? Had he frightened her away because he had not been able to control his own lust? *Impossible.* She needed his touch as much as he had needed hers. He knew that—still knew it. It was something else. He could hardly credit how he should know such a thing. He just did. Damn it, he didn't know why. And he needed to know. Needed to know why she hadn't come to him in over a week. He needed to know almost as much as he needed her.

Every night, every morning, he had come to the hospital, hoping to find her, to glimpse her on her way to or from work. He had seen no one who resembled her. He would know her body, the way it curved beneath her cloak. He would recognize her voice, the way it soothed the storm inside him. But he had seen no one who he thought was Jane. The letters he had sent to the hospital had been returned to him, unopened. He had even gone to the hospital, inquiring after her. The nurse in charge had denied knowing a Nurse Jane.

She was hiding from him, but why?

Pushing off from the fence, he blinked away the rainwater that landed on his lashes. Ignoring the forked flash of lightning and the roll of thunder, he took another step back, unable to bring himself to look away from the gates of the hospital.

Damn her for not returning. And damn him for being such a pathetic fool. What a simpleton he was to come every day, hoping and praying he would find her. Christ, it was utterly pathetic, this slavish need he had in regard to her. How could a woman he knew nothing about become so vital to his happiness? Women had never factored into his happiness before, so why now, did this one?

The ugly truth stared before him and he forced himself to confront his mistake. He had been gravely wrong to believe that Jane was different from the women in his past.

Goddamn her, she had made him hope. Made him feel alive. Made him yearn. Well, no more. To hell with her. To hell with himself for believing in a woman's goodness.

As he flung open the door to his carriage, his coachman leaned to the side from his perch. "Home, your lordship?"

"No," he growled. "To Madame Recamier's."

"The bordello?" his coachman asked with a frown.

"Do you have a goddamn problem with that, Turner?" he snapped.

"I didn't think——"

"You're damn right you didn't think. Henceforth, you will keep your opinions and your thoughts to yourself. I pay you to drive, not talk. If you're not up to the task, I'll find myself another coachman who can do the job."

The young man's face turned crimson. "Begging yer pardon, yer lordship."

"I should say so. If you want to retain your post, keep in

mind the fact that the last bloody thing I want is a lecture from the hired help on my lack of morals. If I want a sermon, I'll bloody well go to church, or better yet, I'll pay a call on my father."

Slamming the door shut, Matthew stretched out his legs and watched the rivulets of rainwater trickle down the glossed leather of his boots. Christ, he was in a black mood. A rage he had not felt for years was gripping him. The image of Jane standing beside him flashed before him. He thrust it aside, just as he thrust aside the feel of her lips beneath his. A feeling that was strongly reminiscent of guilt washed over him when he thought of the brothel he'd ordered his coachman to drive him to.

What was he doing going to a brothel? He wasn't in the mood, nor the right frame of mind to take a woman to bed. However, it was not only his black mood that made him uneasy, it was something far more unsettling than that. It was his conscience that was jabbing at him.

Fuck her, he spat viscously as he crossed his arms over his chest. He owed Jane nothing. He didn't even know her last name. He doubted he would even see her again.

No, he owed Jane nothing, least of all monogamy. She had ruined him. Had destroyed any hope he had left in his life. Damn it, he hated this feeling nonsense. The sooner he returned to his old careless and embittered self the better.

"Madame Recamier's," Turner called as he slowed the carriage to a stop in front of an old Georgian mansion in the heart of Trevor Square.

Matthew pressed forward and peered at the green door and the triangular stone pediment that made the facade elegant and classical. From the outside, the house was the pinnacle of respectability. On the inside, it was a notorious bawdy house that catered to the whims and fetishes of the ton.

"When shall I return for you, milord? Or perhaps I should wait here?" his nervous looking coachman asked as Matthew slammed the carriage door shut behind him.

"I will send word to you, Turner. But I shouldn't think it will be anytime soon."

"Today, milord?"

"Not likely."

"Tomorrow?" Turner's voice cracked with nervousness.

"Perhaps."

"Two days, milord?" he asked in awe.

"At the very least," he grumbled as he straightened his waistcoat and strolled up the steps to the house.

"Ah, Lord Wallingford," Madame Recamier said with a smile as she swung the door wide-open and waved him in. "*Bonjour,* my lord. It has been a long time."

"Good day, madam."

"You are very early this morning, my lord."

"Let us cut to the chase. I am in need of a well-appointed room as I shall be occupying it for some time. I will also require women. *Skilled* women."

"Oh, my girls are the very best, *monsieur.* Surely you remember that."

"That is why you find me here at your doorstep at this ungodly hour. Now, a blonde and a fetching brunette, if you please."

"At once, my lord. I shall send Chloe and Phoebe to you. I trained them myself. You will find them very…accommodating. They are both highly skilled in the more exotic arts."

"Very good," he muttered, slapping his gloves against his thigh. "Exactly what I'm looking for."

Bloody hell he hoped one of them had green eyes. It would make the fantasy so much more real that way.

"This way, my lord," Madame Recamier called as her wide-hooped skirt swished along the marble floor of the foyer.

For the first time in his life he wondered if he would even be able to complete the task ahead of him. He was absurdly numb. Not even the faintest hum of anticipation throbbed in his veins. His cock, he realized, was humiliatingly limp.

"Perhaps three women, madam," he said as he climbed the stairs behind her. "And one with green eyes. Light green," he clarified. "And a bottle of absinthe," he demanded. He was going to need to get ripping sotted if he was indulging in this sort of play. He had no desire for his dreams to come out. With the green fairy, he could shove aside his past, could withstand the touch of them, their scent on his body in order to live out this fantasy. With the green fairy, he could fuck these women and pretend they were Jane. And Christ, it was a pathetic notion that he needed to pretend. *Fool*.

"My lord." The madam chuckled. "We are only too pleased to service you. Who could deny you?"

A woman named Jane, he thought bitterly. There was only one way to drive her out of his blood, and that was with the body of another—or three others—he thought savagely. Hell, he was going to have himself a grandiose orgy and then he would be good and rid of the chit. After this, he would never again close his eyes and see those lovely green eyes flashing at him from beneath black lace.

He wanted to hate her, but he couldn't. Maddening as it was, his desire for her was growing, until it was all he could think about, until it was all he could see, taste, *feel*.

He didn't want to feel. Didn't want to taste. He wanted to fuck. To purge her out of his mind. By the time he was done here, he would have forgotten Jane and the way she had touched him. When he was done, he would be cold and empty once more. Himself, he growled, as he reached for the blonde who had entered the room. Tearing the flimsy night-gown from her body he saw that her nipples were already hard, and he cupped her breast, and bent to take a nipple into his mouth. He did not suckle her as he had Jane, but bit down on the small bud, eliciting a gasp of excitement.

"What is your name?" he growled.

"Chloe." She sighed as he cupped her other breast and rolled the nipple into a hard, little point.

"No, it is not," he commanded. "It is Jane."

"All right," she said, "I'm Jane."

No, you aren't, he thought as he pressed her against the wall, *but it's all I've got.*

She wrapped her leg around his hip and dipped her hand between her thighs, spreading herself as he watched her fingers between her folds. "What are you going to do to Jane?" she teased as she brought her fingers to his lips.

"Make her pay."

When he found her—Jane—he was going to make her suffer. It was one of the things he was good at, making people hurt. That, and fucking. Pain and screwing. It was all he knew.

9

Sunrise. How he loathed the dawn.

It was just another bloody reminder that another interminably long day loomed ahead of him. Hours and hours of idleness and boredom were his daily penance. How the devil did he continue to exist, enduring the endless monotony? His days had been carried out in the same manner for the past eighteen years. His stint at Madame Recamier's brothel had been no exception. He had been bored then, too. Just carrying out the act in a physical, nonemotional manner.

He remembered those days at the brothel. The women who had pleasured him lay in sated sleep around him as he stared up at the ceiling, physically replete, emotionally void. Even two days of debauchery and numerous bottles of absinthe had not made the unsavory feelings of guilt, remorse and unquenchable longing release their hold on him.

Christ, he had not been able to shake the thoughts of Jane. It was obvious that no amount of sex, no matter how skilled or debauched it might be, was going to be enough to drive away the memories of that afternoon when he had kissed and touched Jane. No breasts were as beautiful and full as Jane's. No skin was as flawlessly smooth and sweet tasting as hers. Even when he had requested that one of the women stroke him to orgasm with her hand, the release had not been the same. He had merely emptied himself in her palm. It had been cold and emotionally vacant. The charged shudder, the shattering experience of burying his face in scented skin as he came, had been missing, and he had felt utterly devoid of any feeling.

The memories faded and he felt the warmth of the spring sun on his face. He was damn certain that this morning, with its obscenely brilliant sunrise, would not hold anything other than the usual amusements and diversions that occupied his days. Certainly it would not be like the days when he had waited to see Jane. Those days of hope and pleasure were gone.

Radiant shards of yellow and orange shot through the bed curtains, piercing his closed eyelids. Groaning, Matthew rolled onto his belly, burying his face in the pillow in an attempt to shut out the sunrise and his thoughts of Jane.

"I don't give a bloody damn what the devil he is up to. I pay your wages if you will remember, not the wastrel beyond the door."

The sound of the bed curtains being thrust aside shot through his brain, setting off a mad tattoo of thundering drums in his head. Christ, he was suffering this morning. He was growing too old for the sort of carousing he had indulged in last evening.

Reaching for the corner of the blanket, he covered his head from the unsightly sounds and the unwanted light.

"You will rouse yourself this second, Wallingford! I demand to know what the hell you were thinking when you decided to drag me into another one of your goddamn scandals!"

"What in Christ's name is *that?*" Matthew snapped, his voice muffled beneath the thick woolen covers.

"Sunlight, milord," Marlborough, his valet, murmured with characteristic sarcasm.

"Not that," Matthew growled. "But *that.*"

The irritated, petulant breaths reached his ears once more. Awkward silence ensued and he could only imagine how his poor valet was bearing up beneath the weight of the twelfth Duke of Torrington's glacial glare.

"*That,* milord, would be your father."

Matthew groaned deeply and cursed a filthy expletive, eliciting the desired effect from the duke.

"Get up this instant, you indolent, worthless—" His father's tirade ended in gasping, stuttering outrage as Matthew's bedmate stirred and stretched, purring like a well-fed kitten. Fuzzy images of sex-flushed skin flashed before his eyes.

Bloody hell, who the devil was it lying partly beneath him? And why the devil had he brought her to his home? And why were they in bed? He never fucked in bed. *Never* had women spend the night, for Christsakes.

His gaze caught the absinthe bottle, the slotted spoon and the granules of sugar that littered the table like diamond dust glistening in the sun. That's why, he thought, savagely. Too much green fairy.

"Outrageously satisfying, my lord," came the husky purr. "How do you come up with these naughty little amusements?"

A woman he remembered to be a buxom music-hall dancer slid her delicately arched foot along his calf, oblivious to the fact that another man was breathing fire at the side of the bed.

"Shall we indulge again?" she asked in a throaty whisper, "for you are gloriously large and hard this morning. One would hate for such a magnificent cock stand to go to waste."

"You licentious, worthless…" As the duke struggled to find the words, the woman stiffened beside Matthew, at last aware they were no longer alone.

"Out of that bed, you shameless hussy. Out at once, I say!" his father roared as he tossed her her chemise. "Have you no morals? I will not have any depraved acts being carried on in any home I pay for."

With a derisive snort, Matthew rolled over onto his back and propped himself up against the headboard. A bit too late to consider the thought of depravity. What a damn fool his father was. Her Grace, his father's wife—the woman his father placed on a pedestal as a paragon—had the morals of an alley cat.

Matthew caught the eye of his bedmate as he scratched his back against the headboard. A queer pang began to squeeze in his chest. Refusing to examine the emotion, he reached for the money pouch that sat atop the commode and tossed it to her. "That's for transportation back to Soho. And for the night," he said, letting her know that their interlude was nothing but a transaction. He had purchased her body because he had needed to come, not because he desired anything more meaningful from her.

With a grateful curtsy, the dancer clutched her clothes to her chest and let herself out of his chamber with the help of his valet.

"You will not be taking that trollop beneath your roof. I forbid it!"

"She'll not be my mistress if that is what concerns you. I have no need of a mistress. I never bed a woman more than once. Everyone is well aware how bored I grow after the initial bout of sex."

"Have you no shame, sirrah?"

Sirrah. Gritting his teeth, Matthew strove for composure. He hated to hear that word sneered in his father imperial, auto-cratic tone. Nothing grated his nerves like the duke—especially while suffering through the undesirable effects of too much drink.

"Well? Haven't you an ounce of honor?"

Matthew shrugged and ran his hands through his rumpled hair. "None whatsoever, I am afraid."

"Now, you listen to me," his father growled. "You've been gone nearly a year, traipsing about the East, whoring and drinking, and I'm through with it. Scampering off to Con-stantinople last spring was the last bloody straw. I've indulged you in this reckless behavior long enough."

"Indulge? Surely you jest? Or have you developed a sense of humor, Your Grace?"

His father colored an unbecoming shade of scarlet. Matthew watched as the duke's hands slowly curled into fists. Inwardly he smiled, triumphant that he was unsettling the old bastard.

"You have a duty to this estate and the title. You have a duty to me. *You owe me,*" his father enunciated with chilling ruth-lessness. "Whatever you may think, sirrah, you have an obli-gation to me."

"I have been obliged to you in one way or another for nearly thirty years. *'Be a good boy',*" he murmured in mocking tones, imitating his pompous father. " '*I demand respect, you owe me at least that. Pass your courses, you owe it to me to be intelligent so that you may provide something useful to the title.*' I have owed and owed my entire life long. Pray tell me, how very expensive is one successful drop of your essence, Your Grace? For I have been paying for that dear drop the whole of my life and the cost seems a bit steep."

"Oh, that is so very clever of you," his father thundered. "Be the satirical wit, then, if you must. Lord knows you haven't the brains to be the intelligent wit."

The rebuke stung. Matthew ruthlessly shoved the old barb aside, allowing his skin to thicken even more. "I did not ask to be born into this world as your heir, Your Grace."

"I did not ask for it, either, but there it is. You are my heir and you will start conducting yourself as such."

"Haven't I been doing so? And here I thought I was getting along rather well in the role. After all, it is an heir's duty to sit idly by with too much money in his pocket and too many hours to spend searching for amusement and vice. I thought I was spending your money and succumbing to vice with perfect alacrity."

Matthew continued, heedless of his father's florid expression. "It seems we have both been doing our bit to fulfill the responsibilities of this unwanted relationship we share. I have been playing my role, and you have seen to your duty. Am I not correct, Your Grace, that your duty as the interred duke is to keep the profits rolling in from the estates for my safe-keeping, and then promptly expire, leaving everything to me?"

"Let me assure you, sirrah, I am nowhere near perishing. Your fervent hopes and prayers have all come to naught."

"How very unnerving, to think the great creator has not heard any of my bedtime prayers."

His father's nostrils flared. The old bastard was in high dudgeon, and Matthew took perverse pleasure in seeing it. He, himself, was in a hell of a mood, and as the old saying went, misery did indeed love company.

"In case it escaped your notice, I have a family to consider— *you* have a family to do right by."

"Have I?" he asked, acting bored. "I don't recall."

"You have a mother and three sisters, by God."

"Correction. I have a stepmother who is only seven years my senior. A woman who was nothing but a girl and whom you married the moment your mourning for your wife—*my mother*—was over. Then you saddled me with three half sisters."

"She was of a marriageable age, damn you!"

"She was barely eighteen and you were five and thirty!" he retorted. "She led you around by your cock." He snorted. "And you played the smitten fool perfectly."

"You, sirrah, will treat my wife with the respect that is owed her."

"Why? You never treated my mother to anything she was entitled to. My mother would have done anything to make you happy, yet you ignored her as though she was nothing but a shadow on the wall."

"I refuse to discuss that woman with you."

"*That woman* was my mother. I am the product of your relationship with her. You may have dismissed her, but I am not so easy to send away. You need me. Proof of just how much you need me is evident by the fact that you are standing in my bedchamber while I am half-naked and still in bed."

"You truly are worthless. Oh, aye, you've done a remarkable job making a damn joke out of your life—sitting about doing nothing but chasing skirts and spending my money and painting scandalous, pornographic portraits. Damn me, I had to hear of the whole sordid affair at my club. And you know how much pleasure it brings me when my nightly port is poisoned by reports of my useless, worthless son."

Matthew shrugged and wiped his hand along his whiskered jaw. "Had you not decided to pinch pennies, I would not have been forced to pursue other avenues to secure what I need for my gallery."

"Your gallery." His father snorted. "Painting was for sissies when you were ten, and it is even more so now. Bloody hell, get an occupation. Take a seat in the Commons. It will be no great trial to have you voted in for my riding. Learn the ways of parliament and great men so that when you take your rightful seat in the House of Lords you will be a force to be reckoned with—as any Duke of Torrington has been. At the very least, ride the estates with the steward and learn to do something useful with your days. Christ, a gallery. You'll make me a laughingstock."

"You have done that yourself—and quite admirably, I may say."

His father's blue eyes became angry slits. "From this moment forward you will do as I say or you will find yourself penniless in the streets. Do you comprehend me? Do you understand that I will make it so that you are completely dependent upon me?"

Matthew eyed him sharply, knowing what was to come. He would not be a part of whatever damn scheme his father had concocted for his future. He would not, by God.

"Now then," his father said with a sniff of superiority, "you've spent enough time fucking everything in a corset. I assume, after all these years, you've gotten the skill down pat. You may now set that particular talent of yours in a more useful pursuit and begin by finding a wife to force your infamous member upon. I want another heir to secure my bloodline will continue in the years to come."

Remaining deceptively calm, Matthew crossed his arms against his naked chest and glared at his father. "A wife and brats are the last bloody thing I want in my life."

"A wife and brats are going to be your only means of survival, *my lord,*" his father said with a self-satisfied smile. "You will marry and you will do so within the year. I want her breeding as soon as may be."

"No."

His father looked incredulous. "I beg your pardon?"

"I will not marry because you command it. You, Your Grace, may go to hell."

His father came forward and tried his best to stare him down as if they were two mongrel dogs fighting for the last bone in the rubbish bin. "Obviously you've failed to understand what I am saying. You *will* marry, or you will be cut off from any financial support from me. And just so you know I am not blowing smoke, I will take this time to tell you that your monthly income has been reduced yet again."

Matthew struggled to show little emotion. His father would be searching for signs of it. The last thing he wanted his father to know was that he cared that he might very well wind up in debtors' prison.

"Do what you must," he said with a careless air. "I am still not marrying."

"Are you by any chance attempting to challenge me, sirrah?"

"Consider the gauntlet tossed to the ground, Your Grace. In this matter, I will fight to the death."

"By God, I will make you suffer," his father thundered. "I will reduce you to one of those begging disgraces that litter the East End. I will make it so none of the fine ladies you're so fond of pricking will even look at you. One day, you'll find that the only one willing to raise her skirts for you will be the saddest, poxy whore that walks the length of Petticoat Lane. Even then you will not likely be able to pay for her diseased sex."

"Perhaps you should take one of those common streetwalkers to your bed, Your Grace. Perhaps it would do something to improve your disposition."

His father's expression grew livid. "*Half.* You have now had your income sliced in two. You may bid adieu to your fine boots from Henshaws, and your tailoring from Westons. No more scandalous parties, or trips to the East. No damn art gallery."

"I shall move back to the estate then," he said, knowing he held the ace that would end this conversation. "Imagine waking up every morning to find me at the breakfast table dining amongst your charming family. Imagine the influence I could be to my precious sisters."

His father reeled back on the heels of his boots and his eyes began to bulge with rage. "You bloody bastard, you leave my family out of this."

"You leave my income intact and I will leave you in peace with your wife and your chits."

"I will find your Achilles' heel," his father growled as he stomped to the door of the chamber. "I vow, I will find your one weakness and when I do, God help you."

"God?" Mathew said on a chuckle. "Christ, the devil himself threw me out of hell because I was too much competition for him. Do you really believe God will help me?"

"No, sirrah," his father muttered, his gaze sweeping over Matthew's tousled hair and indolent pose. "No, he will not save you. You are simply not worth the effort."

Matthew watched his father leave, then turned his attention to the commode that stood next to his bed. On it was his sketchbook. He took it, flipping through the erotic sketches of a lovely female form that burned in his mind. He saw it every night, nearly every waking hour of the day. As he flipped through each sketch, he was haunted by the beauty of her, by the increasingly painful ache in his heart. He had drawn her in every kind of pose he could think of, and every position he wanted her in. Her hair was always a different shade. Her face—blank. With a growl, he threw the book on the bed, and impetuously knocked the empty absinthe bottle to the floor where it smashed into a thousand shards. Christ, his life was falling apart, and all he could think about was Jane. Where was she? Who was she with? And did she think of him anymore? Were her dreams clouded with thoughts of him?

Jesus, what was he going to do?

Fisting his hands through his hair, he pressed his eyes shut, willing himself to think of anything other than Jane. It wasn't as if he had nothing else to do with his time but sit around and lament the loss of her.

He'd bought the little run-down shop in Bloomsbury for his gallery with the proceeds from the auction nearly a sennight past. Workers were even now beginning to fit the place according to the designs he'd drawn.

He could go there. Escape to his make-believe world of art and leave the haunting memories of Jane behind. He could take a hammer and bring down walls, with powerful vicious strokes, exorcising Jane from his blood with each thrust.

Destruction…. He could vent his pent-up rage there until he was utterly exhausted, his brain too worn out to think of Jane and all the things he wanted to do to her tempting body.

Jane…. He opened his eyes, focusing on the sunlight that streamed through his window. It always came back to her. When would it stop? he wondered, fearing that it might not.

"My lord, I've run the bath and your trunk is packed."

Matthew glared at his valet. "Packed for what?"

"Your trip to Bewdley, milord. The wedding," he clarified when Matthew gave him a blank look. "You are still Lord Raeburn's best man, are you not?"

Damn it. He had forgotten all about the wedding. In his post-Jane delirium, he had forgotten many things.

"Right," he grumbled, "I'll be along in a second. Marlborough," he called, stopping his valet at the door. "Has the post arrived?"

"Yes, my lord."

"Is there…was there anything of a…personal nature?" he asked, feeling his cheeks crest with embarrassment. But his valet, professional as always, barely blinked.

"No, my lord."

Matthew nodded and fisted his hand in the sheet. It was time to forget her. Forget everything about her. Most especially the way she had seemed to awaken him from his decades of slumber.

"Is there anything else, my lord?"

"No, nothing." There was simply nothing else, he thought morosely as he made his way to his dressing room.

She was gone, disappeared amongst the coal smoke and fog. He had no chance of finding her now. London was the place to hide when you didn't want to be found. And it was obvious now that Jane didn't want him discovering her in her secret hideaway.

Parting the velvet curtains of the carriage, Jane revealed more of the rolling countryside that lay outside the window of their traveling coach. It was early May and the mountainous county of Worcestershire was awakening from a long hard winter.

The trees were in full leaf, and the fields were now a sloping array of light greens and dark emeralds. In the distance, outlined by the horizon, loomed the rugged heath-covered Malvern Hills. The county, a varied mix of mountains intertwined with fields of crops and orchards, was dotted with quaint little market towns that had been virtually unchanged in centuries. Industrialized progress had not ravished the countryside as it had in many of the other northern counties of England. There were no giant stacks belching out clouds of thick black smoke. No farmland destroyed to make way for huge factories or railway tracks. Perhaps if the inhabitants of

Worcester were fortunate, they would avoid the poisonous tentacles of industrialization for a few more years, preserving, in Jane's opinion, the most spectacular scenery in all of England.

Outside the window, tulips and daffodils were growing wild beneath the trees. Tall pussy willows and wild grasses that grew rampant in the ditches at the side of the road swayed and rustled in the warm breeze. It was an ideal spring day, being neither too cool nor too hot. The breeze was just right and the sun was shining brightly, with nary a cloud to be found in the powder-blue sky. *A perfect spring day.*

She had always enjoyed this ride up to see Lady Blackwood's nieces. As a child her world had been London's dirty and gritty East End. She could never imagine that the world, let alone England, could look this beautiful. Every year she and Lady Blackwood made this journey, and every year, Jane still marveled at the countryside. She should have been resting back against the plump squabs enjoying the breathtaking scenery and the tranquil peace. However, she could not stop her mind from continuously belaboring the events of the past weeks, nor could she stem the restlessness that had seemed to grip her for the past two days since leaving London.

There was a strange mixture of fear and apprehension in her that she did not understand. She only knew that as they came closer to Bewdley—a sleepy little Georgian village in the north of Worcestershire—the trepidation grew stronger until she could no longer stem the tide of uneasiness rising in her belly.

It was all because of him, of course. Wallingford. She had tried hard these past weeks, to forget him. She had worked herself into exhaustion, trying to erase him from her mind. Sometimes she thought she had succeeded. It was only in the darkest hours of night when she dreamed of him, and his hands touching her body, that she realized she'd failed. She doubted she could ever forget him, or the kind of pleasure he had awakened in her.

She was loath to see him again, but knew it was inevitable. He was friends with Anais, and her fiancé. He would attend the wedding. And Jane would be forced to see him. Except the last time they had seen each other, he had treated her like rubbish, and she had possessed a cockney accent.

Lord, what was she to do? One thing was for certain, she could not allow him to discover that it had been her who had cared for him in the hospital.

"My favorite niece marrying, and a future marquis at that," Lady Blackwood said with a self-satisfied grin as she gazed out the window.

Jane smiled and nodded, determined to forget Wallingford for the time being. "I am happy for Anais. She deserves her prince."

"Indeed she does. She has loved Lord Raeburn for a heap of years. I have prayed so often that God might have it in his plan to marry them to one another. After the events of last winter, I despaired of it ever happening."

"True love has a way of always coming out the victor, don't you think?"

"What would the two of us know about true love?" Lady Blackwood said with a chuckle.

"Indeed," Jane muttered as she once again focused on the countryside that was whirling past her window.

"I am very pleased that you agreed to act as Anais's maid of honor," Lady Blackwood continued, heedless of Jane's inner melancholy. "I do not understand why you hesitated in the first place. You've been friends for years. Who else should it have been?"

A lady of similar background. The daughter of a marquis.

Most certainly not some guttersnipe who was her aunt's companion. But as always, Lady Blackwood chose to ignore and forget that her companion was not of her world, or that of her niece's.

"Perhaps Ann will suddenly be well by tomorrow."

"Red measles linger, Jane. I doubt Ann will be in any shape to walk down the aisle with Anais. Besides, red spots are most unbecoming in a lady."

Jane halfheartedly smiled and let the curtain drop back into place. "It shouldn't be me. I'm not family."

"Jane, dear, you really must not dwell on your past. I have told you that your humble beginnings and your pedigree do not interest me. Moreover, Anais feels the same way as I."

"I am not fit to act as Anais's maid of honor, your ladyship, and you know it. In fact, I am fortunate to even act as a companion. By rights I should still be living in the parishes or struggling to obtain a post as a chambermaid."

"Nonsense," Lady Blackwood said with a scowl. "You are far too intelligent for such menial tasks. You are a lady of considerable breeding. It is not just a matter of it being in the blood, you know."

Unable to win the argument, Jane let the topic drop. In her employer's eyes, she was simply a young woman who had once fallen on bad times. A woman she had taken under her wing and tutored. When Lady Blackwood had found her, Jane had been a parentless, homeless waif in need of food, shelter and protection.

"Jane, you've not been yourself these past weeks. I can't understand it. What's happened?"

"Nothing has happened."

"Jane, you can tell me."

What, that I was duped into believing that I meant something to Matthew? That my silly, idealistic fantasy brought me nothing but hu-

miliation and hurt? By God, her pride still stung, and her heart continued to weep blood every time she thought of him.

Good Lord, she should be done pining for him and what she had thought he was. He was the Earl of Wallingford. Not Matthew. He was a womanizing blackheart, not worthy of her notice or her favors.

"Dr. Inglebright is worried about you."

Jane met Lady B.'s rheumy gaze. "He worries about a great many things, I am only one of them. He needs a break away from the hospital."

"He is getting that. He told me he has been invited to stay in the country with the Duke of Torrington."

Jane arched her brow. It wasn't like Richard to be courted by the aristocracy. She couldn't imagine it was his doing. More like his father's, she suspected. Even though he was a doctor, Richard still had obligations to his family, and this was one of those occasions where he had to bow to his overbearing father's wishes.

She had heard of the duke, but had never met him, or knew anything about him. Lady Blackwood's reputation did not allow for her or Jane to go to any tonnish events, but that did not stop them from reading, and enjoying, the gossip in the newspapers.

"By the by," Lady Blackwood murmured, "I had an opportunity to question my niece about the guest list for this weekend. I fear that there is a guest who might prove a bit upsetting to you."

"Oh?" Worse than Wallingford? She couldn't imagine it.

"Thurston will be there. It seems the old earl is a bosom bow of the groom's father. I understand he has confirmed that he will be staying the entire weekend."

All thoughts of Matthew flew out of her mind, replaced with the horror of the past. Sweat prickled Jane's scalp beneath her bonnet. She did not want to see the earl. She wanted nothing to do with the lecherous beast. The last time she had crossed paths with the earl, he had decided to beat the day-lights out of her with his brass-embossed walking stick.

That had been fourteen years ago.

Thurston had been an acquaintance of her mother's. No, not an acquaintance, Jane thought sourly, but a customer. After her mother had died from drinking herself to death, her mother's *protector* had sold Jane to the earl to pay her mother's debts. She'd been but a child at the time.

At first Jane had gone willingly, assuming that she would be put to work in the kitchens, but when it was made clear the earl had purchased her virginity, Jane had flown into a fury. A fury that had been matched by the ruthless Thurston who had beaten her, then attempted to rape her. Her struggles and screams had only ignited Thurston's lust, and Jane had barely escaped his clutches with her virginity and life intact.

"We will endeavor not to cross paths with Thurston," Lady Blackwood muttered as her shoulders swayed in time to the carriage movement. "You will certainly not be expected to speak to him. I shall cut him as I always do. If he decides to stiffen his spine and approach me, I shall have Raeburn rescue us. Anais has already spoken to her intended about Thurston. My niece informs me that Raeburn will be watching."

"Perhaps I might just stay in my room for the weekend," Jane muttered as she relived that night, standing out in the rain, hungry and cold and seeking refuge from the elements and the pain in her body from Thurston's beating. Thank God Lady Blackwood had stumbled across her a few hours later after returning from a friend's house.

"If it were any other event, I would have declined the in-vitation, rather than risk a chance of a run-in with Thurston," Lady Blackwood said, pulling Jane out of her memories. "But

I am afraid that I cannot miss dear Anais's wedding. I also fear, that as the maid of honor, you cannot reasonably spend your time cowering in your room."

No, she could not.

"I thought it best that you know ahead of time, dear. I know you will want to be prepared for any surprises."

"Yes, indeed."

Lady Blackwood smiled affectionately and pressed forward. Laying a reassuring hand atop Jane's folded hands, she patted Jane's trembling fingers. "Stiff upper lip, Jane, dearest. The old goat will not get the better of you, or me, for that matter. Show him you are made of better stuff than he. Let him know that he never broke your spirit."

Nodding, Jane continued to keep her gaze averted from Lady Blackwood. The world outside whirled by, all bright and welcoming, while the darkness of her thoughts and the memories of her unhappy childhood raged like a tempest inside her.

For the next hour, Jane waged a private internal war. It had been a long while since she had allowed herself to recall the miseries of her past. Memories that were left best buried threatened to reawaken, and Jane shoved them ruthlessly deeper. She refused to think of her mother—the mother who could not live without a man in her life. Her father, a selfish aristocrat who wanted nothing to do with her. Her mother's protector, who wanted to sell her to a lecherous old man after her mother died. She refused to think of any of them, and the hell the three of them had put her through.

With a little shake of her head to clear her mind of the disturbing memories, Jane leaned forward and squinted against the glare on the glass. Beyond the gentle slope of grass loomed the Marquis of Weatherby's enormous mansion. An Elizabethan palace, three stories high, it was also the home of the marquis's son, Viscount Raeburn. Eden Park, as the estate was named, was the stage for Lord Raeburn's wedding to Lady Blackwood's niece.

The sun-baked limestone country house rose above the valley in which they were traveling, like a mammoth iceberg rising from the sea. Sitting forward on the bench, Jane pushed her spectacles higher on the bridge of her nose, watching in wonder as the mansion grew larger as they approached. Imagine being mistress of such a place, Jane thought in wonder.

Jane finally tore her gaze from the rolling green hills and turned her face from the window. She saw that Lady Blackwood was watching her intently with a mixture of curiosity and concern.

"You know, Jane, that I am always here if you need to confide in anyone. I would hope, dear, that you would trust me in matters close to the heart."

Lady Blackwood was looking at her with shrewd scrutiny. Jane felt herself shrink back from that knowing gaze.

"Thank you, my lady. I do feel quite comfortable speaking plainly with you. Although, I do not have anything to converse with you about at the moment."

Lady Blackwood arched her brow and sat back against the squabs. Jane knew without a doubt that Lady Blackwood's intelligent mind was busily trying to fit all the pieces together.

No one knew her as well as her employer, and Jane was well aware that Lady Blackwood suspected Jane was harboring secrets. God help her if Lady Blackwood ever discovered what had happened at the hospital, or in Wallingford's carriage. What would she say if she were to discover that Jane had once fancied herself in love with Lord Wallingford!

"You are very quiet this afternoon, Jane. You seem to be in deep thought."

"I underestimated him and allowed him to humiliate me,"

Jane murmured absently then caught herself. She had not meant to say that aloud. Fortunately, Lady Blackwood appeared not to hear her.

She really needed to gather her thoughts and her considerable control. Her behavior was irrational, moody, not at all in keeping with her steady character. More than once Lady Blackwood had commented on it. Jane knew it was only a matter of time before her employer demanded to know what was causing Jane to shirk her duties as an attentive companion.

Damn it all! She could not stop from continuously thinking about Wallingford and all that had happened between them.

She had erred. She had done something she had never allowed herself to do before. She had hoped. She had dreamed. And all those dreams had centered around a man she thought was the missing piece of her soul. A man who could read her thoughts and actions so well. A man who truly looked beyond her facade to the depths that were hidden beneath.

Silly romantic twit! Her desire to be desired was nearly her ruination, and all at the hands of the most notorious debaucher in England.

"Look, here we are at last!" Lady Blackwood cried with glee.

Jane looked at the house and swallowed hard, wondering if Lord Thurston would already be there, lying in wait to pounce on her one more time. Or worse, Wallingford.

God, she hoped not. She didn't think she could handle any more surprises.

10

"Smoke?"

Raeburn declined the offered cheroot with a shake of his head. "Anais can't abide the smell of it."

Matthew snorted and put the cheroot to his mouth. Striking a sulfur match, he lit the end of it and puffed, making a great display of smoke. "Seems like a lot of rules and inconvenience when one seeks to please a lady. Myself, I don't give a damn, and I suspect I am happier for it."

Raeburn chuckled and continued to look out the salon window that overlooked the drive and the steady stream of conveyances that carried the wedding guests.

"I am the happiest of men, Wallingford. You, of all people, know that."

Matthew gave an inelegant grunt and blew a cloud of smoke up into the air. "But how long will said happiness last. A year? Two?"

"A lifetime."

Not bloody likely. However, who was he to drive the joy out of his friend, and on this, the day before he was to wed? Let him keep his hopes for a lifetime of love. He knew better. Nothing lasted a lifetime, least of all the love for a woman.

"She'll give me the devil for telling you, but I am afraid I cannot contain myself." Raeburn turned his face from the window. A smug, masculine grin widened his mouth. "Anais is with child."

"Randy old goat." Matthew laughed as he congratulated his friend with a hearty slap between the shoulders. "Christ, you've anticipated the marriage bed. I'm shocked."

"I'm not a saint," Raeburn said with a leer. "I've bedded her every chance I've had."

"Better take it a wee bit slower. You're going to be married to the woman for a lifetime. There are only so many carnal delights. What can be left to experience?"

"Many. For instance, making love to one's wife while she is big with your child is an experience I cannot wait to try."

Matthew frowned. "Fat and awkward. Not my idea of a good tumble."

Raeburn studied him quietly. "Truly? You do not feel a sense of possession when you think of the woman who will bear your sons and daughters? Imagine a woman ripe with your babe inside her. Is there any other thought that makes you feel more manly and virile?"

"I had three wenches at the same time last week at Recamier's. I felt damn virile and manly, I assure you."

"Be serious for once," Raeburn chastised.

"I am being serious. The logistics were a bit trying, but after a few goes, they got the way of it."

Raeburn's smile faded. "Think on what I am saying, Wallingford. The woman you love carrying your child. Watching a part of yourself growing inside of her, feeling it move. The profoundness of it. The *rightness*."

Stomping out the end of his cheroot, Matthew looked away from the intensity and the probing he saw in his friend's eyes. He did not want to think such things, for he knew that the miraculous love Raeburn felt for Anais was not to be his. Any woman impregnated with his seed would be by accident and by the way of a one-night stand or a woman who had the misfortune to become his wife and thus a brood mare for the ducal dynasty.

What Raeburn had with Anais was the rarest love he had ever seen. It had survived through childhood and adolescence, past young adulthood and numerous betrayals to survive and flourish. He had never seen that kind of love, and he knew without a doubt that such a thing would never be his.

But did he even want such a thing? He always thought not. A wife was too stifling, children too loud and dirty. Marriage and brats meddled with a man's routine and a man's home. He did not want a wife and brats, but he could not deny it to himself, he had thought of a woman carrying his babe. *Once.* One unguarded moment in the middle of the night, he had thought of a woman dressed in a drab gray gown, a black veil covering her face, her delicate gloved hand caressing her swollen belly. And he had seen his hand, ungloved and large, reaching out to rest upon hers. That night, alone in his bed, he had wanted a wife. He had wanted a child.

Shaking his head, he focused on a black town coach that was lumbering along the drive. Shaken from his thoughts, he raised his arm to lean against the window frame and assumed his bored, careless air, the one that hid so much of himself from the world.

"The trouble with pregnant wives, Raeburn," he drawled, "is that they tend to lose their looks after they've given you an heir and a spare. In short, they usually continue to look pregnant when they are no longer belly full."

"You're wrong," his friend dutifully protested. "I think they only look more beautiful to a man."

"If you say so," he said with a shrug. "Who is this?" he asked, pointing to the gold crest on the door of the town coach. It had pulled to a stop, and a footman, dressed in a powdered wig and pair of silk breeches and white stockings, was in the process of opening the door.

"That is Lady Blackwood," Raeburn answered with a smile. "An original as a young woman, and a force to be reckoned with as an old one."

"The woman who fancies herself a suffrage leader?" he asked, amused. "She'll swallow her tongue when she finds out that I am in attendance."

"She knows. Anais told her. You will recall that Lady Blackwood is her aunt. So be nice."

"As a matter of fact, I do recall the old bird, and her frosty companion, as well. What is her name?"

"Miss Rankin."

"Ah, yes, the unfortunate Miss Rankin," he drawled, amused. The last time he had seen her had been in the late winter, in Bewdley, at church. She had garnered his notice because of the color of her hair—an unfortunate red mass that appeared unruly beneath her bonnet.

He had seen that particular shade of red before. The sharp-mouthed woman who had stomped on his pound note had sported hair that color. His teeth ground together. He still felt anger over the fact that Jane had run from him. Naturally, that anger extended to the woman who was brave enough to deny him any information of Jane.

"Has Anais informed you that Miss Rankin is to be the maid of honor?"

Matthew promptly choked. "Surely you jest at my expense?"

"She is one of Anais's closest friends," Raeburn said with a grin. "I wouldn't jest about such a thing."

"Christ, Anais could have at least chosen a pretty friend, if for nothing else but for my sake," he grumbled as he watched her fall into step beside Lady Blackwood. "What should I know about the woman?" he asked. "Will she converse, or will making conversation with her be as torturous as having my eyelashes plucked out one by one?"

Raeburn chuckled. "I find her rather a delight, if you must know. Well versed on many topics, and full of opinions—which, of course, should amuse you."

"Of course, because my notion of a delightful woman is one who sprouts opinions," he muttered sardonically.

"Lady Blackwood and Anais treat her as though she were a part of their family. So perhaps you might think of her as Anais's cousin who is tainted by scandal. Lady Blackwood is a divorced woman, you know."

"Christ," he mumbled as he watched the pair make their way up the gravel, to the steps that led to the house.

"Take comfort, old boy. If anyone takes delight in scandal, you do. You'll make a good job of creating one. I know you will. You'll give that drab little peahen a day of excitement."

"What is the peahen's full name?"

Raeburn glanced at him. "Jane Rankin."

The hair on Mathew's nape rose and he glanced down at the woman, watching her disappear beneath the window. It couldn't be…

Jane was an immensely popular name, especially amongst the working classes. It was merely a coincidence they were both named Jane. She was not *his* Jane. Impossible.

"You could have told me!" Jane snapped as she smoothed the long silk train of Anais's wedding gown.

"I had no idea you would be offended by the matter."

"No idea? Ha! The man is a misogynist. He uses women and throws them away like last week's rubbish. To think I shall have to stand up with such a man." *Oh, God,* Jane silently added. What if he remembered her from the sidewalk, when she'd ground her boot into his pound note?

"He is Raeburn's dearest friend."

"Your intended ought to know better than to pick friends of such dubious reputations." What would she say if he did recall their meeting? Worse, what if he thought she was *his* Jane. She was, of course, but she couldn't let him know that. Thank God the shame of being broke had kept her and Lady Blackwood silent about her working as a nurse. No one but the two of them knew. If Wallingford took it into his head to ask questions, everyone would deny that Jane was anything but a companion.

"You should have voiced your complaints last night, Jane, when you first arrived."

"I did, if you will but remember. You chose to ignore my concerns."

Anais met Jane's gaze in the cheval mirror. "You aren't backing out now, are you? I am getting married in three hours and there is no other friend in the world I want witnessing this day than you."

"Of course not," Jane said with a sigh. "Forgive me, it's just that…well…oh, it's nothing. You look stunning, Anais."

Anais laughed and reached for Jane's hands. "Thank you, but you aren't getting off the hook so easily. Tell me, why does Wallingford offend you so? Well, beside the obvious fact he's a womanizer?"

"He trifles with women and their feelings and he hurts them unbearably."

"Does he? I am not so sure about that. I think the women

that choose to be with him know exactly what they are getting. A night of pleasure and a cold spot in bed come morning."

"No, he trifles with them. He makes them feel special and wanted and desired, and then he cruelly takes those hopes away from them."

Anais looked at her curiously. "Do you know someone who has personally suffered such treatment by him?"

Jane looked away and started plucking at the orange blossoms that lay between the tiers of lace on Anais's crinoline skirt. "I know of someone. Naturally her name must be kept in confidence."

"Naturally," Anais murmured. "Jane, is something wrong? You are not yourself—"

"A long journey, I am afraid," Jane said, cutting off Anais. "And more than a bit of excitement. I am so happy for you that you are finally marrying your knight in shining armor."

"Well, he is a bit tarnished, you know."

"All the more interesting when they come a bit dented and tarnished. Isn't that what you used to say?"

"I did."

"You are perfect," Jane whispered as she stepped back and took in the sight of her best friend in her wedding gown. "Your knight is going to fall to his knees when he sees you."

"Do you think so?"

"I know so," Jane said with a smile. "Now then, I have one thing left to do before we leave for the church."

"And that is?"

"I have to confront the devil himself. Wish me luck."

"He's really a romantic, you know," Anais called as Jane reached for the door. "Look beneath the brashness and you will see a completely different man."

"And see what?" Jane asked. "A heartless, black soul?"

"A bleeding one, I think."

"Nonsense, to bleed means that you have a heart and blood in your body. Wallingford has ice in his veins and a mechanical device in place of a pulsating heart. He is an amoral, unfeeling rogue."

And with that, she closed the door in search of her prey. What she was going to say when she found him was something else entirely, and what she was going to do if the lecher had a decent memory and recalled that it had been her standing on the sidewalk was something she did not want to contemplate. But she had to do this before the wedding. She owed it to Anais not to cause a scene.

She found him on the terrace, his black hair shining nearly blue in the brilliant midmorning sunlight. His face was cleanly shaven and devoid of the cumbersome sideburns most men favored. It was strange that a man who was clearly a leader in society was markedly out of step with the current fashions. His tailoring was cut elegantly, and his choice of fabrics was expensive but simple. He shunned the fashion for facial hair and bushy sideburns, and kept his hair neatly trimmed.

A frisson of physical awareness rushed through her as she watched his large hand rake through his silky hair. That hand had once caressed her so softly, so passionately. But that was another time. He had been a different person there with her, and to some extent, she had not been herself, either.

It was those moments at the hospital that continued to plague her. She told herself those memories were nothing but a foggy dream of a faraway time and place. Little remained of that dream now, save for the familiar tremors of yearning that slithered along her nerves whenever her gaze strayed to him.

A beautiful dark angel, she mused, *with a black, fathomless soul.*

"Lady Burroughs," he murmured seductively as a figure in silk sauntered toward him. "Good morning."

Jane froze, her breath trapped in her lungs. What was this? Her mind buzzed with the possibilities and her heart constricted traitorously in her breast. How easy it was for endearments to drip from his tongue. How blasted simple it was for him to insert different women without a care or a thought. Had he even given her—Jane—a parting thought? Had he gone to the hospital to try to see her? Had he been upset when she had not returned? Not bloody likely, she thought venomously. He hadn't cared a fig for Jane—for her.

"Good afternoon, Lord Wallingford. What a delightful surprise to find you standing here on the terrace—and all alone," Lady Burroughs said silkily.

"Surprise?" he purred, and Jane could see that he was leering down the bodice of Lady Burroughs's gown—a bodice that was nothing but a thin-as-water scrap of fabric. "I think not, my lady. This was as calculated a plot as ever I've seen."

"All right," she said huskily, stepping closer to him so that the sliver of daylight between them was snuffed out when Lady Burroughs's blue gown caressed Wallingford's silver waistcoat. "I admit I followed you out here. There, does that please you?"

"It's always pleasing to me when a lady comes to heel," he said with a slow grin.

Jane bit her lip—hard. There was nothing more she wanted to do than reveal herself and rail at him for being such a sexist prig. And good God, was that twittering she heard? She glanced at Lady Burroughs's expression, which should have been one of shock and outrage, and instead found her eyes to be glowing and her mouth pouting in obvious invitation. *Outrageous!* Lady Burroughs was a new bride of not quite three months!

"And what will you do with me, my beautiful lord, when I come and lay myself down at your boots?"

"Chain you there," he said without a second's hesitation.

"Now?" she asked, drawing her index finger down his chest.

"Afraid not," he replied, straightening from her and brushing a speck of lint from the sleeve of his jacket. "All the duties of the best man, you know. Unless, of course, you want to meet me in the vestry later for a little unchristian diversion."

"My lord," she said with a husky purr as she brushed her bosom up against him, "you're utterly scandalous. I can barely wait for a lesson from Genesis."

"The original sin, we could re-create it here, with a dry hump against the wall if you'd like."

"Dry?" she said, arching her brow while she reached for his hand and drew him toward her. "Why, I'm positively dripping for you."

Unable to stop herself, Jane let out an inelegant snort. Was Lady Burroughs deranged? Did the countess hear the same foolish nonsense *she* heard? Why, she was offering herself on a platter to the man. He'd barely even looked at her and yet Lady Burroughs was prepared to do anything to have him.

It was too shameful for words, a member of her own sex lowering herself to please the wishes and indulge the whim of such a man as Lord Wallingford. Good heavens, the man was the devil incarnate, the destroyer of women. She, more than anyone, knew that.

He must have heard her unladylike chortle, for his dark blue gaze slid to where she was standing inside the terrace doors. He looked her up and down with his cool, mocking, assessing eyes for an insolent length of time before he addressed her. "May I be of some service to you, madam?"

She stepped forward and held her head high, refusing to be

intimated by such a man. She had stared him down once before, she could do it again. Keeping her voice controlled and cool, she said, "You are of little service to anyone, least of all me, my lord."

His chin tilted and his eyes flashed—anger, disbelief—she didn't know, but his dark eyes continued to dance mischievously in the sunlight as he watched her stroll onto the terrace.

"I can't image any man wishing to service you with a mouth as sharp as that."

She stood before him, ignoring his stinging rebuke, which she knew was a thinly veiled insult toward her plain looks. What the libertine meant to say was he couldn't imagine anyone servicing her with her sharp mouth because she possessed little else that could make one ignore her tart tongue.

"I'd like nothing better than an opportunity to match wits with you, my lord, but it seems we must put aside our respective feelings toward one another and think of those who would have us, pretend at least, that we are enjoying each other's company."

"Ah, the maid of honor," he whispered, letting his gaze flicker along her, his eyes narrowing in suspicion. "I suspect you are the same Jane Rankin whose boot mark is stamped upon my pound note, for you share the same color hair, and glimmer of defiance in your eyes."

Jane darted her gaze to a spot over his shoulder, but he clutched her chin and forced her to look upon him.

"Where is your accent today, hmm? And what the devil were you doing there, in the East End?"

He remembered. Devil take him. Of course he remembered, but that didn't mean she needed to. "I'm afraid that you have mistaken me for someone else, Lord Wallingford."

His eyes narrowed and she felt his cold stare attempt to pierce her, but she would not let someone as useless and immoral as Lord Wallingford discompose her. She was through with her infatuation of him. He was not the man he had once been with her. That had been an act. Before her stood the true Wallingford.

"Perhaps once you're finished subjecting this woman to un-imaginable humiliation," Jane murmured, "you will be so kind as to meet me in the study. Apparently we have a toast to write for the happy couple."

And then she nodded politely to Lady Burroughs and turned magnificently on her heel back to the house.

"Redheaded shrew," he muttered.

"Insufferable wastrel," she muttered back before closing the door behind her. She caught his stunned expression and took perverse joy in it. It was childish and small of her, but she was not above admitting it. She wanted retribution against him, for making her forget her vow to be true to herself, to never allow herself to be ensnared by a man, to never lose herself to a man. She had been in very real danger of doing so to Matthew. She would have done it, too, had not the Earl of Wallingford shown up to save her the humiliation.

"Excuse me," Matthew grumbled as he stepped away from Lady Burroughs. "It seems I have an appointment."

"Later, hmm?" Lady Burroughs purred. "We will meet later, and I will give you what you have been desiring for months."

With a curt nod, he stalked across the terrace and thrust aside the door. Not thinking about Lady Burroughs and her offer, he stalked onward, inwardly fuming. The little hellion. He was going to give *her* what she deserved. Then he was going to shake her till her teeth rattled and the information he wanted about Jane came spilling out of her mouth, for re-gardless of what she claimed, she was the woman he had spoken with on the sidewalk. It had been her, Lady Blackwood's drab companion, sporting a cockney accent. What the devil she had been doing there was anyone's guess—probably up to no good, hence the reason she had used an accent. They had met before, perhaps she feared he would recognize her, and inform her employer. But the truth was, he didn't give a damn about what she had been doing, all he cared about now was finding out how she knew Jane, and forcing her to tell him where he could find her.

Boot steps pounding throughout the hall, he headed for Raeburn's study. Throwing open the door, he stalked inside and slammed the door shut, taking care to lock it behind him.

Jane Rankin was already sitting in the chair behind the desk, busily scratching away on a piece of vellum with a nibbed pen. She did not deign to look at him when he slammed his hands atop the polished veneer while he leaned menacingly over the desk.

"I see you're already here," she mumbled. "No doubt the lady took umbrage at your primeval attitude toward her sex and told you to go to the devil."

"We have an assignation planned for later in the afternoon, where me and my primeval attitude are going to fuck her senseless."

"I despise that word, and I take grave exception to it when used against my sex in such a demeaning way," she hissed, slamming the pen down atop the paper and glaring up at him.

"Is that right? Well, that's too damn bad because it's one of my favorites and I use it every chance I get."

"Heathen," she spat.

"Drab little peahen," he shot back in a childish display of temper. But the little she-devil did not back down. Instead, her complexion turned as red as her hair, and her eyes flashed behind her unfashionable spectacles. Her voice was shrill, belying how much he was rattling her. *Good*.

"Even so, my lord, we are here because our friends are in love, and they want us to act as their witnesses. For today, we will have to find a way to put aside our mutual distaste and act as though we are civil human beings, which will be a stretch for you, I know."

He smiled, a ruthless cutting smile that showed all of his white teeth. "Don't worry, I can be charming, even to drab little lady's companions."

She tilted her chin defiantly. "There is no need for charm, my lord. I am not interested in your bed."

"Good, because you aren't going to see it, nor are you getting into it."

She folded her arms across her breasts and glared. "Now that we have established the boundaries, perhaps we might begin work on our toast to the happy couple."

"Might I suggest you abandon the toast, and go upstairs to ready yourself. The ceremony begins in little more than an hour."

"I am already dressed," she said on a gasp.

Matthew let his gaze stray down her form. She was wearing a gray gown without any adornment. Not a scrap of lace or satin adorned the cuffs or neckline of her severely styled gown. Her red hair was pulled tightly back into a bun that was secured ruthlessly with one simple silver pin. Her spectacles, large and pitted, had dust motes illuminated behind the lenses.

"You have got to be jesting," he mumbled, not knowing if he meant for the poor creature to hear him. "You aren't going like *that* to a wedding."

"I have no need of fancy gowns and feminine fripperies, my lord. It undermines our sex. It makes us pretty, fluffy ornaments for men's pleasure. I dress for me, not for the pleasures of men."

"That much is obvious."

Her eyes went wide, but she did not cower at his cutting comments, steeling her spine instead. What sort of woman was this standing before him who could withstand the lashing of his razor-edged tongue? What kind of upbringing had inured her to such cruelty?

Just when he was about to speak, to say something to soften the lethalness of his previous words, a cloud shifted, partially covering the sun and the light through the window. He blinked, watching as the shadow skated over her face, transforming her into someone else—someone softer, more vulnerable. *Someone more familiar.*

"Why are you looking at me like that?" she hissed, and the mulish set of her mouth and the shrillness of her voice made him question the impossible thought that had just run unbidden into his mind.

She trembled and he saw that she ran her hands down her arms. Those small, delicate hands. Soft hands.

"Where's your accent," he murmured, his mind blanking at the possibility. "You had a cockney accent," he added, "when we met on the street."

It couldn't be. This drab, plain little wretch could not be his Jane. She was not the soft, vulnerable woman possessed of passion. A well of deep passion that was begging to be let free. A passion he had wanted just for himself.

The shadow danced away, leaving her face glowing in the sunlight. No. It couldn't be. He was seeing things. Thinking strange damn things.

"As I said, you have mistaken me for another. London is full of drab little peahens, sir. Now, then, I'm leaving," she said in a huff.

"To change?" he asked, unable to stop from goading her.

"To write a poem for my toast," she snapped. "And you may suffer, for I will not help you with yours."

"No need, darling," Matthew drawled, his words intending to push her away. "I doubt you know a suitable word that will rhyme with *fuck*."

"Stuck," she said, turning to face him. "For two days, my lord. We are stuck with one another. Let us make the best of it."

"And how do you propose we do that?"

"By giving each other wide berth. We will not stand together, we will not talk to one another and we will most certainly not look at one another."

"No problem from this quarter."

"Good. You may be assured that it will be no difficulty for me, either."

"I didn't think it would. You're cold and heartless, frigid, I daresay."

She glared at him over her shoulder and that strange feeling plagued him again. Bloody hell, it couldn't be. It just could not be…

11

It was a beautiful wedding.

The bride wept openly, and the obvious adoration the groom felt for his beloved was evident throughout the ceremony. Once or twice, Jane felt the stinging warmth of tears gathering behind her lashes. She was happy for Anais's joy, Jane reminded herself, but the faint taste of bitterness stung her tongue all the same.

What would it be like, Jane wondered, to have such a man standing before you, his eyes damp with emotion, his heart on his sleeve for everyone to see? The expression that Lord Raeburn's handsome face had worn when he saw Anais walking down the aisle with her father simply stole Jane's breath. *Such love....*

Pain, regret, jealousy filled her soul. She had never known love, let alone the kind that Anais shared with Raeburn. To look upon such a miraculous thing and know that it was never to be yours was the cruellest torture Jane thought she had ever endured.

Looking around the table at the guests seated for the wedding breakfast, Jane's gaze strayed once more to the happy couple who were seated across from her. Anais was smiling and blushing as Raeburn whispered something in her ear. Not ashamed to show his emotion, Raeburn pressed a kiss to his bride's temple while his fingertip glided down Anais's rose-flushed cheek.

"I believe a toast is in order before we begin the meal," a deeply male voice whispered beside her, jerking her from her musings as violently as the lash of a whip striking her flesh would do.

Wallingford. How could she have forgotten the brute was seated beside her? Every time he moved in his chair, or his arm or thigh brushed up against her, her body jolted as if she had been shocked with an electricity machine. How could she be physically aware of him after the way he had abused her person so abominably? *Little peahen,* he had called her. A drab, color-less bird...

Her pride still stung at the remembered barb. Still-mad tears wanted to gather in her eyes, but she forced them aside. Jane Rankin did not weep, least of all for a man. She had shed enough tears in her lifetime that she had used them all up. There were no more tears left to spill down her cheeks in re-sponse to Wallingford's cruel assessment of her. Even if it was the truth.

She was what she was. Nothing could change her physical appearance. As Lady Blackwood was wont to say, "God makes us as he intends for us to be." Jane had never questioned the validity of that statement, until she had laid eyes on the beau-tiful dark angel that was Lord Wallingford.

More important than her appearance was her personality. She did not want to change who she was. She liked this Jane, this strong, independent person. A person of honesty and in-tegrity, *honor.* She was a nurse, a person of worth. It was her mind that counted, not her appearance. Richard certainly hadn't seemed to mind her plainness. With him, she did not have to worry excessively over her hair and her gowns and manners like all the other young women her age. She was simply herself, not some concoction designed to incite the male ideal and fantasy.

And yet, she could not get the sound of the deeply painful *drab little peahen* out of her mind. Oh, how hurtful he was. He was nothing like the man he was when she had nursed him. There was nothing left of Matthew. Wallingford ruled now.

"The toast?" Wallingford murmured once again. "Or are you ignoring me? Or mayhap you are trying to figure out what shocking word I've chosen to rhyme with my favorite word?"

Jane slid him a disapproving look, and the devil had the nerve to chuckle. "What do you think the old tabbies will do when I say the word *fuck?*"

"Hit you over your head with their reticules if they have any sense."

"What will you do?" he asked, meeting her gaze.

"Nothing. I expect no more out of you than low behavior. Your shocking way of speaking cannot possibly offend me more than it already has. I am prepared for anything, my lord. I only hope that my friend, the bride, is equally prepared."

"Let us all hope," he muttered. "So, shall I begin, or shall I defer to you? Ladies first, I believe."

Her spine stiffened when the word *lady* escaped his mouth. He had not said it in a sarcastic drawl as he did his other put-downs, but Jane knew that he had meant it as an insult. She was not a lady.

Suddenly she was filled with the uncomfortable emotion of pain once again and she despised the vulnerability that followed it.

"Please, you first," she muttered.

Avoiding her gaze, Wallingford pushed his chair back and stood, his champagne glass in hand, his arm raised in the air. "A toast to the happy couple," he said in a loud, imposing voice. The guests quieted and reached for their glasses, their gazes focused on Wallingford and his commanding aura near the end of the table.

"I once told Raeburn that true love was like a ghost. Everyone talks of it, but few have seen it." Polite twitters ensued, and Jane saw a few knowing nods between some of the elderly men present at the table. "But Raeburn," Wallingford continued, "is the luckiest of men, for he has seen it. He has it, what most men yearn for and what few will find."

Jane stared up at Wallingford as he stood beside her, her mouth parted in astonishment. Was this Wallingford? Or had some mischievous woodland faerie sprinkled dust over his head on the ride to the church to turn him into a human being with a conscience? A soul?

This was Matthew, a soft voice whispered to her. This is how he had been with her, when he had thought her someone else, someone beautiful and worthy of him.

"I always believed that men talked of love to make the carnal needs of man more acceptable to themselves and their friends, as well as the fairer sex." Snickers and grins shot up all around the table, but quieted immediately when Wallingford's voice took on a soft, almost philosophical tone. "I know now that isn't always true. For I have seen the strength of it, the power of it to bring together two people who are meant for each other. You have made a believer of me, Raeburn."

Wallingford saluted the happy couple with his champagne flute. "To Lord Raeburn and his lovely new bride, the Viscountess Raeburn. To true love," he said, sipping a mouthful of champagne. "Forever."

"Forever," the guests cried cheerfully.

"Forever," Jane murmured, studying Wallingford as he slowly lowered himself into his chair. This was not the man who had cornered her so churlishly in the study. This was Matthew, the man she had wanted so desperately all those weeks ago.

The very thought that the man who had awakened her to womanhood resided in the breast of London's most notorious scoundrel confused her. How could such a beautiful, sensitive creature exist beside such cruel callousness?

"Your turn, I believe." Again, that same electric frisson swept along her skin. Her hands shaking, she reached for her reticule and pulled the little piece of vellum from the silk bag. "Allow me," he said, standing and stepping beside her so that he could pull her chair away from the table in order for her to stand. She noticed that he did not regain his chair, but stepped to the side, standing with his arms behind his back, watching her intently.

Aware that all eyes were on her, Jane awkwardly cleared her throat and pushed her spectacles on her nose. She refused to look down the imposing length of the table that was lined on both sides with elegant couples. People of status. People of money. People that were *someone.* Standing alone, with all eyes upon her, Jane had never been more aware of how utterly out of place she looked. Never had she felt more of a misfit than she did now, here at her friend's wedding, with twenty couples of importance and means mentally ripping her to her shreds.

She felt Wallingford's dark gaze burning into her back, watching her, scrutinizing, no doubt, her awkwardness. Was he taking delight in her discomfort? Was he thinking of how drab a little bird she was amongst all the beautifully dressed women at the table? Did he see Lady Burroughs's full bosom spilling over her bodice? Was he comparing the outrageously beautiful countess's coiffure and gown against her bright red hair and dull, serviceable gown?

Inadequacy. Inferiority. The emotions washed over her and she tried to gather her spirit, her confidence, the inner strength she prided herself on. She didn't care about looks and clothes. They did not make the woman. *They did not.* It was what resided *inside* the woman that was her worth.

Jane caught Lady Blackwood's little wink out of the corner of her eye. It was an encouraging look. A motherly look that suddenly rooted her flighty nerves and fastened them safely inside her. With a tight smile, Jane unfolded her paper, which shook miserably in her hands. Would that she could hide that telling fact, but the more she concentrated on stemming the trembling, the more the convulsing paper trembled.

"It will be quite difficult to follow in Lord Wallingford's steps," Jane said with a shaking laugh. "For I do not have the gift of speaking so easily. I lack mesmerism and a silky tongue," she said, her voice trembling as she fumbled to make a jest. A few murmurs and a giggle from a woman met her ears, making her face flame red with embarrassment. *Get on with it, then sit down before you humiliate yourself beyond redemption.*

"These are not my words, I am afraid, but the words of Elizabeth Barrett Browning. Words that are most fitting, I think." Clearing her throat, Jane raised the paper to her face and began to read the lines she had scribbled down hours earlier.

"If thou must love me, let it be naught except for love's sake only. Do not say 'I love her smile—her look—her way of speaking gently.' For these things in themselves, Beloved, may be changed or change for thee—and love, so wrought, may be unwrought. But love me for love's sake, that evermore thou mayst love on, through love's eternity."

Lowering the paper to rest upon the table, she turned her gaze to Anais and Lord Raeburn, whose arm was protectively around Anais's shoulders. "That is the meaning of true love. Love through adversity and joy. Through beauty and plainness. A love with no beginning or end, a love which we have been shown today. To Lord and Lady Raeburn. Forever."

"Hear! Hear!" a number of the guests called as they clinked glasses. "To forever."

Anais rose from her chair to embrace her, and Jane hugged her friend tightly to her breast. "Thank you, dear Jane," Anais whispered through a sniffle. "I will remember those words forever."

Nodding, she hugged Anais and watched as Raeburn clasped Wallingford's hand. To her shock, Wallingford embraced his friend and bent his head to say something in Raeburn's ear. What, she would dearly love to know.

"Come, come," Lord Weatherby, Raeburn's father said impatiently. "The food is getting cold."

Taking their chairs once again, the four of them sat. Jane reached for her napkin and placed it on her lap, careful to avoid brushing against Wallingford, whose large frame was taking up most of the space between their chairs. With a deep breath, she reached for her glass and froze, the crystal goblet sliding from her hand when her gaze landed on a pair of green eyes. Mean green eyes. Familiar, haunting green eyes. Unable to hide her shiver, she looked away from Lord Thurston's taunting glare.

"Allow me," Wallingford said softly as he reached for her champagne flute and settled it atop the white damask tablecloth. "Are you chilled?" he asked as she shivered involuntarily. "I can have one of the footmen close the window if you would like."

Jane looked up at Wallingford and saw that his gaze was volleying between her and Lord Thurston, who was making no pretense of staring at her.

"No, thank you," she murmured, flustered by the presence of Thurston, and the uncharacteristic concern she heard in Wallingford's voice.

Wallingford said nothing, but continued to study both Thurston and herself. She could feel his curiosity and hear the questions he must be asking himself. How could a drab servant be acquainted with such an illustrious aristocrat and member of Parliament?

"Bacon?" Wallingford asked, holding the silver tray out for her.

"No, no, thank you."

"All that champagne on an empty belly will make you cup shot, darling," he drawled. "And as we have hours left together in service to our roles, being cup shot with me is not to your advantage."

With a glare, she reached for her fork and stabbed a piece of bacon.

"Wise girl," he said with a wolfish smile.

Matthew was gone, she thought with a sad wistfulness, and Wallingford was back in all his callous glory. It was easier this way, she reminded herself. It was much easier to despise Wallingford than it was Matthew. Now, if only he would remain Wallingford the rest of the weekend, she could then concentrate better on avoiding Thurston.

"So tell me," Matthew said as he swung the bride into a wide swinging arc, "what is the story of your maid of honor?"

"Jane?" Anais asked a little breathlessly. Aware that Raeburn was shooting him daggers from the periphery of the ballroom, Matthew slowed the pace out of deference to her ladyship's delicate condition.

"Yes, Miss Rankin." He was careful not to appear too interested. Anais, despite being a friend for years, was a woman after all, and women were the very devil with stratagems when they thought to entangle themselves in a plot to hatch a love match.

"She is my aunt's companion, and the very best friend in the world to me—well, apart from Raeburn, of course."

"Of course," he said tightly. *Get to the dirt, if you please.* But he could hardly say that. To do so would certainly pique Anais's interest. And why he was interested in the dull Miss Rankin and her equally dull story, he had no bloody idea.

From the second she stepped out onto the terrace and interrupted him with Lady Burroughs he had been interested—even more so after he had realized she'd been the smart-mouthed creature who had stomped on his money.

He had watched her during breakfast. His own reaction was equally interesting. But what was even more remarkable was the little byplay he had witnessed between Miss Rankin and Lord Thurston and the physical reaction he had experienced upon watching the two of them. *Very* interesting, that.

"How long has Miss Rankin been employed by your aunt?"

"About fourteen years, I think," Anais said as he spun her around during the Viennese waltz. "She is a most loyal companion to my aunt, and a most reliable friend to me."

"She doesn't work elsewhere, does she?" When Anais looked at him strangely, he tried to clarify. "I thought perhaps I had seen her somewhere before, that is all."

"No, her occupation is as a companion."

Frustration welled within him. He couldn't get past the idea of Miss Rankin as Jane—his nurse. She was all wrong. Yet the thought prevailed, making him stare at her and wonder if it had indeed been her at his bedside. Her in his carriage—her body he brought to climax.

Christ, he could hardly believe it, that creature shuddering in his arms as he ravaged her quim with his mouth. Miss

Rankin was cold and removed. Jane was warm and soft, infinitely feminine; it could not have been her he had been with.

"And her family?" he asked, his gaze straying from Anais to the lone figure sitting in the corner of the ballroom, the large potted palm nearly obstructing her from view.

"No family to speak of. I should probably not tell you…"

Yes, he wanted to shout. *You should probably not, but devil take it, you must!*

"It would be most upsetting to Jane if you knew…"

"Oh, well, then," he said, acting contrite. "You probably shouldn't. I don't think she likes me much as it is."

A glint twinkled in Anais's blue eyes. A sparkle of interest. A glitter of excitement. She was piqued. God help him, she was no doubt already planning his wedding to the unfashionable and dowdy Miss Rankin.

"My aunt found her." Anais deliberately lowered her voice so the other dancers around them could not overhear. "She was huddled in the rain outside my aunt's town house one evening."

Matthew arched an amused brow. "She wasn't casing the house, was she?"

"She was scavenging in the rubbish bin eating the bits left over from dinner." Anais suddenly looked up at him with sad eyes. "Naturally my aunt could not turn her away. So she offered her protection and employment."

A host of unsavory emotions twisted his gut. Horror, shame, guilt, sympathy…all foreign to him, and all blasted uncomfortable as they sat heavy in his breast. And the feeling that he was looking upon Jane, the nurse, consumed him.

He repeated the words in his head. It was not her. It was not Jane. Jane was gone. She had left him.

"All I know of her parents is that her father was an aristocrat and her mother was his mistress. I do not think it turned out well, for Jane was raised in the stews of the East End. Her mother jumped from man to man, searching for a protector. Jane, of course, followed, but was frequently not extended the protection of her mother's lovers. I am afraid Jane was left on her own, more than once."

"Illegitimate, obviously?" he asked, watching Jane, a flicker of anguish for the child she had once been eating slowly at the little bit of conscience he still possessed.

"Indeed. But none of that matters," Anais said, turning her face up to his. "It does not matter to my aunt, or me. And because Jane is so dear to me, it does not matter to Raeburn. I trust, my lord, that for this weekend, Jane's unhappy circumstances will not matter to you."

"Of course not," he muttered, wounded by Anais's lack of faith in him. "I can be quite charming when called upon."

"Charming is not what she needs, my lord. Constant is what my friend requires. I beg you, as long-standing friends, leave Jane alone. Do not trifle with her or charm her for your own amusement."

The dance came to an end and Matthew walked Anais back to her husband. "You have my word, Anais. I will leave her alone. I don't want her. I don't need her."

But even as he said the words, his gaze searched out Jane. No, he didn't need her. He didn't *need* any woman. Despite his avowal, he nevertheless found himself standing before her, his hand outstretched.

"Shall we?"

Her eyes blinked owlishly behind her spectacles. "Shall we what?"

"Dance," he said in exasperation. "After all, it is the thing to do at a wedding ball."

"It is improper for a lady's companion to dance," she said with a dignified sniff as her gaze traveled over his shoulder to the swirling dancers behind him.

"It is most proper for the maid of honor and the best man to share a dance."

"No, thank you," she replied in a firm controlled voice that brooked no opposition.

"Come, you must," he muttered, perturbed by her refusal. No woman had ever before refused him a dance. He'd be damned if this colorless spinster would be the first.

Grasping her hand, he pulled her from her chair, aware that an elderly matron was closely watching them from between the palm fronds. Jane gasped as her body brushed against his. Matthew stood momentarily transfixed by the image of her bodice pulling tight against her corseted breasts as she struggled to control her indignation.

Magnificently large, rounded breasts, his mind seemed to scream.

"What do you think you are doing?" she hissed.

"Attempting to persuade you to dance with me," he murmured in a disconcerted voice. Lord, what sinfully beautiful curves lay hidden beneath her ugly gown. He could feel the voluptuousness of them beneath his palm, all luscious and full as he attempted to quiet her struggles and lead her to the dance floor. He was hardening in response to them, and he had to stop himself from rubbing his tented trousers against her hips.

"I already declined your offer," she snapped, brushing his hand away from her lower back. "I can say with certainty that I *will not* be persuaded."

"Come," he coaxed, suddenly needing to feel her body moving against his if only to assuage some of the pain in his groin. "You'll enjoy it."

She glared at him. "I most certainly will not."

"You will."

"I do not dance."

"You will today," he muttered, reaching for her hand.

She closed her eyes as if she were in pain. "I do not dance, my lord, because I do not know how," she bit out, every word clipped and hard. "There, are you satisfied? I truly am a little peahen as you say. I am a drab, colorless bird, unable to even dance. Now, release me. And cease looking at me in such a way. I do not want your pity."

"It was not my intent to humiliate you."

She snorted and tilted her chin proudly. "Of course you sought my humiliation. It is retribution, you see, for embarrassing you in front of your latest conquest this morning."

"She is not my latest conquest," he snapped, irritated. Why the devil did she make him feel so bloody filthy when she looked at him through her spectacles like that? Christ, what was she doing to him? He was quite clearly coming unhinged. One minute he was despising her, the next he was erect and wishing he could shove her hand beneath his trousers.

"You claimed an assignation with her this afternoon," Jane said silkily. "Are you now saying that you lied?"

"A man can change his mind." *And he had better change his mind about her, and quick.*

"A leopard, my lord, never changes his spots."

"What the devil does that mean?"

"It means you are what you are. Do not bother to stand before me and pretend you are a gentleman, for you are the furthest thing from it."

He was floundering for a response when the sunlight streaming through the window was suddenly snuffed by a heavy, gray cloud. Matthew watched with a mixture of wonder and horror as it transformed Jane's face. Good God, the shape of her face, the brilliance of her green eyes glittering behind her spectacles…

"You have no conscience, sir. No morals. You care for no-one other than yourself and your pleasures."

"You know nothing of me," he growled, studying her face.

"And you know nothing of me," she said in a voice that had grown soft, wounded.

That voice, that whispering, caressing voice. It was the same one he heard in his dreams. It was Jane's voice. God help him, it truly was her.

Slowly, he lifted her face with his fingers, his stomach churning uncomfortably. Christ, what a fool he had been. Was she laughing at him, at the absurdity of him desiring Jane and despising this Jane? Was she feeling smug and superior?

The volatile emotions began to boil in his blood at her betrayal, and he stopped himself just as he was about to squeeze her chin in a painful grip.

Damn her, she knew who he was. He had not concealed his features with a veil. He had not hidden anything from her. And yet she had stood before him, acting as though they had never met, never talked, never touched.

Rage made his breathing hard, and he fought it, barely able to see anything other than that day in the carriage, when he had desired her so bloody much. When he had talked of himself and allowed her the briefest glimpse into his soul. *Christ!* Was she amused by him whenever she thought of that day that he lowered her bodice and suckled her breasts? Was she mocking him now, secretly laughing at him, remembering how much of a damn fool he had been? Was she enjoying her triumph over him that day when she had stomped on his money—and his feelings?

Fuck! His beautiful, passionate Jane concealed beneath the armor of this little tergamot.

With lightening speed, he shackled her wrist and captured it ruthlessly in his hand. Aware that no one was paying them any heed, he pulled her along behind him, ushering her through the door that led to an empty hall. He did not allow her to tarry, but pulled her behind him until they reached another door. Flinging it open, he steered her inside with only the pressure of his hand on her back. The door shut softly and Matthew saw her stiffen as the sound echoed throughout the room.

He was mad as hell at her treachery. What did she think she was about? He would not be laughed at. He would not have this dull woman mocking him. He would not have the pain that came with knowing that Jane was deliberately hiding from him and...*laughing at him*.

Before she could think of getting away, he reached for her, bringing her back against the door, pinning her against the wood with his chest and thighs. His hand skimmed over her hip while he turned the key in the lock with a soft but determined *click*.

She whimpered. In fear. In longing. He didn't know, and didn't particularly care. He was going to punish her here and now for deceiving him. And once she was sufficiently chastised, she was going to answer each and every one of his questions. He was not going to let her out of the damn salon until he was satisfied that he knew all there was to know about Jane Rankin and her deceit.

Tightening his fingers on her waist, he brought her ever so slightly closer to him. He saw her eyes go round, felt the rush of hot air as she released her breath. He was aware that her fingers held a death grip on her skirts.

"Have you enjoyed laughing at me? Do you count your little game a success?"

Her eyes flashed, but she held her tongue. Impressive. But how much longer could she hold out on him? he wondered. Surely her will was no match for his own.

"I know everything about you, Jane," he whispered darkly in her ear. *"Everything."*

Her gaze flashed to his. "I doubt it."

He smiled slowly as he ran his fingertip down the column of her neck. "London College Hospital? You work nights there, do you not?"

The color left her face, but amazingly she held her gaze steady on him.

"You tended me, didn't you?"

"You're mistaken."

He watched his finger caress the pounding pulse in her throat. "I came in your hand, remember? Remember the feel of me in your little palm, remember the way I suckled your breasts?" He brushed his mouth against her ear. "I had my tongue in your cunt, remember?"

She whimpered, and he groaned. Damn it, he should not be feeling aroused by the sensation of her warm, satiny skin beneath his fingers. He should be angry that she was denying who she was, that she had been with him. But anger was slowly being swallowed up by desire. He could not take his gaze from her throat, or stop himself from thinking how much he desired to stroke the full vein in her neck with his tongue.

"You are mistaken," she whispered as she licked her lower lip nervously.

His fingers bit into her waist. "Do not lie to me," he hissed. "I know, Jane. I know *everything*. Now I just want to know why."

She knew what he meant. He saw the realization in her wide eyes. *Tell me why you have deceived me,* he wanted to roar, but he hung on, barely, to his control. He wanted to hear her say it. Why had she done it? To punish him by wanting a creature who didn't want him? Well, she had succeeded. How he hated to admit it, but she had hurt him—*deeply*—by not returning to him. She had abandoned him after the most beautiful, intimate encounter he had ever experienced, and

Christ, how he despised the feelings of abandonment. How he loathed to admit that weakness in his makeup. Hated to admit that this woman, this cold, calculating woman had deliberately set out to hurt him, to awaken in him feelings he had buried and refused to think on made him feel out of control. He was indeed becoming unhinged.

"Tell me," he growled through clenched teeth, shaking her about the shoulders in an attempt to bully her. But Jane Rankin was beyond such intimidation.

"Say it," he snarled, angling his head so that he whispered the words in her ear at the same time his lips grazed her earlobe. "I want to hear the words from your own lips."

"I have no idea what you are talking about. Now, release me."

His palm slid from her waist to her breast until he cupped her in his hand. He pressed forward so that his chest flattened against her and the side of his face nestled against her neck. "Do you believe in fate, Jane?" She gasped as he stroked his thumb across her swollen nipple.

"No," she murmured so softly he barely heard her. "I do not believe in anything."

"You believed once." He palmed her breast. "You trusted once."

"You're wrong. You've mistaken me for some other woman." She groaned when he flicked the tip of his tongue down the tempting throbbing vein that ran the length of her neck. He should not be doing this. He was weakening, despite the fact he never again wanted to be weak in front of this woman.

"I...I don't want you."

His gaze flickered up from her throat to her face. Her head was tilted to the side, her eyes closed behind the lenses of her spectacles, her lips, pouting and pink, were parted slightly. He parted them more as he rubbed his finger along her lower lip. "Liar."

"I don't want you," she said again, this time harder, more forcefully, as if she was trying to convince herself, as well as him.

"You're afraid of men like me, aren't you, Jane? Admit it. I do something to you that frightens you. I make you aware that you're a woman and I am a man."

"You're wrong," she whispered, pressing herself against the door in order to put some space between them. But he followed her.

"I know what you need."

"No, you do not," she protested. Unable to speak, she shook her head, whispering the word *no* again as she pressed herself against the unyielding wood behind her. Any space that was between them he closed when he pressed his chest tightly to hers.

"I know what you want, Jane."

Her lids opened, and she blinked slowly, her gaze slipping to his as her lips trembled. "What do you know?"

His touch softened against her mouth. Her top lip was scarred, somewhat misshapen. He hadn't really noticed it before now, but now he couldn't stop himself from tracing his fingertip over the uneven skin, feeling himself softening. *Weak.* He hated it. He might even hate her for making him feel that weakness, for making him admit to it. Yet, he could not stop his body from responding to her, from wanting to learn all her secrets and hidden truths.

"I know the depth of the passion you keep hidden beneath this prim veneer. I know that beneath your protests you secretly yearn."

"No. No, you're wrong."

"You were eager all those weeks ago, and you burned in

my arms. I think you yearned to feel me deep inside you. I think you *still* yearn."

"Not for you," she whimpered softly.

"Why lie, when I can feel the truth in your trembling hands. I see it in the way your lips are quivering. Smell it in the way your body is heating, scenting with arousal. There is no one better suited to give you everything you crave, Jane," he murmured against her mouth. Reaching for her hand, he brought it to his chest and flattened her palm against his waist-coat. His heart was beating hard, she would feel it. He was breathing hard, she would feel that, too. He didn't give a damn. He didn't care that she would understand that physically he was aching for her. He didn't care about anything other than feeling her touching him.

Grasping her wrist, he moved her palm lower over his breast, down over the flat hardness of his belly, where it rested at the waistband of his trousers.

"You don't like being reminded you have needs and desires. But you have them, don't you, Jane? It was there in the hospital, in the carriage, all that honest need. The need for a man to touch you, kiss you, whisper in your ear. The need to be filled."

He pushed her hand lower and made her feel his cock, hard beneath his woolen trousers. He forced her palm to flatten with pressure from his own hand. She went utterly still, but did not attempt to pull her hand from out beneath his. She could if she wanted to. He barely held her hand against him now. Their gazes met and her breathing was so hard that he could feel the brush of her breasts rising against his chest.

Closing his eyes, he gritted his teeth, savoring the feel of her hand on his prick, despite the fact it was still innocently covered by his trousers. He was so damn hard. So hungry for the feel of her flesh against his flesh. But whose flesh—Jane's, or *this* Jane's? He no longer knew.

It was absurd. Three hours ago, he despised her. Now, he could barely resist the lure of raising her skirts and filling her body with his cock. He was definitely unglued. He wasn't thinking clearly. It was the lust coursing through his veins that was clouding his thoughts. And that was a frightening admission, as well, because he had never lost his way during sex or lust, or the pursuit of either.

Christ, having her pinned like this, her eyes wide and her mouth parting in invitation, made him so damn excited. It was charged. Erotic. He was becoming addicted to the sensation she—Jane—aroused in him.

"Admit it, Jane," he rasped. "The thought of us sharing our bodies together fascinates you. And yet, you pretend to condemn me, but secretly you yearn for what I can show you. And show you I will."

"You will not."

"I will have either your passion, or the truth you are keeping from me. Perhaps I will even have both."

He pushed away from her and saw that her eyes changed from passion glazed to mutinous. He left her then, aching and unfulfilled. Aroused and confused. It was for the best. It was always necessary to have the last word with an opponent as skilled as Jane.

Positioning himself so that his cock would cease rubbing against his trousers, Matthew grunted with pent-up lust and lingering anger. Christ, he swore as he left the salon. Where did Raeburn keep the damn brandy?

12

Bloody arrogant, presumptuous… *Oh!* Jane seethed as she fought to stem the trembling of her hands. Who the devil did he think he was, abducting her from the ballroom and practically ravishing her?

Fanning herself with her hand, Jane strove to control her wobbly arms and legs. Good God, she had been so close to falling for those beautiful blue eyes and that hypnotizing sensual voice. Squeezing her eyes shut, she rested her head against the cool wood of the door and trailed her quivering fingers along her neck, tracing the path his fingers had taken. *I know what you want….*

The whispering remnants of his words called to her, causing a strange, forbidden tightening in her belly. Her lips slowly parted as if in anticipation of his kiss. The memory of his hard, warm body pressing against hers heated her blood until she thought she would go mad from the memories.

Struggling to fight the ache in her body, she lost all strength and allowed her hand to slip down the stiff ruffled collar of her gown. She could hear her shallow, rasping breaths as her palm descended lower and lower until her fingers lay a hairbreadth from her swollen breast. Her nipple constricted, sending her belly tightening and wetness dampening her drawers. He had touched her before—suckled her until she cried out against him. He had been only Matthew to her then. Today she had wanted it again, but it was not only Matthew she had desired—she had wanted Wallingford, as well.

No! She turned and pressed her cheek against the door while she smoothed her hand against the wood, trying to smother the thought. She would not lower herself to such a level. She would not touch herself, would not give in to the base need *he* had awakened within her.

No, she murmured softly as his words whispered to her. *No, I do not need anything from you. I don't want you. I don't want this…this heat, this fever I feel snaking through my blood.*

But the heat would not subside. Instead, she felt her breasts swell further against her muslin corset, as the memories of that day in the carriage meshed with the memories of those forbidden moments here with him in the salon. The desire those memories evoked only made the yearning deep within her more painful, more difficult to deny or resist.

Somehow he had known she was his nurse. How he had discovered her secret was beyond her. But she knew without question that he now knew she was Jane. She also knew he was furious about the fact. Why? She could not help but wonder. Was it because he thought Jane beautiful and mysterious and he was disappointed because it had only been an illusion? Was that the reason behind his anger? His pride was ravished because he had desired a woman he thought beautiful only to have her turn out to be plain—*a drab little peahen?*

Hearing the angry pounding of his boots on the marble tile, Jane cracked open the door and peered out, immediately seeing a wigged footman step out from the shadows with his white-gloved hand extended.

"A missive for you, my lord," the footman said while bowing before Wallingford.

Wallingford took the missive and glanced at the writing.

"Have my horse saddled and brought around to the front of the house immediately."

"Very good, milord."

An unfamiliar sensation swept through Jane as she watched Wallingford tuck his missive in the pocket of his jacket. It must be from a woman. Jane imagined it contained a revolting amount of flowery perfume and an equally revolting request for an assignation.

Jane had a fairly good idea who the letter was from. *The devil!* How could he go meet Lady Burroughs after what had just transpired between them? Was his body not on fire for her, as hers was for him? That thought alone made her feel murderous. Her body had responded to him, to every little touch, every little word, and he treated the matter as though it was nothing.

It was not nothing! It was everything to someone like Jane Rankin. Damn it all! He had given her cause today to rethink her opinion of him. He had been kind to her during the speeches. To think she had actually believed that there could be more to Lord Wallingford than his rake's reputation. In those fleeting seconds, she had nearly believed that the man she had met still resided somewhere deep in the breast of Wallingford. What a fool she was. That man—Matthew—was just a facade, an illusion to lure and entice an unsuspecting and lonely woman. The man was devious, utterly dangerous to her sex with his conniving ways and sensuality.

Furious with indignation, Jane swept out of the salon and ran for the servants' staircase. She was halted by the sting of fingers on her arm.

"Well, well, we meet again, and in such a private place. How fortuitous."

The chill of that voice swept down Jane's spine, making her cry out in fear as she was slammed against the wall.

"You owe me something, Miss Rankin."

Her eyes pressed shut as she thought of a way to extricate herself from Thurston's viselike hold. The tip of his blunt finger traced the uneven skin of the scar on her lip, making her mouth curl in revulsion. "I see you still wear the impression of my signet ring. Good. It will remind you of what you haven't paid me—yet."

"I owe you nothing," she sneered. "Get your hands off me."

"You owe me the price of your mother's debt, a debt that you should have paid fourteen years ago. Interest is mounting, my dear."

She gagged, and he laughed, pressing closer. "I only wanted you the once, but now, seeing how you've grown into this body of yours makes me almost relieved you've been running from me all these years. Such delightful tits," he said with a leer as he cupped her breasts hard in his hands. "Yes, these will do very well. I do so hope you've kept your hymen intact, for that was the price to wash your mother's debt away."

She struggled ineffectively in his hold. "Release me!"

He laughed and reached for the hem of her gown. "Oh, I intend to, right here, where anyone may happen upon us. I'll ruin you so that you will have nowhere else to turn but to me. And then, dear Jane," Thurston growled as he pinched her thigh hard beneath her gown, "I'll make you pay with every inch of this lovely pale skin."

He moved in to kiss her, but the air moved violently between them, and she heard the sound of skin on skin, and the crunch of bone.

The next thing she knew, a black shadow whirled past her,

picked Thurston up from the floor and slammed him against the wall.

Wallingford.

"Your filthy paws are somewhere they don't belong," Wallingford growled, slamming Thurston up hard against the wall for a second time.

"They're exactly where they belong," Thurston spat through little bubbles of blood that trailed from his nose. "I own her."

"Not anymore," Wallingford sneered. "What is the cost of her debt?"

Thurston's eyes narrowed, and with a sickening leer he glanced at her. "Ask her, the little hellcat."

"Say it now!"

Thurston turned his rapacious glare to Wallingford. "Her virginity."

Jane felt her face flame with humiliation and, cursing, Wallingford shoved himself away from Thurston, and reached for her. She was shocked, trembling, her hands mindlessly trying to smooth her skirts, the ones in which Thurston had had his hands up.

"Jane," he murmured, gathering her close, wrapping his arms securely around her. "It's all right," he whispered.

She nodded and held on to him, taking in the aroma of his freshly laundered shirt, and the cologne that scented his skin. She continued to tremble, even when he squeezed her tight in his arms.

"Leave, Thurston," he commanded. "And if I find you near her again, I will kill you. Do you understand me?"

From the corner of her eye, she watched the old earl slink off into the shadows. She shuddered, and Wallingford ran his big palm down the length of her back.

She pressed her face into his chest. "Thank you," she whispered. "A thousand times, thank you."

"Did he hurt you?"

She shook her head, and he released her, checking for himself that she was unhurt.

"Christ, Jane, what—"

"Please don't ask," she murmured, shame welling up within her.

He nodded, and ran his hands through his hair. "I'm only glad I came upon you when I did."

"I, as well," she said, rubbing her hands down her arms, chasing away the chill and fear that still lingered. It was then that she saw how ashen his color was. How grave his expression.

"I know this isn't the best time, but, Jane, I beg of you, if you are who I believe you are, come with me now."

She would have laughed at such arrogance if it were not for the stricken appearance and the note that was crumpled in his hand. "It's not an invitation for—" He flushed and glanced away. "My sister, Jane. She is ill. I need you—she needs you."

He saw the war waged in her eyes; the refusal to admit who she was still burned there, behind the fear left by Thurston. But this was not a ruse to get her to submit. This was truth. Sarah. She needed him. He didn't ask much of anything from anyone, but this was something he had to ask, even despite the ordeal Jane had just gone through. Himself, he was still trying to assimilate his feelings regarding what he had witnessed. He'd had the irrational urge to choke the life out of Thurston when he had come across the old bastard trying to rape Jane.

The memory of what he had seen made his blood turn to ice. He wanted to reach for her, but instead held out his hand, showing her the crumpled paper.

"This missive is from her nurse." He held the crushed paper aloft, showing it to her. "Sarah's taken ill and is calling for me.

Her health is fragile, and now this… I must leave, and I want you to come with me to nurse her."

"Is there no doctor in the vicinity? The village of Bewdley is nearby, is it not?"

"There's one, and I wouldn't allow him near my dog." He reached for her wrist, wrapping his fingers around the delicate bones. "Please," he said, the words rusty from little use. "She's ill, and frail. Jane——"

With a nod, she gave in, and the weight he felt bearing down upon him suddenly lifted.

"I will need to inform Lady Blackwood," she muttered, swishing past him.

It seemed forever before they were on their way. As the carriage door slammed shut, Matthew realized it had not been more than a few minutes since he had received the note summoning him home.

Sarah. Poor, sweet Sarah, he thought. She was seventeen, with the mind of a child. Instead of balls and gowns and daydreams of weddings, his sister thought of dolls and tea parties and chasing after butterflies.

She was the only person in the world whom he could say he truly loved. And the thought of her ill, possibly seriously, made him hurt like the devil.

"How long to your estate?" Jane asked, drawing him from his thoughts.

"Only a minute longer. It's not far, the grounds border Raeburn's estate."

Jane nodded and looked out the window. In the distance he saw the ducal estate rise from between the hills. He loathed the place, the home of his birth, the prison of his childhood. Even now he felt the familiar unease settle into his breast. He avoided this place like the plague, but with Sarah ill, he had no choice but to go to her and the house that held nothing but nightmares for him.

"Is that it?" Jane pointed in the direction of the obscenely huge mansion which was really a castle. The dukes of Torrington, he thought with a sneer, had a long and noble tradition. But that tradition would end once he came into the title. He had no desire to be a duke, or to see to the running of that monstrosity. As far he was concerned, it could crumble to the ground and disintegrate, along with his father's prized fortune.

"It's lovely," she said, her voice full of awe. "The scenery, it quite takes my breath away. I've always thought Hyde Park stunning, but this…it defies words. The trees." She pressed closer to the window. "What are they, the ones out in blossom?"

"Apple and quince," he murmured, casting a cynical eye over the grounds. Aye, it was breathtaking. There was a lovely bridge that crossed the man-made lake that he used to like to stand upon and gaze out over the vista. There was an old temple—a folly, they used to call it—in which he and his friends used to play hide-and-seek.

Suddenly, he had the urge to show Jane the grounds, to cross that bridge with her. To hide her away in the temple…

She glanced at him, and he met her gaze, and for the first time, he really looked at her. He didn't know what to make of her. She wasn't beautiful, but she held his attention as though she were the most celebrated beauty in Europe.

Behind her spectacles, her eyes were green. A stunning shade, actually. The color of celadon—luminous, otherworldly. They were large, with a lush fringe of curling lashes. Her brows were auburn, and her skin a delicate white. Over the bridge of her nose, a smattering of freckles scattered. He had a mad urge to connect them with the tip of his finger. He studied her mouth next, his heart freezing and missing a beat as he recalled plundering it with his own. Their mouths had melded, their tongues had danced, and he had never once felt the misshapen corner. Why? he wondered.

She was conscious of his appraisal and tilted her head away, preventing his stare. He wanted to turn her head, wanted to trace her mouth, to touch the uneven skin, to put his tongue to it and ask how she had come by it.

Jostling of the carriage pulled his gaze away from Jane and to the window. They were climbing up the drive of the estate. Soon they would be inside his father's home. Matthew had never considered it home, did not consider his father's wife, or her daughters, family. Only Sarah was his family.

The carriage lurched to a stop and the driver jumped down from the box and lowered the steps. Jane inched forward and Matthew held out his hand, stopping her.

"My sister is special, Jane." He swallowed the lump in his throat and willed himself to go on. "Frequently she is misunderstood, overlooked. She is…she is…" He struggled with the wording, always fiercely protective of her. "She is simple. Do you understand?"

He could tell Jane did, by the way her eyes softened behind her spectacles.

"You will have a care for her, won't you? She has feelings, although no one in this house ever considers them."

"Of course."

With a nod, he opened the door and ushered Jane down the steps. Staff were already waiting outside to welcome him home, but he guided Jane up the stairs, rushing her inside with nothing more than a nod to acknowledge them.

Inside, the foyer was dark and gloomy. The familiar shudder swept down his back, and he looked up the winding staircase to see a pair of blue eyes watching him. He ignored the person, and instead placed his hand on Jane's back and motioned her to the right, impatient to get her to his sister.

"Jane? Good God, is that you?"

Matthew whirled around and saw a tall, blond man walking down the hall with his father. Beside them was a man with white hair and thick sideburns, dressed in a black suit and carrying a pigskin bag. A physician's bag.

"Richard?" he heard Jane whisper in disbelief as his form appeared from the gloom and into the beam of sunlight that crept in through the transom window.

"Good heavens, it is you!"

The man named Richard came to a stop before them, his gaze volleying back and forth.

"Lord Wallingford," the man muttered, "I see you are well and truly recovered."

"My son has the devil's own luck, Dr. Inglebright," his father sneered. "It will take more than a bashed skull to do him in."

Christ! He knew the man now and he could not stop himself from stepping closer to Jane. He was marking his territory, he thought as he pressed his hand into her lower back. He was making it good and damn clear to the doctor that Jane was his. Why he wanted her, he couldn't fathom. He did not care to possess females. He didn't want a relationship, but he did not want Inglebright having her.

"What are you doing here, Miss Rankin?" Dr. Inglebright inquired, his gaze straying between them. "Not that I am not delighted to see you, of course."

Jane flushed, and he wondered if it stemmed from nervousness or embarrassment by being seen with Wallingford. She tried to step away, but he placed just the right amount of pressure on her spine to let her know she wasn't going anywhere. "Lady Blackwood is visiting her niece, who happens to be married to Lord Wallingford's friend. We were at their wedding when he asked me to attend to his sister who has fallen ill."

"Good, good," the older man muttered. "Looks like a bit of Providence, Miss Rankin. You can assist Richard here, while His Grace and I have a game of billiards."

"A game of billiards would be just the thing, George. Come, I've had a new table delivered. It's been awaiting its inaugural game."

Matthew fisted his hands at his sides, hating his father and his callous indifference to Sarah. As he watched him retreat with his visitor, he had the urge to throttle him as though he were a punching bag.

"Miss Rankin?" Dr. Inglebright said, motioning her forward. "Shall we?"

Matthew put his hand around her waist, anchoring her. He felt those eyes on the stairs bore into him and he glared back, up at the face he despised. *Still here,* he thought, *haunting these halls.* His attention snapped back to Jane, who was delicately trying to extricate herself from his hold while Richard watched. Their gazes met, and Matthew smiled, an expression that could only be described as chilling.

"You'll not get rid of me so easily this time, Doctor," he snapped, ushering Jane forward.

The room was dark and ominous, sterile, Jane thought as she took in the white walls and plain curtains. On the bedside an oil lamp was lit. The bed curtains were pulled back, revealing a large bed with a carved headboard. In the middle lay a young lady whose beauty was remarkable, even in ill health.

She was blonde, with long curling hair that was fanned out on her pillow. Her skin was flushed and her breathing rapid.

Jane took a step closer, and behind her, Matthew moved her to the side, allowing him to rush to the bed.

"Sarah, pet," he murmured, sitting down on the bed and lifting her hand to his mouth. He kissed her, and she opened her eyes and smiled.

"I told Mrs. Billings you would come."

"I received her note and came straightaway. Sarah, what's wrong?"

"Did you bring me a dolly?" she asked. "You promised you would. A pretty china one from the toy shop in Mayfair."

"Of course I did," he said, smiling as he kissed her hand once more. "But there were none there as pretty as you."

He tweaked her nose and she laughed, which gave way to a groan. "My tummy hurts."

"I think it's appendicitis," Richard murmured beside her. "She has all the signs, and now the fever is coming on. I gave her a dose of laudanum, which had minimal effect on the pain. I'm afraid her appendix is going to burst. Nothing much can be done if it does."

Jane nodded, unable to take her gaze off Matthew sitting beside his sister. Gently he brushed her hair back from her forehead and asked her, "Where on your tummy do you hurt, pet?"

She placed her hand on her right side, low on her abdomen. "Oh, it hurts. Mrs. Billings said it was too many tea cakes, but I haven't eaten any. I swear it."

"I believe you," he soothed. "Here," Matthew whispered, reaching beneath the blanket. "Here is Lady Bess." He withdrew a doll dressed in a ball gown and Sarah clasped it like a lifeline to her chest.

She had the appearance of a young woman, a startling beauty, but her mind was clearly that of a child.

"Oooh," Sarah moaned, "it hurts. My tummy…"

"My lord, your sister is suffering from appendicitis,"

Richard announced from the foot of the bed. "We need to operate before her appendix bursts. If it ruptures and the poison goes into her abdomen—well, the odds are not in your sister's favor. Your father has ref—"

"Don't listen to a goddamn word he says," Matthew snarled.

Richard momentarily froze, before gathering himself. "Yes, well, your father is disinclined to consent to such an operation."

Matthew flung himself up off the bed. "My father wouldn't lift a finger to help her," he hissed, "but I would do anything for her. So if she requires an operation, then you will do it."

Richard flushed crimson. "I cannot just perform a surgery, my lord. Your sister's mental capacity—"

"Is of no matter here. If you value your livelihood, Doctor, you will get started now."

"I...I need consent, my lord, and your sister, in her capacity, is unable to give it. And as her brother you have no say in her care. Now, if you were her legal guardian—"

With a viscous oath, Matthew swept past them. "Prepare your things and be ready for my return. You *will* operate, Inglebright."

13

Throwing open the door of the sitting room, Matthew barged into the room and found Miranda, his stepmother, lounging on a settee, looking at fashion plates. She was dressed in the height of fashion, her throat and wrists dripping with jewels. She did not look shocked to find him standing in her private salon, breathing fire.

"Welcome home, my son," she said with the skill of an actress. "Have you come to give your mama a kiss?"

Christ, he despised this woman who had taken his mother's place. He loathed her, couldn't stand looking at her and the amused glint in her eyes.

Her son...

He cringed at the very thought.

Ruthlessly he shackled her wrist and pulled her up from the settee. She was tall for a woman and able to look him in the eye. She did not even attempt to struggle with him. Instead, her back went rigid and the air of motherly affection was replaced with a venomous, calculating gleam in her eye.

"You will tell your husband to consent to whatever the doctor deems necessary for Sarah," he snarled between set teeth.

She smirked and tried to tug free of his hold, but he tightened it, forcing her to bend back and look up at him. "Your father—"

"You will tell *your husband*," he ground out, "that you wish to consent to the operation. Do you understand me?"

"And how do you expect me to persuade His Grace?" she snapped.

"Why don't you try using the allurements you cast when you got him to agree to marry you?"

Her eyes turned to slits and her lips thinned. "I see your disposition has not improved. You're still the same surly, sulking brat you always were. Darling Elizabeth's little boy," she taunted. "The little boy she didn't want, the one she ran away from."

"Shut up," he roared, tightening his hold. The bitch smiled, and he saw red. She always did know how to bait him. "I hate you as much as I ever did, but never more than now, knowing that you'd let your child suffer in pain."

"It's better this way," she sniffed. "You know that. She has no prospects, no life ahead of her."

"*She's your child!*" he roared. Disgusted with her, he shook her, trying to shake sense into her.

"She's dead to me," she shot back. "What do I want with an idiot like her? She brings me mortification and humiliation whenever I look at her. I *want* to be rid of her!"

He tossed her back and she landed on the settee in a pile of silk and petticoats. In the sunlight, her jewels glistened around her throat. He had the urge to strangle her with them.

"You disgust me," he sneered. "You're inhuman."

She laughed, and Matthew wondered when it was his stepmother had descended into madness. "And how would you know what it is to be human? If you want her saved, *my lord,* then do it yourself."

Matthew barged into Sarah's room and prowled around the bed. Jane had removed her cloak and bonnet and rolled up her sleeves. Before her, on the commode, was a basin, along with a silver tray lined with instruments. She was in the process of pouring steaming water in the basin when he stormed in.

"Begin," he ordered.

Inglebright was on the other side of the bed, his gaze fixed on Jane. When he turned to assess him, Matthew saw the question burning in the doctor's eyes. It was not a question pertaining to Sarah, but Jane.

They stared each other down as Jane worked silently. He watched her pour the water, then bend low to whisper something to Sarah. His sister seemed to calm, responding to the soft lilt of Jane's voice.

Matthew knew what it was like to be on the receiving end of that voice. To feel her hands gently ruffle his hair. It was calming. Peaceful. He needed that calm now.

"Your father—"

"I told you to begin. Now do so. I will deal with my father, you needn't fear any repercussions."

"Richard," Jane admonished, "he will stand by his word."

How Jane could have come to trust him, Matthew had no idea. The fact that she did, however, pleased him. He was scared to admit how much, actually.

"All right then, Jane, you may begin. Two drops of ether."

It was late afternoon by the time they were done. Jane's lower back was stinging from standing so long, and her feet ached. She couldn't wait for a moment of privacy to untie her half boots and rub her toes. But she had a few things left to do before she could seek her own comfort.

Jane went to the bed and checked once more on Sarah. She was breathing easy and her skin, while pale, was warm and dry. Peeling back the covers, she lifted the girl's gown and made certain the dressing was intact. It was. She would have some pain there. Jane knew just how much, for Richard had removed her appendix last year. But it was nothing that a tincture of laudanum could not control. She stood staring at the girl, trying to find the resemblance of her brother in her lovely face. Sarah was fair, and Matthew dark. But both of them were tall and shared the same aquiline nose, no doubt a trait inherited from their father, the duke.

Jane trembled, thinking of the man who had sired Sarah and Matthew. He had come storming into the room in the middle of the surgery, huffing and puffing like bellows. Any sane person, male or female, would have backed down from the imposing aristocrat, but Matthew had stood eye to eye with him, bellowing and huffing just as much as his father. The way he had protected his sister warmed her, gave her yet another confusing glimpse of him.

Which man was he? Matthew, or the notorious rake?

In the end, Matthew had squared off with his father in a verbal barrage, but Matthew had stood his ground, and won the battle. It had been too late to stop the surgery when his father had barged into the room, for Richard had already removed Sarah's blackened appendix, and was in the process of repairing her.

He had done an excellent job of it, Jane mused as she looked once more at the dressing. Sarah was fortunate it had been Richard, and not his father, who had done the surgery.

Covering her up, Jane stood and stretched, rubbing her lower back as she did so. What she wouldn't give for a good long soak in a warm tub.

"Jane, may I see you?"

Richard was standing in the doorway. She glanced in the direction of the chair in the corner of the room, where Matthew had quietly sat, watching them. He had drifted off to sleep.

"Of course," she whispered, tiptoeing past him. Silently she padded across the carpet and into the hall.

"I thought we might go out into the garden. It's spectacular."

"That would be lovely."

She followed him down the stairs and through a dark hallway that led out through the kitchen gardens. "I've already taken a walk," he said as he strolled beside her, "and knew you would be desirous of the fresh air."

She was. On the drive over she had been taken with the view. It would be nice to see the grounds before she returned to Eden Park and Lady Blackwood.

Once outside, Richard led her down a terraced staircase. At the bottom, it was if another world had opened up.

"Oh, my," she breathed. Shielding her eyes from the setting sun, she scanned the vista of trees, shrubs and flowers. In the distance there was a bridge that crossed a lake. On a hill on the other side of the water was a round Palladian-style temple.

"Spectacular, isn't it?"

Jane glanced at Richard. "I...I can't describe it. All this," Jane said, sweeping her arm in a wide arch, "is the duke's?"

"Yes, and some of the forest, too."

Jane could not fathom owning something as glorious as this. To be able to walk out of the house and stroll through such beauty, she could hardly imagine it. There was a peace and tranquility in the vista lying before her that made Jane think of taking moonlit strolls and reading a book beneath a tree by the water's edge.

"There is a lovely little spot over here, with a bench."

She followed Richard down a stone pathway and sat on the iron bench. Beside her were peony bushes, whose buds were swelling, preparing to open. Next to her, Richard's knee brushed her thigh.

"Apologies."

"No harm done."

He smiled and reached out, brushing back a lock of hair that had fallen from her pins. When their gazes met, there was something in his eyes she had never seen before. "You cannot imagine how pleased I was seeing you standing there this afternoon," he murmured, his voice much deeper than Jane had ever heard it. "Almost as though you were fated to be there, at my side. You are a helpmate, Jane. A wonderful nurse. A…special woman."

Jane didn't know what to think, how to reply. A month ago she would have swooned at the thought of Richard speaking to her like this, but now, an image of Matthew flashed in her mind, and she realized that everything came back to him. Despite the fact he was Wallingford.

"I have embarrassed you."

She shook her head, but her complexion told the truth. She was blushing, and she didn't know what to say in return.

"It's been a long day. You're tired."

"It has," she agreed, stretching, trying to alleviate the burning in her back. "It was a rather early morning getting the bride ready, and now this." She indicated the house, and everything that happened.

"How did you come to be here?" she asked, hoping to change the track the conversation had taken.

"Father," he groaned. "He is the duke's personal physician. It was my father who figured out who our patient was. The duke invited us here to thank us, but if you ask me, he brought us here to bribe us to keep our mouths closed about his son's activities that night."

"Activities?"

Richard pursed his lips, as though he was deciding whether or not to answer her question. "Well, I suppose you should know. The earl was in the East End at a gentleman's supper club. He was auctioning off a painting he had done. It was…not in good taste," Richard said with a grimace.

"Oh," she murmured, looking away.

"His lordship has a reputation, Jane—"

"I'm aware of it," she admitted. But there was another side to him. She had glimpsed it.

"So you know what he is?"

A rake. A scoundrel, a womanizer. *A heartbreaker.*

"I have a reasonable idea."

His hand rested on her knee, and he squeezed, forcing her to meet his gaze. "Stay away from him, Jane. He is not a man to be trifled with. From all accounts he is cold-blooded and cruel, and I would hate for you to be his victim."

Too late. She had seen that cruelty, been on the end of it, yet she had also seen such passion and warmth.

"Well, then, shall we?" Richard asked. "I requested tea and you look as though you could use a strong cup."

"I'll follow in a moment. I'd like a few more minutes out here. It's so lovely and fresh. I can breathe," she teased, "without choking on soot."

"Very well. I'll see you in a few minutes."

Jane watched Richard retreat up the path, and up the stone steps that led to the terrace. She waved when he turned back and looked at her. A movement in an upstairs window captured her attention and her hand lowered as she watched the white curtain move.

Someone had been watching them.

The window remained black, the curtain still, and finally, Jane rose from the bench and continued along the garden path, marveling at the fruit trees that were in full blossom. The quince blossoms were her favorite, so delicate and heavenly scented. Stopping, she grasped a handful of blossoms from a low-hanging branch and inhaled the sweet, heady scent. She wanted to bathe in it, to be covered in that decadent perfume.

"Beg pardon, miss, but this is for you."

Jane let go of the branch and reached out for the folded paper on the footman's silver tray. As she did so, she glanced over her shoulder to the steps that led to the house. "I didn't see you come out."

The servant looked straight ahead. "My apologies for the intrusion, miss, but his lordship was adamant that you be given this straightaway."

Jane unfolded the paper.

Dine with me tonight.

Refolding it, she placed it on the salver. "Please convey my thanks for the invitation, but I must decline."

The servant barely blinked as he said, "May I inform his lordship why, miss?"

Jane was taken back, and the servant knew it. His gaze flickered to hers briefly, before fixing on a tree limb that was loaded with blossoms. "His lordship will ask why, miss."

"Tell him I won't be staying for dinner. I expect to be gone shortly, as a matter of fact."

"His lordship has sent a missive around to Eden Park to tell them that you are needed here, miss."

Jane gasped in outrage. What right had he to do such a thing?

"Miss?" the footman asked, knowing she now had no reason to refuse Matthew's offer.

"Tell his lordship that my possessions are not with me, therefore—"

"His lordship has sent a carriage back to Eden Park to retrieve your trunks, miss."

Jane felt herself reddening with anger. "I have nothing suitable in those trunks to take dinner with a duke and an earl," she snapped.

The footman bowed and nodded before turning on his heel and leaving her.

Bloody arrogant…oh, she wanted to spit she was so angry at his high-handedness. Just who did he think he was, ordering her about and organizing what she was going to do and not do?

After a minute or two of gnashing her teeth, Jane stomped back up the path, and ran into the footman who was making his way down the stairs.

"His lordship has made a reply, miss."

Jane grabbed the missive and opened it, feeling her face drain of blood.

Then you may dine with me naked. Flesh is always suitable attire, and a nice accompaniment with wine.
Eight o'clock, on the terrace.

Jane crumpled the letter. As she looked up at the house, she saw the white curtain move once more. Behind it, appeared the Earl of Wallingford. He was looking down upon her, his handsome, fallen-angel face watching her.

With a nod he acknowledged her, then disappeared from the window. Her traitorous heart quickened, and not in anger.

Jane followed the footman and the warm glow of the lantern he held in his white-gloved hands. In the distance, thunder rumbled across the heavens. It was twilight, and with the storm clouds gathering, it was dark, lending the garden an eerie, gothic feel.

As they walked over the stone bridge, Jane studied the still, murky waters below. A white swan swam beside a black one. The black one was obviously the male, for it never left the white one's side, and every time a rumble of thunder would roll, he would swim closer, directing her to the bank.

Jane had never seen a black swan before. There was a quiet beauty to the creature. A sadness, too, she felt, as she watched the pair swim beneath the bridge. They were mismatched, yet they seem to suit one another as they floated atop the water.

She watched them till they faded into the darkness, then took up her pace behind the footman who was waiting for her on the other side of the bridge. Turning down a path, they headed for the building that she had seen early this afternoon.

Obviously, Wallingford was entertaining her outside the dining room. Jane didn't know what to make of that, but her body did. It was already heating up, remembering how he had touched her. His hands, those beautiful, artistic fingers had touched her breasts, her quim, and the memory of it was enough to make her shudder—and not in revulsion.

Climbing the hill, Jane lifted her skirts just as she felt the first drops of rain begin to fall. Damnation, she hadn't brought an umbrella.

"Here, I'll help you, miss." The footman offered her his hand, and she took it, allowing him to tug her along the incline that led to the folly. They were running, but it was of no use, the heavens opened in a deluge, and Jane was soaked to the bone in an instant.

The door of the temple opened, and Wallingford appeared, running down the steps to them. He took Jane's hand from the footman, and ushered her up to the building, exchanged words with his servant, then closed the door.

Jane stood like a drowned rat in the middle of the building, which was decorated with artwork and statues. She was breathing hard, out of breath from running up the incline in a heavy gown. Raindrops marred the lenses of her spectacles, and her hair, which she had carefully pinned up, was wet and curling and slipping from her pins.

"I didn't make it rain," he said as he caught her glare.

Now what was she to do? She was soaked through. And he seemed to be rather pleased by the fact.

"May I?" He reached for her spectacles and pulled them slowly from her face. His gaze never strayed from her eyes, and the searing sensuality of having his attention focused solely on her was too much. She looked away.

"Jane..." He captured her chin and turned her to face him. "Let me look."

"I do not care for your high-handed methods, my lord," she snapped, refusing to look at him.

"What have I done except purchase your services for my sister?"

"I cannot be bought, sir," she gasped, shoving away from him. She ignored his startled expression and moved to the hearth and the fire that burned brightly. She was cold, trembling, but she was damned if she would show that to him. He had purposely trapped her here, and for what? Realization suddenly dawned on her. "Or perhaps, this is how I am meant to repay you for saving me from Lord Thurston?"

His expression turned murderous. "Christ, Jane, what do you think of me?"

"You might think that because I am a poor lady's companion and a nurse, that you have rights to me. Because I am indebted to you for saving me from Thurston, you feel it entitles you to use me as you will."

"I never intended to use you, Jane."

She laughed without humor as she crossed her arms over her breasts. "Then what I am doing here?"

He moved toward her, touching her, and she backed away, refusing to allow it. She was angry, her emotions volatile. And he was looking like Matthew, with his rumpled hair and night beard. He was dressed far too casually in black trousers and a white shirt that was opened, revealing his bronzed chest. The chest she had washed, touched...

"You need to get out of those clothes, Jane, before you catch your death."

She was freezing, her teeth chattering uncontrollably as her wet hair dripped down her neck. He held a blanket and unwrapped it, holding it out to her. "It's all I have."

She had seen too many die of pneumonia from the damp, and she'd be damned if she was going to meet her end that way. With a curse, she undid the buttons of her gown and stepped out of it. Her petticoats and corset came next, leaving her in her chemise, which was damp and clinging to her breasts.

She felt naked and exposed, but the way he looked at her made her blood singe. Even without her spectacles, she could see his expression. Watch his eyes lingering on her breasts, on the apex of her thighs.

"There, are you satisfied?" she snapped, tugging the blanket from his hand, which she wrapped around her shoulders.

"This was not my intention when I asked you here tonight."

"Then what was it, my lord? Why won't you just leave me be?"

Matthew stared at her for a long moment, her question registering in his brain. He had no idea what he was about. The only thing he knew was that he was unraveling, disassembling like a madman. His actions made no sense, his thoughts, his desires ruled him now.

He'd been enraged as he stood at Sarah's window watching

Jane with Inglebright. *Mine.* He had screamed the word inside his head for what seemed an eternity. Goddamn it, he couldn't credit it, but he was envious, no, downright jealous of the bastard. Jane was his. In every corner of his mind and his cold heart, he believed it. There had been something between them those nights at the hospital, and in his carriage. It had been more than the need for sex, and Christ, he wanted it back. He sure as hell didn't want Inglebright getting any of it.

"I believe I begin to understand why it is you cannot leave me be. It is the object denied that is fueling you. You're not used to being spurned, and you cannot abide the fact that someone like me, with my looks and lackluster pedigree, has done so."

A novelty. He had called her that in his carriage. It was partly true. He had never met a woman like her, who could rattle him the way Jane did. Yet she was so much more to him than a body to fuck. Tonight he had brought her here to talk, and yet here she was standing in her chemise, her lovely breasts clinging to the damp material. He wanted to see her bare, to rip it from her. He wanted to paint her with his eyes, and not the imaginings of the past weeks.

Yet, she hated him. He saw it in her eyes, those gorgeous, mesmerizing pools. Christ, his knees had grown weak when he had removed her glasses. She was so…lovely to him.

He thought back to that morning, in Raeburn's salon, when he had confronted her. Rubbing his forehead, he sighed, allowing himself to think, however fleetingly, about those moments and the uncharacteristic feelings that had raged hot in his blood. Anger had been the first to singe him. Hell, he had been so damn angry with the chit. He could have shaken her. But why? *Because you felt something for Jane and she apparently did not.*

Was that it, his pride was pricked? He had wanted her, and she didn't want him, was that what this madness was about?

"You wanted me," he murmured aloud. "You invited me in, Jane."

"And I'm quite sure you found it rather amusing."

"I believed, Jane, I still believe, that I have glimpsed deeply inside you, to a place where no man has ever been invited before."

She glared at him. "You are uninvited, sir, for I have no desire to provide you with entertainment. I'm sure you've mocked me, laughed at me."

"Is that what you truly think, Jane? Did you feel this same contempt and hatred for Matthew as you do for the lord?"

Her lashes lowered, shielding her response from him. Not even the faintest hint of pink on her cheeks gave away the truth. "No."

"Tell me why," he asked, needing to know why she hid herself behind the veil, why she still continued to shield the truth from him. Damn it, he had taken her breasts in his mouth. Had suckled and teased as he had never done with another woman. She had touched him, stroked him—*her*—Jane Rankin. And by God, she had enjoyed every second in his arms. Did that day or any of their time spent together mean so very little to her? Was it only him who had been affected by the current that seemed to run charged between them?

Christ, was he alone in his desire?

When she looked away from him, refusing to answer his questions, he reached into his jacket and removed the slip of black lace he carried with him. The same lace he removed in order to press his lips against her bounding pulse that day in the carriage. "Why, Jane?"

Her gaze swung back to him. She went rigid then, her gaze fixed on the strip of black lace.

"You have obviously mistaken me for someone else, my lord."

"You have already admitted it, Jane, the moment you agreed

to come with me to tend Sarah. You see, I remember everything that led me to come into possession of this lace. Tell me why you still insist on hiding behind the veil when I already know it was you."

He saw something flash in her eyes. Vulnerability. He knew it as soon as he saw it. So, it was the same for her as him. She did not want to admit she had needs—needs she had allowed him to see, had allowed herself to indulge in with him.

They had both been weak, and neither one of them could bear it, knowing that the other had seen them exposed.

"What will it take for you to tell me?"

"You insult me yet again with the suggestion that I can be bought."

"Everyone has their price, Jane."

Her celadon-colored eyes flashed angrily. "Not everyone, my lord."

"Everyone," he said ruthlessly.

She tilted her head and studied him with her shrewd, intelligent eyes.

"Are you for sale, my lord?"

Keeping his expression inscrutable, Matthew hid the shock that lanced through him. He had not expected that from her. "If I were, would you purchase me? Well, Miss Rankin?" he asked, pretending to be bored, pretending that it was not of any import what her answer would be. Although nothing could be further from the truth. Hell, he hadn't even drawn breath in the past thirty seconds while he awaited her answer.

"I would not."

His breath came out in a rush. Her answer did not surprise him. Miss Jane Rankin would never pay for anything—let alone a man of his reputation. He was quite certain that Jane would rather spend her days searching for ways to strip him of his flesh, not paying for it. But what did Nurse Jane want?

"I would not purchase you, my lord, because, simply put, I would want all of you, and you would never allow that."

"All of me?"

"That is the point when one purchases the body of someone, is it not? One wants the rights to that person. When one is willing to trade in currency for the soul of another, one cannot be satisfied with only half measures."

"I don't understand, Miss Rankin. If a person has allowed themselves to be sold, then they must give the buyer whatever it is he or she wishes."

"I assumed you would think in such a way. You are a man, after all. However, my lord, you and your sex are gravely mistaken when it comes to purchasing women. You think that by buying a woman, she will give you all of her—she will not. A body and pleasure are superficial things. One can separate themselves from their body and soul. In the end, you will have the physical, but you will not have the intimacy of knowing the true woman inside the body that you use."

His own body grew hot as he realized just how much he wanted Jane. Not her body, but her, every little thing that made her unique, made her Jane. "You gave me all of you, Jane. I believe that."

She shook her head, denying it, but he felt it. Jane, the woman he had held in the carriage, was her true self.

"It is human nature to hide a piece of one's soul from the sight of another," she said. "If that person is worthy of it, one day, that piece may very well be revealed. If the person is not worthy of such intimacy, then he or she shall have only the body and pleasure. No amount of money can purchase a person's soul."

"Would you try to pry my secrets out of me, Jane?"

"I am one hundred percent certain that if I were to purchase you, my lord, you would give me what you were willing to give, and nothing more. I suppose you would favor me with your reputed prowess in the boudoir, while leaving everything about yourself outside the door. It would be all physical, would it not? Nothing personal, nothing intimate. Just mechanics. There would be no emotional closeness."

If she were any other woman, he would have agreed. However, there was something about Jane that made him want to give her more than what he had ever favored his other conquests with. Something he had been prepared to give Jane, his shy, quiet little nurse.

"My point, my lord, is that you cannot get what you desire simply because you have the pound notes to procure it. And because someone is purchased does not mean that they have to give everything to the one who has bought them. Who we are, what we need—that elusive glimpse into one's soul—can never be bought. It can only be given."

He stopped himself from saying, somewhat impulsively, "I would give you anything you asked for," and instead schooled his expression.

"Are you keeping your soul from me, Jane, is that what you are trying to tell me? Are you afraid now, because I have glimpsed deeply inside you once before? Do you fear I may find out all your little secrets, all your desires and use them against you? Is this why I am uninvited?"

"Don't," she whispered, backing away.

"Why, Jane, are you afraid? You want to give a piece of yourself to me, but you don't want to admit it, do you? You're afraid. You don't know what to do with the need I make you feel."

"Which man are you?" she challenged. "Matthew who I first met, or Wallingford?"

"Why does it matter?"

"Because I liked Matthew, I would have given him anything. I abhor Wallingford. I wouldn't give him anything of any worth, most especially my soul. Which…which man are you?"

The silence was charged, nearly electric between them. Both of them stood watching the other, both trying to hide the fear and truth that threatened to spill out at any moment.

"What is your price for this glimpse into your soul?" he rasped, pulling her closer. "Tell me. I will pay it."

"I am not for sale, my lord."

"Is Jane, the nurse?" he asked, scouring her face, wishing he wasn't being such an idiot. But Christ, he couldn't think. Couldn't control what was coming out of his mouth. "Jane, the nurse, was eager enough for the pleasures of the flesh. Tell me, how much for her?"

"Is Jane who you want?" He detected a sadness, a dejected tone in her voice, and his insides suddenly felt queer and unsettled. "Is she the woman of your dreams, an image you have painted in your mind? Is it that Jane you want?"

"I don't know."

She nodded, accepting his honesty. "My price would be too steep—you would never pay it."

"Ask it."

She looked at him for a long time, her cheeks reddening with a becoming blush as she stood dripping wet, with the blanket around her. Finally she steeled herself and spoke. "My price, if you choose to meet it, would be you, my lord. Not Wallingford," she clarified, "but Matthew. The man you were."

His breath hissed through his lips and he dropped her wrist as if he had been burned. He felt trapped, suffocated. *Retreat,* his mind screamed. *Run away from what she is suggesting.* Yet he wanted her with such fierceness, he wanted to possess her, to take her and bend her to his will. His thoughts stopped, the war within ceased, and he came to her, taking her by the shoulders, shoving her up against the wall as he tore at the slender straps of her chemise.

"You do not know what you're asking for," he growled as he pressed his face into her unbound hair. It was wet, and the coolness did nothing to clear the fire that raged in him.

"I know the man you were," she whispered as she closed her eyes and tilted her head to the side. "I've glimpsed him since. Where is he, Matthew?"

"He's broken," he rasped as he ran his lips down her cheek to her jaw. "He's fucking ruined, Jane, and he'll destroy you."

"No."

"Yes," he insisted, pushing against her, needing her, fearing the connection of her body and his. The last vestige of control left him and he growled into her ear as he captured her earlobe between his teeth, "I will make you hurt, Jane. That's all I'm good at, hurting and fucking. I don't know how to love, how to feel. I don't know how to be with you. I only know how to fuck you, not even you," he groaned, "but your body. That's all I take—a cunt—not a body. Not a woman. Not your beautiful soul, Jane."

Her body went soft against his, and he pulled the blanket from her, smoothing his hands down her supple skin. "I don't want to hurt you, but I will. But I can't let you go." He pressed his eyes shut and fisted the hem of her chemise in his hands. "God," he growled, fighting the memories, the fierce wave of emotions that crashed over him, "I watched you with him today. He touched you. Your knee. He looked at you, Jane."

"It didn't mean any—"

"Mine," he snapped. He traced the uneven skin of her lip then pressed the tip of his tongue to it, making small circles over the scar. "All mine. Even though you'll hurt at my hands, you're mine."

★ ★ ★

Jane could hardly breathe. What was she doing? She had come in, determined to put him in his place, yet here she was, yearning for him. She had glimpsed Matthew, heard the pain in his voice. It had called to her, beckoned her. That tortured voice was her undoing.

Her lips sought his, and she kissed him—softly. A brush, a slide of their mouths until he deepened it, brushing his tongue over her lips, lingering over her scar before he whispered, "All of you, Jane. I need all of you—*now.*"

He tore the chemise from her body, baring her. She was utterly naked. He held her wrists in one hand, high above her head as he studied her body.

"Jane," he groaned as he bent to kiss her breast. She whimpered in protest, but it came out a moan, and when his tongue searched for her nipple, it was hard. When he drew it into his mouth, her whole body tightened, her womb contracting. She was restless against him and he suckled her fiercely. When he released her, he fell to his knees and kissed her belly, her hip. With his fingertip he caressed the black bruise on her outer thigh, then kissed it, washing away the taint of Thurston's touch. His mouth moved up, over the rise of her belly, to her right side. He kissed the scar where her appendix had been removed.

He looked up at her as he traced the puckered flesh, then he was standing, her face clutched in his hands, his mouth hungrily searching out hers. "I cannot stand to think of his hands inside you," he said hoarsely, kissing her with harsh intent. "He did it, didn't he?"

There was no questioning who *he* was. With a nod, Jane admitted it, and it sent him spiraling out of control.

"His hands may have been the one to heal you, Jane. But it will be mine that awaken you."

His mouth moved over hers, his tongue snaking between her lips. Deeply, erotically, he made love to her mouth as his hands swept along her body, caressing her in places she had never been touched before.

How had this happened? she wondered as she reached for his hair and brought him closer to her.

"Jane, let me in," he pleaded, parting her folds, spreading the wetness that lurked between them. "I want to be a part of you." She heard the buttons of his trousers fall to the floor, and she broke off the kiss, shoved him, and he stopped, his face confused as if he, too, was shocked by the events that had transpired between them.

"Who are you?" she asked, her eyes glistening with tears that were part pain, part sorrow. She wanted so much for this to be Matthew, but she feared that Wallingford had swallowed him up.

He ran his hands through his hair and closed his eyes, trying to gather himself. "I don't know, Jane. I don't know who I am."

14

Matthew blew out the match and puffed on the cheroot, watching as the end glowed red. Closing his eyes, he tried not think of Jane's ravaged expression. He tried, and failed. Already he had hurt her.

She had run from him, and he had not chased after her. It seemed a hopeless business, this attraction, yet he couldn't get her out of his head.

Inhaling the cheroot, he rested his head back against the headboard and exhaled a long, steady stream of gray smoke. An image of Jane, her pale body, ripe with curves, came to him, and he savored it as he inhaled again.

How had events taken such a turn in a day? She had run from him, been gone for weeks, and yet, here she was, sleeping three doors down from him.

She was not the woman he had thought she was. It had disappointed him that morning when he discovered her true identity, but now it no longer mattered. He wanted to know *her,* wanted that elusive glimpse inside her, a glimpse he believed, she did not give just anyone. Certainly not to any man. *"Who do you want?"* she had asked. He hadn't known his answer then, but now he did. Now he would tell her, *"You, Jane. Just you."*

Jane…lovely, plain Jane. He reached for her spectacles, which lay on the table. He smoothed his thumb over the delicate silver arms, feeling the remnants of her.

It had been the singular most erotic thing he had ever done, pulling those glasses from her face and revealing her eyes. It had been like stripping her of her flesh and baring her soul. Those eyes…they held such depth, such passion, and sorrow, he believed.

Jane was not plain. He had looked deeply—today most especially—and had seen the loveliness in her. And what was more, he felt strangely possessive of that rare splendor. He wanted her to be his, yet he didn't want her to think that he could be hers—that there could be anything lasting between them. But when he thought of her with another…

He thought of Inglebright's hand on her knee, the way his gaze had lingered on her breasts…

His cock stirred beneath his trousers at the remembered sight. He had wanted his hand replacing Inglebright's. Now, remembering Jane, he wanted to touch himself, to immerse himself in the image of him and Jane together. He wanted to sink down and part his thighs and stroke himself, thinking of Jane lying between them.

It couldn't be, of course. He was ruined for that sort of play. His lover had seen to that. He could no longer abide being touched, stroked and caressed. It made him feel dirty, shamed. But with the absinthe…

With the absinthe he could allow it. *Perhaps.* The ether certainly had allowed him to shed his revulsion of being touched. And Jane's hands…they had felt so damn good.

Unwittingly, his fingers found the waist of his trousers. His pants were already undone. He parted the flap, found the throbbing head of his cock and smoothed his fingers over it. He was hard. He wanted to be touched, to have a mouth love him. He wanted Jane's mouth.

He moaned and slid his hand along the shaft, fisting it, not hard like his lover had wanted, but soft, lazy. Putting out the cheroot, he leaned against the headboard once more, watching his hand holding his cock. He allowed himself to feel the pleasure, and he shoved aside the guilt that came with that pleasure.

He imagined Jane, her red hair glowing like fire from the flames of the hearth. He thought of her, naked, sliding between his thighs. He imagined holding his cock out to her, watching her take it into her mouth and love it—love him.

Yes, this is what he wanted, Jane loving his cock, sucking him deep. He wanted to hold her there with his hands clenched in her hair. He wanted to see her hair spilling over his thighs, to hear the sounds of her mouth sucking, her tongue lapping.

"*Christ, yes,*" he moaned, increasing his rhythm. He wanted to feed her his cock, and watch her suck him until he came and then he wanted to watch her take him in. He would lay his fingers against her throat and feel her swallow him—all the way down. How bloody sinful she would look like that.

But it was more than sex he wanted. There was something else he yearned for. Something he had never found.

He was starved for it, parched, thirsting for a connection with someone—*no*—with Jane. Greedily he wanted to horde her, to hungrily devour every little word, look, soft inhalation of desire, and selfishly keep it, never to return it to her, for it was for him, his alone. Never to be shared, never to leave the confines of his memories. But there was so much more that he wanted from her. Touch, he shuddered at the word, the very thought. Yes, he wanted to be touched by Jane.

Outside and deep within his body he wanted Jane's fingers imprinted on him, branding him and binding him. He yearned for the feel of her body, her touch, her breath against his skin. He wanted it embedded in his mind, his pores. He wanted it entwined with his body and soul, both which hungered and hurt. Both which were empty and so…he swallowed and pressed his eyes shut, finding the strength to go on. Both which had never known softness or kindness. Both which were so frighteningly alone and…afraid.

What he wanted was the sort of elemental connection that would bind Jane to him for eternity, a connection that would see him well fed and safe, forever. Body and soul. His already belonged to her, and he shook, unnerved by the truth and the feeling that, perhaps, the dawn would for once be a welcome sight.

He wanted that morning. A new beginning—with Jane. He thought of her, lying in bed, and the image of her naked, covered in blossoms, made him come.

It was so damn easy. So pleasurable to come like this. His seed burst forth, shooting in hot spurts onto his belly. He had always felt dirty when this happened with his lover who had tutored him in the way of fucking. But this, this climax with Jane, if only imaginary, was not shameful. With Jane, this sex act could be beautiful, freeing.

Relaxed, Matthew closed his eyes, enjoying the minutes of bliss.

Jane nudged the door open, and gasped, unable to move from her spot. What she was watching was so personal she knew she should leave. But how could she, when it was Matthew, looking like this, all male and sensual.

He was on the bed, legs spread. His trousers were opened, and he was pleasuring himself. It was the most beautiful thing she had ever seen, and the sounds of his breathing made her own body shudder.

She should make a noise. Alert him to the fact that he was not alone. But she could not. Instead she studied him, the way his corded forearms tightened with each stroke. She listened to his groans of pleasure and watched his seed spurt onto his stomach.

Jane...

She heard her name whispered in the quiet, and her body trembled, awakened. Her core opened, and she closed her eyes. Images of him on top of her swept before her, and she touched herself through her nightgown and found her core wet.

A soft snore captured her attention. She looked back at Matthew, and saw the gentle rise and fall of his sculpted chest. He had fallen asleep, and she was...curious.

Silently she crept to the bed and bent over him, studying his face. This was Matthew, this was how he had looked at the hospital, vulnerable, beautiful. A fallen angel, she thought, reaching out to touch him.

Just one touch...*one*...a guilty pleasure in the night.

It was dark. He hated the dark. He hadn't always, not until his tutor had made a habit of coming into his room at night. He was tired...so tired, yet he was afraid to go to sleep.

He struggled, trying to fend off the fatigue, but it claimed him and he fell into a dream. It was a dream of sex, and of the maid who changed his bed. He liked the way she looked, with her big breasts and rosy cheeks. More than that, he liked the way his cock felt when she was around.

In his dream, she went to her knees and sucked him.

Mmm, this dream was so real. He could hear the crisp sheets sliding, could feel his cock thickening, being stroked. Then the wet mouth, the bite…

He woke up from his dream, screaming, thrashing. He hated when his lover came up on him in the dark. Hated the things he was forced to do. His mind warred with it as his body betrayed him, selling itself for pleasure.

End…he wanted to put an end to it, but he couldn't. He was help-less, the needs of his body were stronger than his mind, and his lover knew it, used it against him. And in a rage, he shoved, dislodging himself from that mouth.

You'll be back for more, the voice taunted…

"Get the fuck off me," Matthew shouted, hitting her with the back of his hand. Jane cried out and tumbled to the floor. The metallic tang of blood slipped between her lips and she touched her trembling fingers to them. Pulling them away, she saw the crimson drops.

"Oh, God, Jane," Matthew cried as he jumped from the bed and lifted her into his arms. "Jane," he whispered, rocking her. "What have I done?"

He lifted her face from his chest and he swore when he saw her lip. "Christ," he muttered as he wiped the blood away.

"I—I'm all right," she stammered, "I touched your shoulder—to awaken you. You must have been dreaming. It's my fault."

"Never come upon me in the night, Jane, especially in the dark," he said in a harsh voice as he held her face in his hands and studied her mouth. "I have dreams…" He looked at her, his eyes full of sorrow. "Bad ones. I never know who is friend or foe."

Wiping her mouth with the cuff of her gown, she glanced away, aware that the stickiness on his belly had coated the front of her gown. She could feel the wetness against her own belly and it aroused her, made her want to lay him back onto the bed and kiss away the horror she still saw in his eyes. She wanted to take away the pain, she realized, as much as she wanted to feel the passion he could give her.

"What is it, Jane?"

She could not admit to such a thing, that she desired such an intimacy, so she admitted the real reason she had found herself in his room.

"Your sister, she has awakened. She asks for you."

His gaze roved over her face and his thumb slid along her cheek. "I'm sorry, Jane. I...I didn't know it was you."

Jane slid from his lap, and saw that his gaze had lowered to the front of her gown. When he looked up to her face, he reached for her hand and kissed her palm. "I told you I would only hurt you."

And that was when Jane realized that Lord Wallingford was like an onion, waiting to be peeled back, and each layer would make you cry.

Jane awoke that morning to a heady perfume. The sun was shining and the luxurious bed was so comforting she didn't want to waken. It was early yet, and she stretched, wondering if she might go back to sleep for a few minutes.

As she gazed out the window, checking the position of the sun, she saw the vase of blossoms on the table. Quince. She had admired them yesterday in the garden. She sat up in bed, and realized that her bed and pillow had been sprinkled with blossoms, as well.

Matthew...

Jane grasped a handful of the petals and brought them to her nose, inhaling deeply. She was going to put them in her bathwater and bathe in them, just as she had wanted.

But first, she intended to check on her patient.

Sliding from the bed, Jane donned her wrapper and walked to the end of the hall to Sarah's room. The door opened, and she slipped inside. She stopped when she saw Matthew sitting on the bed, holding her hand.

"Forgive me. I didn't know you were here." Her palm came up to smooth her hair. It probably resembled a bird's nest, but there was nothing to be done now.

He looked her over, his deep blue gaze not missing an inch of her person. "Good morning, Jane."

The velvety timbre of his voice slid over her body, warming her, and she found herself stepping deeper into the room.

"It's early yet, I hadn't realized I would meet anyone."

He took in her robe and bare feet before meeting her gaze. "I like you rumpled like this. Here," he murmured, pulling something from his waistcoat pocket. He handed her her spectacles. She slid them on, blinking behind the glass as her surroundings became clear.

"Ah, there is Jane," he teased. "A bed-warmed Jane."

She flushed, and looked away, trying to dispel the intimacy between them. Yet it remained. She remembered the blossoms and realized he must have stood over her, raining those petals atop her. Had he watched her sleep? The answer, she saw, was in his eyes. He had.

Pouring water into a basin, Jane picked up a cloth and dipped it into the cool water. "How is she this morning?"

He placed a gentle hand on his sister's cheek. "She doesn't have a fever."

"That's a good sign." She moved to the bed and sat on the other side, dabbing the cloth against Sarah's forehead and mouth. "I hope she will awaken again today, for she needs to drink."

"Look at me, Jane."

The quiet of his voice startled her, and she glanced up, only to have him capture her chin in his hand. He took the cloth from her and dabbed it at her mouth. "It's swollen this morning, and bruised. Does it pain you?"

"No, not like last—" She caught herself.

"Not like last time," he finished for her. "Who did it, Jane?" His fingers replaced the cloth as he gently brushed the pad of his thumb over her lip.

"No one of consequence."

"Thurston. It was him, wasn't it?"

She could not meet his eyes when she nodded.

"Tell me why, Jane."

"My lord, please."

"I want to know you, Jane. I spent all night beside you, watching you, wondering about you. I've thought of you living many different ways. I thought of you in the carriage and the way you took care of me. I've thought of you on the terrace giving me what for before the wedding. I've wondered who you are, Jane."

"I am me."

"I don't know that person, but I want to. What do I have to do, Jane?"

"You know what it is."

"Very well." He stood up, and kissed her wound with a soft brush of his lips. "There is a cottage on the grounds. Come to me tonight and I will let you in. I will allow you to see a part of me that no person, male or female, has ever seen. I'll give you my secrets, Jane. And hope that you will keep them safe."

15

At precisely eight o'clock, Jane found herself standing before the cottage. It was a beautiful little place with arched windows and a gothic exterior. His studio, he had called it.

She rapped on the door, then waited nervously for it to open. Looking at her surroundings, she could not help but admire the ducal estate. The gardens were breathtaking, and the cottage, surrounded by apple and quince trees out in full blossom, was something out of a fairy tale. It was so different from the dinginess of London. And the sky, she could hardly believe the number of stars beginning to peek out now that the sun was setting.

It had been a long day caring for Sarah, who was making a remarkable recovery. She had dodged Richard as much as possible, fearing another awkward conversation. As well, she had not seen Matthew since their meeting that morning, but that did not prevent her from thinking upon him almost constantly and wondering what manner of man he truly was.

When her knock went unanswered, she raised her fist to rap again, and stopped when she saw a figure emerge from beneath the waving branches of a willow tree. It was Matthew, dressed much the same as he had been that morning, with the exception of his breeches, which he had changed for a pair of black trousers. He was still in his shirtsleeves, but they were done up at the wrists. His waistcoat was black silk shot through with silver thread. His cravat was black and tied simply at his throat.

There was a thrilling intimacy to his attire, despite the fact that she had seen him naked before. He was the only gentleman Jane had ever seen in shirtsleeves, and the forbidden dishabille strangely excited her.

He came to stand before her, his shadowed gaze assessing her slowly, roaming over her hair and then down to her gown. Another serviceable gown—her wardrobe was chockfull of them. She had thought herself frivolous when she had bought the striped muslin gown. Wools and flannels were what she normally chose for herself. As a servant, she should not be dressing in the height of fashion. Flannels and wools were practical and sturdy and much more in line with a lady's companion than silks and brocades. However, some impish impulse had made her purchase the muslin gown she now wore.

The style of the gown was similar to the ones she usually wore—high necked and long sleeved, with no lace or ruffles or other feminine adornments. Her hair was swept back into a bun and secured with the same silver pin she always wore. She had always been quite content with her choice in garments. However, standing here being scrutinized by Wallingford made her feel inferior and plain. Where she once thought the striped muslin frivolous, she now thought it simple and dated. Even if she had wished to dress for him and their dinner, she could not—she did not own anything as fine or as frilly as the women of his sphere.

"What are you thinking, Jane?"

"Nothing of import," she said with a shake of her head. "I was just thinking that I should have looked in on Sarah. I gave her something—"

"A book," he said, coming closer to her. "She told me. She also told me that you promised to teach her to read. Did you mean it, Jane?"

She looked up at him and saw he watched her with carefulness. "I meant every word."

"Is it true that you only learned to read a few years ago?" She flushed red with humiliation and looked away in shame. "One thing you must learn is that you should never tell Sarah anything you wouldn't want repeated. She means well, she would never intentionally hurt anyone, however, her intelligence...well, sometimes she is like an impetuous child, never knowing when to stop talking."

"I understand."

"You comprehend her, don't you? Most people cannot be bothered. Most people cringe and run the other way whenever they see her coming."

"You don't."

"No, I don't. I welcome her. She is my purpose in life. There are few whom I would admit that to, Jane. But perhaps we should have our discussion inside, *hmm?* My valet will be arriving with the dinner cart."

"Very well, then," She turned to reach for the doorknob. Pausing, she took a deep breath and lowered her head. "Wait," she whispered, then turned to face him. "I've been thinking about this. I want to know. How did you know...I mean, how did you discover—"

"That you were the woman at the hospital?"

She nodded and followed the movement of his hand until it came down to rest upon her fingers, stopping her from opening the door.

"Your name."

"There are thousands of Janes in London."

"But none with your voice."

"Matthew…"

"Jane, believe me when I say I was entranced by everything about you, but it was your voice, an angel's voice. When I heard it, it gave me such peace. When your voice grew soft in the ballroom, I knew. I couldn't forget that voice, Jane."

His breathing seemed harsh to her ears. She struggled not to look away from that intense, almost passionate gaze.

"We have done what we promised never to do," he said, his voice husky in the dark quiet. "We—both of us—wished never to expose ourselves to the prying eyes of others. And yet we have done the unthinkable, we have sold ourselves to each other."

She could not help but stiffen at his words. Indeed, they had agreed to complete honesty, to shed the mantle of secrets they both wore, and yet, the reminder of it did little to settle her nerves. She had known what she was getting. She had known that her secrets would now belong to him, yet that had not prevented her from coming to him.

"We are both damaged souls, Jane, marred by darkness and sin. We're both scarred," he whispered, brushing his thumb against the uneven skin of her top lip. "You wear your scars on the outside, while mine are hidden deep. But they're there, Jane. You just have to look hard."

"And will you let me look deep, my lord?"

"You've made it clear that this is the only way I can have you."

"Honesty will set you free."

He smiled, and a soft sound of amusement passed between his lips. "The truth enslaves. It will chain us, bind us in a way that the two of us will fight to get free from."

"I can bear the burden."

"I wonder if you can. Because beyond this door we will cease to be the people we show to the world. Agreed?"

"Yes."

"I will be only Matthew here in this room with you, Jane. Tell me, who am I to expect? Who are you really?"

"I do not know," she said, her voice trembling despite her attempts to appear as though she were firmly in control of her feelings. "I always thought I knew myself so well. But then—" The words froze in her throat and she looked away, but he caught her chin with the edge of his fingers and turned her face to his.

"Only honesty, Jane. We promised. We will not go beyond this door until I have your word that you will be completely honest with me, as I have vowed to be with you."

"I thought I knew what I wanted—who I was—that is, until that night in the hospital. You...you awakened feelings in me that were strange, terrifying yet exhilarating. These feelings were all things I forbid myself—feelings I've never wanted to have. I was quite satisfied with never having felt pleasure or passion, and then when I met you, I questioned everything I have ever believed in. You ask me who I truly am? The truth is, I do not know."

"Do you wish to know?"

"I fear the answer I may uncover."

His expression seemed to soften. She saw the flicker of some-thing in his eye, before he shielded it with his thick lashes as he watched his thumb glide along her mouth, parting her lips. "I, too, am afraid, Jane. I fear what I will find inside me, as well. I fear the things you will ask, and the answers I shall have to give you. Shall we forget this bargain of ours, then? Shall we pretend that we never agreed to bare our souls to one another? Should we forget that we ever met, ever touched. Ever kissed?"

"Is that what you want?" she asked, fearing the answer.

"No," he replied in a hard, almost choking voice. "It is not what I want. I want to know *you*, Jane. I want to understand what makes you different from the women I have known. I want to understand these feelings I had, that I still have."

"Then we will go forward. And we shall never tell a soul what happens in this room. We will never speak of each other's secrets or use them to hurt one another once this week is over. For, a week is all I dare give to you."

"Agreed. Our secret."

Together they released the latch on the door and stepped into the cottage. With a quiet click the door closed behind Matthew. They were now completely alone.

When she turned and looked at him, Jane knew that Matthew would strip her utterly naked, and he would not have to remove one stitch of her clothes to do so.

The room was warm from the fire that blazed in the small hearth. Candles flickered in candelabra that were scattered about the room and atop the fireplace mantel. It was a sitting room of sorts. As she looked about the small parlor, through the dancing shadows of candlelight that cast shifting shapes on the velvet wallpaper hangings, she realized that this cottage was Matthew's private sanctuary.

Taking a few steps forward, Jane came to stand before two oval portraits hanging above the mantel. The one was of a young boy whose black hair was a mass of riotous waves. His blue eyes were shadowed, cheerless. His lips, pink and full, were set in a hard line. His expression was severe, austere. Far too serious for someone as young as he. Jane could not help but reach up to trace the outline of the sad little face that looked down upon her.

"You were not even happy as a little boy, were you?"

"No. I was not."

"And now?"

"I am not certain what exactly happiness means. I do not believe I have ever really experienced true happiness, or if I have, it was so fleeting that it left an unmemorable impression upon me."

Jane did not turn around to search him out. She did not need to see his face to know that he was feeling awkward, defensive. She heard all that and more in his voice.

"I was seven when that portrait was painted. I despised the lace collar my mother insisted I wear. I loathed the artist and how he forced me to sit for hours in that chair and look out the window. It was bloody torture sitting for that portrait."

"How so?"

"It was summer and for the entire week it was sunny and warm. I knew Raeburn and Anais and my other friend Lord Broughton would be down by the river, playing and fishing. I could hear the three of them, their laughs being carried on the wind. I saw them, running, Broughton holding the string of a kite while Anais and Raeburn chased him." He smiled sadly and half turned his face from her. "Raeburn and Anais were hand in hand even then. I remember watching him run with her. I could see her smile, and I saw his, and Christ, I hated him for that, for his happiness. I hated him for his freedom, while I was stuck in my father's ducal estate, trying to be the dutiful son and failing miserably."

"You wanted to be outside with your friends."

"Yes. I wanted to be out of the house. Anywhere away from my father."

"And your mother?"

There was a very long pause in which Jane could hear his rapid breathing. She felt the tenseness in the room grow as the silence stretched on. "I loved my mother. That is her portrait beside mine."

"You look like her. You have her eyes, and her smile."

"How do you know? You've never seen me smile."

"Once," she whispered, "when you shook hands with Lord Raeburn after the wedding toasts. You smiled then. You have a dimple in your left cheek."

Jane heard a shuffle along the floor. She peered over her shoulder to see that Matthew was gazing into the mirror, his head tilted to the side as his hand traced his jaw.

"Your mother has the same dimple as you. The artist has captured it perfectly."

"I am the artist."

Jane started, then swung her attention back to the portrait. In the painting, his mother was dressed in a ruffled pink velvet wrapper. She was posed, reclining against a crème-and-gold-brocade settee. Numerous pillows were scattered about and a tray, filled with glass bottles of perfumes and silver tins of powders rested beside her. Her long blond hair was unbound, cascading over her shoulders.

The painting was intimate, as if Jane had just happened upon her resting in her boudoir. She could not help but compare it to the memories she had of her mother, servicing her lovers with her cheap, harlot clothes and her rouged cheeks and lips.

"I remember the morning I found her sitting just like that," he said as he came to stand beside her. "I ran into her room and found her sitting on the settee, sipping her morning chocolate. I was so proud, I couldn't wait to show her something, so I ran to her room and barged in, ignoring the shrieks of her maids."

"What did you have to show her?"

"A perfect score on my Latin exam. My tutor had just

given me the results, and I snatched it out of his hand and ran to show her. I remember her smile and the way she kissed my cheek."

Jane saw him stiffen then shake his head as if chasing the memory away. "It was one of the last times I saw her alive. I was ten when she died. No one else has seen this painting but you."

"I am honored. Truly. It is so very well done. But I must know something, you said it was one of the last times you saw her alive—"

"Don't," he murmured, closing his eyes. "Don't ask me that."

It was on the tip of her tongue to remind him of their pact, to thrust his words of honesty back into his face, but something in his expression, in his eyes—a pain she had never seen in him before, made her stop. *A soul is never bought,* she reminded herself. *It is given.*

"Very well, I will not ask you. But tell me, how old were you when you painted this?"

He let out his breath and relaxed somewhat. "Fourteen. My father always chastised me for my painting, saying it was for sissies, that if I were to grow up to be a real man, I would put aside my painting and daydreaming and concentrate on my studies. I was a miserable student, only average at best. Every bloody subject was such a chore for me to learn, but I tried, tried so damn hard to please her...to make it easier for her with him."

"And you didn't?"

He grimaced and looked away from the painting. "I rarely pleased anyone, least of all my parents. I'm afraid I was something of a disappointment to both of them."

"And your tutor, did you please him?"

Matthew laughed, a humorless, hollow sound. "Not usually. He was a hard old bastard who was exceptionally fond of flogging."

"Did he flog you?" she asked, thinking of him as he was in his portrait, with his sad eyes and sullen expression.

"Every chance he got. He took perverse enjoyment in it, and I refused to cry, which of course made him work harder."

Oh! She wanted to weep for him, to hold him.

"I haven't the mind for studies and books," he said flatly. "I learn more by seeing and doing, but the English education system is not based that way, therefore I muddled through with nothing impressive to show my father, who would only accept excellence."

She glanced again at his portrait. "He wanted you to quit painting. Did you give it up like he asked?"

"No, I hid it. I would stay in my room late at night when I was supposed to be studying and instead I would sketch. I would never dare attempt to paint for fear they would find out. I never cared about going against my father, but I never wanted to disappoint my mother, so I hid the fact that art was my world. My escape, so to speak. I have never shared my art, with the exception of a few pieces that Raeburn has seen, and the portrait I auctioned off."

"The one that was indecent."

He inclined his head, but held her gaze. "There is so much about me that is indecent, Jane. My entire life has been nothing but. But enough of me now," he said, turning to her. "What of you and your mother?"

Jane stilled and fisted her hands at her sides as the unwanted memories began to float back into her mind. "My mother was lovely—nothing at all like me. She was blonde and blue eyed. Angelic. She was an opera dancer and an actress when she met my father. After…" Jane swallowed hard, ashamed to admit what her mother had been. "After my father left us, my mother was forced into prostitution."

"And your father?"

"An aristocrat. My mother was his mistress. I am illegiti-mate." She looked up to gauge his reaction, but he hardly even blinked at the news she was a bastard. "I barely remember him," she said, gathering her courage to tell him of her past. "He left my mother when I was seven, tossing us out onto the streets. I've never seen him since. My mother always said I have his eyes. The garish red of my hair is a mystery. I am not certain what hateful ancestor be-queathed it to me."

"It is not garish."

"Kind words are not necessary," she said with a fleeting smile. "I'm well aware that it's a terribly bright color. Not at all fashionable."

"You are mistaken. It is not at all offensive. In fact, I like the way it burns in the firelight. It glows," he said as he curled a loose ringlet around his finger. "It feels like silk. I would like to see it unbound and resting over your shoulders."

A little tremor snaked down Jane's spine. She hid it by step-ping away from him and walking about the perimeter of the room. But the sensation of his touch still discomposed her, and she fought to think of anything other than the image of her unpinning her hair for him.

"Is this your studio, then?" she asked, thinking it better to return to a safer, less intimate topic.

"It is. It was my mother's cottage. I used to spend hours here with her, watching her write or read. I began to sketch here. We would sit for hours in our quiet pursuits. It's the only time I can ever remember feeling at peace. Perhaps it was even hap-piness I felt here in this room with her."

"So you left it the same, trying to recapture those days with her."

"Yes, I suppose so. The window overlooks the orchards, and when they are in blossom like they are now it's the most spectacular, inspiring sight. I hope you will come to this room in the daylight and see for yourself."

"Perhaps I will," she murmured as her gaze hungrily drank in her surroundings. Empty frames and canvases were scattered about. Easels and paint jars with abandoned brushes littered the tables. In the middle of the room was a black velvet lounge with gold cording and tassels that decorated the curved arms. Behind it was a black-lacquered screen with painted pink blossoms on it. In the corner, by the window, sat a delicate rosewood desk. Atop it were painted miniatures of Matthew as a child, and a young woman, who, she suspected was his mother.

As she walked, she allowed her fingertips to graze the pictures and the furniture, taking everything in about the room and her rich, luxurious surroundings. Matthew's sentimentally struck her as incongruent with his callous shell. She would never have thought that the Earl of Wallingford would have had a soft spot for his mother.

"I was ten when she died," he murmured, his voice thick. He turned away from her, giving her his back as he looked out the window. Yet he still continued. "She left us—me," he clarified. "My father made it intolerable for her. I was her only method to get to him, you see. It was me, my successes, my failures that made my father either happy with her, or unhappy. He felt it was her fault if I was bad or…stupid," he said, "and I tried very hard to be what my father needed, for my mother's sake. But I was a miserable failure. It was not long before my father turned completely from her. She loved him, but that love turned to melancholy. I tried to replace that love, but she turned from me, as well. She took a lover, and left. I followed her, running down the lane after the carriage, begging her to come back. But she would not. Finally I could run no more and was forced to watch the carriage disappear amongst the dust. When it turned the corner, the harness broke, and it sent the coach tumbling down the hill. She was killed while running away from me."

Jane went to him, and held him, wrapping her arms around his shoulders as she pressed her face against his back. "Matthew."

He stiffened and Jane felt his breath freeze in his lungs before he gathered himself and stepped away, unable, or unsure how to accept her touch.

He turned and looked at her, pain and sorrow etched in his eyes, but there was something else there, as well, lurking in the dark blue depths. He spoke in an urgent rush of words.

"I wish to change our bargain."

"In what way?" she asked skeptically, her instincts suddenly on alert.

"I wish to reserve the right to ask a favor of you in lieu of a question. And you may do the same of me."

Jane stared at him for a long while, trying to understand what he was asking of her. "I thought you wished to paint me. Is that not what you wanted in return for answering your questions?"

"Yes, and I still do. However, I want…" He cleared his throat and tugged at his cravat. "I want other things."

"I will not sleep with you."

His gaze flew to hers. "Are you an innocent then, Jane?"

Any other woman would have been outraged by such a question, but Jane was not. How could the question not have come up in his mind, especially after the events that day in his carriage, and in the hall with Thurston?

Taking a step back, she walked toward the settee and trailed her fingers along the soft nap of velvet. "In the physical sense, yes, I am still innocent. But am I an innocent?" She smiled sadly and walked around the settee watching him warily. "No,

I am afraid I am not an innocent. I have seen things that no woman or child should ever see. I have lived in places that no human should have to live. My innocence, if I ever had any, was stripped from me when my father left my mother and me destitute..." She trailed off and watched as her fingers, so white, sunk into the black velvet. "After he abandoned us, I truly learned what hell was like."

"And you plan on staying a virgin, then?"

"Yes."

"For how long?"

"Until I am ready to relinquish it."

"Are you waiting for marriage, then?"

"No, I am not. I am waiting for love." Lifting her gaze from the settee, she found him standing before her. "You probably find that amusing, don't you? Someone like me, waiting for love. Even I think it is foolish. Love is such a fickle thing, and yet I can't help but desire it. I don't know why, but it is the last wistful desire from my childhood that I have not been able to banish." Shaking herself, she smiled and shook her head. "I am saving the only thing I have of any value for the man I love. He need not be my husband, he need not even love me. But, *I* must love *him*. That is the price of my virginity."

"You confuse love with sex, as do most females."

"Do I?"

"Yes. You needn't have love to have sex."

"You must at least like the person."

He snorted and stalked to the window where he stood looking out at the sky, which was now black. "No, you needn't even like them."

"I cannot believe that one can—"

"Do you know how many I've fucked that I can't stand, that I actually hate—" He stiffened, as if catching himself saying something he should not. A few seconds of silence followed before he spoke again. "I will not mock you for your thoughts on love, if you will not mock me and my views on the same subject. And my favors will not be for sex—your virginity is safe from me."

"Then what will these favors be?"

"I do not know," he said quietly. "I only know that I wish to reserve the right to ask them later on, if I so desire."

"All right then, I will grant you that, as long as you do not ask for my virginity, I will grant whatever favor you ask."

He nodded and bowed his head as he looked down at the ground below. Jane studied him, observing the way his shoulders were set, almost rigid. She watched as the sliver moonlight glinted off his hair. Listened to the even cadence of his breathing as it filled the quiet.

"Why did you offer this?" she asked, unable to stem her curiosity. "Why me?"

He did not turn around, but instead raised his head and sighed. She saw that his knuckles had turned white as his fingers gripped the ledge of the windowsill. "I have asked myself that very same question."

"What, why the offer or why me?" She laughed, attempting to make light of her question. But inside she was not laughing, for she was afraid of what his answer would be.

"The offer, of course," he said, blowing out his held breath as he turned to face her. "I cannot fathom what made me offer such a thing, what made me yearn to open up myself to you and your ridicule, and possibly even your revulsion."

"And you have never questioned why me?" she asked cautiously as she stepped around the arm of the settee. "Why a red-haired, spectacle-wearing spinster could induce a man like you to offer such a thing as secrets."

"I sensed—I still sense—that there is a likeness between us.

I felt it from the first moment I saw you. We are alike in the fact that we are not truly the people we show the world."

"Am I not?" she asked, taking another step toward him. "What makes you think that I am not really cold and indifferent?"

"Because I felt the warmth in you when I held you in my arms. That was not indifference." He turned and half looked at her over his shoulder. "If it was, tell me so at once, Jane. If you felt nothing for me—not even physical need—tell me now and I will release you from this bargain."

"Why would you agree to such a thing when you wanted it so badly last night? You wanted my secrets. You were willing to pay for them. How can you so easily say you don't want them now?"

"I do not want your secrets for a price, Jane. I do not want to share mine with you because of a bargain." He looked away and stared out the window. "I want whatever you give to me to be willingly. I want what we shared before, give-and-take. If you cannot give me that, if you truly felt nothing for me then, then you may go now, for I want *all* of you, Jane, not just the little bits you're willing to give me."

The seconds stretched on, marked by the ticking of the clock that sat atop the rosewood desk. How much he asked for. Did he know how much he asked? Did he know that to answer him would be to look deep inside her, at the place within her she refused to believe existed? Did he know that her answer might destroy her forever?

16

The seconds marched on, marked by the measured tick of the clock. With each passing second, his body grew hotter, his nerves growing rigid with barely controlled impatience. She had wanted him. He knew that.

However, as the silence stretched on, he began to doubt his memories. Perhaps she really had not wanted him. Perhaps it had been all one-sided and his desire for her had clouded his judgment, had made him fail to see that she did not return his ardor. What if she had only allowed him such liberties because he was titled, or worse, she feared she had to in order to keep her job. Had it only been desperation that had driven her to his arms?

"Milord," came a voice from beyond the door. "Your dinner has arrived."

Relief washed across Jane's face and he felt himself growing angry with his valet for arriving at such an inopportune moment. The little minx was *not* going to avoid answering his question. It was time for the truth. Never had he wished to know the truth more than he did at this very moment.

"Milord—"

"Enter," he snapped, turning his back to both his valet and Jane. Christ, his damn hands were shaking—with what—anger, frustration, pain? No, by God, it was not pain.

Shoving aside the unsavory emotion, he told himself over and over until he believed it as the truth, that he didn't give a fucking damn what her answer was. She *had* desired him. He knew it to be the truth. She could say whatever she liked, but he damn well knew that she had, at the very least, felt physical desire for the man in the carriage. And why he cared, why he needed to hear that avowal in her own voice was beyond him. It was so bloody foreign to him to seek anything other than sex from a woman. But here he was, seeking confirmation from Jane Rankin that she had, at least once, desired him.

The clanging of the cutlery and fine china filled the room as his valet hurriedly laid out their supper. When he finished, he cleared his throat and asked, "Will there be anything else, milord?"

Matthew stared down in disgust at his hands, which were still trembling. "You may leave us."

"Very good, milord."

The door clicked shut behind the servant and Matthew turned to find Jane sniffing delicately at the silver dishes atop the table. "Everything smells so delicious," she murmured in obvious appreciation.

"Did you respond willingly to me?" he demanded, refusing to let her think that he was going to allow her to change their conversation so easily. Her eyes narrowed, and he saw her defiant little chin come up a notch. His gut reacted violently, tightening and twisting, and he realized at last what he was experiencing. *Fear.* Christ, he despised feeling this way, but he could not go on with this evening, nor with their bargain, if what they had shared that afternoon had been nothing but a sham.

It made no sense to him that he should care if her desire had been true or feigned, he only knew that right now, it mattered greatly to him.

She stood still, not even attempting to reply to his question. He had to force himself not to stalk to her and take her about the shoulders and demand her answer. Being the overbearing man was not the way to deal with Jane Rankin. It was likely to get him a nasty stomp on his instep and not the answers he so desperately needed.

"I believe I have the right to know whether you actually felt desire, or whether I was duped into believing you wanted me," he said through gritted teeth when she turned her gaze from him.

"Is your pride hurting?" she asked. "I hope it is, for I have lived with such pain since that day you came to take me away."

He felt his face flush as the image of her standing on the sidewalk resurfaced.

"Do you know how much it hurt to look up at you and realize that you had no clue who I was? You looked at me as if you were seeing right through me, as if I were as insignificant as a bug crawling atop your boot." He saw her fingers had curled around the back of the chair and were now white with tension. "It hurt because I trusted you, because I had given everything of myself to you, and it apparently meant nothing. It hurt to know that the man who stood before me, the man who uses women and thinks of them as objects for his pleasure, was the same man who earned my trust. The pain of the discovery was more than you will ever know. I have never...I don't..." Taking a deep breath, she seemed to gather her emotions, steadying them before she focused her gaze once more upon him.

"What is done is done. Perhaps, my lord, we should sit down and eat and forget about discussing things that cannot be taken back or forgotten. It seems a shame to let this dinner grow cold. Your cook has obviously gone to great lengths to prepare a beautiful meal."

She did not wait for him to pull out her chair, but instead did it herself and sat down with a regal elegance, dismissing him and their conversation. Head held high, she stared straight ahead, her expression serene. But he was not dissuaded. He had heard the uncertain emotion in her voice, the pain at his remembered barbs. He took her words for the truth. She had given herself to him because she had wanted to.

He took his seat at the table, across from her, and contemplated her through the flickering candlelight. "Jane, I—"

"There is no need to say more, my lord," she murmured between sips of wine.

"My pride...." He swallowed the lump in his throat. "I daresay it has taken a very great blow these past weeks. I am not used—"

"To being tricked by *drab little peahens?*" Her gaze collided with his. "I can imagine your ego has been dented considerably. It must be quite something for a man of your reputation and tastes to discover that he has been secretly meeting a drab lady's companion and not the exotic and mysterious creature he thought she was."

"That is not it," he growled as he stabbed his fork into a slice of roasted beef.

"Admit it, you were disgusted when you discovered it was really me you had been meeting. I saw the disappointment in your eyes in Raeburn's library. I could see inside to the workings of your mind, and you were questioning how you could have mistaken the nurse for me. How you could have allowed yourself to be attracted to such a woman."

"No, you're wrong."

She arched her little winged brow and glared at him. "Am I?"

Hardly able to swallow, he chased the bit of beef down with his wine and contemplated her as he wiped his mouth with his napkin. "What am I to say, Jane? Either way, I will hurt you. And I have no wish to cause you pain."

"You have claimed to never care about women and their feelings. Why would you care about mine now? No, please, say the truth, my lord. I want the truth."

She looked at him with her penetrating, steady gaze and felt himself shrink back from it. Christ, he didn't want to hurt her feelings; he was a brute when it came to women, yes, but he did not want to hurt Jane, nor destroy her memories of him. Memories he knew he would carry with him for the rest of his days.

"I was taken aback, yes. Not because you are not…pretty," he said, struggling to find the words. She let out a disgusted huff of breath and vigorously began cutting her meat into minuscule bits.

"Oh, for Christsakes," he snapped, reaching for her hands and stopping her. With a squeeze of her fingers, he forced her gaze up to his. "Listen to me. I am only going to say this one time, and then the topic is over. Yes, I was disappointed when I discovered it was you. At first it was because of your appearance—the severity of it, the prudishness of you. In my mind I did imagine you looking different."

Her expression crumbled, but she regained her composure swiftly as she sniffed back the pain. "I'll wager, in your mind, I didn't wear spectacles, or possess a freckled face. In fact, I probably wasn't even a redhead. More likely you imagined a tousled blonde with a flawless complexion."

"I dreamed of you with many different hair colors and styles."

"But no glasses?"

"No," he barked, hating being goaded by her. "I didn't. Christ, Jane, am I to be punished for my imagination? I saw nothing of you those nights in the hospital. Am I to be berated for imagining the face of the woman whom I had kissed and touched so intimately? Am I not allowed to be disappointed that the warm, passionate woman I held in my arms was really nothing but a cold and indifferent spinster? For that was the real disappointment. It was not the fact that you have red hair that you wear so severely. Nor is it your spectacles and dowdy clothes." She sputtered, searching for words, but he squeezed her hand again, silencing her. "I was disappointed in *you,* just as you were disappointed in learning that I was really the notorious Wallingford. Is it really any different?"

"Yes," she snapped, "it is very different! At least I still found you sinfully handsome despite hating you as Wallingford!"

She flushed and pulled her hand out from his and he sat back, surprised, yet irrationally pleased with her outburst. "Your pride was hurt then and now, with my frank admission."

"I do not need to be found beautiful by any man," she snapped, and he knew that she was lying. Whether she realized it or not, she was lying to herself. She was also giving him an understanding as to the root of her anger, something he was certain she would be mortified to discover. "I am what I am, my lord, and I would much rather be admired for my brain and my ability to discuss things with a rational, intelligent mind than to have only my beauty be of any value. I do not care if you find me to be a little peahen. I do not care if you think me a colorless spinster, and perhaps I am. But the fact remains that I will not—*can not*—change what I am."

"Jane—"

"Have you not shamed me enough already with your inquisition? What more do you want from me? I have already admitted I wanted you for no other reason but desire. Was that not your original question, my lord?"

"How did we arrive at this, Jane? There was no quarrel between us this morning. How did we go from the intimacy of our conversation when we first arrived in this cottage, to the hostility that is now flowing between us?"

She refused to answer him and instead fobbed him off, something she was very good at when the conversation struck a nerve or became to intimate for her to discuss. "Perhaps we might continue eating and find another topic of conversation if you wish to diffuse the heat of the present topic. We were doing rather well when we were talking of things other than ourselves."

Nodding curtly, he picked up his utensils and began eating, hardly even tasting the food in his mouth for the unsavory taste that already resided there. He did not like leaving their conversation there, with her thinking he thought her plain and unremarkable.

Tossing his napkin onto the table, he shoved his chair back and walked to her, tugging her up from her chair. She gasped and he saw her lips part invitingly. Unable to control the impulse, he parted his lips and brought them down to hers, allowing them to hover, to widen. Her breathing turned harsh and he saw her lips inch closer to his as if she was going to kiss him. Their lips brushed slowly, just barely grazing, before she pulled away.

She shuddered in his arms, and he gripped her tighter, fighting the impulse to crush her to his chest. "Jane, let us start over, begin anew."

"How? When the past haunts us?"

He captured her chin in his hand. "I do not know how to be intimate, Jane. I only understand sex."

"And I will not allow you to have sex with me. I won't be an empty vessel for you to fill and toss out when you're done."

"Then we are at an impasse."

She nodded and reached for her skirts. "Good night, my lord."

The next morning, Jane awoke from a restless night's sleep, her hair in disarray and her eyes puffy from lack of sleep. *Damn him!* Why the devil did Wallingford plague her thoughts and dreams? Why could she not get that erotic, charged moment of their near kiss out of her mind, and replace it instead with the hurtful admissions he'd told her.

Flinging the bedcovers back, she walked to the heavily carved wardrobe and began tearing the few dresses she owned from the hangers. She would leave this morning. She wouldn't give the ogre a second thought, much less the opportunity to know anything more about her. Such an undeserving man! What did she care what he thought of her for leaving without satisfying their bargain? What did truth and honor mean to a man such as Wallingford?

"I…I see you are going home."

Snapping to attention, Jane straightened her spine and glared at the door. Standing on the threshold, hand still gripping the brass latch, stood Sarah.

"Does my brother know?" she asked softly as her gaze volleyed between the portmanteau that was open on the bed and the empty wardrobe. "If… If I…I have done something, tell me. Don't leave. M–my brother…"

"Sarah, no, it isn't like that," Jane said, feeling anguished at the sight of Sarah's trembling lips and glistening eyes. She ran to her and helped her limp to the bed. "Good Lord, you shouldn't be out of bed. How did you… Never mind," Jane muttered as she helped Sarah onto the bed. "How do you feel?"

"Tired of lying in bed all day. Nobody wants to play with

me," Sarah mumbled like a petulant child. "Everyone leaves me. I am always alone."

Falling to her knees, Jane took Sarah's hands in hers and bent her head so that she could capture Sarah's gaze with hers. "Sarah, look at me."

Tear-filled eyes met hers. "You promised to teach me to read."

"I did," Jane said, nodding, her heart breaking. "But you've been ill and it is much too soon to be out of bed."

"You're going to leave and break your promise."

Jane bit her lip. She could not go back on her word to Sarah. Painful memories of her own childhood came rushing back. The loneliness, the despair. How many times had she been alone as child? How many promises given to her by her mother had been broken? How many times had she seen the retreating back of someone she had desperately needed?

"I am not leaving, Sarah. I was…I was…" Jane looked around her room, at the trunks and the gowns thrown hastily inside, and tried to come up with a suitable excuse.

"Somehow your gowns got packed by magic?" Sarah supplied with a soft laugh that was part sob.

"Precisely." Jane smiled sadly, squeezing Sarah's hands and delighting in the easy forgiveness Sarah offered. "I am afraid your estate is filled with naughty little faeries that are bent on causing trouble."

"Maybe I should check my gowns, too, in case the faeries have gotten into my things."

"That is a very good idea," Jane said with a laugh as she squeezed Sarah's hands once more.

"You need to fix your hair." Sarah looked up at her and crinkled her nose. "It looks like a nest the robins made in a tree outside my bedroom window."

Laughing, Jane smoothed her hand along her hair.

"Miss Jane? Would you teach me to read while on a picnic?"

Bright yellow sunlight filtered in through the windows. It was followed by a warm, whispering breeze that carried with it the sweet scent of fruit blossoms. Gazing out the window, Jane saw the trees in the orchard swaying gently in the spring morning. She imagined being outdoors enjoying that heavenly scented air. "I think it's much too early for you to be out of doors."

"My brother is very strong. He'll carry me."

"Sarah, I'm not sure that this is the right thing to do. Perhaps your brother—"

"Oh, goody!" she cried. "I will tell Matthew. He will be pleased. It was his idea, you know. He loves picnics."

Jane tore her gaze from the window and reached for Sarah as she struggled to rise from the bed. "Wait, what's this about your brother?"

"Help me to my room," Sarah commanded, sounding every inch the daughter of a duke, "before you change your mind."

"What a lovely day for a picnic, wouldn't you agree?"

Jane glared at Matthew from beneath her bonnet brim. He was standing in a patch of sunlight, a wicker basket dangled from the fingers of his right hand, while a green and red wool lap blanket was folded neatly over his left arm. He passed Jane the basket then bent to pick up Sarah, cradling her carefully in his arms. She hugged him, kissing him awkwardly on the chin.

"This is the bestest idea, Matthew."

"I'm glad, pet," he said, his gaze softening as he looked at his sister. "And what do you think, Miss Rankin? It is a far better way to begin your lessons than in a stuffy old schoolroom, wouldn't you agree? I vow, I was getting a headache visiting that sickroom of yours, pet. The fresh air will do you good."

Jane cocked her brow and tapped the toe of her half boot on the grass. The devil had the nerve to laugh.

"Well, then, let us be off. I thought we would take the boat down the river to the west side of the estate. It's lovely this time of year."

Sarah wrapped her arms around his neck. "Shall we, Miss Rankin?"

Jane glared at him, then came out from her spot beneath the leafy canopy of a quince tree.

"How magnanimous of you to allow me to tour you about the estate," he drawled as she came forward.

"Do not think you have won," she muttered quietly, so that Sarah would not hear her. "I have not agreed to this preposterous plan because of you. I have done so for your sister. Nothing more."

"What are you saying?" Sarah asked as she pressed forward and peered at her over Wallingford's shoulder.

The devil had the nerve to lift his brow in challenge. She shot him a look of barely concealed contempt before addressing his sister. "I was asking your brother if he thought it prudent for him to escort us today. After all, he must be very busy with business and ledgers and land tracts. Far too busy I would think to spend the day entertaining his sister and her nurse."

"Ledgers and land tracts?" Wallingford said with an amused laugh. "Obviously you have mistaken me for one of those aristocrats who actually sees to the running of their estates, Miss Rankin. I am not of those nobles, darling," he drawled, and the warmth, the intimacy of it trailed across her skin like the tips of his fingers caressing her arms. "I am very indolent, you see. I would not recognize a land tract from a ledger, or a hedgerow marking my property from my neighbors. My knowledge lies elsewhere—primarily in the diversity of corsets and petticoats."

"My lord!" Jane scolded, her gaze darting to his sister, who seemed, to Jane's relief, to be occupied following the fluttering orange wings of a butterfly that was busy suckling the nectar from a flower.

"Do not concern yourself," he murmured. "I have no thoughts to business today. I have spent my morning doing far more productive things, like organizing our little excursion and this afternoon's entertainment."

"What are you about, sir?" she asked, unable to keep from wondering what nefarious plan he had in store for her.

His grin was devilish. Jane felt blinded by the beauty of it. She was quite certain that if Wallingford chose to smile, his lips, combined with his lethal predatory grin, could make a woman swoon from at least fifty paces away.

After last night, his mood was too light, and Jane was immediately on guard. She didn't trust him. Nor did she trust herself with him.

They'd reached the dock. Carefully he stepped into the boat, placing Sarah just so, covering her with a blanket and propping her with cushions that were already in the craft. He took the basket from her and placed it at the bow, then he turned his attention to her and held out his hands.

"I don't like being manipulated, my lord."

"'Matthew' is fine, especially when we are alone."

"I mean it," she said, furious with him. "You are pushing your sister, sir."

"Inglebright thought it a grand idea. Was I mistaken that you value his opinion? Did you not inform me he is one of London's best physicians? Besides, it was you who told me that Sarah needed to get up and moving."

She scowled, not liking her words thrown back in her face. "You deliberately set out to manipulate me by using your sister and my obvious affection for her."

"I did no such thing. I merely suggested a picnic."

"You did it to blackmail me after the debacle last evening. You cannot simply plan a picnic and think that I will forget about all we said to each other last night."

Ignoring her protests, his hands encircled her waist, lifting her off the dock. "I wanted at least another day with you, is that so very bad?" he whispered next to her ear.

He held her up by the waist so that they were eye level and Jane was forced to put her hands on his shoulders and look straight into his blue eyes. "I did not attempt to manipulate you in order to have you stay. If that is what you think. Sarah is her own person, capable of forming her own stratagems." Then, unceremoniously, he deposited her into the boat, leaving her gasping in indignation and burning for more of his touch.

Hmph! she huffed before settling herself against the side of the boat. She watched as he expertly untied the rope, and with his booted foot, pushed them away from the dock.

"I thought we'd spread the blanket beneath the apple trees," he said cheerfully as he picked up the oars. "No better time, the blossoms are in full bloom."

Jane struggled to tear her gaze off the bulge of muscle beneath his jacket. With every stroke of the oar, the material bunched and tightened, fascinating her, making her dream of feeling it tighten beneath her fingers. She remembered the way his body felt, all hard and sculpted—and warm—growing hotter as her hands traced the planes of his broad shoulders and sculpted back. As if aware of her thoughts, he suddenly turned his blue gaze on her and grinned wickedly.

"I was looking at that spot over there." She pointed, just above the outline of his shoulder.

"Indeed?" he drawled, allowing his gaze to linger on the front of her bodice. "And what did you think of that particular spot?"

She shot him a severe, disapproving look and focused her attention instead on Sarah who was busily looking through the stack of books she had brought with her. With a deep chuckle, Wallingford set the paddle once more into the water, plunging it deep to turn the boat to their intended direction.

As the oar dipped in the lake, she followed the ripples of water, her gaze lifting in time to see the black and white swans, swimming together. They stopped, floated for a second, then the black one began nuzzling the feathers of the white swan. He was grooming her, and Jane watched with rapt attention as the male indulged his female. Matthew followed her gaze, and studied the swans, as well.

"They're beautiful together, aren't they?" Jane murmured. "So different, yet the same."

He cocked his head, studied her, and Jane looked away, fearing she had said too much. She was determined not to speak another word to him.

Within minutes, they had traveled the width of the river and were approaching the dock. "I'll moor the boat first, then help you ladies out. The water is rather deep here, you'll have to have an extra care."

"Will you lift me out?" Sarah asked, looking up from her books.

"Of course, pet."

"I will not need that sort of assistance," Jane muttered, refusing to allow herself to think of Wallingford lifting her out of the boat and bringing her to his chest. Absolutely not. Her hand still burned where his fingers had held hers, and her heart had not slowed to its usual pace.

Damn him for making her feel like this, like a giggling green girl.

"I am afraid that is the only way out of the boat," Wallingford said. "The area where we are picnicking does not have a shore, so to speak. The dock, as you see, is quite a distance away from the riverbank. It's deep here, and the dock is high, making it quite difficult for a lady in layers of petticoats and a heavy gown to step up from the boat to the dock. I'll have to lift you."

Jane glared at him while secretly waiting to feel herself being lifted in his arms like a helpless heroine. But she was no fainting girl, and she would not be one for him.

Jane leaned back on her wrists and inhaled the heady fragrance of the apple blossoms. "Mmm, it smells so good."

Matthew offered her some cheese and a piece of freshly baked bread.

She shook her head and gazed up at the canopy above her. Sarah had already eaten a small portion and was curled on some pillows, fast asleep. The outing had been good for Sarah, but exhausting, as well. She needed a nap before they returned to the house, and Jane, enjoying the breeze on her face, closed her eyes. She could get used to this quite easily.

"What are you thinking of, Jane?"

"How lovely it is here."

"But that is not all you're thinking of."

How well he knew her—already.

"Jane?"

She glanced at him and heard the truth spill from her lips. "I'm just mulling over the fact that I know very little about you, and yet, we have…"

"Been intimate? Yes. I know what you mean. It seems we should know one another better…. After all I already know your taste."

She blushed. "My lord—"

"Matthew," he interrupted. "We need not be so formal when we are alone. We've moved past that, have we not, Jane?"

She nodded awkwardly, not knowing how to disagree with him. They had moved on. She'd felt it last night, and now, sitting beneath the tree, surrounded by nature. Something was drawing them together, and she was helpless to resist it.

She felt him move, and she opened her eyes to see him sprawled out beside her, his head propped up with his hand. "Last night ended in a disaster, Jane. I don't want it to be like this."

"I am…not used to the company of men, and the conversation was rather…"

"Painful?"

She nodded. "Honesty can be as cruel as a lie."

"I am not accustomed to caring about other's feelings, Jane, but last night, after you left, I was…stunned by your anger. Confused. I couldn't understand what I had done to earn your fury. It took me most of the night, but I finally came to realize that it was because I had been so rude, so damn hurtful to you as you stood before me on the sidewalk."

"Don't go any further, please."

"I'm sorry, Jane," he said as he lowered her face so that he was gazing directly—and deeply—into her eyes, "that I did not see you, that I treated you and your tender feelings so horribly."

"I would have rather died than admit to you that you had hurt me, but now…" Jane closed her eyes and fought for the strength to open herself up to him. "Now I will admit that your appraisal of me more than stung. It hurt. It tore me apart inside until I was left with nothing but pain—and the desire to hurt you just as horribly. A flaw, I'm afraid."

"I am full of flaws, Jane, but with you—" He swallowed hard, his Adam's apple bobbing up and down, making Jane wish to press her lips to it. "With you, Jane, I have the very great desire to be the sort of man that cares. That feels. A gentleman, I believe the ladies call that sort of man."

Jane smiled despite herself. Matthew, Lord Wallingford, would never be the gentlemanly sort, and the knowledge secretly thrilled her.

He reached into a satchel that lay on the grass and pulled out a book. "Look."

She flipped through it and scanned the elegant nudes he had sketched. They were of a woman with a lovely body, sprawled in many positions. The woman was faceless in every sketch, until the last. There she saw her face. It was her in bed, blossoms covering her.

"I want to paint you like this," he murmured, taking the book from her hands. He pressed her back onto the blanket with his palm on her belly. "I want you naked, surrounded by blossoms."

Matthew slid in beside her, his hand resting beneath her breast. The breeze blew across them, sending a few blossoms wafting down, landing on the exposed flesh of her chest. She moved her hand to brush them off, and Matthew clasped her hand in his, threading his long fingers slowly between hers.

"Let me." Then, lowering his head, he gently blew the blossoms off her gown.

Jane couldn't smother the small cry that escaped her, nor could she hide the goose bumps that sprang up to cover her flesh. His hand tightened on hers, then his lips brushed over her skin in much the same way as his breath had. Her skin tingled, and an ache developed in her breasts.

"You taste so sweet," he breathed against her flesh. "Your skin is so soft, so warm."

Jane cried out when he unlocked his hand from hers, but her protests ceased when she felt his fingers beneath the edge of her bodice.

"It all went so wrong last night, Jane. So wrong," he murmured as he tugged the bodice lower and ran his tongue along the edge. "You thought I believed you insignificant, but the truth is, I find you fascinating. You think I suppose you're not pretty, but, Jane," he said, looking up, "I find you stunning. Your eyes…your imperfect mouth. It's beautiful, and I want to paint you how I see you, sensual and womanly, dying to break free of an ideal that imprisons you."

His fingers unhooked the top buttons of her gown, and she glanced over to Sarah, who was quite a way away, partially concealed by the trunk of a tree.

"She sleeps deep," he whispered as he parted her bodice to reveal the swells of her breasts, "and I need you. I know your body is not mine, that you will not give it wholly, but could you give me *something* of you, Jane?"

She closed her eyes and allowed him to bend his head to her breasts. He nudged the gown lower with his mouth, nipping her skin. "Yes," she murmured. Tentatively, she ran her fingers through his hair. "Yes, Matthew."

He exposed her, pulling her breasts free of her corset. The warm breeze kissed her nipples, hardening them, and she opened her eyes to see him tracing one areola, his circles becoming smaller and smaller until his fingertip caressed the very tip of her nipple. Reaching above her head, he picked up a handful of blossoms and dropped them onto her chest, then he lowered his head, and blew them so softly away from her. Her nipples crinkled further and he brushed his lower lip against one.

"I have never seen a nipple this color before, such a deep coral. I wonder how I shall find the right shade."

He sipped her, his lips working her nipple until she was moving restlessly beneath him. "I want to watch you come, Jane."

He reached for her skirts and tunneled his hand beneath her gown and petticoats. Up her stocking his palm smoothed, making his way to her garter, which he traced with his fingertips. "I want to sear the image in my mind so I can paint you pleasuring yourself."

She gasped as his fingers found the opening to her drawers and smoothed over her sex, spreading the wetness that had been slowly building since she set eyes on him that morning.

"Matthew," she pleaded, needing him to touch. His eyes closed and he rubbed his finger between her folds.

"Again."

"Matt—" Her voice broke off as he buried one finger inside her, and she moaned as he slipped in another one and stroked her. "Matty."

She felt him shiver, his broad shoulders trembling beneath her hands. She could feel the muscles there, beneath his white lawn shirt, tightening and stretching, matching the rhythm of his fingers.

"Oh, God, Jane," he whispered. "Open your eyes, and let me see you. The *real* you."

She obeyed him and found him looking down into her face as he slowly moved in and out of her body with his fingers. Her womb contracted and she felt herself grow slick, coating his hand. His lashes fluttered closed and he removed his hand, making her clutch at his shoulders.

"I want to know what you'll taste like mixed with quince."

Jane watched as he brought his hand to his mouth, the one he had used to pick up the blossoms, the one he had pleasured her with. He licked his fingers, which glistened, then brought his mouth down on hers, kissing her, erotically sliding his tongue inside her mouth as he slipped his way inside her body, his fingers building her up, slowly pulling her orgasm from her. And all the while he kissed her, until she began to tremble. Only then did he pull back and watch her unravel in his arms.

"Say it, Jane," he whispered as he circled her clitoris and

shattered her mind, body—and soul, if Jane were being completely truthful. "Say it."

"Matty," she whispered, catching his gaze. A tear slipped from her eye, trickling beneath the lens of her spectacles, before sliding down her cheek where he brushed it away with his lips. "What have you done to me?"

17

That evening, Raeburn and Anais came by to check on Sarah. Jane had been happy to see her friend, and Matthew had enjoyed watching her, remembering that afternoon when she had shuddered in his arms.

He had not washed after their intimacy, wanting to smell her on him. He needed to be close to her, needed to be part of her.

She had admitted she wanted him, but in what way, he didn't know. What intimacies she would allow, he could only imagine and hope for. He wasn't stupid enough to believe that Jane would give him her virginity. He knew he would not ask for it, for it came with a price, a price he would not ask Jane for.

Still, though, he had thought of little else but claiming her virginity, of molding her body to fit him—only him. He had never cared about that, being the first man to claim a woman, except for Jane. There was something very primitive about breaking her, forging his way in, making her accept him, feeling her blood on his cock.

It was base, monstrous how he was thinking, but he

admitted that he would take great pride in seeing Jane's virgin's blood coating his shaft.

Raeburn shifted against the balustrade and Matthew followed his friend's gaze and saw that it was focused intently on Jane. He didn't care for the amused glint in Raeburn's eye, nor did he care for the smug smile that parted his lips.

"My God," Raeburn drawled as his smile widened. "You've gone and done it. You've fallen for the little peahen."

Matthew stiffened. "Don't call her that," he snapped, his gaze lingering on Jane and the curve of her graceful neck and the wisps of red hair that caressed her skin.

"Why not, you do," Raeburn taunted. "I specifically recall hearing you say she was nothing but an unremarkable and dour spinster."

"Well, perhaps I might have been wrong," he said.

Raeburn placed a hand over his heart and took a mocking step backward. "Wrong? The Earl of Wallingford mistaken about a woman? Impossible, my friend. You are never wrong where women are concerned."

Glaring at his friend, Matthew fumbled inside his jacket pocket, searching for a cheroot. After locating the wooden box of matches, he irritably swiped a sulfur match against the stone railing and lit the cheroot, inhaling deep breaths of smoke before waving the flame out and tossing the match to the ground.

"Admit it, Wallingford, the peahen has somehow managed to catch your eye."

He caught Jane laughing as she sat down beside Anais. Even through the French doors he was aware of her, aware of the way the lamplight reflected in the glass lenses of her spectacles—aware of the way the firelight would dance along the deep auburn highlights in her hair that was pulled so severely back.

Despite the distance between them, his body was as aware

of her as if she were standing beside him. He saw her laugh again, then clasp Anais's hands in hers. Her face turned pink and he was drawn in by the simple pleasure of watching her unguarded and laughing. She was full of life and exuberance, and her skin fairly glowed as she laughed with Anais. He thought of her, lying beneath him, her face awash in pleasure, her skin glowing pink with arousal.

"She is no colorless bird," he murmured, not knowing if he had intended to say the words aloud.

"Is that so?" Raeburn asked as his gaze narrowed on Jane.

"Indeed. There is something about her," he said, unable to keep his gaze from her. "Something I cannot describe or understand. She is not the least bit beautiful by society's standards, and yet I have not thought of another woman since I met her at your wedding. There is something about her face that draws me in."

"You find her beautiful?" Raeburn choked out.

"Is that so damn hard to believe?" Matthew growled, tensing as his body filled with anger and a fierce protectiveness he had never felt toward a woman.

"Aye, it is," Raeburn said with a grin. "It is almost unbelievable. I've never known you to look at a woman with more than a passing glance. Your gaze strays to the most superficial trappings. But it seems you have looked deeper where Miss Rankin is concerned. You've seen beyond the spectacles and her severe manner of dress and seen the beauty within."

"You're talking rubbish, Raeburn," he grunted as he took a long, calming drag on his cheroot. "Obviously your honeymoon has made you into a romantic halfwit. You're romanticizing whatever this…this attraction is I hold for Miss Rankin. An attraction, I fear, that is fueled not by lust or affection, but by pride. She won't have me, you see, and I am afraid that my ego cannot bear it."

As soon as the words were out of his mouth, he knew them for a lie. Knew that at first, when he had pursued her at Raeburn's wedding, it might have been a case of bruised pride. However, he had to admit that those were not his feelings now.

"I don't believe you, you know," Raeburn said beside him. "You see, I've known you too long, and I've seen you with too many women—women, I may add, that you have never looked at quite the way you look at Jane."

"I don't know what you mean, Raeburn, nor do I care."

"You don't have to pretend, my friend. I understand how damnably confusing the whole thing can be."

"What whole thing?" he asked as he studied the blunt end of his cheroot.

"Giving your heart to another."

He laughed, a hollow, bitter sound from deep in his chest. "I have no heart to give, surely you know that."

Raeburn looked at him with a strange intent gaze. "You have one, I'm sure of it, you just have to find it. However, I'll wager it's locked up tighter than the crown jewels."

Raeburn knew nothing. Matthew grunted and looked away. He had no heart. He was heartless. He was not kind, he was selfish and merciless. He could not give anything—most important, his heart—to Jane Rankin. And what was more, he didn't have it in him to offer anything meaningful to any woman.

"Well, then," Raeburn muttered as he looked up at the night sky. "I suppose it is time to retire. Anais has been exhausted. I don't want her overdoing it."

"How is she feeling?" Matthew asked as he stomped out the end of the spent cheroot.

"She is feeling very well, just tired. Everyone is trying to assure me that it is very normal for her to be so tired this early in her pregnancy."

"You're worried," Matthew stated, hearing the fear in his friend's voice.

"I am." Raeburn took a deep breath and blew it out in a great rush. "I fear what could happen. Childbirth is so damn unpredictable. I couldn't bear it—living through the agony of losing her."

Nodding, he studied his friend, marveling at the true fear he saw in Raeburn's gaze. He had never thought of childbearing in such a way. Children were heirs, and the begetting of them was nothing short of a breeding practice, much like a good broodmare being paired with a stud. He had never stopped to think of the emotional bond that tied a man and woman when a child was created out of love.

He was not fool enough to believe that he would ever have that bond with a woman. His children would be heirs to the ducal dynasty, and the woman who bore them, nothing short of a vessel to ensure the propagation of his family's lineage. Such a cold, calculated scheme—nothing at all like the way Raeburn and Anais had conceived their child.

Raeburn seemed to pull himself out of his morose thoughts while he only sank further into his. "Night, old boy," Raeburn muttered. "I'll see you in the morning for a few hours of fishing?"

Nodding, Matthew turned his back on the French doors and the glittering lamplight pouring out from the salon, and looked up at the black-velvet sky. Christ, his mind was a mess. He was thinking things he had never once thought of—never once cared about. A wife and children? He'd never wanted them. To continue the ducal dynasty? He'd always wanted it to die out with him, thereby exacting the cruellest revenge on his father. But he was thinking of these things tonight, and what was worse, he was looking at Jane Rankin when he thought them.

"Matthew?"

He stiffened, as though he'd been hit with a lash. Jane's voice, low, husky, tore into his flesh and he curled his fingers around the stone balustrade. How the intimacy of hearing her call his name in the dark made his blood grow hot. How he hated the weakening of his resolve. He was not the man Raeburn was, he reminded himself. He did not love women, or care for their feelings. He did not think of them as wives and mothers and lovers. He thought of them as sexual beings—beings to be fucked and discarded. He was callous and cruel, and he was only deluding himself into believing that he was something other than a libertine.

He doubted that whatever transpired between him and Jane this week would mean a damn to him once they returned to London. He doubted he would even care, or remember all her sordid little secrets. He was damn certain he would not remember the feel of her wet body clinging to him, or recall the way he had felt strong and masculine, protecting her and whispering away her fears with soft words. He would not allow himself to remember the way she had looked up with admiration as he carried her along the dock. No, damn it. He was no goddamn knight in shining armor. His past was a cesspool of debacles and debauches. He could not change what he was, and what was more, he didn't think he could bear to. Because caring who he was would mean that he would have to care about Jane and her opinion of him; and caring about Jane Rankin was something that would only cause him pain.

"Matthew?" she whispered, but this time she rested her hand on his forearm. The image of her small hand on his coat sleeve played havoc with his mind. He felt himself begin to soften, begin to believe in this that could not be. As he looked down at her hand, anger began to rage inside him. And as irrational as it was to feel angry with himself, it was even more irrational to wish to lash out at Jane.

"Do you wish for me to meet you in your studio?" she asked, her voice quiet and unsure. "Or perhaps—"

"It is our bargain, after all, isn't it, Jane?" he snapped, hating the venom he heard in his words, and the sound of her startled gasp. Christ, he despised the fact that he was lashing out at Jane because he was confused by what he was feeling. He felt utterly worthless and undeserving. "Yes, I want you in the studio. You are here for me to paint, and I am here to tell you whatever it is you want to know about me."

"I think I learned all there is this afternoon," she whispered, and he saw a fleeting glimmer of what he thought might be hope in her eyes. Hope that perhaps his reputation might be overblown, hope that he was really a gentleman who carried ladies safely from danger. Hope that he was anything other than the notorious earl.

"Is that what you think?" he asked, lowering his head so that he was glaring at her.

"I think I know you better than you think I do."

He whirled around and smiled cruelly. "My dear, you haven't even begun to know the worst of me."

Running to keep pace behind Matthew, Jane struggled for breath and found herself being thrust forward into his studio. With a slam of the door, she was alone with him.

"You aren't shocked, are you?" he drawled, untying his cravat and tugging it from his neck. "You might have thought I was a gentleman, but I am afraid that I rarely act as such. I take what I want and leave what I don't. In general, I really don't give a damn what anyone thinks of me."

"I don't believe you."

"That is your mistake then, Jane."

"What is your most painful secret, my lord? What is it that makes you despise women so much?"

He shut his eyes, pressing his lids tightly together as if he was under a great deal of pain. "Do you mean my painful secret, or my most shameful, Jane?"

The rawness of his words sent gooseflesh rising along her arms, but she refused to allow him to intimidate her. "You said just a few minutes ago that I did not know the worst of you. Perhaps you were right. Perhaps I want to know."

He laughed and tossed his cravat onto the settee. "All right, then. I will acquaint you with the real Wallingford. The real Wallingford doesn't give a damn about women and their sensibilities. He doesn't care what people think of him or say about him. He just doesn't care about anything or anyone at all."

"I don't think that is entirely true."

He stared at her, his eyes narrowing. "Really? And what makes you a goddamn expert?"

"I saw a different side of you when you were ill."

"And I saw a different side of you, as well. You basically told me that what I saw was an illusion. It is not the real you. Well, Jane, that was not the real me."

"You're lying. I know you are."

"Am I? You seem to be under the misapprehension that I am a gentleman. I am not."

"You claim to not care for anyone or anything, but I know that for a falsehood. You love and care for your sister."

"I love and care for her when it is convenient for me to do so."

She shook her head, knowing he was acting in such a way to protect himself, pretending that he didn't have a conscience, when, in fact, she knew he did.

That afternoon, she had seen the real him. It had been there.

She wanted to see it again, wanted to give in to that man, that man she was falling hopelessly in love with despite her intentions not to.

"You're a gentleman—"

He laughed. "Perhaps I was the gentleman at the hospital because it suited me. It amused me to play the part because you were so obviously smitten by it."

"You attempt to hurt me with words, but I have learned to have a thick skin, my lord. I will not be persuaded by you and this show of anger and hostility. It will not prevent me from learning all I can about you."

"What makes you any different from the scores of women I've bedded? I never gave them anything. What makes you think I'd give you what you want?"

"You make it a habit of speaking lightly of the women you have made love to."

"I never call it that. I despise the term. It is never about love. It is about lust, the sort of animal-like emotion that every male, of every species, succumbs to."

"Has there never been one special woman whom you thought highly of, whom you felt something for?"

"No, I have never allowed a woman to touch me with anything more meaningful than sexual superficiality. I fuck women, Jane. I do not make love to them. I do not let them into my soul. I do not feel them creep into my heart. Women are for physical release, nothing more.

"You are no doubt wondering about that afternoon in the carriage. You are probably questioning if that was only fucking, too. You are wondering if I felt anything more for you than fleeting physical lust."

"You are wrong," she said, her voice trembling with hurt even though she tried to disguise it. "You forced me to admit that what we shared was not an act for either of us. You made me tell you the truth. Now, you tell me the truth. Tell me why you would pretend, still, to be the heartless roué."

With a flash of anger, he had her pressed up against the wall. "I *am* heartless. Haven't you realized that yet, Jane?"

"Matthew—"

He shoved his body against hers, trying to intimidate her. "Why do you insist on seeing the good when it is not there? Go back, Jane, before I ruin you."

She smoothed her hands down his chest and he moved away. "Don't...paw me," he gasped, shuddering.

What she saw confused her. She had touched him before, while she had cared for him. He had wanted it, yet now he recoiled from it. What had happened to him to make him so angry, so full of pain?

The dreams, the crying out in his sleep. She remembered, when he was ill, he had fought the night men. He hadn't wanted to be touched then.

Suddenly she wanted to hold him, to love him, to erase the past with her body.

"Matthew, tell me the truth, what happened in your past to make you abhor being touched."

He looked shocked at her assumption, but it was swiftly replaced by anger. "You wouldn't be able to listen to all the sordid details, Jane. You couldn't possibly fathom the atrocities I have committed with this body."

She reached for him but he evaded her touch. "Christ, leave me alone. Get out of my life! I don't want you in it."

"What of your soul, Matthew? Will you be able to relinquish me there?"

He glared at her, his chest heaving in agitation. "I haven't got a soul, Jane. Besides, it's been all of what, two days? You are hardly embedded inside me."

"It's been weeks, Matthew. I think we became entwined the

moment you arrived at the hospital. There is no denying what we shared."

"What? Lust?" He laughed. "I wanted sex, Jane. *Fucking.* Can't you understand that? It's still what I want, to fuck the virginal spinster. I want to see if I can make you pretty as I shove my cock into you. There? Is that what you wanted to hear?"

She shook her head, denying his words, his purposefully hurt-ful words that he intended to use to make her run away from him.

"Do you know what I do to women like you, Jane? I look down my nose at them and laugh. I stomp all over their ten-der little feelings and don't look back. You amuse me, Jane."

"What has made you so full of hate?" she whispered. She reached out to touch him, but he captured her wrist before she could do so. Her lip quivered and she blinked back the tears that threatened to spill. He was hurting, lashing out because she had glimpsed a side of him he didn't want her to know about. She wanted to soothe him, but oh, God, his words hurt, and her heart…it was being crushed.

She ran, ignoring the roar of her name in Matthew's an-guished voice.

18

He ran out of the cottage, dragged her back against him as she kicked and flailed. He turned her in his arms and kissed her, hard, forcing her to accept him. She felt the vibrations in him, the anger, the pain, and she gave in, allowed him to carry her back inside the cottage and put her against the wall.

"This is the only way I can do it, Jane," he rasped as he lifted her skirt and ran his palms down her thighs. "I'm ruined for anything soft. I…I can't allow your body on me, my past—" He choked back the thought and reached for her, gazing deeply into her eyes. "I'm broken, Jane, and I want so desperately for you to fix me."

He tore at her dress, pulling the tapes free, sliding the bodice down until it was at her hips. The petticoats came next, then were discarded in a pile. Her drawers, he tore at, shredding them. He turned her around to face the wall and untied her corset strings with impatient hands. When he reached her bottom, he palmed her buttocks, pinching them, squeezing them.

Jane knew what Matthew needed. It was not softness or tenderness. He needed the demon from his past purged, and she was willing to be the method.

Her corset fell to her feet and he removed her chemise, leaving her naked with her back to him. He was not soft. Not romantic in his words.

"Bend forward," he ordered, "so I can see your pink folds."

She did as he asked, supporting herself with her hands on the wall. He touched her, spreading the wetness up the crease of her buttocks.

"I want to fuck you like this."

Her body heated.

"You've already creamed," he whispered hotly in her ear. "You flow thick with excitement, Jane. Could it be that you are just as deviant as I in your needs?"

"Don't say that," she gasped as he circled her high between her crease. "You are not deviant."

He laughed as he sunk his wet finger into her. "No? Would you think I was if I were to tell you that I have had fingers here," he murmured as he gently moved his finger in and out of her bottom. She groaned. It didn't hurt, but it didn't feel like his fingers had this afternoon when they had filled her quim.

"It's sinful, isn't it?" he whispered into her ear. "But it feels so good."

He pulled out and turned her around. Reaching for her leg, he wrapped it around his waist, exposing her. He touched her, parted her, watching as he worked her sex. She wanted to hang on to him, but he reached for her hands and made her grasp the curtain behind her.

He undid his trousers, and his cock sprang free, jutting out at her. "This is fucking, Jane. It's all I do. Do you want it?"

She whimpered and watched as he stroked the head of his phallus down her sex.

"Do you want this dirty thing inside you?" he asked. He

met her gaze, and Jane realized that he was not there with her. His body was, but his mind was somewhere else, some past time when he was young and…abused.

"I want to sink it into you," he whispered. "I want you to want to claim it. Claim me."

Her heart broke for him, for the yearning she heard in his voice.

"I want you to watch me inside you and…not turn away in disgust as you see me buried deep, knowing it's me."

"Matthew," she whispered, reaching for him. "I want you."

He pushed the head inside her, not far, only enough to feel that he was there. He looked down and watched as he inched farther inside her. She saw his lashes flicker, then look up at her. "You give me this, your virginity?"

"Yes."

"Do you love me, then, Jane?"

She did. God help her for loving such a tortured beast, but she did. She didn't know how, or why, just that she did, and that she wanted nothing more than to give him what he wanted. It was the only thing of value she possessed. The only gift she could give to the one she loved.

Guiding her hand to his shaft, she shoved him forward.

"Jane?"

It was a question, and she gazed into his eyes and arched her hips forward. Her one hand was still holding the curtain, the other was wrapped around his thick phallus. With a nod, she gave her consent to him to take what he needed from her.

With a swift thrust he buried himself deep and moaned, pressing his face into her neck. She wanted to clasp him to her, but was afraid he would stop, so she clutched the curtain and felt his cock make love to her.

She wished it was his body loving her, too, but he wasn't ready for it.

"Won't you watch?" he asked as he kissed her cheek. She didn't understand his need, but she looked down to where their bodies were joined. His hard shaft glistened with her body's excitement as it moved in and out of her. His hand left her buttock to trace the rim of her vagina. He was feeling himself stretching her. "You're so full of me," he murmured, his words a hot caress against her cheek. "Stretched wide, with me inside you."

She nodded and watched him pull out and sink in again, her body and heart leaping at the primal possession of him taking her.

"I never watched, Jane," he whispered. "I couldn't bear to. It was shameful, sinful. But this…this looks beautiful. *Right*." He reached for her hand and brought it to her sex where he made her touch, made her feel him moving in and out of her. It was arousing, so much so that she gasped, her nipples beading in pleasure, and she closed her eyes, enjoying the sensation riding within her.

"Open your eyes, Jane. I want you to know that it's me here with you—in you."

"I know it's you." She sighed, feeling her climax steadily growing.

"I need to know," he said, his voice pleading. "I need to know it's you. I need to see *your* eyes."

Their gazes met, held, and he looked deep within her eyes as he moved inside her. He stroked her, his hands rubbing her bottom, stroking in caresses before he teased her clitoris and stroked her harder when she begged. When she clamped her thighs tight around him, he captured her face in his hands and withdrew from her, emptying himself onto her belly. Then he fell into her, his head buried in her neck, and Jane wrapped her arms around him, holding him through the storm.

★ ★ ★

Hours later, Matthew sat in a chair near the hearth. He had dressed Jane in her chemise and petticoat and had placed her on the settee, exhausted, languid. He had watched her sleep and felt his chest hurt with a mixture of euphoria and heart-ache.

What had he done to her?

His limp cock was dusted with drops of Jane's blood. He had taken her virginity, a gift she said she was saving for the man she loved. Damn it, he had coerced a vow of love from her. He had not given her his vow in return.

Was that what this was, this pain in his chest? Was this love? Or was it guilt?

No, he couldn't bring himself to feel remorse for what he'd done. It had been beautiful to watch her take him, to accept him as he was. Unfortunately, he could not accept himself as he was—damaged, broken. He was beyond repair, despite her hoping that Jane might put him back together again.

She stirred, and her eyes opened. Her glasses were on the table, and he thought about reaching for them and passing them to her, but he decided he wanted to look into her eyes with nothing in between. She had seen enough of him when he had been taking her. She had glimpsed deeply into a part of himself he locked away from the world.

"What are you thinking, Matthew?"

His lashes lowered, shielding his eyes, disguising the shame he felt. "How much I loathe myself. How I despise what I have done to you, Jane. I have wronged you. Not only…now, but in the past, after…" He swallowed hard, his lashes finally lift-ing, meeting Jane's direct, unwavering gaze. "When you look at me like that, Jane, I feel compelled to confess everything I am to you. Your eyes, they pierce me, down to the very depths of the darkness inside me. I wish what you saw was clean and pure, but I know there is only dark obsidian there. I wish what was there could please you, but I only know how to hurt, to seek to punish.... Jane, I sought out prostitutes after I left you on the sidewalk. I took them, knowing they weren't you...pretending they were. Wishing, in vain, that they were."

Her gaze softened, filling him with remorse. "I think both of us retreated to the comfort of familiarity. You returned to sex to numb your feelings. I hid myself behind a veneer of self-righteousness. I sought to punish you, as well. In our own way, we both mourned for what might have been. You owed me nothing, Matthew. Most especially your fidelity. In truth, if you had asked for mine, I would have refused you, purely out of spite. You see," she whispered, "I, too, have flaws. We are both human. As you said, both scarred. By retreating to the way of life that has kept us safe after our abruptly aborted childhoods, we sought not to add to those wounds. We've learned to live and survive, the only way we knew how, behind a veil of detachment."

"How can it be that you can see behind this mask of me?"

She smiled, one of sadness and perceptiveness. "Because I look out through the same sort of mask, Matthew. Because...we share the same fears. The same flaws. Our hearts, our souls yearn for the same things, except we cannot give voice to that fact. Can't accept it because of the horror, the loss of control. Because behind the mask, we are only human. Fragile and frightened. And lonely, I think."

"Yes, lonely," he murmured, studying her face, which suddenly was luminous with beauty, which glowed with wisdom and insight and a soul-shattering amount of understanding and absolution.

"Neither of us wishes to drop the mask, to allow others a glimpse beyond the facade for fear that our humanity will show. Our humanity, which we fear because we cannot control who we are, deep on the inside. We can only hide it, bury it deep and hope our frugality does not show."

"I have seen yours, Jane, as you have been witness to mine."

"Yes. We both have been hurt, destroyed by human deceit and capriciousness. Yet we have managed, in each other's arms to lower the masks, if only an inch, to see inside each other's guarded souls. I offer you forgiveness, if that is what you seek, but more important, I give you my understanding. That is the beauty of being human, I think, to understand another's pain, as though it were our own."

She was breathtaking in her beauty and her human spirit, he thought, unable to speak as he gazed upon her. Hers was the sort that would not fade or grow jaded with time and years, but flourish, grow more radiant with life and its experience. Hers was a beauty that no other possessed. A beauty he longed to keep, to hide away, to bask in, himself alone. She had become his. He didn't know when, whether it had been the moment her fingertips had touched him when he was hurt, or if it had grown like a seed, slowly spreading until Jane had become the root anchoring the shattered pieces of his heart, pulling then tight together until it resembled the organ it should.

"Talk to me," she whispered, her voice unsure, vulnerable. "Please, say something."

When he looked at her, he felt his chest burn, then words erupted from deep within, words he couldn't hold back. "You have complicated things, Jane. You have taken an act that was simple and straightforward and turned it into something I no longer recognize—something I can't understand."

She sat up and brushed her hair from her face. "How so?"

He wanted to touch her, to sit with her and brush her hair. He wanted to feel her lying over his body.

"It has become all about you, Jane, about how I want to

pleasure you—to show you passion, to make you experience it at my hands. It has become about us, the picture in my mind of us pleasuring each other. I never pleasure women. I touch them, arouse them, but with only one goal in mind, *my* pleasure. I never care about the act, or them. But you have made me care. You have made me see beauty where none existed before. You have made me yearn, when I only ever had a need."

He walked to her, lifted her into his arms. "I want so much to show you that need, Jane."

Matthew's arms felt strong beneath her as he carried her to his bed. He wore a linen shirt that was unbuttoned, allowing her to feel the hot skin of his corded neck beneath her lips. Aware of the steely strength in his shoulders, she slid her fingers beneath the opening of his shirt and caressed his chest. His flesh was taut over the thick muscle, warm and scented with the smell of eastern spices and man.

Jane threw caution to the wind and allowed her hand to slide farther into his shirt. Cupping his breast, she discovered his chest was nothing but chiseled muscle that felt as unyielding as rock and as contoured as a sculpture.

Tilting her head back, she looked up into his face and saw that he watched her with unblinking eyes. His irises had turned to a brilliant, glistening shade of india ink and she could not help but think once more how beautiful and mysterious his eyes were.

He reached the bed and instead of tossing her on it, he gently placed her atop the blankets, which were folded back, and followed her down until his body half covered hers. Pressing against her, his weight sank them both deep into the mattress. She should have felt smothered by his strength and the strong, large bulge of his arousal that pressed eagerly at her sex, but she felt only desire and comfort and a strange sense of safety and rightness.

"Can I touch you?" she asked, smoothing her palms along his shoulders.

He nodded. "I will tell you if it becomes too much." He kissed her, partly to stem any questions, she knew, but she allowed it. Permitted him to choose their path.

"I was too anxious. I did not take my time to explore you as I should have—as I wanted."

She covered his sculpted mouth with her finger, stopping his words of regret. "You gave me what I needed, Matthew. And I needed you so fiercely, and somehow you knew that. My body has not stopped crying out for more of it."

His eyes darkened further and his lashes lowered. She followed the path of his gaze and saw that he was busy untying the strings of her chemise and she became mesmerized by the beauty and elegance of his long, dark fingers pulling and tugging and freeing the perfectly tied bow. Her breathing became rapid and she felt the light brush of his knuckles along her belly as he parted the cotton over her hip.

"I want to give you more, Jane. I want to savor you, to kiss and lick every inch of you. I want to tongue you," he said in a deep, provocative voice. Then he flicked the tip of his tongue between the seam of her lips. "Everywhere. Your lips, your neck, your breasts, your rounded belly. Your beautiful little cunt," he growled, sending a wicked, forbidden tremor throughout her limbs. "I want you to tell me your desires. I want you to tell me what you want me to do to you."

She lay partially beneath him in only her chemise and she felt his wide palm slide up her calf, then thigh, nearly engulfing her flesh in his hand. He caressed her to her hip, running his hand appreciatively up and down the rounded contour.

He reached up, above her head, and she froze, stiffening

beneath him. It was a silly response, but she could not hide it, nor could she look away from his gaze that studied her so quizzically.

"Please don't," she whispered, seeing how his hand was against the bed curtains. "I don't want it to be dark, not with you. I...I want to see you—*us.*"

"I would never want you in the dark, Jane. You were made to be seen beneath a man."

"I want to see you, too." Slipping her hands beneath his shirt, he helped her tug the linen over his shoulders and when his head pulled free, his hair was mussed and she ran her fingers through it, thinking how rakish he looked peering down at her with his disheveled hair.

Sliding his hand beneath her pillow, he raised himself slightly above her. Her gaze skimmed down to his belly that was fashioned out of the same hard muscle and resembled a washerwoman's washboard. Black silky hair ran in a straight line from his navel, disappearing below the waistband of his black trousers.

"You're beautiful," she said on a sigh, sounding awed even to her own ears. "You feel like steel beneath this soft skin."

She traced the tattoo above his heart. "What is this?"

"The Arabic symbol for peace."

She kissed it, let her lips linger against his chest. He held her head there, letting her touch him with her mouth.

"I'm going to get a blossom for the next one, and place it over my heart. My offering to you, Jane."

She let out a deep satisfied sigh as he pulled her chemise from beneath her.

Matthew looked down between their meshed chests and studied Jane's lush body. She was naked, and he watched how the raindrops on the window dappled shadows on her skin. He saw the reflection of a crystal-shaped drop snake over the roundness of her hip. He traced it with his finger until it ran down her thigh, racing to the shadow of her apex, until another drop followed, then another, reminding him of tears.

Brushing his cheek against her thigh, he closed his eyes, smelling Jane's skin, relishing her fingers running through his hair, absorbing the feel of her naked body against his. His heart hurt, despite knowing what they would share. It ached at the loss he knew was coming closer day by day.

They would go their separate ways soon. The secrets and pleasures they shared would forever be kept within the confines of this cottage. Every time he gazed out this window, he would see rain and the shadowy droplets on Jane's flesh. He would think of tears and forever wonder if Jane would shed any for him.

"Matty?" she asked, and he pressed his eyes shut, willing the pain to subside. "What is it?"

She lifted his head from her lap and he smiled, a sad smile, mixed with joy and desire, loss and loneliness.

"I want to make you weep with pleasure, Jane." He slid up the length of her luscious body. "I want to take your tears away on my lips and keep them with me forever. And after, I want to paint you like this, with the shadows on your body and the remnants of pleasure casting a glow over your body."

His palm roved to her softly rounded belly and the suppleness of her flesh reminded him of silk and rose petals. She was almost luminescent and he watched how the dark rain clouds outside his window cast shadows along the hollows and curves of her body.

Every once in a while, the wind and the splattering of rain hitting the window would drown out her breathing and he would find himself holding his own breath as he waited to hear hers once again.

She stirred restlessly, her knee sliding up to shield her shadowed sex and he held her still before slowly raising his gaze to hers. "Don't hide anything from me, Jane. You're beautiful. You have the body of a woman made for making love."

And he meant every word. She was amazingly lovely and utterly arousing.

Raising himself on his elbow, he moved just enough so that he could see her completely. Perfect, full breasts with coral-colored nipples and large dusky areolas greeted him, and he brushed his hand along the outside of her breast, watching as it gently swayed, beckoning him to play.

"I want to touch your breasts and suckle them." He let his gaze slowly meet hers. "Do you want that?"

She nodded and reached for his hand, placing it atop her breast. But before he could take her nipple between his thumb and finger, she reached for his head, bringing him to her so that she could offer her breast to his mouth.

She arched so beautifully, like a taut bow when he curled his tongue around her distended nipple. Her fingers gripped his hair and her head was thrown back by the time his hand was palming her and his mouth was slowly and steadily devouring her nipple.

He was frantic to suckle her hard, but she was so wanton beneath him as he teased her with slow, erotic tugging motions that he could not allow himself to indulge his lust. So instead he sucked slowly, savored her taste, the feeling of her nipple lengthening and hardening in his mouth, the sounds of her passion as it whispered between her parted lips.

Her hand flew to her belly and he allowed his palm to slide down below her rib cage to lie atop her hand. Suddenly he wanted to bring her to orgasm while he suckled her. He wanted to feel her womb contract as he brought her to orgasm with his mouth.

"You're going to come for me with just suckling, Jane. I want to hear your cries of pleasure as you feel my lips drawing your nipple deep into my mouth."

She gasped as he nuzzled his mouth against her nipple, making it harder, making it strain against his lips before he mouthed his way from her breast to the soft, scented valley between, only to capture her other waiting nipple between his lips.

On a hiss, she arched into his mouth, and he covered her hand more forcefully until he could feel the flesh of her belly quivering, and he could imagine her sex trembling and aching for his cock. Until he could almost sense her arousal seep from her body and onto her thighs. And still he sucked and sucked until she was gasping and gripping his hair, and her breasts were swaying wantonly with desire and the need for release.

"Oh, God, Matthew, you are so beautiful like this."

"While I'm tonguing your pert nipples, or when I'm drawing you deep into my mouth and sucking you hungrily?" he asked as he mouthed her nipple, which was now red and swollen. He blew against it and watched the areola crinkle in response and her nipple jut out even more. His cock pulsed at the sight and he felt a dribble of come seep out and roll along his shaft. With a groan, he grasped her breast and teased his lips with her nipple before he drew it into his mouth, suckling her deeply, over and over again.

"I never knew…" She trailed off, her body tightening, her hand clenching on her belly. "I never thought…"

"Shh," he murmured when he felt her belly contract beneath his hand and he saw her lashes begin to flutter. "Let it come to you. Savor this. Love this," he said against her mouth as he saw her orgasm wash over her.

"Matty!" she cried, shattering his soul.

Nothing tore through his defenses like Jane saying his name.

The wonderful splintering of mind and body had barely settled before Jane felt Matthew slide down the length of her, his tongue burning a path down her midriff to her belly. *I want to tongue you…* His words filtered through her mind, and she rubbed her thighs together, feeling the slickness pooling between them.

If it were any other man she might have been ashamed of her response and what she wanted him to do to her with his mouth and hands. She might have been mortified to find her legs spread and Matthew's hard, muscled thigh rubbing her mound as he played with her nipples.

His thigh was riding against her, and she could feel the woolen fabric of his trousers abrading her sex. She was so wet that his thigh seemed to slide along her as he pressed forward— harder—rubbing intimately against her clitoris with his knee, and she gripped the bedsheets tightly in her fists.

"Not the sheets, Jane," he said, reaching for her hand. "Score my back with your nails. Pinch my shoulders with your fingers. Tug my hair as you ride my thigh. I don't care," he said, his voice husky. "I just want to feel the pleasure coursing through you."

"Matthew, oh, God!" she screamed as one hand snaked its way through his hair, and her other hand bit into his shoulder. She arched beneath him, but he pinned her still with his heavy thigh and held her steady with his burning gaze. "I want to tongue your quim. And I want you to watch as I do it."

He was sliding down her and his big hands were gripping her bottom, angling her sex to his mouth, and then he was greedily lapping at her, and she watched him make love to her with his lips and tongue. His eyes were closed as if he was relishing a rare, exotic dish. And the way his tongue slowly slid up the length of her made her ache to hold him there.

But soon she was so restless and he was going too slowly and she was rubbing against him, struggling to find the right rhythm, the right pressure that would make her shatter once more. And he ignored her, doing what he pleased with his tongue in slow, stroking, flicking movements.

And then, just when he moved his tongue against the spot that ached, she moaned and felt two of his fingers sink deep inside her, drawing out her arousal, then sinking inside again. He set his tongue to her clitoris and pressed against it. It throbbed beneath his tongue. She became restless and he moved his tongue in a furiously fast rhythm that had her nearly convulsing and crying out his name.

He continued to lick and murmur soft words of passion as she climaxed beneath him, and slowly, she floated back down to earth. She watched him nuzzle her, watched her fingers rake through his black hair, thinking how beautiful he looked making love to her this way.

She also saw that his erection was still thick and protruding from behind his trousers. Her fingers, shaking still from her climax, reached for his waistband and unbuttoned his trousers.

"Touch me, Jane. God, I need to feel your hands on me."

She did, stroking her hand up and down the long, thick length of him, watching in amazement as the already distended veins filled more, coloring the head of his penis a dusky plum color. She felt the shaft widen in her palm and she gripped him harder, stroking him more determinedly, knowing that she wanted him thick and hard plunging inside her.

A drop of pearl-colored fluid leaked out the slit of his sex. Her tongue came out and moistened her lip and she wondered how she could think of taking his swollen tip into her mouth and tasting him.

Matthew's groan caught her attention and her gaze flew to his, and she knew he had guessed her thoughts as she watched him catch the drop on his thumb and bring it to her lips.

She did not hesitate to accept what he offered. With a flick of her tongue, she captured the drop and tasted him.

He straightened away from her and tore off his trousers. His erection soared to the ceiling and she tried to capture it again in her hand, but he evaded her touch and settled himself between her thighs.

She ran her fingers over his cheeks and stared into his eyes. "Beautiful fallen angel," she whispered, the words coming from deep within.

"Help me to find my way back to heaven, Jane. But I want to go there while I am inside you."

He thrust into her and caught her cry on his mouth. Slowly he loved her as his body, slick with sweat, moved atop hers. She clutched him, his back, his bottom. She arched against him, feeling his body crushing hers. They kissed, their tongues touching, as was every part of them.

"Jane," he whispered. He pulled out and came, coating her belly, then fell atop her. "Thank you," he whispered, and she watched him clutch her to his chest, and close his eyes.

19

The dawn of a new day had never looked promising for Matthew, but this particular morning held hope. As he trudged through the gardens, his boots caked in mud, his jacket flung over his shoulder, he thought of Jane and the night they had spent. Somehow, he had been able to allow her touch. She had chipped away at his defenses, letting herself in, bit by bit.

As he rounded the lane, he ran up the small incline and saw an unfamiliar carriage in the drive. Perhaps it belonged to the Inglebrights. They were preparing to leave today, which suited him fine. The further Richard Inglebright was from Jane, the happier he would be.

Climbing the stairs by twos, he let himself in the house and was greeted by the butler.

"You're wanted in the library, my lord, straightaway."

"I'll change first."

"No, my lord, His Grace demands your presence now. He's been searching the grounds for an hour for you."

"My boots are caked in mud."

The butler ushered him along as though Matthew were keeping God himself waiting. He despised doing his father's bidding, acting like a faithful hound at its master's boots.

He turned away from the library and headed for his rooms.

"Get in here, now, sirrah."

Gritting his teeth, Matthew halted on the steps and looked down at his father. "I'm not dressed for an audience."

His father's face went florid and his sideburns twitched. "When has that ever stopped you? Now, get in here."

Wishing to get the discussion over with, Matthew strolled into his father's sanctuary and slammed the door.

"What has gotten you out of your bed before noon?" his father growled as he took a seat behind his desk.

"A walk."

His father's brows rose. "You're hardly the type for a daily constitutional. Indolence is your routine, sir."

Matthew refused to be baited. "Get to the heart of the matter, *sir*."

"Very well. We have a guest."

"Congratulations. Now, if you will excuse me—"

"Constance Jopson, your future wife."

Matthew froze partway to the door. "I beg your pardon."

"Constance Jopson and her father are here. You're going to marry her."

"Like hell."

His father glared at him over his bushy brows. "It's all been arranged. Now, go and change your clothes and make a proper appearance."

"Just what do you take me for? I'm not your damn lackey that you can order about."

"No, you're my heir, but that still means I can order you around. Now do as I say, you're getting mud and sheep dung on my carpet."

"Fuck your carpet, sir," he snarled.

"You will marry the chit, or you will be penniless," his father stated coldly. "I'll not hear another word about the matter."

He thought of Jane, of leaving her behind. He thought of being married to another, another woman's hands all over him. He started to sweat, to begin to shake with rage.

"I'll be penniless, then." His father growled as he glared up at him. "But the rights of heredity still mean that I will be the next duke of Torrington."

His father hated it when he was right.

The duke came barreling out from behind his desk and stormed up to him. "Aye, you'll be the next duke unless you manage to get yourself killed. But I have not worked myself to the bone to make this title and estate what it is for nothing. No, by God, you will do as I say. You will marry Constance Jopson and inherit her dowry, which includes a railway factory and a good deal of land and currency. All commodities this estate needs. Money for a title, it's done all the time."

"So now you're a cock bawd?"

His father slapped his face, and Matthew barely blinked. He wanted to punch him but he knew if he did, he wouldn't stop. He'd kill the old bastard, for what he was doing now, and for what he had turned a blind eye to before. "How dare you," his father growled.

"No, sir. How dare *you?* You sold me for steel and coin."

His father flushed and straightened his waistcoat. "You will marry the girl, give her your title, and in exchange you will give me her dowry to further the ducal coffers, and you *will* provide me with an heir. Hopefully a more competent one than you are."

Matthew saw red. "No."

His father pounded his fist on the desk. "By God, you'll

do as I say. I know your Achilles' heel, sirrah, and I will not be afraid to use it."

Jane. He felt the dread, feared that his father had somehow learned of his feelings for her, and now was going to take her away from him. Oh, Christ, his father was going to do something to Jane.

Matthew ran to the door, needing to find her when his father's words chilled him. "It's too late, sir. What is done is done. Present yourself in the crimson drawing room at one for tea with your intended."

He found her standing on the bridge, leaning on the railing as she watched the swans swimming. He ran to her, caught her up in his arms and held on to her tight.

"Jane." He pressed his face into her neck and inhaled the familiar, comforting scent of her.

"Good morning." She laughed, but he was in no mood for humor. He needed her, to know she was safe. She knew it, too. When she tilted his head away from her and looked deeply into his eyes, he knew what she saw there.

She offered him her soft hand, and he clutched it, leading her to his cottage.

Inside, he closed the door, shutting out the world, his father, that woman he was supposed to marry, and just focused on Jane.

"Shall you paint me today?" she asked.

"No." He couldn't be parted from her, couldn't still his emotions or quiet his thoughts to paint her. He reached for her, wrapped his hand around her waist and pulled her to him.

"Dance with me, Jane."

Her eyes lit up behind her spectacles. "I don't know how."

"I know, and I thought it the saddest thing when you said that. Every woman should know how to dance."

"Not wallflowers."

"Especially wallflowers. I make a habit of dancing with at least one of them at every ball."

"You're teasing me." She laughed again. "Besides, when will I use this skill?"

"Whenever you're with me."

He moved her around, and she tripped and stepped on his foot. He smiled and held her steady. "Take off your gown, to your chemise. Your shoes, too."

She looked at him for a long minute, then removed her clothes. He watched her, feeling a rush of emotion swell through his chest. He could not lose her, not now that he had just found her.

And he would not marry Constance Jopson. He would live penniless with Jane until he came into his title before he wed another woman.

She was stripped down to her chemise. Around her neck she wore a red satin choker, which was tied in the back with a bow. She had no jewellery to speak of, and the thought made him glad of it. He wanted to give Jane her first piece.

"Come here." He motioned her forward and she put her hand in his. He lifted her onto his feet, her breasts brushing up against him.

"Oh," she cried, holding on to him.

"Now let me do it, Jane. Just follow where I lead."

He turned her around, counting the time in his head, humming the tune to his favorite waltz. He glanced at her and her eyes were closed, her body moving against his.

There were no words said, just their breath being shared, and the flow of their bodies. He moved to the bedroom where he stopped.

"I knew you would lead me here."

"Jane. I need you," he said with a shudder as the memories

of his father came rushing back. The fear started to creep up, and he reached for her.

"I'm here, Matty."

Jane followed him down onto the bed, her soft body resting alongside his. Pulling the pin from her coif, her long, red hair fell in thick waves to drape over his shoulder and chest. He inhaled the scent. *Sensible soap.* The aroma aroused him and he reached for a handful of the silken mass and inhaled deeply. Jane. *His* Jane.

Closing his eyes, he willed his heart to slow, his body to relax and absorb the heat of the woman lying against him. He wanted her with a frightening intensity that made him want to run away and hide from the emotions he was beginning to experience.

If he were smart, he would either take her and spend himself inside her tight, beckoning quim, and thereby exorcise her from his life, or if not that, then he should push her aside and end this, this emotional intimacy that had sprung up between them. How it had was beyond him, yet there it was. Emotionally they were connected in a way that he had never been connected to another human being in his life. Not even Raeburn and Sarah, whom he could admit he loved, had provoked such a bond.

Why now, after twenty years of fastidiously hardening himself, after two decades of slow, interminable death, did this one woman's voice call to him? Why did his soul answer that voice? he wondered.

"Matthew?"

Their gazes met. Hers, as always, was forthright and clear, centered firmly in the here and now. And his, he knew, was glazed, drifting to the past where his world, and what he might once have been, had died a sudden death.

What did she see there, in his eyes? Lust? Avarice? Unworthiness? Did she see the same thing he did, every morning when he forced himself to stare back at the debauched image that glared back at him in the looking glass?

"Matty?" she whispered again, only this time worry had replaced the huskiness. He closed his eyes not wanting her to see him like this, weak and vulnerable. He did not want her to know that he possessed a heart, or that it had begun to beat again, beneath the gentle ministrations of her hands.

He did not want to think of the possible future waiting for him back at the estate.

Her lips, red and pouty, lowered to his, and he watched, suspended in longing, as they came slowly to his. "Won't you kiss me?"

His thoughts were a blur, his actions sluggish. She did not wait for him; instead, she kissed him, inserting her warm tongue between his lips. It was slow, lazy, drugging as she increased the intimacy of their joined mouths. Small fingers wrapped around his wrists, holding his hands to her hair as she slid atop him.

His breath caught and the familiar urge to stiffen and withdraw nearly consumed him, but she refused to release him, and he tried, so hard, to allow himself to submit, but he couldn't allow the intimacy. But he wanted to please her, to be the kind of man she deserved, the kind of lover she needed.

Rolling over, he captured her, bringing her body beneath his. *Perhaps like this…*

"No, Matthew," she murmured, shattering the heart that had begun to beat too fast.

No? Was she saying she did not want this, his sex thrusting into her? How could she deny it when he could feel the sticky wetness of her cunt coating his thigh?

"You want me, Jane," he growled as he rubbed his knee against her swollen folds. "I can feel how much."

She struggled beneath him, but he refused to lift away from her. He ached to sink himself in her core, to feel her heat wash over him. He wanted to rid himself of the memories that had started to creep in, like the suffocating vines of ivy against bricks.

"I'm good at this, Jane, you'll like it."

All you're good for is fucking. It's the only thing you do well…

The poisonous voice of his past returned, haunting him. Yes, he knew how to fuck, but he didn't know how to love, to pleasure without intent. To give, expecting nothing in return.

Swooping in, he tried to capture her mouth, but she turned her head and his mouth landed in her hair. His heart sped up, not from the chase, but from fear. Why was she turning from him?

Beneath him, she bucked, forcing him off, but he refused, and captured her chin in his hand, forcing her to look into his eyes, to find the man that lurked deep within him. Could she find him? Did she see him there, struggling to be free of the past?

"I can make you want this!"

She fought beneath him and he reached for her wrists, pinning them above her head. "I can feel how wet your cunt is. It's dripping, my thigh is wet, yet you pretend indifference."

"Matthew—

"You want me! Say the words, Jane. Tell me you want my cock deep within. Tell me you ache for it. Admit the power I have over you."

He shoved against her. "Don't pretend you're not weeping for it," he rasped against her ear. "Me inside, fucking you."

She refused to look at him, and he forced her to feel him, so hard and heavy pushing against her. "I could make you beg for it. Even now your little quim begs for my cock, and don't you dare deny it."

She went utterly still beneath him. Her beautiful eyes dulled and her voice was soft and quiet—painfully quiet. "I cannot deny what we both know so well. You are right, you can make me want you. You have that power, Matthew, to control me, my body and mind. You've taken my free will, I can't refuse you. Is that what you want? Does knowing you have that kind of power make you feel happy? Manly?"

He growled, hating her words and the pain they caused him. He shoved his engorged cock against her, parting her slick folds through her chemise with the tip, making her feel him. "I could force you. I could make you forget that you said no."

"Yes. You could. Forced seduction they call it." When she looked at him, her gaze was full of sadness. "I am so hungry for the feel of you that I may even like it."

Horror gripped him, and Matthew pulled away. He could not force Jane. He knew what it was to be forced, coerced, *lured* into something he didn't want but could not resist. He did not want that for Jane. Did not want to be the same sort of monster that had corrupted him.

Pulling away, he was shocked when she lunged up and lay on him. He couldn't breathe. He was smothered by her body, by the curtain of long hair that cocooned him.

"Jane," he gasped, struggling for air and words. But she surprised him with her strength, with the speed of her nubile fingers. Before he knew it, his wrists were in her hands. Knuckles scraped the headboard, and he felt something smooth and cool slide around his skin.

Binds...

His mind fractured and he was no longer in his cottage with Jane, but in a darkened room in the ducal estate, half waiting, half fearing the sound of the bedroom door creaking open in the night.

Blinded by the impending onslaught, he struggled against

her, aware of her still, and not wanting to hurt her as he had the last time when she'd awakened him and he had flung her from his bed. He didn't want to hurt Jane, yet he could not allow himself to be subjected like this. *To submit.*

"Release me," he growled, struggling harder against the pulling ties that shackled his wrists.

"I want to discover you, Matthew. To touch you as I did that night in the hospital. I need to feel you beneath my fingertips. And what is more, you need this, to be touched. To know what it is like to be *with* someone, not simply in a body."

"Damn you, Jane, there is nothing I need from you."

Even as his body cried out for Jane's hands on him, his mind warred with it. He could not lie here, helpless, his hands shackled. He could not be at another mercy's. Not again. *Never* again.

Bucking, he looked up and saw the crimson ribbon she had worn around her throat tied against his wrists. Panic at seeing himself bound flooded him and he twisted, feeling the slippery glide of the satin loosen.

"Matty..." Her angel's voice cut through the haze of rage that clouded his thoughts, his vision. "Let me. *Trust me.*"

His vision blackened, snuffed out by another sash of satin.

"Jane, no," he groaned, half begging her. He could not do this.

"Shh," she whispered. The soothing touch of her fingertip against his lips made him jump, which only put his body into contact with hers. His flesh burned where their skin touched. He reminded himself to breathe, to slow the racing thoughts that were thundering through his brain. This was Jane, he reminded himself.

He tried to focus on how she would look, her breasts full and pale. Nipples, a deep coral, marred with red circles from his sucking mouth, the red patch of hair that enticed him, damp with her excitement.

Hands reached for him, and he arched, fighting the sensation of his body being touched. "Don't," he cried, despising himself for his inability to hide this part of himself from Jane.

She said nothing as she continued to glide her soft, gentle fingers along his shoulders and chest. Matthew felt his breathing grow too shallow and fast, felt his stomach tighten and his muscles quiver just as they once had with his lover, who had taught him to crave perversity. Who had made him commit a most unforgivable sin.

He had to put a stop to it, these memories, these feelings, Jane smothering him. There was only one way he could.

"The feel of your body disgusts me, Jane. Get off."

A beat of silence. A heavy pause in which his heart took one last beat and stopped. He could feel the pain his words caused her, and he forced himself to steel his spine, to forget her pain and think only of his own.

"What part of me disgusts you? My body, or the effect it has on you?"

"Sod you," he snapped, tugging at his binds so fiercely he made the headboard rattle. He gasped as she found his cock. He was huge, thick, straining to be touched and taken into her hot mouth. His body wanted it, his traitorous dick was weeping for it, but his mind could not allow it.

"I said get the fuck off me," he snarled.

"Not till you tell me why."

"Because I hate you!" he roared.

The rushing of his blood in his ears died, followed by the sound of him tearing out Jane's gentle soul with his poisonous tongue. Oh, Christ, he didn't want to hurt her, to lie to her, but he couldn't do this. It was the only way to make her stop…hurt her…break her…

"Who hurt you?" she murmured as her fingertips glided against his lips. So soft, like the fluttering of butterfly wings.

It broke him. Those three words seemed to rend the crack in his heart wide-open, until he was bleeding out into his body. "Jane, don't," he begged, "please. Let it go. Let *me* go."

Her touch persisted, only this time he felt her breath, humid and warm, against his mouth. "You ache to be touched, Matthew. Every human does. It is what differentiates us from all the other mammals of the world, the need to touch and be touched."

"Jane, you mustn't."

"I must," she returned, and then she kissed him, her lips soft, pliant, nondemanding. She traced the edge of his nose, the shell of his ear, the contour of his mouth, which continued to protest in shallow rasps that were part terror and part heart-wrenching longing.

"Be easy," she purred as her hands left his face and traveled over his shoulders and down his arms. She was quiet in her exploration, and it unnerved him. He was used to common talk when his lover would force him to endure touch. Those times had been base and animalistic, not reverent and quiet like it now was with Jane.

He tried to focus on her hands, Jane's hands. In his mind he knew who they belonged to, but every once in a while, the voice of his lover would cut in, and he would feel the sting of pain on his skin.

"So big and strong, like an ox. So proud, yet here you are, crying, broken."

He shuddered, his entire body growing taut. He felt his stomach churn as Jane's hands traced the muscles of his torso, snaking slowly, but intently, down.

"Look at the size of you. And you say you want to stop this? What a liar you are. You can't stop this, your cock wants it, your body wants it, and your mind is too weak to fight them.

Gasping, he curled his fingers into his palms and tried not

to struggle, but Jane sensed the turmoil in him and crawled up higher, until her body was flush atop his, and he felt every inch of her, every curve and indentation, even the beating of her heart against his breastbone. When she kissed his tattoo, he actually heard the small exhalation of air whimper past his lips. When he felt Jane's hand slide between their bodies and reach for his cock, he gritted his teeth, trying to focus on the pleasure, not the past.

"Jane, talk to me," he cried as she stroked him. "I need to hear your voice." *To keep the other one at bay,* he silently added.

"I am here, Matthew." He felt the sensual drag of her hair sliding down his chest and belly. "I'm with you, touching you, discovering you. You're beautiful," she murmured, her voice full of awe. "I want to touch you forever and marvel at how perfect you are."

An unchecked tear seeped from his eye. Mercifully the blindfold caught it, preventing him the shame of having Jane know he was weeping.

"I want to taste you," she said, circling his nipple with her tongue. The hot lash made his cock jump in her palm, and he allowed himself the sinful pleasure of imagining her mouth answering the beckoning call. He wished he could allow it, but he hadn't been able to bear it, his cock in another mouth. His lover had ruined that for him. He had tried it, over the years, drinking absinthe so he would not hear the voice, or see the face that haunted his dreams. But not even the absinthe allowed him that pleasure. He could never retain an erection whenever he allowed such intimacy.

He would be damned to hell if he grew flaccid now with Jane.

Her soft palm continued to stroke him, her clever thumb swirling around the swollen head, spreading the evidence of his desire along the cap and down to the ridged neck of his shaft. Incredibly he heard her lips part, felt her thumb leave him, then the unmistakable sound of her lips sucking.

"I want to take you deep in my mouth," she said between kisses that moved along his ridged abdomen. "I want to feel your strength, taste you…"

"I…I can't," he murmured, his voice cracking. "I can't abide that act, Jane."

He felt her move on the bed. "Why?"

"Because," he whispered, thankful he was blindfolded, "I was forced to watch it being done to me, and it was…wrong. When I looked down, between my legs, the person…my…tutor…it was wrong."

She stilled. "What if you saw me?"

He thrashed his head. "No, Jane."

"I want to take you in me."

"Jane, no!" he cried as she slid all the way down his body and fitted her curves between his thighs. His shaft was in her hand, and it was moving downward, to a mouth he knew would be open, hot and wanting. He whimpered, and she stopped, and instead of a warm wet mouth, he felt something else trickling along his shaft. Jane's tears.

"Matthew," she murmured, her voice breaking. "How can I save you?"

"Release me, Jane."

She reached above his head and untied him. She pulled the blindfold off, and he looked at her with what he knew was more than need.

He said nothing, but lowered his mouth onto hers. He swept his tongue inside and for the first time, allowed himself to stop thinking—to only feel.

Matthew took his time exploring her mouth, delighting in the weight of her resting atop him. He willed his blood to slow. Every liaison in his past had been nothing but the frantic mating of bodies. Clothes had been shed and torn. They had panted and lusted and satisfied their carnal desires—and then he had left, physically replete, emotionally empty. He didn't want that with Jane—he wanted more. The slow seduction, the exploration of her body, the commitment of her beauty etched for eternity in his memory.

Her body grew restless against his, and he rolled atop her, taking her with him, holding her so that she was cradled in his arms. Their eyes met and he stared into her luminous gaze, losing himself.

Pressing her back, he studied her lying beneath him, waiting for him. White linen had never looked more erotic to him than it did now, shielding Jane's curved form.

Delicate embroidered pansies dotted the neckline, and instead of buttons, the gown was held together by a long line of white, silk ribbons tied into perfect bows. He was going to untie them, one at time, slowly, assuredly.

His eyes met hers as his fingers reached the first bow, tugging at the end, unraveling it until it was only two strings crisscrossed against the other. Placing his finger beneath it, he parted the ties, hearing her inhale and hold her breath when the linen gaped teasingly open.

The second bow came undone and still she held his gaze, her breasts rising and falling, her breathing increasing every time he loosened a silk ribbon. The third bow slipped between his fingers and he could not resist glancing down between their bodies.

His bronzed hand rested partly inside her gown, the snowy linen contrasting with his skin. The chemise was undone to her midriff and it would not take much effort to slide the thin straps along her arms and part the material over her generous breasts to reveal her silken belly.

Without a word, he rose to his knees, straddling her legs before reaching for the straps of her gown and revealing her fully. A fine flush covered her skin, and he looked up to see her blushing.

"My God, how will I ever capture this beauty on canvas?"

Her eyes were misty when she looked into his and her lips trembled a fraction. "Truly?"

"I could not have conjured up such loveliness." He ran a hand along her side, relishing the soft, curved feel of her. "I'll make this beautiful for you, Jane. I swear, you will never regret this with me."

And then, he lowered himself atop her so that her breasts scraped his chest and their eyes were locked together, and he sunk himself deeply inside her.

He did not ask if she could take all of him, for he knew she could. He was so deep inside her, he felt her pulsating around him. And when he began his dance of enter and withdraw, and he heard each gasp, each creak of the bed with his measured strokes, he knew that he had found the one person who matched the passion he had swimming in his veins. The one person who could accept him as he was—damaged, soiled goods.

He looked at Jane's hair fanned out against the white pillow, down to her breasts, which swayed and brushed his chest, down to the red thatch that meshed with his black hair, to the sacred place where he joined inside her. The beauty of it hit him all at once, and he realized that he had never before thought of the act of intercourse as a magical dance. But as he watched himself enter her, watched as she took him—his length, his thickness—deep inside her, he knew he was watching something much more profound than two bodies seeking pleasure.

As if to confirm his thoughts, he looked up and saw their reflection in the cheval mirror that sat in the corner of the room. His body, so much harder and darker than hers, slid along her curves and he saw how her hips moved with his, saw how his hips undulated with each stroke of his cock deep inside her until they moved together as one.

He slid a bit to the right, still partially covering her with his body and she tried to follow him, but he stilled her and whispered against her ear, "Look and see us."

Her head moved against the pillow and he saw her eyes go wide with wonder and desire as she studied their bodies sliding along one another in the reflection of the mirror. He slowed his rhythm till it resembled an unhurried rising and falling of hips and legs, breasts and breaths.

They watched their bodies moving slowly together and after a long while, Matthew lowered his face to hers and kissed her cheek. "I only see you now, Jane."

Jane placed her hand palm up against Matthew's and they stayed like that, palm to palm, for long seconds before he entwined his fingers through hers and brought their hands back behind her head as he thrust deeply into her.

He had never felt this—this oneness of mind, body and spirit. As they looked into each other's eyes, as his hand gripped hers tightly and his body slid along hers, he knew that he would never, ever, feel this connection with anyone else.

"Don't close your eyes. I want you looking into my eyes as you come. Show me everything inside you, Jane."

He'd never before been struck by the beauty of lovemaking—the graceful movement of a female body in motion beneath him. He'd never taken the time to savor every sound, to watch as lips parted on a silent moan, or a plea for more. He'd never studied how lashes fluttered open and closed.

He'd never felt his heart fill with emotion, or his soul come alive when eyes, glazed with passion, met and held his. He had never made love until he reached for Jane's hand and pulled her up, encouraging her to watch him enter her body. She watched, wide eyed, as her body took him in and loved him.

When he could no longer fight off the desire to spill himself, he pulled her to sit atop him, wrapping her thighs around his hips while he buried his lips in her hair. His hands squeezed her lush bottom, forcing her up and down, driving her to take all of him.

He'd never experienced love until she clasped his head to her breasts and clung to his hair, her hips moving instinctively as *she* made love to *him*.

"Loveliest Jane." The strangled endearment was ripped from his throat and with a rough shout and a final deep, penetrating thrust, he pulled out, allowing his seed to splash between the cleft of her bottom.

For minutes they sat, clinging to the other, arms clutching and hugging, faces buried in each other's necks, a fine sheen of perspiration trickling down her back and his chest. Slowly he came back to earth, his angel still secured in his arms.

He looked at her, traced the freckles on her nose, then kissed each one, sighing as he did so. "I love you, Jane Rankin," he breathed, holding her tightly. "I love you more than you will ever comprehend."

20

They walked back together, hand in hand, stopping to watch the swans swimming. Stepping behind her, Matthew wrapped his arms around her waist and kissed her neck. "I adore you, Jane," he murmured. "It was not the height of orgasm that made me say it." Jane felt light, as if she was floating as she turned in his arms. "I love you, Jane," he said, his lips lowering to hers.

She kissed him, and caressed his cheek. "I love you, as well. So much."

He captured her hand in his and brought it to his lips. "You're going to have dinner tonight with me," he whispered, kissing her fingers. "In the cottage. Just the two of us."

"And will you paint me?"

He tweaked her nose. "Yes, naked with blossoms scattered around."

Jane kissed his knuckles before she released his hand. "I'm going to see Sarah now. It's been hours since I've checked on her."

"All right, I'll meet you shortly, I have some business to attend to."

Jane walked the short distance to the house, lost in thought. She was in love. Oh, God, she was in love with Matthew, Lord Wallingford. And he returned that love. It still astonished her.

They hadn't talked of the future, no plans had been made, but Jane felt it, that deep, abiding connection that would see them through. They were of different classes, but that did not matter, because what they had defied the strictures of money.

Strolling into the house, Jane passed Her Grace who was walking alongside a young woman dressed in the height of fashion.

"Miss Rankin, won't you come and be introduced to Miss Jopson?"

Obediently, Jane strolled to where they stood outside the crimson drawing room.

"Miss Jopson," she murmured as she curtsied.

The woman eyed her with amusement. She did not return the curtsey. "This is Miss Rankin, our little nurse that I was telling you about."

"Ah, yes," Miss Jopson said, her eyes glittering with what Jane thought was malice. "Charmed."

"Miss Jopson will soon be joining our family," the duchess murmured. "Won't you wish her well, Miss Rankin?"

"Indeed." She was confused, not comprehending exactly what position this Miss Jopson was going to be filling.

"Well, it's teatime," the duchess announced as the hall clock began chiming. "Good day, Miss Rankin."

The door promptly shut in her face.

Jane had never cared for the duchess or the way she seemed indifferent to everyone, especially Sarah.

Determined not to let Matthew's stepmother sour her thoughts, Jane ran to Sarah's room only to find her gone.

★ ★ ★

Not bothering to change, Matthew barged into the drawing room, eliciting gasps as he slammed the door shut behind him. In the room were his father, stepmother and a young woman whom he supposed was going to be his wife.

Miranda, his scheming stepmother, spoke first. "Wallingford, meet Constance Jopson. Won't she make a lovely bride?"

He glared at his stepmother and barely looked at his prospective bride. "I won't be marrying her, or anyone else you pick out."

Miranda's eyes glittered. "Make him see reason, darling," she cooed, brushing her hand along his father's arm. Clearing his throat, his father glanced curiously at Constance. "Oh, Miss Jopson and I have spent the morning having a little tête-à-tête. It is all out in the air, Your Grace."

Matthew glared at Miranda who smiled and rose from her chair to look out the window. Just what damn deal had she struck?

He caught Constance's cool expression and realized that she was a younger miniature of Miranda. His stepmother caught his gaze from across the room and smiled knowingly, setting his hair rising on his neck.

"You will marry Constance," his father announced. "It's been all arranged."

"No."

His father's right eye twitched, and he glanced at Miranda who motioned him on. His father pulled at his cravat as if it was choking him. "If you do not, then I will send Sarah away to an asylum for the insane."

His world came crashing down. "No," he roared, thundering toward his father. Miss Jopson wisely jumped up from her chair and ran for the door, opening it, preparing to flee. His father stepped back, but maintained his position.

"She will be locked up, shut away from the world with all the other idiots no one wants."

"I want her!" he stormed.

"And you have no rights to her or her care. I am her father and I will decide what it is best for her."

"And locking her away where she will be mistreated and ignored is your idea of what is best for her?"

"Then marry Constance, and she'll be safe."

There was a gasp at the door, and Matthew snapped his attention to the horrified sound.

Jane.

He ran to her, but she disappeared down the hall and out the front door. Miranda followed him into the hall. When she smiled, he pushed her back against the wall and wrapped his hand around her throat.

"How could you?" he snarled. "How could you do this to your own flesh and blood?"

She clutched at his wrists, clawing for air, and he squeezed, wanting to crush the windpipe he felt beneath his hand.

"You know I love her, and you can't stand it."

He thrust her back and she coughed, falling onto the floor.

"I won't let you take her away from me."

"It's too late," she gasped. "She's already gone. She'll return once you've agreed to the marriage."

"I won't," he roared. "I'll tear this house down looking for her. I'll search the countryside, but I'll *never* marry Constance Jopson."

Miranda sent him a scathing sneer. "You pathetic fool, she's already been taken away, and you'll never find her. Never."

Jane ran until her lungs burned, till she couldn't see any longer. Until she was at the temple and leaning against the wall, crying.

What had she thought? That they could be together? There was no future for a woman like her and a man like Matthew. He was going to be a duke, and she was… nothing. *Nobody.*

And Constance Jopson. She sobbed as she thought of the beautiful, fashionable creature. She was perfect for him, the sort of wife he should have on his arm.

But what they had done, what they had shared that afternoon, it had been more than their bodies. They had held one another, touching and whispering. They had confessed their love—and she had believed him.

"Jane."

He came up behind her, wrapping his arms around her, holding her tight. Rocking her, he whispered in her ear. She held on to him, sobbing, not caring that she was acting silly. He had made her no promises, offered her nothing but pleasure. It had been her own naïve fantasies that had made her think that they had a future together.

"Jane, I must," he whispered, clutching her. "I'm sorry."

She flung herself from his arms. "Why?"

"Because I must wed," he said, coming to her and taking her hand. "But it needn't interfere with us."

She slapped him hard across the cheek. When he looked at her, his eyes were dark, stormy. "I love you."

She hit him again, hating him. "And what am I to be?" she cried. "Your…whore?"

He held her wrist. "My lover? My mistress?"

That word ended any hope she had of any sort of future with Matthew. She could not be a mistress, not Matthew's, not any man's.

"No."

"Jane," he said in a nauseating placating tone that made her want to slap him for a third time. "Be reasonable."

She couldn't. Not when her heart was breaking into a million tiny pieces.

"I need you to understand that this is out of my hands."

"Why must you marry her?" she demanded.

"Because she is who my father wants."

"And you have no say?" His gaze flickered to hers, and the muscle in his jaw tightened.

"No. I have no say."

"I don't believe you. You're a liar," she spat.

"The truth is, Jane, that I must. They will send Sarah away to a lunatic asylum if I decline. You know she won't survive that. She won't…" He looked away and fisted his hand against a pillar. "I can't let her go, Jane."

"And what of me?" she asked, trying to stem the pain in her voice. "Will I just go on and survive, then? Why? Because I am tougher? Because I am not a lady?"

He took a step closer, and reached for her, but she backed away, stumbling as tears clouded her vision. "Or am I just easier to replace, and therefore, the logical choice to go?"

He looked at her with such agony that Jane knew the answer.

"Don't make me choose, *please,*" he begged.

"I'll make it easy for you, my lord. You won't have to."

She turned and walked away, and he roared her name, which she ignored. He came after her, stomping down the incline. He grabbed her arm and she pulled viciously, freeing herself from him.

"Jane, don't leave this way."

She didn't reply, but she picked up her skirts and hurried her pace. She was going to sob uncontrollably and she didn't want to do it in front of him.

"Jane, please, you don't understand. I can't let her go."

But he could let *her* go, and the knowledge was killing her.

Despite the pain, Jane continued marching down the incline. She had no idea that he had followed her until she felt his touch on her arm, halting her.

"I can't choose, Jane." Her heart broke and she looked away, but he caught her chin and forced her to look up at him. His gaze faltered, and he looked away, then immediately it swung back to her.

"Jane, Sarah is my child."

21

The words were out. His shameful secret was known.

"Your child?" she asked, the words just a whisper. He hated to see the tears in her eyes, the pain his actions were causing her. He longed to wipe them away, but he knew he no longer had the right to touch her—not with his filthy hands.

"My daughter. Yes."

She stumbled, her expression dazed. He helped her to sit, and he sat down beside her, wishing he could hold her. He needed her now, more than ever. Her mouth opened, then shut. She looked at him, then away. He feared her response, the horror of her thoughts as she wrote the story in her mind.

"I was fifteen when Miranda, my stepmother, came to me one day in the stable." He stopped, blinked a few times and took a deep breath. He had never said the words aloud—to anyone.

"I was big, nearly full grown. She used to look at me," he said, unable to say the words. "And…and…"

"Don't," Jane whispered, tears were streaming down her face, but he couldn't stop, not now that the words were out.

"That day in the stable, she cornered me. She had been looking at me for months, leading me on, a glance, a brief touch, whispered innuendos. I...I didn't know what to think. But that day," he said in a quiet voice, "she came to me. She dropped to her knees and undid my britches."

"Oh, God," he heard Jane whisper beside him, but he had to go on. The words were spilling out of his mouth.

"She handled me so well. I'd never been touched, only by my own hand." He closed his eyes, refusing to relive the visuals that threatened to come upon him. "I was so damn hard," he said through gritted teeth. "And when she took me into her hand, and then...into her mouth..." He clenched his jaw. "Christ, I didn't want it to end. I...hated it, seeing her there between my legs with my cock in her mouth, but I liked the way it felt. She made me watch, her eyes looking up at me. It was wrong and shameful. She was my father's wife. But she was only twenty-two at the time and had already given him two daughters. I hated her, but I loved what she did to my body. She would come to me in the dark and wake me with her mouth. She tutored me in sex, and it became dark and disturbed.

"I hated her more for what she was making of me. I tried to degrade her, but she liked it, found the perversion tititlating. It destroyed me, Jane."

She reached for him and held him, her tears trickling into his hair. "She raped you."

He looked up at her and shook his head. He wished to God he could lie and say she had, but he couldn't. He couldn't lie to Jane. "No, Jane. I agreed. I wanted it. Sometimes, I searched her out, too. Some nights I lay in bed, playing with my cock, hoping she would come to me."

He lowered his head and rested it against her breast, hiding his face from her gaze, ashamed by this necessary admission.

"It was my first sexual experience, Jane. I was only fifteen. I didn't know how to control my body or my needs. I was just learning about sex, and Miranda…she taught me to use and be used. And all the time she told me not to tell. Who was I going to tell?" he scoffed. "She was my stepmother, for Christsakes. No one has an illicit affair with their stepmother, and at fifteen."

"Matty," she whispered kissing his brow. He clutched at her gown and rubbed his cheek against the swell of her breast.

"It went on for months, and then she became pregnant with Sarah. She came to me in a panic. She was pregnant and had not slept with my father in months. We planned his seduction, and she convinced him that she had conceived that night. I tried to break it off, but she wouldn't hear of it. I tried," he said, clutching Jane. "But she would return to me night after night, and when you're fifteen, Jane, and hard whenever the wind blows, you want it. God, my body wanted it so much that it won out over my mind. I hated her, even as she pleasured my body. She would come to me, pleasuring me as my child grew within her. It disgusted me what we were doing, especially when I saw what I had created with her. But I…I couldn't stop, Jane. And then she had Sarah." He paused and looked up at her. "I named her, you know. When I saw her, I loved her. Not because of Miranda. But because she was a piece of me. *My own*. Miranda hated that I loved Sarah. She was perversely jealous. The summer I was seventeen, Sarah was turning two. I was leaving for university and Miranda didn't want me to leave. We were still…fucking," he said, remembering those times with disgust. "On the day before I was to leave, I met her down by the lake. As I crossed the bridge, I saw something floating in the lake. And then I saw Miranda, she was holding Sarah beneath the water."

Jane held on to him, clutching him as he began to tremble.

"I thought she was dead as I pulled her out. But she lived, and she is how she is because of me. Because of what I did with Miranda."

"Matthew," Jane sobbed. "My heart is breaking."

"Then, stay, Jane, because the thought of you leaving is making my heart break, as well. Stay because I need you. Because I love you. Stay because I cannot live without you."

Later that evening, after Jane had had a bath and cried until she had no tears left, she sought out Matthew and asked him to walk with her.

He followed, silent, pensive, until he reached for her hand and brushed his thumb over her knuckles. Stopping her, he kissed her palm, and then wrapped it around his cheek. "Stay."

She closed her eyes, blocking the desperation she heard.

"I can offer you everything you could ever want, Jane."

She looked away, biting her lip. No, he could not. It had taken hours for her to admit that. Hours of introspection and tears and heartache.

"Jane, look at me."

They were standing on the bridge with the sun setting behind them. He lifted her chin, and she saw him through a veil of mist. She heard his breath catch. His voice shook.

"You undo me with your tears, Jane."

"I do not mean to."

"Your happiness is now vital to my existence, *you're* vital to my survival."

"Matthew, it cannot be. To skulk and hide…to love in secret like it is a crime, a shame—"

He held on to her, stepped close to her so she was forced to tip her head back to see him. "Is it so very bad to want me, Jane? To want the pleasure I feed your body and soul? Is it so very sinful to love me?"

Am I that sinful? The question burned in his eyes. Reaching for his hand, she brought it to her lips, kissed his chafed knuckles and pressed his hand to her warm cheek. A tear fell from her eye, and she let it roll down and splash onto his hand, where it trickled between his fingers.

"Jane, I live for you now," he whispered, his voice breaking. "How can you not know that? How can you not believe it?"

She believed it, felt it with every fiber of her being. She lived for him, as well. Her heart beat for him, and always would.

"Jane, believe me when I tell you I can give you everything you ask for, and things you don't. I will hand you the moon and stars if they be your desire. I can make love to you every night, every morning. I can let you touch me. I will cherish those touches, will welcome them—*crave them.*"

"But you cannot give me the one thing I have yearned for my whole life."

He sucked in a breath, his hand trembled in hers. "Jane—"

"You cannot give me respectability, Matthew."

He exhaled long and deep, a tortured sound from deep in his wounded chest. "What is a piece of paper worth when it's only a signature? What does it mean when the heart is not in it? It means nothing, Jane. It is just a document. I have spoken of my love, my feelings. I have given you something much more important than my name, I have given you my trust. My body. My heart."

He tipped her chin up and smoothed his thumb along the wet trail of her tears. "What I have shared with you—my love, my body, the secret I have kept for seventeen years—it is more sacred, more powerful than any wedding vow. Jane, you are my confidante, my helpmate, my friend. My lover. You are everything the word *wife* means to me. In my heart, we are wed. In my soul, you are mine. Does the title mean so very much to you, Jane?"

His fear shone in his eyes and she ached to soothe it. "No, Matthew, your title means nothing to me. I do not need to be a countess. I do not aspire to be a duchess. I only aspire to be your wife, in name, Matthew, not in a higher, philosophical plane. But the mortal plane, where society dictates the rules. I do not want to be hidden away in a cottage by the sea, waiting for you to come to me. I do not want to be called whore or mistress. I do not want any children we might be blessed with to be labeled bastard."

He squeezed her hand hard, fighting to keep her within his clasp. She gripped him back, showing him the violence of her feelings. "Jane, you are breaking my heart."

"I am broken, too, Matthew. I wish it could be different for us. But if we are to stay true to ourselves, then we must do what is best for us. You must marry Constance to save Sarah, or hate yourself...or worse, hate me for making you choose. And I must leave you, because you cannot offer me what I need. Passion. Love. Lust...it is so very strong between us now, but will it be that way in a year? Two? Will we despise ourselves later for our weakness now?"

"Shh, don't say it, Jane."

"I could never make you choose between Sarah and me, Matthew. It is not in my nature to do such a thing. You are an honorable man, and I would not ask you to do something that would mar your sense of right and wrong. It is right to do this, to give Constance your name. And while I wish it could be me, I can say that I have fallen even deeper in love with you today, knowing the sort of man you are."

He reached for her, held her about the shoulders. His eyes were glowing with unshed tears. "Stay, Jane. I have not asked for anything since I was a ten-year-old boy chasing after my mother's carriage...but I am asking now...no, I am *begging* you. *Don't leave me!*" Crushing her to his chest, he buried his face in her hair. She felt the warmth of his tears trickle down her neck, and she clutched him tight, holding him safe. "Don't leave me, Jane…don't, please." He shuddered.

"I will never fully leave you, Matthew. Somehow I think you know that. A part of me will always belong to you, as you will always belong to me. What we've shared cannot be taken from us. I will clutch the memory of you—of us—to my breast for the rest of my days."

He clung to her, murmuring over and over, "No. No, you will not leave. I will not allow it. I forbid it. I can't bear it. Jane, I will not know how to go along without you. I cannot go back into the cold, not when I've been thawed by your warmth."

Standing at the window of his study, Matthew watched as the door of the carriage shut behind Jane. Their gazes met, and despite the fact that Jane had asked that he not see her off, he had not been able to resist one last look at the woman who had changed him, who'd awakened not only the man, but the heart inside him.

Jane… Resting his flattened palm on the glass, he tried to connect with her, if only for a fleeting second. *I need your touch…*

Despite the silence, Jane heard him and his desperate plea. Her own small hand, devoid of a glove, rested against the carriage window, holding him palm to palm, despite glass, brick and mortar. The sun chose that moment to shine, illuminating the copper curls that had escaped her bonnet, and the glistening trail of tears that slid down her pale cheeks.

Pressing his forehead to the cool glass, he held her gaze, her palm, his eyes pleading with her. *Don't go. Don't leave me.*

Suddenly he was ten all over again, running down the lane after the carriage that was carrying his mother away. He had been hurt and confused then, afraid of the future. He knew now what the future would bring for him and he could not bear it, couldn't stand to awaken to another morning without Jane lying there beside him. Could not endure feeling his newly mended heart shatter once again.

I love you, he mouthed, and watched as she covered a sob with her hand.

The driver cracked the whip, and slowly the heavy coach lumbered forward. He watched her leave him, the black carriage rumbling down the gravel drive. His palm and forehead still rested on the window until the carriage was nothing more than a tiny speck on the horizon.

He was heartsick. Devastated. Numb.

Jane was gone, and with her, she had taken his heart. His pleasure. His reason for living.

Come back, Jane, he pleaded as he closed his eyes. *Come back.*

"I see the nursemaid has left at last. A wise decision."

The coldness of that voice cut him to the quick, and he found his old armor, his indifference, his contempt, his tongue that could cut down anyone unfortunate enough to be caught by it.

"You will not come into this room unannounced ever again."

Constance laughed as she shut the door behind her with a soft click. "Why? Is this where you entertain your little nurse?"

"You will never speak of her again, do you hear me?"

Softly she came up to him. He watched her movements in the reflection of the glass. She circled behind him, much like a shark circling an unsuspecting swimmer. Oh, she was every inch a predator. He saw her scheming expression and he hated her. Despised everything she stood for.

"Very well, my lord. Now that the obstacle is rid of, let us get to the ground rules of our alliance."

He whirled on her, his voice dripping with coldness and venom. "The ground rules are, we will be married and you will be the Countess of Wallingford. Once my father dies, you'll be a duchess, entitled to all that the position allows. But you will *never* be my wife." Her eyes flared, and he stepped closer, intimidating her. "In exchange for my title, you will keep out of my way until I summon you. Then you will lie on your back, and I will fuck you for however long it takes for you to bear the next heir. For your sake, I do hope you're proficient."

She had the audacity to smile. "Proficient in bed?" she asked. "Like your little whore, the nurse?"

He gritted his teeth, trying very hard to shove the unseemly idea of choking her out of his mind. "I expect no pleasure out of you." He raked his gaze over her body, and felt nothing but contempt. "Likewise, you should expect none from me. I desire your proficiency be in conceiving. I have no desire to fuck you more than absolutely necessary."

"You may very well like it, fucking me, as you say."

He scoffed, unable to credit it. He still had the taste of Jane on his tongue, her scent on his fingers. He hadn't been able to wash them away, knowing he'd never again smell her on his skin. He could hardly believe that he was looking at this woman, knowing he would have to enter her body and spend himself. It sickened him, made him violent. An act that had once meant nothing to him but the pleasure of release was now the most sacred of acts. But it never would be hallowed with Constance.

"You look at me, my lord, as if I were a hideous beast. We both know I am not. I daresay I could be quite pleasing to you in bed."

His head was pounding, the pain shooting into his eyes. He

wanted to quit this conversation, this room, this house, and barricade himself inside his cottage with his art, and the bed that still smelled of Jane.

"My lord?" she purred, pressing into him, "I know my attractions. They are the very sort that you've long admired in your lovers, are they not?"

He stiffened, hating the truth of her words. There was a time that he would have found Constance worthy of a tup, but that was before a green-eyed imp had stolen his soul. All he could see now was Jane, her lush body naked and adorned with orange blossoms.

"What do you say, Wallingford?"

He straightened out of his trance, trying to forget the days and nights he had spent with Jane. "In future, you will not discuss the physical act with me. Save it for the paramours you will take."

She smiled, her eyes glistening with challenge. She was by no means put off by him and his cold disdain. "It all sounds so very reasonable. I get the title and the freedom to do as I please. You get your father off your back by getting yourself legshackled to a rich heiress who will provide you with an heir."

"You've a very good understanding of matters, Miss Jopson."

"But there is one other thing, my lord, I believe needs clarification. That sister of yours. I won't put up with her. She's an embarrassment I will not abide. How can I be expected to entertain with ease and style when at any moment an imbecile may come into the room?"

"You will put up with her, or you will find yourself in the streets, penniless, do you understand? She is none of your concern, nor will she ever be. Your only task in this house is to spread your thighs."

"Then I assume if you are to humiliate me with your sister, then I may humiliate you by being seen with my lovers."

"I don't give a damn what you do. As long as you've provided me with my heir, you can move out and live in town with a harem of men. Just do not make the mistake of taking a lover before you conceive. If I am to have an heir, I want it from own tainted bloodstock, not that of a footman, or God above, a poet."

"Is that a promise, my lord? You will not later decide to curb my…amorous pursuits with other men?"

"It is a promise you can take to the bank, Miss Jopson."

"It seems we have reached an amicable solution to our marital discourse. I will be a vessel for your spawn, and you will be my way to all the finer things in life that I have come to covet. A woman could not ask for a better arrangement."

Jane would, he silently thought as he slammed the door to his study. Jane would have asked for much more.

"What the devil do you mean you're marrying that pit viper? You're in love with Jane Rankin, for God's sake."

Matthew reached for a cheroot and tossed it back onto his desk. How easily he had fallen back into old habits. Jane had been gone only a few days and here he was descending into dissolution once again.

"Tell me why," Raeburn demanded, "you would give up Jane for Constance."

No one knew why. Only Jane. He wasn't about to change that.

With a shrug, he muttered, "Because it suits me."

Raeburn glared at him. "Your father. He's blackmailing you."

Damn Raeburn and his clear logic. "I liked you better when you were an opium addict," he mumbled, fidgeting with the tip of the discarded cheroot. "You never cared about anything then."

"I always cared for you, and now that I am free of opium, I can see more than I ever have before."

With a sigh, he said, "Believe me when I tell you that my father has a vise grip around my throat. He wants the money Constance will bring, not to mention the railroad connections with her family. He's willing to use Sarah to get it."

Raeburn's green eyes darkened. "How?"

"He's threatened to send her to an asylum if I don't wed the pit viper, as you call her. You know very well what those places are like. I cannot stand aside and allow her to be thrown to the devil, Raeburn. Damn me, my conscience has chosen to rise up, and I can't shove it back down."

Raeburn's eyes closed. "I know of my own happiness with Anais. I wanted the same for you. Is there any chance at all that your father might change his mind?"

"About as much chance as me being welcomed into Almack's with open arms."

"And what of Jane?"

Matthew swallowed hard as he avoided his friend's direct gaze. Christ, his head hurt. He was going to wind up with another one of those migraines, he thought with disgust. The damn things had plagued him since Jane left. And there was no Nurse Jane here to rub his temples and whisper to him in her angel voice.

"We have broken off," he said in a voice he barely heard himself. "It's for the best. I would only have ruined her. It was just a matter of time before I did."

"Think this through, man!" Raeburn pleaded. "You can't stand Constance. She'll make your life hell. What comfort will she give you—"

"This is a business contract, Raeburn," he snapped as he

pressed his fingers to his temple. "It isn't a bloody romance novel."

"You love Jane."

"Well, I can't have her," he shouted as he punched the glossy top of the desk.

"You deserve her, Wallingford."

"Don't," he thundered, pounding the desk again. "I don't want to hear it. Leave it be. It's over and done, and Jane is out of my life. Constance will be my bride."

"And what sort of marriage will you have?"

Not the sort he had increasingly begun to dream of.

"We needn't have any pretense between us, Raeburn. Both of us know exactly what sort of marriage it will be."

"Why don't you explain it to me, then?"

"Very well. We will marry in the estate chapel, and then I shall take my bitch of a bride to the bedchamber, do the deed and hope like hell she's impregnated. Once she spits out an heir, she is free to see whomever she wants. Father gets her money and an heir, and Sarah will be safe."

"Seems like a cold deal to me."

"Downright glacial."

"You cannot want this."

"Of course I don't want it," he growled. "But life is full of bullshit we don't want."

"Anais will be devastated by this news. She had hoped... well, she thought that perhaps you and Jane might find happiness together."

They had, he wanted to say, but then it was snatched away. Memories were all he would have now.

"How is your wife, by the way?" he asked, wanting to put an end to talk of Jane and his farce of a marriage.

"She's fine," Raeburn muttered. "But let us return to your life."

"Why? It's in utter shambles, and I prefer not to think about it. So, tell me, will you do me the honor of being my best man, or am I to ask Broughton?"

In the quiet of the night, Matthew sat down at the small secretary in the corner of his cottage. From his chair, he looked out into the room where he had spent so many hours with Jane, loving her, touching her. It was hard to believe she had been gone for a week.

So short a time. Yet a lifetime of changes had filled his hours. He was betrothed to a woman he despised. He would father a child with yet another woman who meant nothing to him.

Damn her, he cursed, pounding his fist against the desktop, why did she have to leave him? Why wasn't it enough for Jane what they had, why did she have to ask for more than he could give? Didn't she understand that he'd give her his lifeblood to make her happy?

The sins of his past roared up, along with the vision of Miranda. He had ruined his life, succumbing to her charms and his body's urges. He had ruined Sarah's by incurring Miranda's wrath when he was about to leave for university. Now, he feared, he had destroyed Jane.

Anger and pain seared through his body and he jumped up, pacing the small perimeter of the cottage, searching for the safety of the coldness he had once used as an impenetrable shield.

Tears heated his eyes, and he fought them, refusing to weep, to feel.

"Why?" he screamed, letting the noise bellow out loud and ferocious. "Why can I not have some measure of peace?" he questioned.

"Matty…" He heard Jane's soothing voice as he collapsed

onto the bed and rested his head on the pillow that still smelled of Jane's soap.

"I love you, Jane," he whispered. "I will love you for eternity, and God curse me, I will love you beyond."

22

It should be easier now, to wake up in the morning and move through the motions of the day. But the fact was, it was not. For the past two months, Jane had thought of nothing but that morning when she had left Matthew standing at the window of his study, his palm pressed to the glass. She could not close her eyes for fear that the image of him standing there, telling her he loved her would sweep across her eyes. She was doomed to think of him. Every day without Matthew was increasingly harder to bear. She thought of him nonstop, dreamed of him every night. It was her hands, not Matthew's, that traced the contours of her body while she tried to relive those beautiful moments in his arms.

When they had met, he had been in need of love. He had needed her touch. Now it was she who was shattering from the pent-up need to feel his hands caressing her. She wanted his breath in her ear. His words, uttered in his deeply masculine voice, piercing through her desire.

After all this time, her desire for him had not abated. She

doubted it ever would. He would always be there, an ever-present unanswered echo in her soul.

She was only glad that their stations in life would prevent them from crossing paths. He was lost to her now, and while it had been by her own hand, Jane still felt the decision was the right one for her. She wanted to be her own woman, living on her own terms, not a gentleman's mistress who would shower her with gifts and pleasure when it suited him, only to discard her when he was through with her.

Jane had seen that happen too many times with Lady Blackwood's friends. She heard the women at the hospital whispering amongst themselves about their ill-fated love affairs. She had lived it with her own mother.

A woman's worth was more than a comfortable home and bedsport for a man. She had always believed that, with every ounce of her being. But lately, she had to remind herself that it was a mantra still worth believing.

She had wanted an honest relationship with him. A marriage, legal in the eyes of the law and the church. She did not want to live in sin, despite that it was love that had brought them together.

"Ah, there you are," Lady Blackwood said as Jane entered the breakfast room. "How was your night at the hospital, dear?"

"Quite well, thank you," she replied as she sat down and poured herself a cup of tea. It was increasingly difficult to hide behind the facade she had constructed. She didn't want Lady Blackwood to suspect she harbored a wounded heart, as well as a pining one, for Wallingford.

"You're working too much, gel. I see the weariness about your eyes. Take a break from the hospital. Inglebright will take you back whenever you desire. You know that. Besides, I'm certain you've tucked away the tidy sum you made while caring for the duke's daughter—there is no reason to work for wages at the hospital."

She couldn't give up being a nurse. It was the only thing that kept her from going insane in the long, dark hours of the night.

Lady Blackwood's rheumy gaze clouded even more. "You know, Jane, that you do not have to continue like this. It's no secret that I am not rich, but I have put aside a portion for you after I depart this life. It will allow you to live quite well, I think."

Tears stung her eyes, and Jane tried hard to swallow the tea without choking. A life without Matthew, and now the thought of losing the woman who was like a mother to her. "How can I ever repay you?"

"You already have, with years of exceptional care and friendship. I do not believe you have an inkling of your worth, Jane."

"Thank you, my lady."

Lady Blackwood cocked her head to the side and studied her. "Will you not confide in me, Jane?" she asked in a gruff voice. "It pains me to see you hurt like this. You try very hard to hide it, but you never were one capable of deceit."

"I don't know what you mean," she murmured as she reached for a slice of toast and the crystal jam bowl. "I'm just a bit tired." Jane nodded to the newspaper, which was folded up and resting beside Lady Blackwood's plate. "What gossip is there to be had this morning?"

"Oh, the usual," she replied, resting her wrinkled and gnarled hand on top of it.

"Come now, you love to tell me of the gossip."

"No, nothing of any import."

"Well, that is a first, for every morning for the past fourteen years you have regaled me with the flummery of the society pages."

"Jane, don't," she commanded, struggling to hold on to the paper as Jane pulled it out from beneath her hand. It was more than a command, Jane thought, freezing, it was a plea.

Very slowly, Lady Blackwood lifted her wrinkled hand and met Jane's gaze. "The paper says that Lord Wallingford is to wed Constance Jopson today at his estate."

The toast turned to sawdust in Jane's mouth. She struggled to keep her facade, to find the right words that would throw her employer off the scent she had obviously discovered. But the thought of Matthew's marriage, the finality of it all, made her disguise crumble.

"How very nice," she replied, glancing out the window. "It's lovely and sunny today. I hope the weather is the same in the north of the country."

"Jane?" Her name was a question filled with worry.

"Is there any other entertaining news," she asked, smearing more jam on her toast and averting the conversation her employer was bent on having.

"This came." A white envelope with a red wax seal appeared from beneath the paper. One glance at the seal, and she knew who it was from. Her heart leaped in her chest, even as her hand tightened around the knife.

Lady Blackwood rose unsteadily from her chair. "I am rather tired," she murmured. "I don't believe I will need you today, Jane. Have the day with my blessing."

A warm, leathery hand pressed affectionately atop her shoulder. "I am always here for you, Jane. Please remember that."

With a nod, Jane struggled to hide the wetness in her eyes as her gaze strayed once more to the letter. With a gentle pat, Lady Blackwood left her alone.

When she picked up the missive, she brought the paper to her face, smelling the ink, the faint scent of his cologne and the acrid aroma of a cheroot. Closing her eyes, she rested the missive against her cheek, holding it there as though it were his hand cradling her face.

She was at once eager, yet terrified, to read it. Either way, its contents would only bring pain. She could not go against her desires to be an independent woman and become his mistress. A mistress was chained to a man, bought by him solely for pleasure.

And what if he was not renewing his offer, she thought sadly. In all honesty, that would hurt her even more.

She wouldn't read it, she decided. But she could not toss the letter aside, or throw it into the fire. She would keep it safe and in a place where she could look at it whenever she felt the need to be close to him once again. And one day, she might find the inner strength and emotional peace to read it.

The drizzle was cold. Damp. The sort of chill that found its way through woolens and down to the bone, yet he didn't feel a thing. The sky, a gunmetal gray, was ominous, as the heavy rain-filled clouds hung low on the horizon. Leaning against the stone railing of the bridge, Matthew stared down at the deep, dark water below.

He always loved the garden in this weather. It looked hauntingly beautiful in this light. It looked ghostly and lonely, the drizzle only adding to the ambience, echoing what was inside him, the place where his soul and heart should have resided. A place that was now a desolate wasteland of emptiness.

It had been two months since he'd seen Jane, or heard her soft, whispering voice. Yet he recalled her face as clearly as if he had just left her in bed. He heard her voice—*constantly*—whispering to him throughout the day and night.

The throbbing in his chest, the need to see her once more had not dissipated over time, but only grown until it had become a consuming compulsion. He had all but moved into his cottage, painting and sculpting all day and night, only to sleep fitfully in the bed they had once shared. Everything always came back to Jane. Even the sculpture of orange blossoms he had carved had been about Jane. His whole damn life revolved around her, and likely always would.

Not a word from her, he thought, fisting his hands together as he looked out on to the still waters of the lake. Every damn day he scoured the salver, searching for a letter, but none ever came. Did she even think about him anymore?

Pathetic though it was, his entire days were spent thinking of her. Wishing it could be different, wishing *she* could be different. If only she had been rich. If only she wasn't so strong in her convictions. If only she could be bought…

But then she would not be his Jane. She would be Constance. It wasn't Constance he wanted. He wanted Jane. The woman who had opened his eyes to life. The woman who had borne his cruel tongue and coldness. The woman who had slowly and carefully pulled away each of his defenses to see the bleeding core of him. The woman who understood his past and how he could have committed such reprehensible sin.

Jane…

Between his fingers, he watched the blood-red satin ribbon ripple in the breeze. She had freed him with this bind, yet once again he was bound. The memories of that afternoon constantly replayed in his mind. Alone in bed, he thought how much he wanted to be touched. How he craved the feel of Jane's delicate fingers caressing his chest. He fantasized of her mouth on his cock, sucking him in deep, her tongue slowly trailing along his shaft. With her it had not been dirty and shameful. With her, he had not looked down between his thighs and seen something sinful and wrong. When he had closed his eyes, allowing himself the pleasure of experiencing Jane's gentling suckling mouth, he had not seen Miranda between his legs. He had not heard her cruel words. He had not been fifteen. A boy. He'd been a man. *Jane's man.*

Last night, alone in his cottage, he sat in bed, his back to the headboard while he lazily stroked himself. It had felt good, his fisted hand sliding up and down his shaft. He had thought of Jane, her hand, her mouth, and his release had been explosive, coming in hot spurts on his belly. He had gone to sleep like that, spent, yet still hungry for more.

"You're going to get sick."

Drawn out of his thoughts, he saw Sarah standing beside him. She offered him part of her umbrella. Standing close to him, she sheltered them. "What are you doing out here at this time of the morning, it's not much more than six," he asked.

"I saw you leave your cottage. You looked sad."

He could not look her in the eye, so he turned his gaze to the water once more.

"You're always sad now," she said quietly. "My heart hurts when you're sad."

He said nothing, and she pressed closer to him, resting her head on his shoulder.

"I want to make you smile again, brother."

His eyes closed, hating the lie on her lips. He'd done nothing but lie to her, and here she was, trying to give him solace. She would never understand the circumstances of her birth, or what Miranda had done to her and why. He would never be able to tell her that he was not her brother, but her father.

"Matthew, does your heart hurt because you miss Miss Rankin?"

"Yes." He could not lie to Sarah, not about Jane. It felt wrong to lie about someone he loved so much, someone who meant so much to him.

"I miss her, too. Maybe she'll come back."

"She will not be coming back," he gasped in a choked voice.

"Lady Raeburn says that if you want something bad enough, that you must pray for it. I've prayed every night for her to come back to be my friend. Have you prayed, Matthew?"

"Yes." His voice was a pained whisper. Christ, he had prayed, begged, bartered for some miracle to be created so that he would not have to go through with this marriage. So that he could have Jane once more.

Sarah reached for his hand and clutched his fingers. "I know it's not the same, Matthew, but I will be your friend."

Clinging to her hand, he finally brought his gaze to her face. Such a beautiful face, with honest guileless eyes. The color was his, but his eyes had never shone with such open trust, his eyes had always glittered with mockery and pessimism.

He kissed her forehead, taking her strength. "You are the very best of me," he whispered.

They stood quietly for a few minutes, before Sarah brightened.

"There is the black swan that Miss Rankin liked so much," she said, pointing to a spot where the branches of a weeping willow dipped into the water. Paddling through was a lone swan, its feathers black as midnight.

"Its mate died. He swims about all day looking for her. It would be awful to be alone all the time, wouldn't it?" she asked.

"Yes. Terrible," he replied, thinking how he had floundered about these past months searching for a way to be with Jane.

"Do you know that swans only mate once in their lives?" Sarah asked him. "That poor swan will be alone without his mate for the rest of his life. How long will he live?" she asked.

"Mercifully, not long," he replied, thinking of the decades he had lying before him.

"Humans are like swans, they only love once, too, don't they?"

His voice became choked. "Yes, they do. But sometimes love is not enough to keep the one you love with you."

Looking down at his hand, he opened his fingers and allowed the crimson ribbon to flutter down. He watched it spiral down to the water, a feather falling from the sky.

It began to rain then, the drops heavy, landing on the satin as it floated atop the water. It reminded him of teardrops, and he was thrust back to his cottage when he chased the shadows of raindrops on Jane's skin.

"Goodbye, Miss Rankin," Sarah murmured quietly beside him.

Matthew watched as the water took the satin beneath its depths. "Goodbye, Jane."

Like an automaton, Matthew reached for the handle and opened the door to his wife's bedchamber. Christ! His wife. He'd been married that morning, only a few short hours after being on the bridge, saying his goodbyes to Jane.

It had been a simple, short service. Without any of the fripperies that came with a wedding. The vows had been shortened to within an inch of what was considered a legal marriage. He absolutely refused to say "with my body I thee worship."

But the vow had run through his thoughts all day, as he imagined Jane standing before him, him vowing to love her, and her body, until death do they part.

"At last," came the husky voice from the depths of the lavishly draped bed. "I was starting to wonder if you would ever come out of that cottage of yours."

His body tensed and he paused, just inside the room, wondering if it was too late to turn back and run away. He'd never been a coward before, but this night…what would happen, made him want to run and hide, never to be found again.

"I see you needed liquid courage," Constance purred with amusement. "I rather wondered if your reputation was misplaced."

Drowning the amber contents of his glass, Matthew set it on the table beside him and closed the door. He hoped to God that five glasses of brandy was going to allow him to crawl into bed with this creature.

As he stepped farther into the room, he saw Constance lying in the middle of the bed, artfully arranged. She wore a sheer gown, which hid nothing of her body beneath. Her long hair was unbound and spread over both pillows. One leg was bent, and she let it fall to the side, exposing her sex to him.

His body did not react. His stomach, however, protested. He could not do this, sink himself inside this woman. Not after what he had shared with Jane. With her, he had learned that sex brought more than the physical release of animal lust. With Jane, sex had been about mutual pleasures, a shared connection both physical and emotional. With her, there had been touching, whispering—love.

"Well, my lord? Am I not to your liking?"

Constance knew very well that she was any man's dream. Her body was trim and long legged. Her breasts pert with ripe, pink nipples. Any man would pursue her, any man but him.

Drawing a finger along her sex, she parted her outer lips, showing him that she was already wet. She was an erotic picture lying like this, and before Jane he would have fallen atop her and taken her, amused by her blatant sexuality. But now, he felt only repulsion.

"Come to bed," she murmured as she pleasured herself. "I'm quite certain we will both find it an enjoyable ride." Her gaze flickered along his body and he willed his cock to respond, but it wouldn't, and it wasn't because of the half bottle of brandy he had downed, either. He was simply ruined for anyone but Jane.

"Take off your robe," she commanded, "and let me see what I've got myself, along with a title."

He tore the silk dressing gown off his body, angered that he was not only a prize, but a stud to service her, as well. He was breathing hard, and the muscles of his chest and abdomen responded to the inner rage that was roiling within him.

"Very nice," she said with an appreciative sigh. "Even in this state, you are rather large."

His cock was limp. He would need to toss off to get it hard, but he didn't want her eyes on him as he did it. And he didn't want her hands all over him, either. He was able to have no other hands over his body but Jane's.

She kneeled before him as he stood beside the bed. When she looked up at him, her eyes were filled with malice.

"I will be anything you want tonight, my lord, but there is one thing I won't be—and that's your little nurse. So if you're thinking of pretending I'm her, you can shove that notion aside. I'd rather have you take me as a whore than to make believe I am that pathetic creature beneath you."

Never in a million years could he make the mistake that Constance was Jane. The eyes looking at him were nothing but manipulating, scheming eyes, and Jane's had been so trusting, so understanding.

"Will we consummate this marriage tonight?" she asked, reaching for him.

"Alliance," he growled, shoving her hand away and reaching for his member. He did not leisurely glide his hand up along the shaft as Jane had done. He did not enjoy the first sensations of his cock filling with blood the way he did last night when he had masturbated. He felt dirty doing it like this, the way

Miranda had liked, sitting on her knees with his cock before her face. She had liked to watch him pulling and tugging. *"Harder,"* she would tease as he grew excited and dangerously aroused.

Constance watched him with the same lascivious gaze as Miranda once did.

"Look at the size of you," she purred appreciatively as his cock grew in his hand. "I can't wait to have it filling me. Your merits certainly have not been overblown. And you certainly know what to do with it, don't you?"

Closing his eyes, he tried not to see Constance or Miranda. Tried not to hear Miranda's voice, saying, *"This is all you're good for, fucking...."*

Harder and harder, he shoved his hand up and down, strangling the shaft and making the head swell. He saw Constance sway, her mouth opening, preparing to take him in, and he froze for the briefest of seconds.

"On your knees," he growled. "Face the other way."

If she was disappointed by his lack of finesse in foreplay, she showed no outward signs. Making a show of it, she slowly slid the gown from her body. Her attempts were all in vain, for he could never be ensnared by her charms.

This was fucking, pure and simple. A way to procreate. Not create a child as Raeburn had done with Anais. No, he was fornicating to produce an heir and build the Torrington dynasty. And this woman, this conniving...*viper*...would be the mother.

"Come to me, my lord. You tease me with your cock."

"Don't talk," he commanded as he reached for her hips. With one swift thrust, he sunk his cock into her depths. She was wet and she moaned, her hands fisting the coverlet as she rolled her hips.

"Oh, God, yes, you do know what to do with that glorious staff."

If he had thought she was a virgin, he would have been more careful upon entering her. But she was, as he suspected, well used to physical pleasure.

Her hips rolled beneath his palms while her quim gripped his cock. He shoved up against her, impaling his entire length into her. She moaned, and he hated her for enjoying it, for feeling anything but dirty and shamed.

He felt dirty. And guilty.

"Faster," she begged, throwing her bottom out at him, and he heard Miranda's voice, all those years ago as he sweated atop her, driving his cock deep into her cunt. *"This is the only reason why women will want you, this,"* she had said as she scratched her nails down his back and ass. *"This body, this cock. It's the only thing you have that's worth anything."*

Fingers pressing into her hips, Matthew drove deep into his wife, not to feel pleasure, but to exorcise the voice in his head, the memories of all the meaningless sex he'd had in his life.

He had never taken Jane like this, just fucking and fucking without thought. Without feeling. Without pleasure.

"Yes!" Constance cried out, screaming as he pounded into her. He was sweating, breathless, as he increased the depths and speed of his thrusts. He was mindless now, feeling nothing but contempt and hatred for her, and himself. He didn't know how he would come like this. And he didn't want to think of Jane, to sully the nights they had shared as he fucked Constance.

But in the end, it was the only thing he could do, pretend that he was pounding into Jane, punishing her for leaving him, fucking her so hard that she would never, ever think to leave him again.

He hated how he was thinking, despised Constance before him, on her knees, begging for him to give her more. Christ, he was empty, just a shell of himself. He had nothing to give, not even his seed.

He did not want to make a child with another woman he de-spised. He did not want to give Constance anything of himself. She could have the title, the money, the estate and the house in London, if she would but leave him be, if she would make no demands upon him to take her to bed and breed with her.

But Sarah would not be safe from the clutches of his father. As her brother, he had no power. The only power he had was to come, spill his seed and give his father an heir. That was the only way Sarah would remain safe at home.

He prayed then, like never before, begging for anyone, God or devil, to give him release so he could end this torture. He wasn't certain who heard him, but he felt his seed speed up his shaft and pulse through the slit in the head.

He watched his shaft bob up and down, still buried deep in Constance, and all he could think about was how he had never once bathed Jane's womb with his essence.

Constance collapsed against the bed, her face glowing with the last vestiges of pleasure. Closing her eyes, she smiled. "Miranda was right, you are a beast in bed."

23

"Jane?"

Wiping her eyes with the back of her hand, Jane knew it would be impossible to hide her feelings, or her swollen eyes, from Lady Blackwood.

The sound of her cane thumping slowly across the hardwood floor made Jane's heart pump faster. Her mind raced for an excuse for the tears.

"I have a terrible headache," she mumbled into the pillow. "Please forgive me for missing dinner."

She felt the bed sag, then the warmth of Lady Blackwood's hand on her hip. "I understand you ache, but I doubt it is your head, Jane."

Fresh tears filled her eyes, and Jane pinched the feather pillow in a fruitless attempt to stop them and the sob that swelled in her throat.

"No words are necessary, gel. I can see what it is in your heart, and it pains me to know that you're hurting. I know of your love for Wallingford, Jane. There is no need to protect me from the truth. Let it out, dearest," she whispered. "A good cry always makes thing seem better."

"I couldn't do it," she sobbed. "I couldn't be his mistress."

"Oh, Jane," she whispered. Jane fell into her arms and cried as Lady Blackwood gently rocked her.

It was dark outside, the moon high in the sky. Matthew would be wed now, and no doubt would be in bed with his new wife. Jane choked through sobs at the thought of his body loving Constance. His beautiful hands touching and caressing, his wicked lips whispering…

Her gaze fell to his letter, which had fallen to the floor. She had not been able to resist opening it, and the pain she knew it would cause her was ten times more horrible than she had imagined.

Dearest Jane,

I do not know what to say, how to tempt you. If you had a price, I would pay it. If you desired particular words, I would say them. I would be anything you want, Jane. Just come back. Please come back.

I am utterly miserable without you. It's rained every day since you left, and I have done nothing but stare out my cottage window and remember you, lying in my bed, your skin flushed with excitement. I remember the way you felt beneath me—atop me. I can still taste you. I think I always will. My memories are all of you, Jane, and your image will not leave. It haunts me day and night. You fill my dreams, fuel my erotic fantasies.

I miss you, Jane, the sound of your breathing, the feel of you lying next to me.

Tell me you're miserable, too. Tell me you're lonely, that you think of me in the night. Tell me you dream of me and the pleasure you once found with me. Tell me that you regret leaving and that you are coming to me on the next train...

You know there are circumstances I cannot change. I wish I could turn back the hands of time, but that is not possible. The only possibility is to tell you that I love you, over and over again, and that I want to be with no one but you, Jane. You are my life. My love. My soul.

I am begging, Jane, come back and let me love you. Let us live in this little cottage, away from the world and worry about only us.

All you need to know is that I will wait—forever—Jane, for you to come back. One day you will...you have to.

My eternal love,
Matthew

"My darling, there is something I wish to say to you, and I'll only say it once. We will talk about it no more."

With her gnarled fingers, Lady Blackwood brushed Jane's tears from her face. "When one is as old as I, one cannot go through life without regrets. I have a few, but do you know what my biggest regret is?"

Jane shook her head and Lady Blackwood clasped her cheeks and forced Jane to look at her. "It's going through this life as though it were a dress rehearsal."

Jane frowned, and Lady B. smiled. "I've been living my life, trying to get it right for the next go-round, Jane, and there's no guarantee that we're going to get it, that chance to live life perfectly. What if this is our only chance?"

Lady Blackwood stood at the side of the bed and smiled down at her. "Once the tears are all dried up, Jane, think of what I've said."

Jane watched her leave, then picked up Matthew's letter. Had she made a mistake? Would time tell her?

She looked out the window and up at the sky, searching for answers. There was no message, no fork of lightning to let her know what she should do. But the answer was there, niggling deep down inside her.

She thought of Matthew. And missed him so much.

Lying back on the bed, she read his letter again, this time allowing herself to trace the words as she imagined him writing it to her. Her heart hurt, more than she ever thought possible.

She wanted to go to him, but pride was the only thing she had left. So pride kept her in London.

The crisp autumn air was pungent with the smell of drying leaves. The air was chilled, and Matthew took a sip of his tea, trying in vain to warm himself. London in autumn was always dismal and damp, and this autumn in particular was miserable.

It had been five months since he'd wed. Five months of feeling cold and empty. He took another sip of tea and savored the fleeting warmth as he set his cup back into the saucer and reached for the *Times*.

The slap of a hand on top of his newspaper made him look up. It was Constance, buzzing about the breakfast table. The sight of her irritated him. He always ate breakfast alone, while her ladyship slept the day away. He wondered what could possibly have her up at this hour, interrupting his meal.

"Guess what?" she teased.

"I don't care for games," he grumbled.

"You'll like this one."

"No, I won't. Say what you need to say."

She leaned down and looked into his eyes. "I'm breeding."

His spoon clanked against the saucer and her grin widened

in triumph. Her smile, he noted, was pure venom. "Dr. Inglebright has confirmed it."

"Which Inglebright?" he demanded.

"Why, the younger, of course. You didn't think I would allow that old man to touch me, not when his very handsome son is quite capable."

Matthew swallowed the bile that rose from his stomach. "When?"

"When? Why, our wedding night, it was the only time you ever demanded your husbandly rights."

He shut his eyes, prayed for patience. "When did you see Inglebright?"

"Yesterday. I made certain to tell him that we would be overjoyed and most thankful if he would share the news with Miss Rankin, who, I believe, is his nurse."

He reached out and shackled her wrist. "Do not play games with Jane."

She arched her brow but said nothing.

"When is the child to arrive?"

"Spring. April, perhaps," she said with a shrug.

He sat back in his chair. A host of emotions swirling inside him.

"I saw Miss Rankin at the Crystal Palace yesterday. And I saw you. Were you meeting her?"

"No." He picked up his paper and took a sip of his tea. But he had followed Jane. Had followed her for weeks, since they had returned to London. She hadn't seen him, but he had watched her, and agonized over every second he was parted from her.

He had written to her, but she had not responded to his letters. He had called on Lady Blackwood only to be told Jane was out. Discreetly he had inquired about Inglebright and discovered that he was courting someone, someone he feared was Jane.

"I will not be in for dinner this evening," Constance announced. "I'll be dining with friends."

Which was not different from any other night, he mused. "I have to go to the gallery and will not be home for dinner, either," he said, rising from his chair. "I…" He flushed, not knowing what to say. "The babe—" He stopped, tried to grapple with what he wanted to say.

"I hope you recall our alliance, my lord. Your brat for my freedom. I will be returning to London as soon as it is safe to rise from childbirth."

He had expected no maternal feelings from Constance. But the fact she held nothing for the life growing inside her sickened him. Suddenly he felt sorrow for his child. It was a product of an alliance. Not love. The child's mother would never willingly be a part of his or her life. It was up to him alone to love the child. Yet another one of his children he was left alone to care for.

"You are not going back on our bargain, are you?" Constance asked, her shrewd gaze raking over him.

"I haven't had a change of heart," he mumbled as he returned to his paper. Good God, his heart could never change toward Constance. She truly was a pit viper, as Raeburn had so succinctly and correctly described her.

"When will you leave for Bewdley?" he asked, attempting to be civil out of deference for her condition.

She frowned, as he knew she would despise the fact that once she began to appear in the family way, she would be banished to his father's country seat. How she would rail against leaving London and her cronies. "Another month, perhaps. Longer if I can conceal this monstrous belly."

"Shall I go with you?" he managed to ask, more out of politeness than desire. Hell, he'd nearly choked on the words.

She snorted and reached for the teapot. "There is no need

to dance attendance upon me when both of us know that this is nothing more than a business transaction. I will be gone in a month, banished to the hell on earth that is the north country. I will deliver this infant and pray with all my might that it is a son, so that I might never be forced to endure this again. And then, after my lying-in period, which Doctor Inglebright assures me won't be any longer than two months, I will be off with my friends on a well-deserved vacation. The continent, or America, perhaps," she said with a little shrug. "At any rate, you and I will no longer have any reason to get along as the terms of this *marriage*—" she sneered the word "—will be met."

He inclined his head, feeling chilled to the bone. He despised Constance, but the child she carried was an innocent, a pawn created by his father's greed and his overwhelming need to drive Matthew to his knees.

As he sat staring at Constance, he could not help but compare her to Jane. He had wanted to see Jane round with his child. He had wanted to place his head on her belly and stroke her. He was repulsed even giving fleeting thought to doing any of that with Constance.

Their gazes met, and he didn't know what to say. Congratulations were not right, nor was any expression of happiness. It was relief, for both sides. The end of their acquaintance was at hand, but only if this child was a son.

He thought of Sarah, his daughter. Thought of this babe, and knew without a doubt, that he would care for and love this child, this innocent life who was going to have the misfortune of being brought into the world by two people who could not stand the sight of one another. No, he vowed, once this babe was delivered, he would not think this way. He would love it. Raise it. Forget that Constance's blood also flowed in its veins. The task would be made all the more easily when Constance was off, traipsing about the world, spending as much money as she desired, leaving him and his child alone, to see to their own happiness.

Shoving back his chair, he stood and addressed her. "Well then, I'm off. The gallery opening is tonight. I'll be late."

She waved him off as she spread jam on her toast. "I'll be shopping."

Jane shuffled through the entrance of the gallery, hidden among the throng of other guests. She wore her best gown bought with the money she had been saving forever, and slipped her spectacles into her reticule.

Nervously she walked in, hoping that opening night was the right time to come. It was packed and he wouldn't see her. Just one more time, she told herself. She wanted one more glimpse. And to see his artwork.

Moving with the crowd of women, she hid behind a large woman wearing a feathered hat.

"There he is," one of the women hissed. "Is his wife with him?"

Jane strained to see beyond the feathers. Between the shoulders of two women, she saw Matthew, dressed in black, looking lethally handsome, standing at the front, greeting guests.

"Of course she's not. That harpy is too busy out gallivanting."

"No too busy to conceive, though," the lady in the feather hat whispered. "I was at Fortnum & Mason's this morning and heard her announce it. She's with child."

Jane gasped, a loud choking sound. Oh, God, it was more than she could bear. She needed to leave before she became ill.

"Five months along," the woman said knowingly. "A honeymoon babe."

Unable to hide the little squeak of pain, Jane tried to move, but she saw that Matthew had turned as if searching for the source of the noise. Then he began to move toward the group of women she was hiding behind. Trapped, she turned her back, hoping he would think she was looking at the art, and not him.

As she turned, a slash of pink caught her eye and she whirled back to a portrait done in creams and pinks. It was a nude. A woman with a voluptuous body was sleeping on a bed, quince blossoms scattered over the sheets and her hair—which was red. Her arm was lying crossed over her eyes and her lips were parted as though she was having the most delicious dream ever.

Jane bit her lip and told herself she would not cry.

"Aren't you beautiful," a darkly sensual voice whispered into her ear. "That's how I've always seen you, Jane. That is the moment I fell in love with you."

She whirled around and came face-to-face with him for the first time since their separation seven months before. The effect was dizzying and she fought the urge to fall into his arms.

"Jane," he whispered, taking her hand. "There is a door ahead of you," he murmured, urging her forward. "Wait there. I won't be but a minute."

Blindly, Jane went through and heard the door close behind her. She found herself seated on a lounge by the hearth, her shoulders trembling from tension and self-inflicted pain. Why? Why had she come tonight? Had she thought she could watch him and feel nothing? Did she actually believe the drivel she had concocted that she could think of him as a friend, could think on their time together as a period of sexual enlightenment?

Fool, she gasped and choked back a sob. She had not thought those things. She did sob then, a small strangling sound, and she covered her mouth and leaned to the side so that she could press her cheek into the curved arm of the lounge and allow her tears—fat and scalding—to slide down her cheeks.

The door opened and her gaze darted to it, only to see Matthew shouldering his way through and pressing his back against the door until it clicked firmly shut. His gaze met hers and then suddenly he was on his knees before her, his face pressed into her skirts as he rubbed his cheeks against her thighs.

"I am in hell," he groaned, and his fingers fisted into the silk of her skirts. "Seeing you tonight has been my salvation and my agony."

Lifting her face from the arm of the lounge, she bent over him, kissing the top of his head and running her hands through his tousled hair.

"When, Jane," he asked, his voice gruff and full of emotion, "when will I look at you and think of you as a friend? When will I see you and not feel my body harden and ache to be inside you?"

His hot hands slid down her calves and snaked their way beneath her skirts so that he could wrap his fingers along her ankles and slide them up along her stocking-clad leg.

"When will I stop dreaming of you wearing nothing but crème stockings and lace garters?"

He bent to kiss her ankle, then slowly he raised her skirts, pushing the silk and petticoats up so that her stockings were revealed to him. His mouth was everywhere, nipping at her calves, her knees and the inside of her thighs. He hesitated for a moment, then ran his lips along her mound that she had not been able to bring herself to cover with drawers.

"I dream of this naked, wet flesh. I crave it," he whispered, and dropped a kiss amongst her curls before wrapping his arms around her hips and clutching her close to him so that his face rested on her bare thighs, and his breath caressed her apex.

"When I saw you tonight without your spectacles, I nearly went mad." He raised his head and looked at her, and she had never seen him look more handsome than he was peering up at her from behind the crinkled blue silk. "I'm supposed to be the only man to see behind the glass." Her lips trembled and smothered a soft sob of longing. "It is only me that should be removing them. Only me you should see atop you."

"Matthew," she whispered shakily, raking an unsteady hand through his hair.

"God help me, Jane," he cried, grasping her to him as he buried his face in her lap. "I cannot do this! I cannot let you be. I would forsake her—desert little Sarah for one more taste of you. I swear, I need you—need the little piece of heaven you can give me. What sort of a man am I?" he cried.

"What am I?" she asked shakily as his fingers pressed into her thighs, parting her, exposing her glistening need to him. "What sort of woman am I that could wish—hope—that you would do such a thing? What sort of wicked wanton am I that would turn you, an honorable man, into a shell of himself, and all for an illicit taste of sin."

"Never illicit," he whispered, looking up at her. "Never sin. Just beautiful and passionate love." He blinked and she saw moisture shine in his eyes. "I have never loved before you, Jane. And I shall never love after."

He needed her. She felt it in his taut shoulders. Saw it in his eyes. Heard it in his words. Felt it through his trembling fingers. And she needed him—so desperately.

He rose from his knees and reached out to her, his hand trembling as he offered her something she wanted so badly. She reached for him and he grasped her around the waist and swung her up into his arms.

"There is so much to say, Jane," he said, his voice harsh with need. "So many things we must say to each other, but I cannot take the time. I need you. Let me show you with my body what I feel, what I cannot find words for."

He carried her to his desk, their mouths a frenzy of heated, hungry kisses. They tore at each other's clothes, their hands stroking, caressing, grasping at silk and flesh.

"Jane, oh, God," he moaned as she pulled his shirt over his head, and raked her nails down his shoulders. "God, yes, score me. Mark me."

She was hungry for his love, for the sex he could give her. The emotions created a tempest, and she rode it, allowing herself not to think, only to feel.

Her bodice came free, and he found her breasts beneath her chemise. He groaned when he realized she hadn't worn a corset and was bare beneath the thin linen.

"I need you," he growled, and he pushed her back onto the desk. He climbed onto her, tore at her chemise, ripping it— and thrust it aside, baring her breasts. Greedily, he lifted her breasts up to his mouth.

"Matty!" she cried as he suckled her fiercely.

His hands, warm and large, lifted her skirts and she helped him, dear God, she actually lifted them for him and spread her thighs, giving him room to touch her, take her.

With his teeth, he pulled and nibbled at her nipple, and snaked his hand beneath her gown, then his fingers were parting her sex.

"You're wet, Jane."

"Please," she gasped as she pulled at the front of his trousers. But he slid off the desk, depriving her of his body. Then he was bending over her, kissing her thigh, then her sex.

"Very wet," he whispered. "I want you on my lips, my tongue."

His tongue wickedly licked her, and she clutched his head, allowing it, begging for more. It felt so good, but it wasn't enough She wanted him inside her, his cock filling her.

Suddenly, she was pulled to the edge of the desk. He tugged her up so that he was standing between her legs, and they were eye level. When their gazes were locked, he filled her with one thrust, the sensation so beautiful that she said, "Again."

He did it again. Over and over, filling her with firm strokes, and all the while they looked into each other's eyes.

"I want to fill you," he said, his voice hard. "I want you to have me inside you as long as possible, forever," he whispered.

"Matthew," she cried as her orgasm built. Yes, she wanted that, too. A piece of him.

His hips moved faster and faster against her, and then his hands were cupping her bottom, lifting her up from the desk to meet his strokes. The penetration was more forceful, deeper, *feral*.

"Fuck me," he rasped next to her ear.

She did. She wrapped her legs around his waist, scored his back and bit his shoulder. He filled her hard, his chest, damp with sweat, rubbed against her breasts as she took him deep, the sounds of their mating filling the small room.

Harder and harder he stroked her, pounding into her. He got no closer, no deeper, yet she wanted more. Deeper, harder, she gasped, and he gave it to her.

"Jane, oh, God, it's not long enough," he growled as he slammed once more into her, but she clutched him tight to her as he flicked his finger over her sex and made her tremble.

She screamed, and he caught it on his mouth, kissing her, his tongue touching hers. With another thrust he filled her hard, and Jane's fingers found his buttocks. She squeezed, holding him to her, and she felt him pour himself into her in hot spurts.

"Jane," he whispered, "please." He touched her hair, her cheeks. "Will you not come back? Please?"

She kissed him, felt the tears that once again welled in her eyes. "No, I cannot. It is not in me to be a man's mistress. I need more."

"I can give you what you want, Jane."

She slid down the desk, and fixed her gown. "Except one thing."

24

A whole year had passed since she had first met and given her heart to Lord Wallingford. It seemed so quick, yet so long. She had only been with him a few short weeks, but a year later he was still in her thoughts.

Besides that one glorious night at his gallery, Jane had not seen him. There had been no more letters. No more sightings of him in London. He had returned to the country, where Constance had been delivered of a son.

Edward, they had called him, or so the newspaper had reported. Matthew's life had gone on, while Jane's remained stagnant.

A dress rehearsal, Lady Blackwood had called it.

She had learned much about herself this past year—her strengths, her flaws, her humanity. About what it meant to love and what it was to live with a broken heart and regrets that seemed more unbearable day after day. But most important, she had learned who she was on the inside. What sort of woman she needed to be. At last, she knew the recipe for her own happiness.

She had wept and grown melancholy, allowing the days to pass to weeks, and the weeks to months, until she had finally grown sick of feeling sad and empty, and decided to move on with her life. That was what she was doing today, leaving the past behind, and embracing the future. But the past, she knew, could never be put to bed, without some measure of closure.

As she climbed the hill, trudging through long grass, she stopped and enjoyed the vista and inhaled the scent of spring. It was a lovely day, warm and sweetly scented with the May air.

Pausing, she shielded her eyes and looked across the water, which glistened like gems in the sunlight. Taking a deep breath, she realized that she had come full circle.

The baby began to cry, and Matthew waved away the nurse. Reaching for the babe himself, he brought his son up to his chest and cradled his little head in his palm.

Six weeks old and growing like a weed. Edward nuzzled his fists and was soon placated as Matthew gently rocked him. He would have to go to the nurse soon, but Matthew was not ready to give him up.

Whispering nonsense words, he picked up his brush and began painting again. It was a garden landscape that he hoped to finish soon. He wanted to send it back to the gallery, which he had neglected since Edward's birth. His son fussed again, and Matthew jiggled him as he had seen the wet nurse do. Unable both to paint and soothe his son, Matthew placed his brush into the jar and held his son up tight against his chest. Edward cried, then stopped, having found another source of amusement.

Matthew looked down to see his son chewing on the pendant he wore around his neck. It was a portrait of Jane he had painted. He never took it off.

"Had it not been for her," Matthew said, "I could never have loved you."

"Yes, you could."

Matthew bolted up and the baby cried in surprise. Turning, he found Jane standing in the grass at the side of his cottage. "Jane?" he murmured as though he were seeing an apparition.

"Hello."

She smiled and her gaze drifted down to the baby who stopped crying to look at her. "He's beautiful, Matthew. Oh—" She covered her mouth and smiled up at him. "Oh, just perfect."

He stroked Edward's head, kissed him, then passed him over to the wet nurse who carried him off to the house. With a heavy heart that at once ached yet leaped at the sight of her, Matthew turned to Jane.

"You look well, Jane."

She flushed. "Thank you. As do you."

His tongue felt thick in his mouth, and he glanced around the garden, searching for something to say. "How long have you been in the area?"

"But three days. I'm staying with Anais and Lord Raeburn." She smiled. "I'm enjoying their son."

"They never said…" He trailed off, feeling desolate that his friend had not mentioned Jane staying with them.

"I asked them not to." She swallowed hard and lifted her gaze to his. "A year is a long time, Matthew, and…things, people change."

"Yes, they do."

She nodded, her fingers gripping the strings of her reticule. "Sarah? How is she?"

"Well, very well."

"I'm glad."

"And Lady Blackwood?"

"She'll outlive everyone, I think."

At a loss for words, he could only smile. They stood there for a few seconds, awkward strangers. "Is Inglebright with you?" he finally asked.

She looked puzzled as she cocked her head to the side. "No."

"I understand he's gotten himself engaged."

She flushed. "Oh," she said, her voice falling flat. "He has."

His heart shriveled in his chest; even after all this time, he still thought of her as his and it ruined him to know that she no longer desired what had only grown steadily in his heart.

"Are you happy, Jane?"

"I believe I am. For the first time in many, many months."

His tongue felt thick in his mouth. "When are you to marry Inglebright?"

"Oh, it's not me, he's marrying," she said, laughing nervously, "but Lord Ascot's youngest daughter. It's a love match."

The tentative flare of hope infused his heart with life once more. "I thought his love lay elsewhere."

"For a time it did, but I could not return the sentiment," she said quietly, "for my heart was engaged most passionately elsewhere."

He took a step closer to her. "And is it still, Jane?"

"It is."

"My son needs a mother."

Jane's gaze flew to his face. Matthew stepped close, and reached for her. "I need my lover."

She nodded, cried and smiled all at once. "It has taken me all of a year, but I've finally come to discover what an independent woman is."

"Yes?" Their fingers touched, grasping, entwining.

"It's someone who does what she damn well pleases, and says to hell with the rest when people talk. It's someone who believes in her worth because of the deeds she does and the loves she gives, not because of her status in society."

"Jane, you have always been a woman of worth to me."

"Is it too late?" she cried.

He opened his arms and let her fly into his chest. "I love you, Jane. And I have been waiting, not so patiently, for you to come back to me."

"Matty," she whispered, squeezing him, "I love you, and that love has only grown. I need you. So much."

"I knew I would not have to wait forever for you, Jane."

"Shall we?" They stood outside the cottage, and Matthew paused on the threshold.

Jane nodded, took his hand and kissed his knuckles. "Yes."

Opening the door to the cottage, he ushered her through. She felt the trembling of his fingers against her back, and she was nearly undone by the passion he had kept so well hidden on their walk through the garden.

Suddenly, she was picked up and clutched to his chest as he strode through to the room where they had made love, so long ago.

"I'm starved for you, Jane."

The words were torn from his throat as he pressed her back onto the bed and followed her down. His hands, shaking, began to unbutton her gown. "So many nights I dreamed of this, you coming back. I fantasized so many different homecomings, Jane."

She kissed him, and when she pulled away, he was looking down into her face. "I prayed every day for you to come back."

"I am here, Matthew," she whispered. "And I'm never leaving again, if that is what you want."

"I want so many things. A future with you, my child growing inside you. I want to talk with you by the fire while

I paint you. I want to wake up beside you and feel you against me in the darkness of night. But right now, Jane, I want you, body and soul. I need…I need so much to be inside you—so deep inside that I cannot feel any separation between us."

He captured her mouth hard with his. His hands divested her of her clothing, ripping and pulling, until she lay completely naked beneath him. He was breathing hard as his mouth worked over hers, his hands tracing her body. The gentleman he had been on their stroll was gone, replaced with this fierce man who was passionate, who held nothing back from her.

They rolled together and Jane landed on him, sprawled atop him. She felt his body tense for the briefest of seconds, before he murmured her name. Pulling her hair free, he let it slide slowly from its mooring. He watched the mass cascade over her shoulders. "Beautiful Jane," he whispered again. He traced her mouth, his fingertip lingering over the scar on her lip, then up to her spectacles where he caressed the arm. She reached for them, tried to pull them off, but he stayed her, his gaze lingering on her face. "Leave them. I can see you very well behind the glass, and what I see is so breathtaking."

She bit her lip, stemming the tears that burned her eyes. She would not cry, even though her heart was bursting with pleasure and joy. Instead, she turned to kissing him—his neck, his shoulder. She parted his shirt, and he pulled it up over his head, revealing strong shoulders and arms. She wanted those arms holding her. She wanted his warm flesh against her, the taste of his skin on her tongue. She bent and kissed his breastbone, then moved her lips over to the tattoo. She stopped and looked up to see him watching her.

"My offering to you, Jane."

She stroked the ruffled outlines of the blossom tattoo that he had placed alongside the other one.

"Peace and Jane," he said as he ran his hands through her hair. "Both are synonymous. Both as essential to me as air and water."

The tears did trickle out, unchecked, as he captured her face in his palms. "There cannot be one without the other."

His mouth caught hers, kissing her with all the hunger that had grown for them both over the past long year of separation. Her hands found the chain around his neck, her finger skimming down the pendant—the portrait of her. His body bore her marks—the tattoo, the portrait, they were all a gift to her. She had nothing to give him, except what she held in her heart and body.

He broke off the kiss, trailed his lips along her jaw, and over to her ear. "I thought you long gone, Jane. I imagined you lying in Inglebright's arms, his bed, your body loving his."

"No," she gasped, hating the pain in his voice. Richard had tried, and in honesty, she had, as well. But she could never allow Richard's touch, his kiss, without thinking of Matthew.

"It was only ever you, Jane. There will only ever be you."

Jane held him, felt his strong arms hold her tight. She kissed him and slid down the length of his body, licking his nipples, which were hard points as she whispered over and over that she loved him. That she desired him. That she needed him in her life.

He had given her so much of himself, and she yearned to do the same. Her mouth lingered over his navel, her finger trailing down the fine length of black hair that disappeared beneath the waistband of his trousers. She undid the first button, hearing his breath catch and hold.

Carefully she parted the flap, freeing him, feeling the thick shaft press against the globes of her breasts. She touched him—with her hand, and he shackled her wrist, holding her. Glancing up between their bodies, she saw that his eyes were pressed tightly shut, and his jaw was clenched as he struggled within himself.

"Let me give you this," she begged.

"No." His voice was full of desire and pain. He moved up, sitting with his back to the headboard. "Come, here, Jane."

She reached for him, brought the tip of him to her mouth and licked, making him cry out. His head was thrown back and his hands fisted in the sheets.

"Jane, no."

"Yes, Matthew," she whispered before taking the swollen head of him into her mouth. He was thick, large. He felt powerful and masculine in her mouth, filling it.

"Jane, you mustn't…you shouldn't," he choked out, his hands leaving the sheets and finding her hair. She sucked the head of him and he moaned, a deep guttural sound that made her womb clench.

"You are so very beautiful here," she murmured before running her tongue along the veined shaft.

"It's dirty," she heard him say in a dark whisper as he clutched handfuls of her hair. "Sinful."

"Those are memories of your past, Matty. What is between us is beautiful and right. This is a sharing—between only you and me. She took from you. I only want to give to you. Please let me."

He swallowed hard. His eyes were still closed, but the incredible tension in his body seemed to loosen. Slowly, his eyes opened, his gaze landing on her. He choked, shocked, aroused, she didn't know, but suddenly his shaft was in his hand and he was holding himself out to her, offering himself up.

The strength of him humbled her, and she took his offering, wanting to love him, to save him from his past.

She took him into her mouth and sucked him deep, feeling

him grow impossibly larger within her mouth as she pleasured him with all the love and desire she had held in her soul.

Matthew moaned as he held his cock out to Jane. Watching her take him into her mouth was at once terrifying and arousing. He had wanted this, Jane's red hair glowing like fire, lying across his thighs. He had wanted to hold his cock out to her, watching her take it into her mouth and love it—love him.

Ah, Christ, yes, he wanted to scream as she swallowed the length of him. She sucked him in deep. He wanted to hold her there and feel her throat. He wanted to come and spill himself in a mindless swirl of rapture. He *did* want to feel Jane swallowing him down, filling her veins with him. He wanted to flip her on her side and ravish her silky quim as she sucked him. He wanted to come with her, lying side by side.

But Miranda's voice began to sneak in. He heard her voice taunting him, and he stiffened, but he willed himself to relax, to shut out Miranda and focus on Jane. With a deep breath, he clutched her hair in his hand and opened his eyes, allowing himself the erotic pleasure of watching Jane loving his cock. Their gazes met, and he held on to hers, allowing it to anchor him into the present. This was Jane with him, loving him, gifting him with her mouth. He allowed the sounds of her mouth sucking, her tongue lapping to wash over him. Everything he heard, each sound and breath, was not shameful but beautiful.

"Ah, Jane," he moaned, fisting his hands even tighter in her hair. "God, you make this so good."

Their gazes locked, making the scene so erotic he could barely hold himself back. This was what he had wanted, this connection, this moment with Jane, when all he could feel was her, hear was her, see was her.

Beautiful Jane looking up at him, loving him in a way that

no woman ever had. Miranda had not loved him when she did this. It had been about dominance and lust. But this…he felt his eyes sting, his vision blur. This was true love. The giving of one soul to another. And he needed this, her soul to fill up the empty place where his had once resided.

"Jane," he whispered, his voice cracking as he watched her soft lips move along his hardness. "Thank you." Touching her face, her hair, he allowed the tears to come streaking down his face as he watched her. How he had longed for this, this healing. Miranda was gone now, exorcised from his mind, purged from his body. There was only Jane there with him now, and he cried harder and reached for her, bringing her up to straddle his lap.

He clutched her face, drawing her close to him so he could see her through the tears he had not allowed himself to shed when she had left. They flooded him now, all the pent-up emotions breaking free, like the rushing waters through a dam.

He clutched her face, holding her tight. "Is it really you?" he asked, fear creeping into his voice as he openly wept. "My God, Jane, is it really you in my arms, and not just a dream? I will not awaken and find you were never here. God, please tell me that this is real—"

She fell into his arms, sunk her body onto his. He felt the warmth of her tight quim sinking down onto him and her own warm tears mingling with his. "I am here, Matty," she whispered. "Oh, please, hold me," she gasped through her soft cries. "Fill the empty place inside me that has only grown since I left you."

He clung to her, burying his face in her hair as he forced his hips up, filling her full of him. Joy and ecstasy tore through him and he held her harder, drowning in Jane and the way she covered him.

Their lips met and they kissed, lazy drugging kisses as their bodies spoke the words they could no longer form. When he was close, he turned with her, wanting to feel her beneath him as he poured himself into her.

"Jane," he whispered, "you have given me my soul back."

She clutched him tight, her body trembling, and he came in hot, spurting waves into her body, which accepted him without prejudice or reservations, sins and all.

"That night in the gallery, I told you you could not give me the one thing I desired."

His gaze clouded. "I still cannot."

She kissed him, and their gazes met as she pulled away from him. "I was wrong. Marriage isn't the one thing I need. *This* is what I need, Matthew. You here with me. Us in a bed loving each other. Your love that has never wavered for me in the year I took to make up my mind to come back. That's what I need."

"Love, passion, monogamy, I can give you all that, Jane. If you will but let me. I can be a husband to you, in every way that truly matters."

They were on their sides, facing each other. He was tracing her freckles, and Jane purred like a well-fed cat. "I was so wrong to have left you."

"As bitterly painful as it was, I realize it was what you needed to do in order to come to me without any regrets."

"I have no regrets, Matthew."

"You are my wife, Jane. In every way that counts. Constance has my title, but that is all. You...you have everything of worth that I could possibly give to my wife."

Jane glanced at the plain gold band on her ring finger that he had placed there after their lovemaking. Yes. She had something that Constance would never have, and that was the man who was Wallingford. The title meant nothing to Jane, it was the man she desired.

"There's a lovely manor home in Evesham," he murmured as he caressed her mouth with his fingertip, "with at least five bedrooms, and a fabulous view of the blossom trail. Would you care to go for a ride tomorrow and see it?"

She kissed his hand. "I would love to."

"It is not a home for me to tuck you away in, Jane, but a home for us, for you and me, Sarah and Edward, and the children I want to give you. I won't hide you away like a mistress, Jane. You're not."

"We won't be received anywhere proper."

"I never was before I met you." His smile softened. "I am no longer alone, or broken, and you've done that, Jane. You've given me back my life. I have no need for society, only for the people who most matter, Raeburn and Anais, and Lady Blackwood will still be our friends, just as they always have. Jane, don't you see that what matters to me is your happiness?"

"I am most happy in your arms. I know that now. I just...had the need to make certain that you understand our life cannot be what it would be if we were married."

"Of course it can, because this is how it would be between us, Jane."

"I can, and want to live with you, Matthew. Life is too short to worry about such matters. And I knew, as each day went by, that leaving you was a regret I could not live with."

"You will have no need to worry about Constance. She will not bother us. She's off to America. And once my father, whom you should know enjoys very good health, is gone, and the title of duke passes to me, I will divorce Constance—"

She pressed a finger to his lips. "I know, my love. Protecting Sarah is important to me, as well. I am satisfied to have your love, and you in my bed. I don't need to be your duchess."

"Ah, Jane," he said, rolling on top of her, "I love you more than I could ever say."

Wrapping her arms around his neck, she smiled. "I love you, too."

"Show me this love, then," he whispered as he lowered his head to kiss her neck.

"My lord, I was hoping that you might take me to meet my son. I am anxious to become his mama."

His eyes flared wide when she said those words, and she knew immediately how much they meant to him. "He wants to meet you, too, but first, I need you again."

"Sinful man," she whispered. "And I would have you no other way."

★ ★ ★ ★ ★

Hungering for more of the sinful Lord Wallingford?
Visit www.charlottefeatherstone.net for one last glimpse
of Wallingford and Jane and their happily ever after.
Epilogue will be available to readers on May 2, 2010.

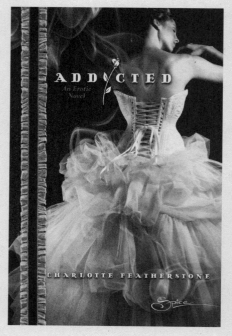

naughty bits 2, the highly anticipated sequel to the successful debut volume from the editors of Spice Briefs, delivers nine new unapologetically raunchy and romantic tales that promise to spark the libido. In this collection of first-rate short erotic literature, lusty selections by such provocative authors as Megan Hart, Lillian Feisty, Saskia Walker and Portia Da Costa will pique, tease and satisfy any appetite, and prove that good things do come in small packages.

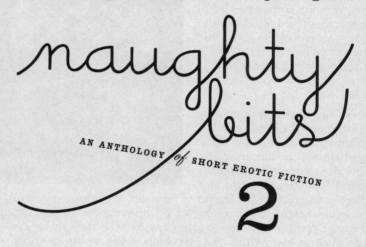

naughty bits
AN ANTHOLOGY *of* SHORT EROTIC FICTION
2

on sale now wherever books are sold!

Since launching in 2007, Spice Briefs has become the hot eBook destination for the sauciest erotic fiction on the Web. *Want more of what we've got?* *Visit* www.SpiceBriefs.com.

www.Spice-Books.com

SV60541TR

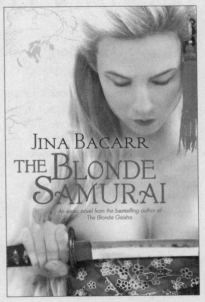

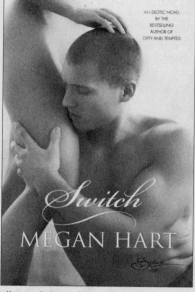